To Elizabeth,

In memory of John. — I hope he would have approved of my effort!

Best Wishes
   from Janet (aka ~~J Dean~~)

J S Downs is in her sixties, recently retired, married with two sons and lives with her husband in North East Lancashire. This is her first novel but she is currently working on a sequel. She enjoys walking, socialising with her many friends and travelling. All of these combine to generate the ideas for her writing.

Dedication

In memory of John Travis, MBE, FRSA (1934–2013) who was my English and drama teacher and a source of inspiration and encouragement to I and many others.

J. S. Downs

An Ordinary Woman

Copyright © J. S. Downs (2015)

The right of J. S. Downs to be identified as author of this work has been asserted by her in accordance with section 77 and 78 of the Copyright, Designs and Patents Act 1988.

All rights reserved. No part of this publication may be reproduced, stored in a retrieval system, or transmitted in any form or by any means, electronic, mechanical, photocopying, recording, or otherwise, without the prior permission of the publishers.

Any person who commits any unauthorized act in relation to this publication may be liable to criminal prosecution and civil claims for damages.

A CIP catalogue record for this title is available from the British Library.

ISBN 978 1 78455 251 0 (Paperback)
ISBN 978 1 78455 253 4 (Hardback)

www.austinmacauley.com

First Published (2015)
Austin Macauley Publishers Ltd.
25 Canada Square
Canary Wharf
London
E14 5LB

Printed and bound in Great Britain

Acknowledgments

Thank you to my husband and family and all my friends who have listened to me and encouraged me throughout the last few months.

Chapter 1

Sue Barnett, sixty years of age, average height, short cropped hair coloured a honey blonde, reasonably pleasant face to look at, a bit pear shaped, but with good legs still. Not bad considering all things – just an ordinary woman.

Born to working-class parents in the early 1950s, the younger of two children, she had been quite bright at school but nothing outstanding. She gained a handful of GCE's and started work at the age of seventeen in the banking industry. She was always a hard worker and liked to think that she did a good job. She married her childhood sweetheart Mark in the late 1960s and they had three children, two boys and the youngest, a girl, within seven years of being married.

Life progressed in a normal way, in so far as she continued to work full-time, look after Mark and the children (Peter, James and Nicola) whilst managing to earn enough to pay most of the bills so that Mark could be self-employed in the building trade without the pressure of having to totally support the family financially. Sue was a good manager of money – her mother had taught her that much – and so long as there was enough to pay the bills and provide food and clothes for the children, with a bit left over for minor luxuries, Sue was quite happy. Mark was able to provide for extras, like repairs or improvements to the house as required. However, there never seemed to be quite enough to gather any significant savings. Everything Sue and Mark had was tied up in their home.

The children eventually left school, got jobs and either married or found partners to live with, and Sue and Mark were left on their own in a large house in a 'good' part of the town where she was born in northeast Lancashire. Sue was generally happy with her life, but the one thing she had missed was going on holiday. Mark never wanted to go away and always found some reason not to, so they had never done the package holiday thing like most of their friends. Sue told herself for years that it didn't matter and made do with having odd days out here and there with female friends, or later on in her life, visiting friends in the south of England. She thought that what you never had you never missed.

Mark was happy for her to go away on her own as it meant he wasn't put under any pressure to go with her and he could stay in his cocoon of security. In fact, he rarely had time off work, preferring to treat each day the same all year round with the exception of staying at home on bank holidays, Christmas etc. When he was at home, his main hobby was restoring old motorbikes. He had two: a Velocette and a Triumph Bonneville. They were his pride and joy and he called them his girls – Velo and Bonnie.

Sue's urge to travel was awakened at the age of fifty when she became quite ill and for several years she endured a catalogue of ill health resulting in several major surgical procedures along with frequent hospital stays (all of this whilst still holding down a responsible job at the bank). Once she had recovered what she deemed to be the majority of her health, she promised herself that she would take a holiday on her own. She mentioned this to Mark and the family and they were encouraging, but they didn't bargain for her announcement that she was going to take up the offer of a visit with friends living in Australia, Steve and Grace. They didn't quite believe that their mother was capable of taking herself off to the other side of the world even if she was going to be met at the other end. The trip went well and convinced Sue of what she had been missing. She decided that she wanted to travel to as many different places as she could, but obviously she could only do that within the constraints of her holiday entitlement at work and her budget.

Now, at the age of sixty, Sue was facing retirement. Having been given the opportunity of leaving her job with a lump sum in addition to her pension, she decided that the time was right to call it a day work wise and try to enjoy some time doing what she had always wanted. After all, her health wasn't as good as it once was and the added pressure of work was having a detrimental effect. *'Life's too short'*, people would say and she repeated this mantra to herself throughout her last few months at work. She became disillusioned with the work culture and the ever increasing demands being put on her, many of which she considered to be unreasonable and in some cases without logic. Going to work each day was becoming a real chore and no longer provided her with the fulfilment and mental stimulation she had always previously gained. It was, she thought, time to go.

Her parents and sister had all passed away as had Mark's parents (he was an only child), so apart from their children and grandchildren they were on their own. But what would she do with her days? Well, she liked to walk to delay what seemed to be the inevitable curse of the older generation – stiff joints and to provide her with the fresh air she had missed when working behind a desk. Sue felt that she did her best thinking when she walked alone. If she had a problem the solitude provided her with the space to work things out logically and practically.

She also liked to go visiting friends who lived a little further afield so she was sure that this would be much more enjoyable when she could do it at leisure instead of having to fit it all in at the weekends or in holiday time. She would be able to keep the garden tidy and enjoy warm sunny days in the summer, (subject to the English climate that is). She had a good relationship with her daughter, Nicola and both her daughters-in-law, Lynne and Emma, so she thought she would make the most of that and go out for little excursions from time to time. Peter and his wife, Lynne, had two daughters, Karen and Rebecca, both in their teens but James and his wife, Emma, had no children and neither did her youngest child, Nicola.

Nicola and her partner, Simon, lived and worked in Manchester. She didn't see them often but she spoke to Nicola on the phone at least once a week. However, her daughters-in-law, Lynne and Emma lived locally and she could see them more often. Jean, one of her closest friends, who lived nearby, would be able to walk with her and they could go shopping or take the occasional visit to the theatre – something they both liked to do. Jean was a widow and had lived on her own for about twenty years, so she enjoyed getting out with Sue when she wasn't working. She would probably be glad of more opportunities to walk with Sue. In addition, Sue had a really close friend, Erin, with whom she had worked a number of years ago and who now lived in the east Midlands. She was always asking her to go and stay, so she would be able to do this more often. Oh yes, there'd be plenty to do and she couldn't wait.

Chapter 2

The first few months of retirement were like being on holiday from work and Sue enjoyed having the odd spending spree on things to wear and on a few decorating jobs around the house to 'tart it up a bit'.

After six months her thoughts turned to holidays. She wanted to see something of the world, go a bit further afield than Europe, where she had been a couple of times with Jean, and do something special. After all, what had she actually done with her life apart from rearing three kids and work bloody hard? She decided to make a list of places she wanted to visit. She started to jot down a list in no particular order as a starter for ten. This included:-

Canada

America (north) – maybe The Grand Canyon, New England, New York

America (south) – Peru, Brazil

Australia – The Great Barrier Reef, Melbourne, Adelaide, Sydney (again but different things)

Hong Kong

New Zealand

South Africa- Garden Route, Diamond mines

She decided that this was a large enough list for now and of course she could add to it as she thought of other destinations. She'd need rather a lot of cash to do all this and she would have to spend her money wisely she knew that much.

She saw an ad on the TV for a train journey in the Canadian Rockies – The Rocky Mountaineer – and decided to check out the details. She told Mark that she was interested in doing something like this and he was, as always, encouraging and upbeat about the idea. "If you can afford it Sue, then do **it.** You're only here once so go for it**,**" he said. The rest of the family were equally positive about it. Therefore, after much deliberation and research on the internet she finally booked an eleven day trip to the Canadian Rockies, starting in Calgary, taking in several locations and ending with a two day train trip on the Rocky Mountaineer train from Jasper to Vancouver. For this last phase, she decided to upgrade her ticket to the Gold Leaf Service which meant she would travel in luxury for the train journey with a panoramic view of the landscape along the Thompson and Fraser Rivers.

She couldn't wait – she was so excited and told all her friends most of whom were green with envy. Jean couldn't afford the cost of the trip so Sue would be travelling alone in a new continent with no-one familiar to meet her like they did when she went to Australia. The thought was a bit daunting but exciting at the same time. She knew that once she reached Calgary, she would meet other people doing the same sort of thing and that most of her holiday would be organised for her. She would, however, have some free days to 'do her own thing' so there would be an element of adventure as well. She had made it clear to the travel agent, who helped her to sort out the package together that she didn't want to be herded about every day so she was pleased with the itinerary. It was a start and she would learn from any mistakes for the next trip. She had to start somewhere and this was going to be it. *Look out Canada, here I come.*

Chapter 3

The day of her departure arrived – it was on a rather cool Thursday morning in early June at 6.00am that she was dropped off by her younger son, James, at the airport. She had said her farewells to Mark the night before as he said he wouldn't want to be awakened early in the morning. It was a bit of a struggle getting showered and dressed without making too much noise, but she managed it. The adventure was about to start. She was sure her baggage would be over the limit – she hadn't known what to pack. She had been watching the weather in western Canada on the internet for a couple of weeks and it was changeable but the forecast and the travel guides she had read said that June would be reasonably warm, so she had opted for lighter clothes, the only thing was, there were a lot of them. She had really enjoyed shopping for them though! However, in the end she was about five kilos below the limit. *Phew! Thank goodness for that.*

Sue's nervousness was tinged with excitement and anticipation of what she was about to experience. After a very smooth check-in and security check process, she began to relax a little and set about getting something to eat while she waited the three hours or so before boarding. This turned into four hours as a delay was announced just as Sue was settling down to eat her bacon sandwich. Would this holiday ever start?

Finally, at just before 10.00am Sue seated herself on the end of the centre aisle of three seats on Row 38, next to a couple of recently retired teachers from the Midlands, George and Heather. Having good travelling companions certainly made the long journey – nine hours – more bearable. As they relaxed for the long journey ahead, Sue chatted with Heather who told her that she and George were also travelling through the Rockies but they were doing a fly-drive and had chosen their own itinerary. They compared notes and to everyone's surprise, there was going to be one night when they would be staying at the same lodge in Jasper. It was agreed they would meet up for dinner on that night.

Sue couldn't believe the coincidence and she was, she had to confess, quite pleased that there would be one night when she would have company for dinner. That was the only aspect of travelling alone that she found a little sad. Although she was used to sitting in a restaurant at her lonely table while other diners seemed to be in twos or in groups, it always made her envious. She would listen to their laughter and obvious pleasure at sharing their day's experiences whilst she could only write things down in her journal and try to explain to Mark when they spoke on the phone how wonderful things were. He could of course never appreciate it fully when he hadn't actually been there. She longed one day to be able to go away with Mark but knew that the chances of that happening were very slim. He was stubborn when it came to even discussing the prospect of him going away. Never mind, she was going to enjoy it whatever happened. Nothing was going to spoil this adventure and she would look for challenges along the way.

Chapter 4

When the plane arrived at Calgary airport, the temperature was a pleasant 18 °C. Well that was a good start anyway. She could manage that if that was what was in store for the trip. She said goodbye to her travelling companions as they went through to baggage reclaim from the Immigration lounge. She was truly on her own. She asked a lady in a green uniform where she could get a bus into the city, but despite her badge saying she was *'Here to help'*, she was unsure and in the end Sue opted for a waiting taxi outside of the arrivals hall on the concourse.

The first hotel was in the centre of Calgary and quite modern – a twenty-six storey building. Sue stood outside looking up at the hundreds of windows above her. She gulped nervously and with a confidence she didn't feel, she strode into the Reception. "Welcome to Calgary, Mam," said a rather young but pleasant lady on the Reception desk. "We have you down as staying for the one night and we have your room on the twenty-fourth floor overlooking the river. Here is your key and the bell boy will take your luggage and show you to your room." She smiled proudly as she handed over the key card.

Shock horror! This was obstacle number one. "Oh," said Sue, "I'm not sure I can cope with that. I'm not too good with heights. Do you think you could find me a room a little closer to the ground?"

Looking rather deflated, the desk clerk recovered quickly and said, "No problem, Mam, we can change that for you. How does the fourth floor sound?"

"That will be good thank you and I'm sorry to be difficult," replied Sue gratefully. *How bloody stupid is that?* she thought to herself. *I'm offered what's probably one of the best rooms in the hotel and I turn it down. I must be mad. How the hell am I going to cope with the helicopter trip over the mountains tomorrow if I can't manage a room with a view? Why did I book a trip to a place that's going to be packed with such experiences? Well, this is not the time to be worrying about that Susan. Just relax and enjoy it. You wanted a challenge. Embrace it and just deal with it calmly and rationally like you used to do with obstacles at work or when you were facing another daunting bit of surgery. It can't be worse than any of that! Why am I thinking negative thoughts all of a sudden? This is a holiday of a lifetime. Get over it woman and move on!*

Finally, having settled herself in the room, or what was more like a suite of rooms, Sue decided that there was time to have a little stroll and familiarise herself with the immediate surroundings of downtown Calgary before having a bath and changing for dinner. She planned to eat in the hotel tonight. She wasn't very hungry, having had a couple of what passed for meals on the plane and really she was more tired than anything what with the time difference of eight hours and the long journey.

After a couple of hours of window shopping and strolling down the very busy streets, Sue returned to the hotel. She had taken note of where she had started out and the direction she was walking so that she wouldn't get lost. At this point, she thought about her friend, Jean, with whom she had spent many a time wandering around city centres trying not to get lost and not getting too much direction from her friend. Jean had no sense of direction whatsoever and relied totally on Sue to ensure they safely got back to their starting point. They had gone horribly wrong when on holiday in Rome on their first day there. They had taken a wrong bus and ended up miles away from where they needed to be. Added to this, Jean had thrown their bus tickets into a very large rubbish bin, thinking they didn't need them any more. As there was nowhere to get any more tickets they had to walk for about two hours at dusk in a strange part of the city and were mighty grateful to eventually find their hotel in time for a late meal – a very late meal! They had laughed about it many times since, but at the time it had been pretty scary.

Jean would have been scared today, Sue thought. Jean would have hated the fast pace and the vastness of the busy street junctions with four lanes of traffic coming in all directions. Noisy cities full of commuters and shoppers were not Jean's idea of a good time. She was much more at home in the country where the pace was slower and the only noises were made by the wild animals and birds that made it their home. Yes, Jean definitely preferred the peace and tranquillity of open spaces. It was a pity Jean couldn't be there with her in the Rockies. That part of the holiday would be right up Jean's street. Sue made a mental note to tell Jean about Calgary when she got home.

Dinner was a bar snack in the hotel and it only took one glass of red wine to make Sue begin to feel really sleepy. It was about 10.00pm local time when she finally flopped into the huge bed that was separated from the lounge area by a sliding door. She closed it instinctively, feeling that it was more private that way. How silly she thought it was really as she was the only one there. Her last thought before she fell into a deep sleep was wondering what the next day would bring. The itinerary said that she would be picked up from her hotel at 8.30am by coach, and en route to Banff there would be the dreaded helicopter ride over the foothills of the frontal range of the Rockies. She hoped the weather would be clear so that she could take some good aerial pictures. At least she would get that bit over with on her first day. After arriving in Banff at lunchtime, with a swift look round to grab some lunch, a ride in something called the Banff Gondola was scheduled for the afternoon before being dropped off at the next hotel where she would stay for two nights. *Oh no, not more heights* she thought. *Sue, stop being a wuss and go to sleep. Tomorrow is another day and you **will** enjoy it!*

Chapter 5

As Sue boarded the coach the next morning, along with four other passengers, the driver introduced himself as John. The first half hour was spent picking up the assorted travellers from various hotels in Calgary and loading them and their luggage on to the coach. John seemed to have a passion for boiled sweets and he noisily sucked on them while speaking into his microphone as they headed for the foothills of the Rockies. Sue managed to get a prime seat at the front of the coach opposite the driver, so she was able to hear his commentary easily (when he wasn't munching his sweets that is) and also could see the road ahead with enough time to get her camera ready for shots of the scenery and of the promised wildlife further ahead.

Her first impression of the landscape was that of its vastness. On the Trans Canada Highway they passed huge farms on the plains outside the city with thousands of cattle. Her first glimpse of a mountain in the distance was what she had been expecting and they ate up the miles on roads that were only occupied by the coach, the occasional camper van and a handful of large articulated lorries travelling in the opposite direction towards Calgary. It was difficult to appreciate how fast the coach was travelling as the roads were so wide and there was so little traffic on them. The plains gave way to hills as they climbed all the way, to the first range of mountains. What a sight they were thought Sue. It was early June, and yet there was still snow on the peaks. She hoped it wouldn't be as cold as it looked, even with the blue skies.

After about two hours, they reached their first scheduled stop – the Annanaskis Park Helicopter and Visitor Centre. This was it. The dreaded helicopter flight. Sue's heart began to beat a little faster in anticipation of what was to come. The first blow came when each person who was scheduled to fly, was required to be weighed on a giant weighing pad. Apparently this was to ensure that each helicopter was not carrying too much weight and the passengers could be grouped accordingly. Some travellers had opted out of the flight, preferring to stay in the comfort of the Visitor Centre and check out the gifts on display. Sue had to admit that it might have been a more sensible option, but then again, it would have been a cop out and she couldn't consider herself to be an adventure seeker if she chickened out of the first challenge. Sue did however wish she had been more vigilant with her weight watching prior to coming on holiday, but it was too late to worry about that now. Fortunately, the various weights were not displayed to the travellers, so that was a relief. After this they were grouped and posed for a photograph outside the waiting helicopter. Sue hated having her picture taken and could only imagine how bad she must be looking at that point. She was probably slightly ashen-faced and wearing a wrinkled mask of terror.

Sue was placed in the first group with four other people. They included a middle-aged couple from the States and two young female passengers from Australia. One of the females was selected to sit in the cockpit with the pilot, an honour she obviously relished, especially as he was rather a dish. Sue wondered if it was part of the requirements for sightseeing helicopter pilots to be good-looking. Perhaps it distracted anyone who was particularly nervous and helped take their minds off their anxiety. Unfortunately, Sue was not going to be able to put this to the test as she was seated with her back to him. Oh well, never mind.

The passengers were all supplied with headphones and attached microphone so that they could speak with and hear each other in-flight and of course, hear the pilot's commentary.

Once the preparations were complete, the pilot wasted no time in getting off the ground. This was it. As the ground dropped away beneath them, Sue felt a momentary surge in the pit of her stomach but she found to her surprise that she was not only able to look out of the window, but she could actually focus on the landscape to take pictures. Bill, the American sitting opposite her, seemed to sense her nervousness and chatted to her. She couldn't believe she was actually enjoying this. It was far more pleasurable than she had imagined it would be. Why had she not tried this before? The flight was over before she knew it and it wasn't until the group had assembled in the Administration building for a coffee (and of course to be given the opportunity to purchase the commemorative photo of themselves along with souvenirs), that Sue noticed the sky was becoming overcast and grey. Large clouds were forming and the tops of some of the peaks that they had just flown over were shrouded from view. The coach driver remarked that rain had been forecast and the further up they climbed on their way to Banff, the colder it would be so it might be a good idea to have coats handy. He added that Banff was about 4000ft above sea level.

After another hour and a half travelling, the coach pulled into the centre of Banff. Although there was some blue sky visible and the sun was out, it felt a good deal cooler than in Calgary. Sue began to wish she had packed some warmer clothes, but reassured herself that this was only a blip and the rest of the trip would be better.

After a little exploration of the main street in Banff and a hurried snack for lunch, the passengers were asked to return to the coach for the afternoon sightseeing experience. According to the literature Sue had with her, there was to be a trip on the Banff Gondola which afforded 'marvellous views of the town of Banff' followed by a brief tour of the town surroundings including Bow Falls, before being deposited at their respective hotels.

The sunshine gave way to drizzle which became heavy rain by the time the coach reached the Banff Gondola station. Sue had to admit that although she had survived and indeed enjoyed the morning's excursion, riding in a helicopter with an experienced pilot among stunning scenery, was not the same as sharing a draughty swaying carriage on wires ascending a mountain in near blizzard conditions and being unable to see anything below, except snow attaching to the passing trees and the carriage itself.

She was visibly shaking as much from the sudden drop in temperature as the apparent instability of the carriage in the wind. Why had she imagined that this was some sort of excursion on the river or a lake? It must have been the inaptly named Gondola. She gritted her teeth and declined the option of a hot chocolate at the summit, preferring to return immediately to ground zero before she became reacquainted with the contents of her stomach. On arrival back at the visitor centre below, she made a hurried dash for the loo and a chance to calm herself before re-joining the other passengers. She had survived a second challenge and was glad to tick it off the list of things to do and see in Banff.

Bow Falls was the next place on the itinerary. However, by the time they arrived, the pathway running alongside the river at the falls was closed due to flooding. Apparently, they had been experiencing unusually high levels of rainfall in the last couple of weeks (a veritable home from home then) and all the rivers were very swollen. Bow Falls on the River Bow was a raging torrent and consequently quite spectacular. However, this also meant that Sue's plan to spend her free day tomorrow walking by the river would have to be revisited. Ah well, that's the beauty of travelling by oneself. There was no-one to debate alternatives with except yourself.

Chapter 6

It rained all through the night – very heavy rain that turned to sleet and then snow. "Snow in June for God's sake! What's that all about?" muttered Sue to herself. She had to get up to go to the loo on several occasions that night – perhaps it was the jet lag catching up with her and her throat was so dry and her head started to ache. She hoped she wasn't getting a cold.

When she rose early the next morning still with the headache and the dry throat, she washed and dressed and wondered why her skin was so dry. It was pouring with rain and when she looked out of her window, she could see that the tops of the mountains that surrounded Banff were completely white. She switched on the TV and found the news and weather channel. According to the jolly weather girl (a little too jolly for Sue's liking) it was going to continue to rain for the rest of the day.

Remaining undaunted, Sue decided that she would get some breakfast in the hotel and then head out into the town and browse around the shops, maybe pick up one or two small gifts to take back home and have coffee in a nice café. This wasn't really what she had thought she would be doing, but at least she could please herself.

The breakfast was a hot and cold buffet. Diners were offered tea or coffee by the waitress and then given the opportunity to select what they wanted from the buffet. There was apparently no limit to the amount each person could have, or how many times they went back for more. It was early and so Sue was one of the first diners that morning. As she sat eating her scrambled eggs and bacon at her little table for one in the corner, two new diners entered the restaurant. They looked like a mother and son. She looked to be in her sixties but it was difficult to tell as she was rather dumpy and fat. The one Sue took to be her son looked in his early twenties. To say he was large was a gross understatement. He was about six feet tall but must have weighed at least twenty stones. His Chicago Bears sweatshirt was as tight-fitting as cling film round a turkey.

They took a table close to Sue and were deep in conversation when the waitress offered them the choice of tea or coffee. The mother opted for coffee while the son requested a glass of diet Pepsi! Sue almost choked on her bacon at hearing this and had to cover her mouth with her napkin to prevent a laugh from escaping from it together with its contents. *Diet Pepsi! I ask you* thought Sue to herself. *I think it's a bit late for that son.*

Sue's shock at the request turned to horror when the young man returned from the buffet with a plate piled so high with food that it was in danger of avalanching onto the table. There looked to be a mixture of scrambled eggs (Sue estimated there to be the equivalent of about ten), baked beans, sausages and bacon all topped off by two enormous waffles! Sue couldn't help staring and didn't realise that she was, until the young man turned in her direction and nodded a "Mornin' Ma'am." She said good morning back and hastily finished her tea, rose and left the restaurant thanking the waitress. Somehow she didn't feel like eating the rest of her breakfast after that.

As she walked into the fresh air she realised that the weather girl had actually got it right when she said the temperature would be about 2°C. She hadn't believed it but now she did, dressed in lightweight cotton top and a fold up raincoat. She would have to buy a fleece or something warmer as an extra layer. She stayed out until about 2.00pm after having exhausted the shops and cafés on the one main street in

Banff, and then both fatigue and cold got the better of her. She had purchased a fleece earlier on and had asked the girl in the shop to remove the labels so that she could put it on straight away. Unfortunately, she had already begun to feel chilled by that time. The headache was still in evidence.

She returned to her room and collapsed exhausted on the bed. It was 5.00pm when she woke feeling much better after her rest. She hoped she would be able to sleep in the night because she had another early start in the morning on her next stage to Lake Louise. She had checked out the eating places in the town during the day and had decided that she would eat at the Chinese place called the Silver Dragon. It was not too far from the hotel and it looked quite busy so she thought it must be good. She planned to go about 6.45pm – not too late as she couldn't cope with eating after about 8.00pm.

When she stepped out from the hotel, the rain had finally stopped and there was some late evening sun. The mountains looked stunning and she planned to get up early in the morning to take some pictures before the coach arrived to pick her up.

Her meal was very enjoyable and she ate far more than she knew she should. After finishing the second of her two large glasses of red wine and refusing the offer of a doggy bag for the remaining food, she paid her bill and made her way back to the hotel. As she walked along the main street, she was surprised to see two familiar faces walking towards her. It was Heather and George, her travelling companions on the flight over. They were on their way to get something to eat and so she mentioned the Silver Dragon which seemed to be of interest to them. After a brief chat about what they had done so far, they parted company. Sue thought it was a shame that she hadn't seen them before she went for her dinner. They might have asked her to join them. On second thoughts, she decided it was unfair to 'latch on' to other visitors. No, she had decided to travel alone, so she shouldn't impose herself on couples who might prefer to be just with each other.

She entered the lobby of the hotel and went straight up to her room. It was only 8.30pm and far too soon to go to bed, besides her stomach was full and she didn't want to lie down until it had digested a little so she decided to check out the bar downstairs. Yes, another glass of red wine would go down very nicely. There was only one other person at the bar – a young man who Sue guessed to be in his thirties. He was talking to the barman about the ice hockey game being screened on the TV.

Sue ordered a glass of Merlot and stood for a moment looking for a suitable seat. The young man offered her the bar stool next to him so she made the best attempt she could to get her backside on it without struggling. *Why did they make these things so high and difficult to manage?* Eventually, when she was seated, the young man offered his hand, introduced himself as David. He said he was a computer software developer and was in Banff for a two day conference starting in the morning. "What brings you here to Banff?" he asked.

"I'm here on holiday," said Sue and added, "I'm Sue by the way."

They chatted freely about all sorts of things and Sue was amazed at how quickly the time went. The barman joined in the conversation in between washing glasses and serving the odd customer that drifted in from time to time. An hour and a half had passed before she knew it and after consuming a mineral water to ease her dry throat, she made a move to leave. David said he would have an early night as he was speaking at the conference and needed to go through his notes before turning in. "Well, we probably won't meet again Sue but it's been great talking to you and thanks for your company," said David as he stood to leave. Sue said she had also enjoyed it and they said goodnight.

Back in her room, Sue felt elated and considered the evening to be a minor triumph in so far as she had actually made someone's acquaintance in a strange place and found it easy to chat. It had been quite pleasurable and all part of the 'doing your own thing' experience. Who knew what she might get up to tomorrow? *Steady Sue, don't get too carried away.* She laughed at her own joke.

Chapter 7

The next morning dawned quite bright and warmer than the day before so Sue was looking forward to the morning's journey and sightseeing on the way to Lake Louise. According to the itinerary, they should reach Lake Louise at about 1.00pm. There were only four other passengers on the coach and this meant that the day's driver was able to give them a more intimate commentary and they could spend a little more time at the places they visited.

The way Sue had planned her trip meant that she wasn't travelling every day and so would meet different passengers from one stage to the next, because other travellers might only stay one night in a location then move on the next day or even stay two or three nights. Either way she would not be travelling with the same group all the time and this, she thought had to be a bonus, especially if there was someone whom she found difficult to get on with.

Today's driver was called Greg, and before they set off on their journey he pointed out some bottles of water in a case on one of the seats. "The water is for you to take freely. It's very important that you drink as much as possible while up here in the Rockies. Although we've just had a day and a half of rain the atmosphere is very dry as we are quite high up – about 4000ft above sea level. The air is thinner and drier and we find that visitors very often get dehydrated. You should look out for the symptoms which include dry throat and skin, headaches and nausea. Don't wait until you are very thirsty before you take a drink of water. You should just keep taking frequent sips throughout the day. You'd be amazed at the number of visitors we end up taking to hospital every year, because they don't recognise the signs early enough and eventually, they collapse."

So that's what's been up with me, thought Sue. *I need to keep drinking a lot more water than I have been doing'*. She grabbed a couple of bottles from the case and promised herself she would be more vigilant with the hydration.

Emerald Lake was one of the stops on the way that morning and it was very aptly named. The minerals in the water mixed with the snow melt from the mountains gave it a very distinct green tinge. The scene was idyllic and Sue made the most of the opportunity to take loads of pictures. She'd thought that she might choose a couple of her favourite ones when she got back home and have them enlarged and framed as a constant reminder of her trip. So far, the scenery was living up to and even surpassing all expectations.

About ten minutes after leaving Emerald Lake, they came to what probably passes for a traffic jam on the road. Apparently, this is a sure sign that someone has spotted a bear ahead and everyone wants to get a good view to take snaps. Sure enough as they rounded a corner, over to the left of the coach in a clearing in the woods, was a brown bear foraging for food among the shrubbery. Her first bear sighting – how exciting it was. She managed to get a couple of shots as they came alongside but not close enough for too much detail, even using the camera's zoom. Oh well, better luck next time.

The coach arrived at Lake Louise about 1.30pm. They were further into the Rockies now and were even higher up above sea level – about 6000ft. The road climbed up out of the town to the next hotel on the trip – The Fairmont Chateau Lake Louise, apparently built in the style of an Austrian chateau. Sue had planned to stay here for two nights and nothing could have prepared her for the sight that met her eyes.

Firstly, the hotel itself was the size of a small village, with a main building consisting of about eight storeys and a separate conference centre that was almost as big. As she entered the main reception area she almost dropped her handbag in shock. The area itself was the size of a large house, with solid wood panelling, sumptuous carpets and a magnificent carved staircase that swept down from one side. There were stuffed bears and moose heads mounted on the walls and the hotel porters were all dressed in a uniform consisting of green woollen jackets, leather lederhosen and long green knee socks. They all wore Tyrolean hats with feathers in them and highly polished brown leather shoes.

At the opposite side to the staircase was a wide hallway that led onto an avenue of shops selling what looked to be designer goods and a huge restaurant overlooking the lake. Within the reception area were a number of grouped sofas and seating areas. These were mainly occupied with visitors waiting with luggage to be picked up or those just passing time, people watching, or writing postcards. Sue had stayed in some pretty smart hotels while on business trips for the bank, but nothing compared to this. It was fabulous.

The reception desk had all the paperwork ready for Sue in advance, so check-in was swift and efficient. She was given the key card for a room on the 4th floor and advised that her luggage would be there in her room already. She was also advised to book a table in advance if she wanted to eat in one of the hotel's six restaurants on the two evenings of her stay. The menus were posted on the board at one end of the reception area. In addition, she was told, there was a twenty-four hour delicatessen that served sandwiches, pastries, drinks and snacks.

Sue decided that this was one place where she was going to spoil herself and eat in different restaurants on each evening. She would go and get settled in her room, freshen up and then her first task would be to book her tables. She got lost on her way to her room, but eventually, she found it. Room 465 was tastefully furnished with mahogany furniture and pale blue wallpaper. The carpet was also of a pale bluish grey colour and it matched beautifully with the grey and silver bedspread and curtains. There were old pictures of climbers and early explorers including women dressed in tweed jackets, hats and long skirts carrying very heavy-looking ropes around their shoulders.

The window blind was pulled down, presumably because the sun – yes, it was out today – shone into the room. Sue walked over to lift the blind and as she did, she gasped at the sight she saw. Lake Louise in all its glory surrounded by firs and pines whose pointed tips reached up towards the snow-capped mountains above. The lake was a blue unlike anything she had seen before – almost turquoise. The travel guides she had read prior to coming to Canada had mentioned the Lake's unique colour and they had not been wrong. There were crowds of day trip visitors milling around the lakeside, taking pictures and sitting with packed lunches on the benches and tables provided. The lake was a popular visiting place for coach parties in addition to residents at the hotel and Sue could see why it was so popular. There were walkers heading off through the woods around the lake and other visitors paddling canoes. Sue fancied setting off on a short walk with what was left of the afternoon, but first she needed to sort out her evening meal.

She went to the huge board in the reception area to study the menus for the various restaurants and to decide which of them she would choose. Fortunately, the prices were listed opposite each dish. She got a bit of a shock when she looked at the prices for the menu for what was probably the premier restaurant, The Fairmont. It was very formal dining, and dinner jackets and cocktail dresses were the preferred attire. She ruled that one out, not just because of the price, but because she had not brought a dress or skirt with her. She had some smart linen trousers and some 'dressy' tops, but she hadn't thought a dress would be needed.

She decided on The Brasserie for tonight and the Italian restaurant called The Lago for her final evening, and went to find the Concierge's desk in order to book. The Concierge's desk was situated in a small booth to the side of the main desk and there was a German couple making a booking for a guided walk for the next day. Sue waited patiently while they discussed the details with the Concierge. As she did so, she saw an elderly gentleman sitting in an armchair in the corner. He had a panama hat on his lap and he was casually rubbing the rim between his fingers. As he did so, he was staring at her intently but not in an intimidating way, more in a far away manner. When Sue smiled back at him and he realised that his attention had been noticed, he rose from his chair and came forward, tipping his panama hat as he did so.

"I do beg your pardon Ma'am," he said. "I don't make a habit of staring at people, it's just that you remind me of someone I used to know and for a moment I was a bit thrown. Do forgive me."

"Oh, that's okay," said Sue. "Believe it or not, I'm always doing things like that, thinking I've seen someone I know and then feeling really silly when I call to them and it's not who I thought it was. I put it down to age you know. I've just retired and I'm sure my brain has decided to start its retirement as well."

He laughed loudly at this and said she didn't look old enough to be retired. Sue blushed and said that her body knew it was old enough. That produced another burst of laughter from the old man. The Concierge had finished dealing with the German couple and had obviously been taking note of the conversation. She smiled at Sue and asked if she could help her. "I think this gentleman is before me," said Sue but the old man waved his arm and said, "Oh, I'm only having a rest in the chair so go ahead it's fine."

Thanking him with another smile, Sue proceeded to ask for a table in The Brasserie for that evening.

"Just for one is it? I'll just check the availability but I think we are very busy tonight. The hotel is quite full at the moment. The only table for one that I have is at 9.00pm."

"Oh that's a little bit late for me to be eating I'm afraid," said Sue, "perhaps I'll just get something from the deli instead."

At this point the old man stepped in and said to the Concierge, "Excuse me, but if this lady doesn't mind, I would be honoured if she would share my table at 7.00pm." He looked at Sue questioningly, and to her surprise she didn't hesitate in replying, "Well that's so kind of you. Are you sure you don't mind?"

"Of course not my dear," he said, "I will be dining alone and as you will be also, it seems the obvious solution."

Looking somewhat startled, the Concierge said, "I'm sure that can be arranged Mr Carter. Consider it done. Please may I take your room number Madam?"

"Oh, Room 465," Sue replied, and with that, she turned to the old man and said, "Well, as we are going to be dining together I'd better tell you my name. It's Susan, Sue to everyone who knows me and I'm from England."

"Well, it's lovely to meet you Susan," said the old man extending his hand. "I kind of guessed you were English. The accent does tend to give it away," and he winked as he said it. "My name's Sam, Sam Carter and I'm Canadian born and bred."

Feeling a bit foolish Sue said, "Nice to meet you Sam and you're right, it's pretty obvious where I come from. How stupid of me. I'm a Lancashire lass from the north of England and I'm afraid I have a strong local accent."

"Well, I love it and I'll meet you here in the lobby at about 6.50pm shall I?" said Sam.

"Yes, that will be fine," said Sue, and as she was about to turn and leave, he said, "I'll look forward to it and to listening to that lovely accent of yours."

Sue walked off to her room in a daze. She couldn't quite believe what had just happened. She had actually arranged to have dinner with a total stranger without turning a hair. Was she mad? No, she decided she was just taking herself out of her comfort zone, and anyway, he must be at least 80 years old. What harm could he do to anyone, especially in a crowded hotel dining room? In the lift she realised that she hadn't sorted out her dinner booking for the following evening. *Oh god, I can't think about that now. I'll save that task until tomorrow. I need to get through this evening first. What am I going to wear? I'm going to have to iron those linen pants. They've been in my suitcase for the past four days. Goodness knows what they'll be like. I think I saw an iron and ironing board in the closet. Bloody Hell! What have you done Sue?*

Chapter 8

As she soaked in the bath, Sue was thinking more about the encounter in the Concierge's office. She suddenly remembered that the Concierge had called the old gentleman by his name, as if she knew him well. He said he was just resting in the chair so maybe he was familiar to the girl. He had probably been here for a few days already and she had seen him before. Yes, she thought that must be the explanation for it.

As Sue made the finishing touches to her make-up, she couldn't help feeling the butterflies that were floating in her stomach. It was as if she were a young girl, anticipating a first date. How ridiculous that was, especially at her age she thought. It wasn't as if she wasn't used to meeting new people and dining with them when on business for the bank, so why should she feel like this now? This was different though. She wasn't on business now. She was just an ordinary woman on holiday, in a strange place, and she had arranged to meet a total stranger for dinner. It was too late to change her mind now anyway, even if she wanted to do so.

At just before 6.50pm, Sue made her way to the lift and pressed the button for the ground floor. It was fortunate that she agreed to meet Sam in the lobby, because she had no idea where The Brasserie was and she had not had a chance to explore the hotel a bit more. He was waiting for her when she arrived in the lobby and he greeted her with a warm smile. He offered his arm gallantly and she took it readily thinking what a gentleman he was. They made small talk as they negotiated the stairs to the floor below where the entrance to The Brasserie became immediately visible.

The Maitre'd smiled warmly by way of greeting. "Ah, Mr Carter Sir and Madam. Welcome to The Brasserie and please follow me to your table."

Again Sue noted that he was instantly recognised by the staff who fussed around them ensuring they were comfortably seated. The table was in a prime position in the corner, where they had a view of the Lake. A bottle of champagne in a silver ice bucket was placed on a stand next to the table already and as the wine waiter came to pour it, Sam said, "I took the liberty of ordering this in advance, as an aperitif. I hope you like it. I don't know a woman who doesn't like champagne but I guess there's always a first. I can get something else for you if you don't want it."

"Champagne is fine, I love it, thank you. But I think I should get something clear from the start. I agreed to share your table, but I will be paying for my part of the food and drink okay?"

"Oh let's not talk financials right now Susan. I find it gives me indigestion when I'm eating." He smiled at her and offered a toast, "Here's to a good meal and pleasant conversation."

Sue raised her glass in response. "Cheers, and it's Sue." She gave him a wry smile that said 'I meant what I said about paying for my share'.

The food was wonderful and their conversation was easy. It wasn't long before Sue began to relax and enjoy herself. The couple of glasses of what was obviously very expensive champagne also helped her mood. She remembered how they had met and asked, "You said I reminded you of someone you knew this afternoon in the Concierge's office. Who was that?"

"Well, actually, it was my late wife, Ellen. Don't be offended by that, I meant that you look like she used to when she was younger. In fact, the resemblance is quite striking." At this point his look became pensive and he paused as if recalling some memory. "She died ten years ago this September and there isn't a day goes by when I don't miss her. You have her eyes and the same complexion. She was also the same sort of build as you. Then, when you spoke and the way you joked, just reminded me of how she was. I'm sorry, I don't want this to sound morbid, but when you couldn't get a table for tonight, I seized the opportunity to share your company in the hope that it might give me sense of being with her again. Please don't be disturbed by that. I'm not some weirdo, but when you get to my age, you look for any little chances to feel young again, even if it's only for a brief time."

Sue wasn't quite sure what to say. She decided that it was best not to dwell too much on what he had said and so replied, "I'm glad I can be of service to an old man, and anyway, it means I get to eat at a reasonable time. My digestion doesn't take kindly to late eating, or to very rich or spicy food, so I err on the cautious side most of the time. This is an exception because I'm on a holiday of a lifetime for me and I'm determined to make the most of it whatever the fallout is."

He laughed and she did too. It felt good to be having this pleasant evening and sharing some good company rather than sitting on her own watching everyone else laughing. During the meal they talked about each other's background. Sam said he was a retired cattle farmer from just west of Calgary. He had two married sons who had followed in his footsteps and now farmed the land and tended the cattle as he had once done. The farm had been in the family for three generations and he had lived there all his life. He had finally retired with Ellen when she was coming up to her 70th birthday and he was 73. They moved into a small bungalow on a corner of the farm so that he could be near his boys and help out occasionally.

"That was ten years ago. We retired in the spring of that year and we decided to come up to Lake Louise in the June as a retirement celebration and a birthday treat for Ellen from me. We stayed for a week and had the most wonderful time. We were spoiled by all the staff here who somehow knew that it was Ellen's birthday. They made a real fuss of her on our last evening. We ate in The Fairmont at the back of the hotel on the ground floor – have you seen it yet? It's a lovely place – a bit pricey, if you know what I mean but worth every cent."

Sue said she had seen it briefly when she arrived that afternoon and agreed it was quite splendid. She didn't tell him why she had decided not to choose that venue for her meal and secretly, she was glad she hadn't because she might have been able to get in there and she wouldn't be sitting here sharing this lovely meal with this wonderful old man.

As if he hadn't heard her speaking he continued, "We ate our meal and were the last people in the restaurant. Although it was late, the staff didn't bother us. There was a pianist playing a Viennese waltz and we got up to dance. Ellen loved to dance and she was actually very good. She tolerated my clumsy steps but never said anything. She had this knack of being able to make me feel good about everything I did. All through our married life it was like that. She was my rock. I know it sounds a bit corny but it's true. When we finally retired to bed (mainly because the pianist had had enough), there was a beautiful bouquet of flowers on our table in our room and a birthday card from the manager and staff of the hotel. Ellen thought it was great and said it had made her feel so special. I remember she cried and said she wanted to remember that moment forever. We left the next day and when we arrived home, the boys and their wives had organised a surprise party for Ellen's birthday. There were about fifty people there when we walked through the door. Not really what we were planning after a long trip in the car but we enjoyed it and she managed to look radiant as always.

A few weeks after that, she took ill. She didn't say anything to anyone, not even me, but I noticed her complexion was a bit grey looking and she had lost a little weight. In August she finally got the boys and me together and told us that she had a tumour on her kidney that the doctor had said was inoperable. She'd known for a few months I think. She said she had been for another scan and it had spread to her bones and there was nothing the doctors could do. Of course we all wanted her to get a second opinion but she wouldn't hear of it. She said she had made all the necessary preparations and she would carry on as normal for as long as she could. She accepted pain relief eventually and we got a nurse to come in to help, but we only needed her for a week before Ellen passed away in her sleep. I was with her when she died and the last thing she consciously did was to smile that lovely smile she had, the one she kept for me."

He paused for a moment and Sue noticed his eyes were glazed over. She didn't know what to say or do, but then she lifted her glass and said, "Here's to Ellen and all the good times you had together. She sounds like a very special lady."

Sam composed himself and brightened, raising his glass in response and taking a long drink. Then he said, "She died on the 3rd September 2002 and there isn't a day goes by when I don't talk to her. I know she's keeping an eye on me from up there and she's probably shaking her head right now and telling me not to be such a sentimental old fool." With that, he grinned at Sue and asked her to tell him a little about herself.

Sue gave him a brief outline of her life and said that she was fulfilling a long held wish to travel, explaining a little of why she hadn't done it before. He listened intently and chuckled when she made light of some of the situations she had found herself in with Jean on their travels.

They left the table for a more comfortable place to have a coffee and a nightcap in the lounge adjacent to the restaurant.

Another hour passed by so quickly, and before they knew it, the time was a quarter to midnight.

"Well," said Sue, "I've had a lovely evening and thank you Sam for your company, but I really do need to get to bed. I'm shattered."

"What do you have planned for tomorrow Susan?" asked Sam.

"I'm not really sure to be honest and it's Sue by the way. I know that I want to explore the lake surrounds a little more and take lots of pictures. The scenery here is just stunning. I might see if I can join an organised walk. I'm told there have been bear sightings in the last few days, so I'm not sure I want to go wandering off on my own."

"No, that's not such a good idea," he replied. "I wonder if you would care to join me for a short stroll around the gardens later in the afternoon and then a coffee on the terrace outside. The forecast is quite good for tomorrow and as the terrace faces south, the sun's on it for most of the day. I don't do long walks these days."

"Yes, I'd like that, and then I can tell you what I get up to."

Sue turned to look for the waiter and miraculously he appeared with the bill as if he knew what she wanted before she did. Sam moved to take the bill from the waiter but Sue got there first. She drew in a quick breath when she saw it. The total for everything came to $230 – about £160. Sue had never had such an expensive meal before but she was not going to let Sam pay for her. She turned to the waiter and asked him to bring two separate bills for equal amounts and she would charge her half to her room number. The waiter looked a little unsure and glanced at Sam who shrugged and said, "Do what the lady says please and bring two bills would you?"

"You really are an independent lady aren't you Susan?" he said, shaking his head.

"I told you I would pay for my own meal. I'm not a scrounger and never have been, and in any case your company has been more than pleasurable for me tonight, so thank you once again. Now, I really must get to bed and as I said before, it's Sue."

They said goodnight as Sue left the lift on her floor. She had noticed that Sam had pressed the button for the 8th floor and she smiled to herself. *You lovely old man Sam, you've come back here to remember your dear wife and I bet you're staying in the same suite as you did 10 years ago. You must have loved her very much. I envy her having had someone who loved her so much and showed it openly.* Her thoughts turned to Mark and she wondered what he would make of this. He'd probably laugh at her having dinner with an old man but he wouldn't be surprised it wasn't some young hulk. Was she really that predictable?

Chapter 9

Sue woke early the next morning. She looked at her watch – it was quarter to six. It would be about early afternoon at home. She got up and looked out of her window. The sun was just coming up over the lake and mountains. The lake was perfectly still and gave a mirrored version of the landscape. It was absolutely breathtaking. There was only one thing for it, she would dress quickly and take her camera to get some shots before all the Japanese visitors came out with theirs. Although it was early and there was a slight chill to the air, Sue felt that the day was going to be a cracker. She made her mind up to go to the deli for her breakfast and then book herself onto a guided walk – nothing too ambitious though – she knew her limits.

She thought of her evening meal with Sam whilst she ate her croissants and coffee, and of the things he had told her. He must have saved up hard to bring Ellen here ten years ago and give her the best room in the place. He was probably spending the last of his savings now trying to recapture the memories. How sad and poignant she thought it was, but also what a beautiful thing to do. Whatever the rest of her trip had in store for her, Sue knew that her stay here in Lake Louise would be hard to follow.

Sue booked a half day walk that was due to leave in about half an hour, so she just had time to freshen up and give Mark a ring. "What's the weather like?" she asked him. "Bloody awful, it's pissing down and blowing a gale. You'd never think it was June. What's it like with you?"

She told him about the snow in Banff and the difference in the weather today. She told him she had eaten dinner with an old man and shared his table because there was no room at the time she wanted to eat. He laughed and said he thought she might find a toy boy on her holidays not an old codger. She said she would ring again in a couple of days.

There were only five walkers including Sue gathered at the guide's office. The German couple were not among them. They were probably doing a much more difficult walk. They looked like they were the hardy types. The guide finally arrived – his name was Bruce and he looked like an old trapper, with a huge brimmed leather hat, chequered shirt and braces holding up khaki coloured corduroy trousers tucked into well used leather boots. He carried a large rucksack with an assortment of objects including a whistle and a map hanging from loops sewn to the bag. He had a large grey moustache and wore dark glasses. He inspected everyone's footwear and when he came to Sue said, "I think you'll need something more substantial than that little lady. We'll be climbing about 1500ft today and I'm told there's about eight inches of lying snow from halfway up. Come with me and I'll see what we've got in the kit room."

Sue followed him into a small locker room and eventually was set to go wearing a pair of very well worn leather boots that he had insisted she tuck her trousers into. He also provided her with a pair of walking poles telling her that he would give some instruction in their use once they were outside. The other walkers waited patiently whilst Bruce showed Sue how to use the poles once they left the lake surrounds. They headed up on the long incline through the woods. They were heading for the Bee Hive Tea House near the summit of a small mountain called the Bee Hive. It got its name from its shape and it was covered in pine trees.

Bruce said it would take about two hours to get there and they would have time to sample the different varieties of tea served there and a snack if they wanted one. Then, they would come back the same way. "There's only one track," he said, "so once you've been up, you'll know the way back down."

Bruce proved to be a first-class guide. What he didn't know about the area wasn't worth knowing. He lived locally in the town of Lake Louise as did most of the staff working at the hotel. He was especially kind to Sue on the walk, making sure she walked where it was safe once they reached the upper part where the snow lay. He made frequent stops so that they could all have sips of water and take photos of the Lake and its surrounding scenery form every conceivable angle. He also had a detailed knowledge of the flora and fauna and talked about the history of the area as they walked.

When they finally arrived back at the hotel, it was after two o'clock and Sue was famished. She went to her room and had a swift wash and changed her trousers. She also discarded a layer of clothing as the weather was decidedly milder this afternoon – 18°C according to the thermometer in the reception.
By the time she reached the front of the queue in the deli, she only bought a sandwich and a cup of coffee, which she decided she would eat outside on the terrace. As she made her way through the open French doors, a familiar voice called her name. It was Sam, and he was seated on the upper terrace with a newspaper spread out on the table and a pot of tea. She made her way over and he folded up his newspaper to make room for her sandwich and coffee. "How was the walk?" he asked.

"It was really good," she replied, "and very tiring too. I thought I'd get a sandwich and coffee before thinking about what to do tonight."

"Oh, I'm glad you mentioned that. It sounds like you haven't got anything planned. Am I right?"

"Well, not exactly, but I was going to check availability for the Italian place, the Lago. I meant to book it yesterday but forgot when we had our little encounter." She smiled and he grinned back.

"In that case, would you be my guest tonight in The Fairmont? It's my last night here as it is yours and it would be just great if you would join me?"

Sue thought about her wardrobe choice and replied, "It's very good of you to offer, but really I couldn't do that. You have been so kind to me already."

"Oh rubbish," he replied, "all I've done is allow you to share my table for one meal and you even insisted on paying your own way. You would be making an old man very happy if you would join me, honestly."

"Okay, Sam, I'll be honest with you. I can't afford the prices they charge in there and besides I didn't bring anything suitable to wear. It said on the board that dress was formal and ladies should wear dresses and the simple fact is I haven't brought one with me. I had to iron the life out of my linen trousers last night to even look half decent! So thanks for the kind offer but I can't accept."

Sam started to laugh out loud.

"What's so amusing?" she asked trying not to laugh and pretending to be serious.

"Well if those are the only two reasons you have for not wanting to dine with me then, that's okay. I was afraid that I had somehow put you off." He rose from the table and said, "Would you excuse me for a few moments. There's something I have to do." With that he disappeared into the hotel. By the time he came back Sue had finished her sandwich and was just draining the last of her coffee from the paper cup.

"It's all sorted," he said. "Where we're going to eat, dress code won't matter and as for the prices, this one is on me and I'm not taking no for an answer." He looked at her triumphantly.

"Well, if you put it like that and you are absolutely sure then I'll accept, but no champagne tonight because I haven't recovered from last night yet. Where are we eating?"

"There's a private dining room on the 8th floor and you can come dressed any way you like and no one will bother. Anyway, there was nothing wrong with what you wore last night, you looked enchanting."

"What do you mean a private dining room? Are you a member of a club here or something? The staff seems to know you by name and although I know you are quite memorable, they do seem to treat you with additional reverence."

"Let's just say I tip well and they love a good tipper," he replied tapping the side of his nose. "Shall we say 7.00pm as last night? Just take the lift to the 8th floor and someone will meet you and take you to where you're going. Now, tell me about your day whilst we have a little walk by the lake, that is unless you have done enough walking for one day."

"Oh, I give up, come on then before it starts to go a bit cooler."

Chapter 10

Sue managed to locate the second pair of linen trousers she had brought in the bottom of her suitcase. That was one downside to a holiday like this one where you were on the move. You didn't get chance to unpack and hang things up for any length of time, so everything had to be ironed before it could be worn, especially linen. *Oh well, you live and learn,* she thought, and proceeded to get out the ironing board again.

She chose a pale dusky pink top to go with her trousers and some sandals with a relatively flat heel. In fact, most of Sue's footwear was quite flat or only had a very small heel. She wasn't good with heels and wondered how women walked on stilettos, especially with those awful pointed toes which were bound to result in bunions when they were older.

Jewellery was another thing that Sue preferred to be plain and understated. Mark had bought her a number of items over the years as Christmas and birthday presents and they were nearly all gold with small diamonds. She wore a white gold pendant with three diamonds in the shape of a teardrop all the time together with a pair of matching earrings each with one small diamond. She didn't think that anything else was needed and most of the time, that was true.

After a final look in the mirror, she was satisfied that nothing more could be done to improve the wrinkles that seemed to be multiplying by the day, grabbed her bag and headed off to the lift for the eighth floor. The lift stopped smoothly and as if by magic, a porter was waiting for her when the lift doors opened. "Good evening, Mrs Barnett?" he said.

"Yes, it is," she replied a little startled at hearing him call her by name. *My god they're efficient in this place,* she thought.

"Would you care to follow me Madam, it's just along here."

They walked along a wide corridor carpeted by the thickest carpet she had ever seen. The pile must have been at least two inches deep! The decor was even more sumptuous than the rest of the hotel – if that was possible- and the doors leading off the corridor were enormously wide. Finally, the porter knocked on a door that had a sign on it saying 'The Beehive Suite'. *Oh, how lovely,* she thought. *I bet this room overlooks the lake and has a view of the Beehive. What a lovely setting for a small dining room.*

Sam opened the door and smiled broadly at Sue and the porter. "Come in my dear." With that he waived her in and gave the porter a tip before closing the door behind him. Sue walked into what looked like an entrance hall with a number of doors leading from it.

"The dining room is through here," he said, ushering her through a door on the left. The room was quite small with just one table set for two with crystal glasses, silver cutlery and a crisp white linen table cloth. It was placed in front of open French windows that led to a balcony. "Come and have a look at the view," he said, leading her towards the French windows.

Sue was speechless for a few moments. Her brain was frantically trying to take in all that she was seeing. This wasn't a private dining room – well, it was, but it was part of a suite, Sam's suite. She was right about him coming back to the same suite to relive old memories. But she hadn't figured she would be the unwitting stand-in for Ellen. The thought made her feel uncomfortable. He obviously sensed her unease and said, "Is something wrong?"

"Sam, all this is magnificent but I really don't think you should be spending your hard earned retirement money on me. I can understand you want to relive some old memories but I'm not Ellen and it makes me feel uncomfortable that you think I can somehow play a role for you here. I think it would be best if I just left you now and went to eat in the deli or something. We'll both be going home tomorrow and will never see each other again, so let's just part now and be glad that we met on our travels and shared some good conversation."

Sam moved toward her and took hold of her hand. His eyes were pleading and he looked as if he was about to cry.

"Oh Susan, please don't go. I never intended to make you feel like that, truly I didn't. I know only too well that no-one could take the place of Ellen. But it's just that when I saw you yesterday, I was genuinely taken aback by your likeness to her, I just wanted to talk to you. Then, when we started chatting, I really enjoyed myself and it lifted my spirits so much I just wanted to share this last evening with you. You are right my dear, we will never meet again but tonight of all nights I really don't think I could be alone with my memories. You see it's exactly ten years ago tonight that Ellen and I shared that last meal here in the Fairmont restaurant. Call it an anniversary if you like. I wanted to come back one more time and soak up the atmosphere and be near her again. Just indulge an old man and I promise I won't be miserable."

"Well, when you put it like that, I suppose it would be a shame to leave the table set like that, with no-one to appreciate it. Anyway, I'm quite famished with all that walking." She smiled at him and his face broke into a wide grin.

"Thank you my dear. You don't know what this means to me. By the way, did I tell you how lovely you look? I don't know why you thought you would be out of place in The Fairmont. Come and sit down and we'll get some wine and see what's on the menu."

A waiter appeared with the menus without having to be summoned. Sue hoped he hadn't been eavesdropping in one of the rooms that led off the small dining room. They chose some wine and food and settled down to enjoy the evening. The meal was delicious, but Sue couldn't help noticing that Sam only ate a small quantity of each course. He chatted freely and they laughed at each other's stories.

Sam talked a bit more about his family. His sons were named Adam, who was 52, married to Kate, and Greg, 49 married to Adele. Adam and his wife had one son, Ryan, and Greg and his wife had two girls, Katherine and Sophie. Adam, the eldest, lived with his family in the big house on the farm and Greg and his family lived a mile away on a plot that connected to the main farm track. Sam had a sort of housekeeper/cleaner who lived in the village nearby and came in each day to cook for him and run errands. Her name was Sarah and she was a spinster in her fifties. He said the boys would tease him that she fancied being the next Mrs Sam Carter and Sam said he couldn't repeat what he said back to them. Nevertheless she was a good woman who did her job with the utmost efficiency.

Sue talked a little more about the family and the burning desire she had to travel to as many places as she could afford. "You see Sam," she said, "I don't feel like I've done anything with my life. I've had three children and worked damned hard if I say so myself, but they are normal things that most ordinary people do. I haven't achieved anything outstanding or done anything really interesting, so I'm trying to make up for lost time before it's too late. It's such a big world and there is so much to see."

"Susan," replied Sam in a serious tone, "Don't underestimate the courage and strength it takes to bring up a family and hold down what was probably a very responsible job. I get the feeling you are a bit of a perfectionist where work is concerned and I'll bet they miss you like mad. Your family probably rely on 'good old Mum' to be there whatever and that takes commitment and guts so don't sell yourself short."

"Is that the end of the lecture Sam?" Sue finally said mockingly. "Oh and for the umpteenth time, my friends call me Sue, but you seem to insist on calling me by my Sunday name."

"That's because I like it better and I have the utmost respect for you my dear, so please allow me this small indulgence."

Sue was touched by Sam's obvious care for her and she agreed that he could be the exception to the rule.

The evening flew by and before they knew it, the time was almost midnight. They had left the table after their meal and were sitting on the balcony. The moon was shining on the lake and it truly was magical. Eventually, Sue said she had to go. She had an early start in the morning – the coach was arriving to pick her up at 8.30am – and she needed to try to refit everything back into her case and have it outside her door for collection at least an hour before that.

"Susan," said Sam, as she was rising from her chair, "will you do one more thing for me?"

Sue wondered nervously what the something was going to be but she said, "What's that Sam?"

"Would you consider being a kind of pen pal and keeping in touch by letter – you know, just telling me how you're getting on and I'll do the same? It would mean a lot to me to know that you were doing okay. Call it an old man's fancy if you like, but it would give me something to do and to look forward to – getting a letter from you and writing one back".

"Yes, okay if you like," she said. "Do you have an email address? It would be even easier and more instant if you know what I mean."

"No, I haven't. I can't be bothered with all that internet stuff. I leave all that to the boys. I'm a bit old-fashioned you know. I like the pen and paper method to be honest. I think it's more personal."

With that they wrote each other's address on some hotel paper on the desk in the entrance hall. Sue turned to Sam to say goodbye and to wish him a good journey home. He took her hand in both of his and kissed the back of it very gently but deliberately. "You know Susan," he said, "if I'd had a daughter I just know she would have been like you. You have made my holiday and you will never know how grateful I am for that. Have a safe journey back and I look forward to hearing from you when you get home with all the news from your end. Take care my dear and don't stop travelling and following your dreams."

"Goodbye Sam and thank you for your company. It really has been a pleasure." She kissed him on the cheek, turned and left him standing at his door. She turned around just before she got to the lift and he was still standing there watching her until she was out of sight. As she travelled back to her own floor in the lift, she felt so very emotional. It was almost like saying goodbye to her father when he was frail just before he died. When she got back to her room, for no reason she could think of, she burst into tears and sobbed until she was exhausted. This holiday was full of surprises.

Chapter 11

Sue didn't see Sam before she left that morning, but she hadn't expected to because he had looked quite tired when she had left him the night before, although he was putting on a brave face. She had to admit she was relieved in a way, because she was still feeling quite sad and she wouldn't have wanted to appear upset in his presence. She couldn't quite get her head around why he had made such an impression on her or why she felt the way she did. Obviously he was a very genuine old man and in some ways he reminded her of her father with whom she'd had a great relationship. Yes, perhaps that was it. Perhaps she was subconsciously thinking about her father and that's why she was feeling melancholy.

She rang Mark before leaving the hotel and updated him on where she was going next. She'd left him a copy of the itinerary on the hall table so that he could see where she was on a particular day, but she knew he probably wouldn't think to look at it. She mentioned that she'd had dinner with the old man again last night but she didn't go into detail about the venue. She wasn't sure why she didn't say. There was nothing wrong with what she had done, but she just decided it didn't need to be mentioned. She'd get enough stick when she got back anyway about having dinner with an old man when most women of her age went for the younger man. No, she'd leave out that bit of detail.

Today's driver was called Alan. He was a real character who had been a National Park Ranger for fifteen years prior to becoming a tour coach driver. As with the previous drivers, his knowledge of the national parks and their history was excellent and he was able to answer any questions levelled at him by the travellers, who again, were a different bunch from previous days. Among today's travellers was a middle-aged couple from New Zealand, Heather and Barry. Sue thought it rather a coincidence that she had met two ladies called Heather in such a short time as she didn't consider it a particularly popular name. They were en route to Vancouver but were taking a cruise up to Alaska from there. After that, they were returning to Vancouver and then flying to Australia to attend their daughter's wedding in Perth, before returning home in another four weeks' time. Sue was reminded once again how happy her fellow travellers were as couples. Every couple she had met were sharing these marvellous experiences and would be able to relive them once back in their homes either by watching the videos and looking at the snaps they were taking, or just talking and laughing about their experiences.

The coach had only just left the hotel and was heading for the main highway on its way to the Athabasca Falls in the Jasper National Park, when two bears were spotted by the driver high up on the grass banking next to the road. The driver was particularly excited and Sue thought this a little strange as he was surely quite used to seeing bears. The reason for his excitement became clear when he explained that one bear was a Black bear and the other was a Grizzly bear and they were sworn enemies. Also, they were almost never seen in the same vicinity. Alan explained that they were obviously unaware of each other's presence otherwise there would probably be a battle which would almost certainly be won by the Grizzly as it was a lot larger and heavier than the Black.

After the required stop by the roadside for pictures to be taken (from the safety of the coach), the journey to the Athabasca Falls continued. The largest falls Sue had ever seen were the ones at Ingleton in North Yorkshire, and she had considered those to be quite splendid, but they were nothing on the scale of these. The snow melt from the mountains combined with the recent high rainfall resulted in the most spectacular display of turbulent, cascading water imaginable. Huge, raging torrents of water poured from the mountains over one rocky shelf to the next, tens of feet below it and onto the next one and the next one until it finally reached the river in the valley below. The noise was thunderous and the spray formed a mist at the top of each cascade. The travellers were all advised to take extreme care when taking photos. There was always one though who wanted to get that unforgettable shot and nearly met his end but for the watchful eye of Alan, the driver, who spotted the potential disaster and managed to pull him back before it was too late.

The next leg of the journey was to take them to the Ice Fields and the Athabasca glacier. They reached the ice station at an altitude of about 8000ft. The weather was dry and sunny but the wind was strong and very cold. Everyone had been advised to wear warm clothing, sun block on their faces and a pair of sunglasses. Sue was so pleased she'd bought that fleece in Banff!

Following lunch in the Ice Station visitor centre, they were called to the meeting point to board a different coach to take them up the mountain to the start of the Ice Fields and transfer to the Ice Trains. These were enormous vehicles with special tyres that gripped the ice without damaging it. The guide on the Ice Train explained to everyone how each of the tyres lasted about 3 seasons (from the end of April to the beginning of October) and cost 5000 Canadian dollars each.

As it was the beginning of June and the sun was out, there was some significant melting, and by the side of the track going up the glacier, the melt had formed small blue streams of glacial water. The sight was breathtaking. There was mile after mile of blue ice that reflected the sun and dazzled the eye. Sue understood now why they had been requested to wear sunglasses. Once they stopped and got out of the Ice Train, one or two of the visitors went to fill their empty water bottles from the blue stream running along the edge of the parking area on the glacier. A guide warned them not to drink it quickly because it was so cold, it could cause them to stop breathing or even bring on a heart attack!

Everyone was frantically taking pictures. Groups of young students from China and Japan snapped each other in silly poses and serious poses. All Sue could hear was their chatting, laughing, and the clicking of their cameras as they took snaps of each other taking snaps – how weird. After about fifteen minutes, they were called back onto the Ice Train to be taken back to their coaches for their onward journeys.

The remainder of the afternoon was spent on the coach but there was more wildlife spotting including more bears with cubs this time, squirrels, a coyote, and the odd Rocky Mountain Long Horn Sheep. Finally, they reached Jasper where Sue would stay for two nights.

The Lodge was just about as different as you could get from the Fairmont Chateau Lake Louise. Sue's room was a small chalet on the ground floor, but it had all the amenities she needed for two nights and most of all a comfortable bed. Perhaps it was the excitement of seeing so many bears and the bracing (slight understatement) air on the glacier, but she was absolutely shattered. She made herself a cup of tea and then decided to have a short nap before showering and going to the Lodge bar for something to eat. An hour and a half later she woke with a start and couldn't think where she was. It took her a few seconds to get her bearings and when she saw the time – 7.15pm – she dashed off into the bathroom to get showered and changed.

There was a roaring log fire in the Lodge bar, which was just as well as it had started to rain again and the air felt quite cold. She chose a burger and fries – it was a change from the very rich food she'd had the two previous nights but she enjoyed its simplicity and she thought that her digestive system would appreciate it as well. After a couple of glasses of Merlot – she was beginning to get used to this now – she felt full and content. She looked around her at the other people in the bar. There were two couples, one young and the other older, eating and chatting quietly, one young man who looked like a local just in for a beer, talking to the barman and two young females having coffee.

She wondered how the hotel made any profit with so few people in the bar but decided that as it was midweek, it was probably quiet anyway. She pondered her journey so far and felt a sense of achievement for the way in which she had coped with everything. She also thought about Sam and hoped he had arrived home safely. She had been surprised when he had said that he would be driving the two hour journey back to the farm. He was 82 he had said. Then she had thought about her aunt who had still been driving at the age of 85, so it wasn't that remarkable after all. She made a mental note to write to him when she got back home as she had promised, though what she would say she didn't really know. Away from the atmosphere at Lake Louise, she wasn't sure she could tell him anything that he would find interesting.

She left the bar at 10.00pm and decided she would have an early night ready for the half day sightseeing trip in the morning. The coach would pick them up at 9.00am and return them to the Lodge at lunchtime, so that they would have the afternoon free to explore Jasper or do some other activity themselves.

The next morning dawned rather grey and overcast, and by the time Sue had finished her breakfast it was pouring with rain. Alan, the coach driver from the day before was waiting for them again this morning. He promised them a memorable if rather damp morning of sightseeing in the Jasper National Park. They spotted more bears that morning and a couple of eagles. Their journey took them alongside the Frozen Lake –

so called because the majority of it was still frozen on the surface, even in June!

The next stop was Maligne Lake and the even more spectacular Maligne Canyon. In places, the canyon was 180ft deep and running through it was a series of waterfalls that could be viewed from foot bridges and walkways that crisscrossed the rocks. They had a twenty minute stop to get a coffee from the café next to the car park and they all took advantage of the shelter from the rain. Sue shared a table with Heather and Barry, and as usually happened they asked her to take a photo of them. Finally, the weather began to improve and by the time they were returned to the lodge, the rain had stopped.

After a quick freshen up, Sue decided to walk the ten minutes into Jasper to grab a coffee and see the sights. Jasper was a busy little town and Sue managed to get a coffee and a cake from the much recommended pastry shop and café pointed out by Alan on the way through earlier in the day. It was every bit as good as Alan had said. After doing some window shopping, Sue made her way back to the lodge to have a shower and wait for a call from Heather and George, the couple she had met on the plane, who had said they would meet her for dinner.

As promised they stopped by her room to say they had just arrived and were going to change, ready to get something to eat. They would meet her in the reception in an hour. They chose a small bar and restaurant to eat and enjoyed a couple of hours catching up on what they had each been doing since they had bumped into each other in Banff a few days earlier. Sue mentioned that she had met an interesting old man at Lake Louise and had shared a meal with him. She didn't go into detail. For some reason she didn't want to talk about it so she confined her chat to the wildlife spotting. They compared notes on what they had seen along their journeys.

Finally, they strolled casually back to the lodge where Heather and George were going to be staying for a further two nights. They said their farewells and wished each other a safe journey back home. Tomorrow, Sue was embarking on the last leg of her trip to Vancouver on the famous Rocky Mountaineer Train. This leg would take two days with an overnight stop in a town called Kamloops. The train journey was to be a highlight of the trip for Sue because she had upgraded her ticket on the train to Gold Leaf. This meant she would have a seat in one of the two-tier carriages that had a domed glass roof for better viewing and she would be treated to five-star dining along the way. She was really looking forward to this part of her trip and to taking lots of photos from the viewing platform at the end of the carriage.

"Better get a good night's sleep tonight Sue", she said to herself as she locked the door of her room. She sorted out what she was going to wear the next day – the travel details had included a note that the dress code for the Gold Leaf carriages was smart - choosing a pair of trousers and a thin jumper that she had bought for her trip and decided she would dress it up a bit with a string of beads.

Another three days and she would be home and back to normal. There would doubtless be lots of housework to catch up on and washing, oh and of course she would need to go to the supermarket to get some food. She doubted that Mark would have done that. He probably had only shopped for his needs whilst she was away. She resolved to try not to think about that just yet. There was the train journey to look forward to. She collapsed exhausted into bed and slept soundly.

Chapter 12

Sue waited on the platform at Jasper Station along with the other passengers on yet another grey drizzly morning. She hoped the weather wouldn't spoil the views from the train. Exactly on time, the gates were opened and passengers were guided to the appropriate carriage as indicated on their tickets. Sue was in seat 60 in carriage number four. The platform was covered in a red carpet that led to each carriage entrance that was flanked on either side by attendants immaculately dressed in dark blue and gold uniforms and waving flags bearing the emblem of the Rocky Mountaineer train company.

The Gold Leaf carriages – there were four of them – were two-tiered and passengers were assisted up the steps and directed to the top tier by a steep flight of stairs that spiralled round to reveal the domed-roofed travelling area. The seats were made of cream leather and resembled armchairs rather than railway carriage seats. Sue thought that even the first class seating on intercity trains at home didn't come close to this luxury. She was shown to her seat at the window and the one next to her was left empty, so she had loads of room to spread her legs and deposit her handbag and camera on the empty seat. This was going to be just fabulous!

As the train slowly pulled out of the station, the train Director announced the staff that would be looking after their carriage for the two day trip. There were three of them – Andy, Greg and Rachael. They came to each of the passengers in turn and introduced themselves whilst handing out a glass of Bucks Fizz to toast the trip. Apparently this is a traditional start to each trip and Sue had to admit that this was shaping up to be a great two days!

There were sixty passengers in carriage four and there would be two sittings for each of the two meals that would be served each day. On the first day, the thirty passengers seated at the front of the carriage would eat first followed by the remaining thirty passengers at the rear of the coach. This would be reversed on the second day.

After about thirty minutes into the journey the first sitting was announced and the passengers went downstairs to the lower level to the dining room. Whilst they were being served their breakfast, the remaining passengers who included Sue, were treated to some pastries and coffee (just in case they felt that they would starve whilst waiting for their sitting). *My God,* thought Sue, *I'm going to put pounds on in the next two days at this rate.*

When the second sitting was called for breakfast, Sue made her way downstairs to the dining room. There was a mixture of tables for four or two, so Sue naturally went to sit at one of the tables for two as she was on her own. Andy approached her and said, "I hope you're not thinking of sitting here on your own. We don't allow people to be on their own whilst they're with us. Please follow me to another table where we have another passenger who is travelling on her own."

Sue hesitated momentarily, but then rose and followed Andy to a larger table where she was introduced to a lady called Valerie who spoke with a distinct Australian accent. She said she was on the last leg of a six week trip that had started in the States. She was due to fly back to Melbourne on Saturday from Vancouver. Sue estimated that Valerie was in her late sixties, and from what she said, it was obvious that she had travelled extensively throughout her life.

They chatted freely throughout the meal which was one of the best breakfasts Sue had ever had. If that was breakfast, she couldn't wait to see what was on the menu for lunch, although she doubted she would be able to eat anything else for quite a while. When they had finished breakfast, they agreed to sit together for all the meals and Sue looked forward to the prospect of getting to know Valerie a little better.

Once all sixty passengers had been served with breakfast, Greg announced that the bar was open and he and the other attendants would be coming round to take orders for drinks – alcoholic or otherwise. There was a wide selection of wines, beers and spirits, as well as soft drinks, tea and coffee which were all complementary. Sue smiled to herself at this last statement. Nothing was complementary really because she had paid what she considered a massive amount of money for this two day part of her trip. Nevertheless, it was good to know that she didn't have to think about opening her purse now.

The rain continued to come down steadily but Sue still managed to get some snaps of the landscape as the train wound its way through pine forests that bordered the Thompson River. The recent wet weather and the late thaw had combined to intensify the power of the many cascading waterfalls that appeared en route. Whenever the train was approaching a place for a photo opportunity, the train would slow down to a crawl and Greg would provide commentary on the history and background to the area. Sue was very impressed with the level of knowledge that all the attendants possessed. She guessed that as part of their training they would have had to study the routes of the trains and learn all about the flora and fauna together with some basic geology.

The remainder of the first day passed in much the same way, with good conversation among all the passengers mixed with the seemingly never ending stream of liquid refreshments. Sue sat with Valerie at lunch and they talked about their hobbies and interests. Valerie was an avid cricket and tennis fan and she and Sue exchanged stories about their visits to Wimbledon. It was remarkable, Sue thought later, that they had so much in common and seemed to agree on all sorts of issues such as world politics and law and order. Sue mentioned that she was planning to visit Budapest later in the year and Valerie told her that she had been born there but was among thousands of refugees who fled the Nazis in the Second World War. She had lost a number of her relatives including her father and uncles. She said that her brother, her mother, and herself had seen some very tough times in the early years following their evacuation from Hungary. She had gone back there for a holiday while her husband was still alive but he had died several years ago and she hadn't been back since.

Finally, after eight hours of travel, the train pulled into the small station at Kamloops. This was a kind of stopping over place, a town in the middle of nowhere really, where everyone said the temperature would be warmer than that of the other places Sue had been so far. Apparently, in the summer months of July and August the temperature regularly reached 30 °C. However, today it was a pleasant 20 °C. All the passengers were efficiently transferred to coaches to take them to their respective hotels for the night and collection the next day. Sue's hotel was a plain-looking concrete building right in the centre of the town and her room was on the eighth floor. To be honest, Sue wasn't too concerned about where it was, just as long as her case was waiting for her in her room and she could have a nice relaxing bath. It sounded silly to say that she was tired but actually she thought that all the eating, drinking and talking in between taking pictures of the scenery had really tired her out. She definitely didn't want a huge evening meal. She decided to have a quick shower, change into some comfortable clothes and footwear, and have a walk through the town. Maybe she would get a coffee and a snack. She would see what was on offer.

The early evening sun was pleasant on her back as she walked along the street from the hotel. She took a note of which direction she was going so that she could retrace her steps on the way back thinking once again of her friend Jean. After about forty minutes of walking, and not finding anywhere that she felt she could get a small snack, she decided to go back towards the hotel and find a convenience store where she might get a cold drink and a sandwich. She wasn't in the mood for company tonight and didn't want to sit in the hotel bar. She found a supermarket that had what she wanted and made her way back to her room to enjoy a quiet evening watching a film on the television.

She ate her sandwich and some prepared fruit she had found in the chilled cabinet in the store and started to watch an old black and white film – a period drama. She soon fell asleep on her bed and when she awoke it was 10.30pm. She changed into her pyjamas and crawled into bed.

As she lay there, she thought about the day and its events. Meeting Valerie and chatting to some of the other passengers too and the beautiful scenery the train had travelled through, even though it had been drizzling for most of the day. Perhaps it would be fine tomorrow for the second leg of the train journey and the final leg of her trip. How quickly it had gone and how soon it would be when she would once more be back home and back to normal. She was looking forward to seeing Mark and the family of course but she would be sad to leave all this behind her. She was determined at that point that there were going to be more holidays of discovery and started thinking of where her next destination might be until she fell into a deep sleep.

Chapter 13

As if someone upstairs had heard her prayers, the next day dawned bright and sunny. The train would take them away from the mountains and down to Vancouver at sea level. They would follow the Fraser River all the way and she had been told to expect a much different landscape than the one the day before.

The coach came to take them to the train and the boarding followed much the same pattern as the day before, with the now familiar attendants waiting on the platform to greet them. Sue and Valerie were on the first sitting for meals today and breakfast was a repeat of the day before so Sue picked something a bit lighter from the menu. They discussed their evening. Valerie had been booked into a different hotel, and she had said that she too was tired, so she had ordered a light snack from room service and washed it down with a glass of Merlot – her favourite wine. She had gone to bed early.

Another wonderful day unfolded, with fabulous scenery and great hospitality from the carriage attendants. Andy, the youngest one, was a budding singer songwriter and he treated the passengers to a couple of songs, one of his own compositions and the John Lennon classic, 'Imagine'. He was very good and the atmosphere was so intimate and quite poignant. As he finished Sue looked around at the assembled passengers. There wasn't a dry eye in the house, including hers.

Just before they arrived in Vancouver, Sue and Valerie exchanged email addresses and agreed to keep in touch. Valerie had asked Andy to take a couple of snaps of her and Sue on her camera and she said she would email them to Sue when she returned home. Sue pondered the pact they had made to keep in touch. People always say things like that but then they never do, but somehow, Sue had a feeling that they would. She felt that she had made a friend for life. This holiday had certainly delivered some surprises and Sue thought once more about Sam Carter. She had enjoyed Valerie's company immensely and knew they would have lots to say to each other by email. However, Sam was a different thing altogether. She would keep her promise to write to him because she felt some sort of duty to do that. But also, she had a strong feeling that she needed to do it. The old man had touched her heart in a strange sort of way that she couldn't explain. She put it down to him being a little bit like her father whom she still missed and thought of frequently. Along with the souvenirs and the things she had bought for herself, she had made two friendships that were so different yet so memorable. They were more valuable than the nice clothes she had bought and she knew their memory would last a lot longer.

Sue stayed the last night in a city centre hotel in Vancouver. She didn't venture out into the city that night, preferring to eat in her room and prepare for what was going to be a long flight home the next day. Her flight was scheduled for late afternoon so she resolved to get up early the next morning (Saturday), go out for a walk and take some snaps of Vancouver before checking out at lunchtime.

Saturday morning was a dull overcast affair and the rain soon appeared. It was a steady downpour all morning so Sue dodged the rain by stopping for a coffee in between snapping shots of the huge tower buildings and landmarks. She thought again of her friend Jean, as she negotiated the busy street intersections and the bustling crowds of shoppers as very soon the city came to life.

Finally, after cramming as much as she could into her case, she checked out of the hotel and took a taxi to the airport.

Her flight home was very tiring and although she was tired she only slept for about half an hour. The route took them over Iceland and although part of their journey was at night, it never really went dark. There were several small children on board and they seemed to take it in turns to scream as loudly as they could. Sue had a window seat and her travelling companion was a British expat, in her sixties, who was now a Canadian resident but was going to Bristol to see her sister who was ill. The flight must have been particularly tedious for her as she was going to have to get a coach in Manchester to take her the rest of her journey. That would be a further three hours after landing and clearing customs. Sue was so grateful that James was coming to meet her to take her straight home.

Chapter 14

James was waiting for her at the Arrivals hall as planned. It was lovely to see him, and Sue began to relax instantly, knowing that she didn't have to drive the hour or so it would take to get home. She briefly covered some of the highlights in answer to his question about whether she'd had a good time. However, as the car got nearer to home, she began to feel a little tired and agitated for some reason. Maybe it was the thought of having to come back down to earth as soon as she walked through the door that was weighing on her mind, but she couldn't get rid of a kind of sinking feeling in her stomach. *Jet lag probably,* she thought and tried to put it out of her mind. James said everything was as it had been before she left and there was nothing much of interest to tell her. He said he would just drop her off home and leave her to get sorted in her own time and say hello to Dad who was there waiting.

Mark was at the door on her arrival and helped her in with her bags before going to make her a cup of tea. "How was it then?" he asked as the kettle boiled.

"Fabulous," she replied, "everything is so big there and the people were really friendly. I met some nice people along the way and I never once felt threatened at being on my own in a strange place. It was a real experience."

"Good," he said. "You seemed to be enjoying yourself from what you said when you rang. As long as you've had a good time that's all that matters. Nothing much has happened here. The weather's been crap as usual. I've been busy working. I wasn't sure what you wanted to do about tea today so I just got something for myself for yesterday and I thought you'd probably be going to do the shopping when you got back."

Sue groaned inwardly. "I'll just unpack one of my bags and put some washing in and then when I've had a brew I'll get some food." She carried her largest suitcase upstairs and started to unpack. *Oh well Sue, might as well get on with it. Back to normal eh?* she thought as she looked at the unmade bed.

Chapter 15

It took Sue a couple of days to begin to feel as though she had overcome the jet lag and regained control of the household chores. Mark had washed some clothes while she was away but everything was stuffed in the airing cupboard all creased up. She supposed she should be grateful for small mercies in so far as he had made some effort at least.

After about a week, Sue's thoughts turned to Sam and the promise she had made to write to him. She sat down with the intention of writing a brief letter for now but found that she had written several pages before she knew it. She mentioned meeting George and Heather in Jasper and making friends with Valerie on the train. She said she hoped he had arrived home safely and that he was well and rested after his holiday. She posted the letter later that day when she was in town.

Life carried on much as usual and Sue met a couple of her friends for a coffee the following week. She told them all about the trip, briefly mentioning the old man and promised to show them her photos once she had loaded them onto her laptop. She suggested they make a night of it with some wine and supper and a film show of sorts. They wanted to know where Sue was planning for her next trip.

"I'll have to get over this one first and start saving some money instead of spending it before thinking about another holiday," she said with a raise of the eyebrows. She had planned a week away in Budapest with her friend, Jean, in early September, so she would just be happy with the odd day out between now and then.

Three weeks after arriving home, Sue received a letter from Sam.

Mr S W Carter
Triple C Ranch
Caldrane, Bow Valley
Alberta
CANADA

7 July 2012

My Dear Susan,

It was wonderful to receive your letter the other day and to hear about the rest of your trip. I'm not surprised you made more friends along the way because you are such an easy person to be with. I hope you will be able to keep in touch with the lady from Australia and maybe even visit her one day.

The boys are busy with the cattle, getting ready for the Stampede in a couple of weeks' time. They are showing a couple of prize bulls so we'll see if we can do well. We've also got one or two new calves so it's all hands needed. I keep out of the way as much as possible these days because they don't want an old duffer hanging around getting under their feet.

I don't get up to much apart from going into town to meet with some old guys I know and have a few coffees and put the world to rights. Once a fortnight I catch a lift into Calgary with one of the boys or their wives, and have a look around while they do their business.

How is your husband – Mark I think you said he was called- and your family? I imagine they were glad to see you back and I hope they had a 'welcome home' meal ready for you. Family is so important don't you think? Ellen and I used to love to see the grandchildren and have them over but they don't want to come visiting their old Grandpa now they're growing up. They've got more important things to do these days.

I do miss Ellen so much. We used to talk to each other all the time – never got tired of conversation with each other. Always remember Susan, that whatever happens in marriage, always keep talking because if the talking stops, so does the understanding and that leads to bad feeling and unnecessary conflict.

Listen to me being all morbid. Sorry about that. Anyway, on a brighter note, don't leave it too long before you get away on holiday again. I think you said you were planning a few days in Budapest with your friend Jean. My Dad was in Europe – France – during the Second World War, but never any further east or south. The Jews in Budapest suffered badly at the hands of the Nazis as in many other big cities. I believe that the architecture in Budapest is stunning so if you like to look at old buildings and are interested in history, then you should have a great time. Send me a postcard.

Well, I've taken up enough of your time for now so I look forward to hearing from you soon.
Sending fond regards and best wishes
Sam.

Sue thought about Sam's words and found herself thinking about her homecoming. Not quite a 'welcome home' meal – more of a 'do-it-yourself' job. As for talking, she and Mark seemed to do less of that lately. He was always working and when he did come home, once he had finished his meal he would invariably fall asleep in the chair. However, she supposed it wasn't all Mark's fault. She made a mental note to try a bit harder.

Chapter 16

As the months passed, Sue continued to write to and receive letters from Sam. She would mention them in passing to Mark and he would usually nod and mutter things like 'oh that's nice'. Sue hated that word 'nice'. It was such a nondescript word. What did it mean? Usually, it was used when people couldn't think of anything positive to say about something. She wondered what Mark really thought about her corresponding with an old man of 83 who she'd met on holiday thousands of miles away. Did he even care enough to have an opinion? She doubted it. He didn't seem to care about anything she did these days, so long as his meal was ready when he got home from work and he had clean socks etc. in the drawer.

Usually, Sue sent and received one letter a month from Sam. She sent him a postcard from Budapest as promised. At Christmas he had included in his letter a beautiful card addressed to all the family. She didn't seem to have any problem writing about all sorts of things when she wrote to Sam – even trivial things that she wouldn't bother to mention to Mark, she would put in her letters in detail, and, he in turn, seemed to love hearing about them.

Sue told Sam about her bucket list of possible destinations and said she would be having a think about where to go next once she had recovered from the Christmas festivities and expense.

No letter arrived in February and Sue wondered if Sam was ill. She remembered that both her parents had struggled with their health in the winter months, and in fact, they had both died in that season. She tried not to dwell on it and wrote a short letter enquiring if he was all right as she hadn't heard from him.

On the 4th March, she received a letter with a London post mark. On opening she saw it was from a firm of solicitors in SW7 by the name of Fearnley and Gordon. It advised with regret, that Mr Samuel Watson Carter had died on 24th February 2013. It further advised that they were acting as administrators of his estate and Sam had bequeathed a small item of jewellery to Sue in his will. The letter went on to request that Sue contact a Mr James Fearnley to arrange a suitable appointment to collect the item from their offices.

Sue's first reaction was one of shock followed by an inexplicable grief at the news of Sam's death. She sat down on the sofa to try to digest the news. "Poor Sam," she said out loud although there was no-one to hear her. She wondered how he had died. Had it been sudden? It must have, because his letters gave no indication that he was unwell. What about his family? His two sons – how were they coping? Had there been a funeral? No, it was only just over a week since his death so there wouldn't have been time.

Then, her thoughts turned to the bequest mentioned in the letter. What could the item of jewellery be? She wondered if it was a family heirloom, and if so, surely it should remain within the family, especially if it had belonged to Ellen. She couldn't possibly accept it. She would contact the solicitors and tell them that although she was grateful for the gesture, she didn't feel able to accept. How would Sam's sons and their wives for that matter, feel about their father giving away something personal that might have belonged to their mother to a complete stranger? No, that wouldn't be right. She was about to pick up the phone to call Mr Fearnley, when her mobile rang. It was her friend, Jean, calling to see if she was walking later that day. She tried to sound normal but was sure Jean picked up on her strange manner because she asked if she was feeling okay. "Oh yes, I'm fine. I've just received some mail and I was pre-occupied with it that's all. Yes, I'll meet you at a quarter to two at the bottom of the lane. See you later."

Sue decided she would discuss it with Jean whilst they walked. She needed to tell someone and it seemed like fate that Jean had rung her at that moment so she wouldn't do anything until she had spoken to her to gauge her opinion.

Later that day, as they walked along the river bank, Sue told Jean about receiving the letter and asked what she thought she should do.

"It's no-one's decision, only yours Sue and you have to go with your own instincts. But I think he obviously wanted you to have the jewellery otherwise he wouldn't have included it in his will. I understand what you mean about the family's view but have you thought that they might be offended if you refuse it? For all you know, Sam might already have mentioned it to them so they already knew. I can't believe he didn't tell them about meeting you in Lake Louise, so they will have gathered what a lasting impression you made on him. Anyway, as I said, it's your decision but you need to think about it carefully before you do anything rash."

"I hadn't thought about it that way Jean. To be honest, I'm still a bit shell-shocked and not a little upset. I really liked the old man you know. He reminded me so much of my Dad and although I thought it might be a bit of a chore writing to him regularly, I actually began to look forward to his letters and to telling him my news in return. I'm really going to miss that." As she finished her sentence she started to cry again, and Jean put a caring arm around her shoulders and gave her a squeeze.

"Why don't you talk it over with Mark at teatime? See what he thinks?"

"He won't have much to say about it I'm sure – he doesn't show much interest in anything I do these days unless it affects him in a bad way."

"I'm sure he'll have a view on this. After all, it's not every day you get left an item of jewellery in someone's will – especially someone you don't know very well."

"That's exactly it, Jean. What will Mark think I did with Sam for him to leave me something in his will?"

"I'm sure he knows he can trust you Sue, especially with a man who was old enough to be your father."

That's just it, I never know what he thinks because we hardly have a conversation outside of what's for tea and have I got a clean pair of jeans."

"I think you need to tell him about this as soon as possible and then decide what you're going to do, but I think you should go to London and collect whatever it is and be happy that you'll have something to remember Sam by."

They walked for about an hour and by the time Sue had left Jean and carried on up the path to home, she had practically made up her mind what she was going to do. She wouldn't call the solicitors until she had spoken to Mark.

Chapter 17

Mark was later home than usual that night. *Typical,* thought Sue. However, she wasted no time in showing him the letter from the solicitors and asked him what he thought.

"You obviously made a big impression on him Sue, for him to leave you something in his will. Course you have to go and see these people. I know this might be a silly thing to say, but they are above board aren't they? Have you checked them out on the internet or anything?"

"I haven't done anything yet, to be honest, because I was quite shocked when I got the letter. I had a walk with Jean this afternoon and told her about it but that's all I've done."

"What does Jean think you should do?"

"She says I should go and accept the gift."

"I think she's right – once you've checked them out. You never know it could be a scam to get you to give some personal information about yourself."

After Sue had cleared up from tea, she went on the internet to look up the Solicitors' details on the Law Society website. She found the firm's name quickly. It showed they had offices in Toronto, Calgary, and London. Mr James Fearnley was the senior partner at the London office but another Fearnley, Robert, was the senior partner at the Calgary office together with a Mr Richard Gordon. The partner listed in Toronto was a

William Gordon and there were several other solicitors named at all the offices. They were clearly a large practice. The telephone and fax numbers listed on the letter matched those on the website as did the email addresses. Everything looked normal and this made Sue feel a bit better. She told Mark and said she would ring them in the morning.

"Why don't you take Jean with you and have a couple of nights in London – enjoy yourself while you're there. You might as well if you're going to the trouble of getting train tickets etc."

"Hmm, I might do that. I'll probably feel less nervous if there's someone going with me."

"What's to be nervous about? You're going to be given a gift – it might be worth a bob or two- you never know."

"Oh, I doubt that. Sam wasn't a wealthy man from what I gathered, and anyway, that's not the important thing is it?"

"No, but all I'm saying is it might be worth more than you think so you should be prepared to have it valued or something."

Sue sighed inwardly. Her overriding feelings were of sadness and she was going to miss corresponding with the lovely old man she had become fond of. Jean was right. The jewellery would be a constant reminder of Sam and his friendship. She went to bed that night and knew she would not be able to sleep. She lay awake thinking about what she would say when she rang the solicitor. She must remember to ask him how Sam had died and what the funeral arrangements were. She would get a sympathy card and send it to Sam's family.

Chapter 18

Sue keyed out the numbers with trembling fingers at 9.30am the next morning. She was quickly connected and put through to Mr James Fearnley's secretary who sounded ultra-efficient.

"Mr Fearnley has asked me to speak to you to arrange a time suitable to you to see him regarding the matter in his letter. What day would be suitable Mrs Barnett?"

"Well, I don't think I can manage this week as I have appointments on Wednesday and Thursday and I need time to arrange train tickets etc."

"How about next week then? Let's say Tuesday? Mr Fearnley is in court all day Monday and he will need some time to attend to his mail in the morning, so how about Tuesday afternoon around 2.30pm?"

"Er, yes that would be fine I think."

"Good, it's in the diary and we look forward to seeing you then Mrs Barnett. Goodbye." With that she rang off and there was silence at the other end of the line.

My God! thought Sue, *she was in a hurry. I didn't get chance to ask her anything. Never mind, I'm sure it'll be all right.*

Sue set about booking train tickets and a hotel on the internet after speaking to Jean and asking her to go with her for moral support. Jean had agreed readily and Sue began to feel a little less worried about it. Everything was set for travel down on Tuesday 11th March at 9.30am which would give Sue time to check in at her hotel before going to the solicitors. The hotel she had chosen was one she had stayed in before, and after consulting a map of the city Sue realised that it was conveniently located within walking distance from the solicitors' offices on Harrington Road in Kensington.

Mark rang her later that morning to check if she had spoken to the solicitor and she told him she had. She went into town that afternoon and bought a sympathy card to send to Sam's family. Choosing just the right one was difficult as Sue didn't know how the family would react on receiving it. She settled on a blank one so that she could write a brief message herself. However, when it came to doing it, she found it hard to think of the right words to say. In the end, she simply offered her sympathy to all the family and said that she had known Sam briefly but had liked him and was sure he would be missed by all. Whatever she said she knew it would sound inane, but she had to write something. It was common courtesy and she couldn't just leave it.

She posted the card later that afternoon and called on her daughter-in-law – James's wife – to say hello.

Emma was just making a cake so she chatted to her in the kitchen while she got on with it. She told Emma about the letter and the trip to London.

"Ooh, that sounds exciting Sue, when are you going?"

"The week after next – I'm taking Jean with me and making it a short break."

"Good for you," said Emma. "If you don't mind my saying so, you've looked a bit tired lately and the change will do you good."

Jean was a bit surprised at Emma's comments because she hadn't thought anyone noticed her much these days, let alone be aware of how she looked. She had to admit to herself that she had felt a little jaded of late but she put it down to winter blues. It had been a very long one.

"Well, thanks for the brew and chat Emma. I'd better be going or else the tea won't be ready when Mark gets home and that would never do would it?"

Emma grinned and shook her head. "He doesn't know when he's well off. You really spoil him you know that don't you?"

"Try telling him that. Anyway, perhaps we'll see you at the weekend?"

"It depends on what James wants to do, but probably we'll drop in to see you."

With that, Sue left and drove the short distance home to get tea sorted.

Chapter 19

The weather was cold and blustery on the morning Sue and Jean travelled to London. Sue had spoken to the conductor on the train and had upgraded their tickets for a small charge, so they were sitting comfortably in the First Class carriage sipping a glass of rosé wine. They chatted freely about all sorts of things. As usual, the subject of age came up.

"Don't you think Jean, that when a woman reaches her sixties, she becomes invisible?"

"What do you mean exactly?" replied Jean.

"Well, you don't get noticed by men in the street. You know, men don't look twice at you do they? In fact, no-one really takes any notice of you. It's like you're anonymous. Even my husband doesn't notice me any more, so what chance is there for me in the outside world? Don't get me wrong Jean, I don't want to have an affair with anyone (except perhaps Mark, though chance would be a fine thing), I just would like someone to smile at me every once in a while, or at least acknowledge that I exist, just so that I felt like a woman again."

"Oh yes, I see what you mean but Mark loves you really. He's maybe not that good at showing his feelings – keeps them hidden."

"I'll say he keeps them hidden. He's so matter of fact about everything. We live like brother and sister rather than a married couple."

"Well, I can't comment because I've been on my own for a long time now but maybe that's what happens when you've been married as long as you two have. Perhaps that's a better guide, the number of years you've been together. If he didn't love you he wouldn't still be around."

"Don't kid yourself Jean. You know what they say about people not changing their bank account because it's better the devil you know and all that – inertia and apathy I think they call it – well I feel it's a bit like that with Mark. No Jean, I'm sure that when you get to sixty, you have a label stamped on your forehead – 'I am sixty – beware! Do not look at me or you may turn to stone!'"

They laughed out loud and toasted all women in their sixties. The other passengers in the carriage – mainly business men tapping away on their laptops and tablets – looked at them, some disapprovingly and the rest curious as to what the joke was.

"We'll be getting turfed out of here if we're not careful," whispered Sue as she noticed a couple of the stares from fellow passengers.

"This is great!" said Jean, enjoying the comfort. "Thanks for this Sue but you shouldn't be spending all your money like this. You won't have any left at this rate."

"You can't take it with you Jean, and anyway, I could be dead next week."

"What a cheery thought."

"Well, you know what I mean. You can't take it with you and all that, and to quote my Dad, 'they don't put pockets in shrouds'. Let's just enjoy the next two days- after I've seen the solicitor this afternoon that is."

It was almost noon when they reached Kings Cross station. The weather in London was slightly warmer and there was a bit more brightness in the sky than back at home, so this lifted Sue's mood a little and once in the taxi on the way to the hotel, she resolved to be a bit more positive and enjoy herself.

They checked into the hotel and sat in their room drinking a cup of tea Jean had made from the in-room facilities.

"I don't know about you Jean, but I'm not hungry after the sandwiches we had on the train. I think I'll have a quick wash and re-apply my make-up ready to go to the solicitors. According to the map, their offices are only a couple of streets away, so we can walk it. I'm assuming you want to come with me."

"Oh yes," said Jean, "but I'm not sure what help I'll be when we get there and I think you should go in to see the solicitor on your own. After all, it's your private business and I don't want to be in the way. I'll be happy sitting in the waiting room."

"Well, if that's what you want, okay, but I don't mind you being in the room with me you know. Nevertheless, I'll be happier just knowing you are outside the door. I know that sounds a bit daft but that's what I feel. Now, what should I wear? I've travelled down in my jeans because I didn't want to crease a pair of trousers on the train."

"I don't think it matters really," said Jean, "but if it helps then wear something that makes you feel more confident."

Sue chose a pair of grey trousers teamed with a dusky pink angora sweater and patterned scarf. She had a black wool three-quarter length coat and she decided that, together with her black leather ankle boots and matching handbag, she looked reasonably smart.

At 2.15pm, Sue and Jean set off on foot to walk the couple of blocks to Harrington Road. As Sue thought, it was only a short walk away. The Georgian properties on Harrington Road seemed to be taken up by professional occupants – solicitors, doctors and dentists. The door of Fearnley and Gordon at number seventeen was typical of that period. Three steps led up to a huge black gloss-painted door with brass fittings. The only concession to the present day was a keypad mounted on the wall with an invitation to visitors to 'press for attention'.

Sue did as requested and a voice from within asked for a name.

"My name is Mrs Barnett and I have a 2.30pm appointment with Mr James Fearnley."

A buzzer sounded and the door glided open as if by magic. Sue and Jean entered through a further frosted glass door.

Fearnley and Gordon's reception area was quite magnificent to say the least. It reminded Sue of something she had seen out of the TV drama 'Upstairs Downstairs'. The black and white checked marble tiled floor gave way to an enormous sweeping staircase of marble stairs with an ornate wrought-iron rail topped in mahogany that had been polished to within an inch of its life. Directly in front of them was a mahogany desk occupied by a smart young woman, Sue guessed to be in her mid-twenties. She asked them if they would like a drink while they waited and they declined and seated themselves on a brown leather Chesterfield in one corner of the reception.

From where they were seated, Sue had a view of the staircase and after only about two minutes waiting, a pair of very shapely legs appeared on the stairs from the floor above. The shapely legs gave way to a black pencil skirt and crisp white blouse, and belonged to a very tall but extremely elegant woman with black hair tied beautifully in a French pleat at the back. She wore a single string of pearls with earrings to match and, as she negotiated the last step, Sue's eyes were drawn to a pair of impossibly high stiletto heeled, black, patent shoes. *This has got to be the secretary I spoke to on the phone,* thought Sue. She was right. The vision held out a hand and introduced herself as Laura, Mr James's personal assistant.

"Mr Fearnley is ready to see you now Mrs Barnett. Please follow me."

Sue followed Laura up the marble stairs to the next floor. There were a number of doors leading off from the wide landing and at the third one, Laura stopped, knocked and after a slight hesitation, walked in. "Mrs Barnett is here to see you Mr Fearnley." Laura stood aside and a tall fair-haired man in his late forties walked across the floor to greet Sue. He held out his hand and Sue shook it with a confidence she did not feel. (An old manager of Sue's had once told her that you could tell a lot from someone's handshake so it was important that you should make it firm and make a statement up front as it gave you a psychological advantage and gave a good impression).

"Good afternoon, Mrs Barnett. I'm James Fearnley, senior partner. Thank you for taking the time to come down to London. Did you have a good journey?"

He motioned towards a leather armchair in front of his desk and Sue sat down saying, "Yes thank you, it was quite pleasant. First Class was quiet so my friend and I had a peaceful journey."

Sue instantly felt ashamed of herself for saying that but she wanted him to think of her as someone used to travelling first class not some hick from up north. If he thought she had said that for effect, he didn't show it and went over to a small table near one of the two bay windows that flanked either side of his enormous desk. On the table was a silver tray with tea and coffee pots, several cups and saucers, a milk jug and sugar bowls with white and brown sugar. There was also a silver box that Sue decided must contain biscuits.

"May I offer you a cup of tea or coffee Mrs Barnett?"

"No thank you, I seem to have been drinking all day so far – tea and coffee of course," she lied.

He sat down behind his desk and looked at her intently for a split second longer than she felt comfortable with. She wondered if he was weighing her up on behalf of the family so that he could report back later. She wondered what he would tell them.

"Well, let's get down to the reason for your visit," he said, taking a large brown envelope from his desk drawer.

"As I said in my letter, Mr Carter sadly passed away on February 24th this year, and in his will, which was amended recently, he gave instructions for you to receive this item of jewellery. It is a small pendant that belonged to his late wife and as such it is an item much valued by the family. I hope you will enjoy owning it."

He took a small, square, red leather box from the brown envelope and slid it towards her on the desk. The box was plain except for a fine gold edging. Sue hesitated and looked at Mr Fearnley as if to seek his permission to open it. She took an inwardly deep breath and lifted the lid.

It was no ordinary pendant that met her gaze, and an instant flash of light shot from the inside of the box. There, mounted on a raised section of cream velvet in the centre of the box, was the most beautiful diamond object she had ever seen. The small oval pendant – about one inch in length, contained a centre stone surrounded by twelve smaller ones, all cut exquisitely and mounted in a platinum setting. The pendant hung on a chain of what Sue guessed was white gold. She gasped and put her hands to her mouth to stop herself from speaking. Tears instantly came to her eyes and she looked towards one of the bay windows to avoid the solicitor's face. She tried desperately to control her voice and could only manage to shake her head.

"I know it's beautiful isn't it?" he said. "It took my breath away when I first saw it a couple of days ago. Would you like me to take it out and put it on for you to see it in all its splendour?"

"No, I mean, not just now. I need a moment or so to take this in. Mr Fearnley, I can't imagine why Sam, er, Mr Carter, has left this to me. You probably know that I only met him last year when we were both staying at the Chateau Lake Louise and we had dinner a couple of times – that's all, nothing else I can assure you. I wouldn't want you to think that I'm that sort of woman."

"And what sort of woman would that be, Mrs Barnett?" said a voice from the far right corner of the room. The voice was that of a very handsome man in his early fifties who had apparently entered the room from the door now behind him. Sue instantly knew who he was – the likeness was striking. It had to be Adam, Sam's elder son.

"Allow me to introduce Adam Carter to you Mrs Barnett." said the solicitor rising quickly from his chair.
"Adam, this is Mrs Susan Barnett."

For a moment there was silence as all parties looked from one to another as if suspended in time. Adam was the first to break the spell, moving towards Sue with his hand outstretched. Sue gathered her wits and shook the offered hand with even more vigour than she had earlier with Mr Fearnley, but she pulled her hand away quickly to let him know that she was merely being courteous. Sue rose and looked at both men. Then she launched into speech:

"Mr Fearnley, I came here at your request, and might I say, after a great deal of deliberation, to accept a 'small item of jewellery' – I think that's how it was phrased in your letter – that had been left to me by the Late Samuel Watson Carter. I did not come here to have my morals scrutinized or to be interrogated by anyone. Mr Carter, as I said, I only knew your father for a very brief time, but one thing I know is that he would be ashamed of your behaviour today. You do your father a disservice by acting in this way. You have rudely interrupted my meeting with Mr Fearnley by barging in unannounced and instantly trying to intimidate me. I may not have known your father for long but I would never dream of sullying his memory by treating one of his friends like this.

I was about to say to you, Mr Fearnley, that I couldn't possibly accept the pendant when I had not even met Sam's family and they surely would want it to stay in their keeping. I am not a gold digger or a loose woman or whatever you want to think. I am just an ordinary woman who happened to meet an old gentleman quite by chance on holiday. We just got talking and found that we shared the same values and enjoyed each other's company. It was actually your father who approached me if you must know. It was your father who asked me to share his table the first evening because there were no more places left and I was on my own. It was your father, **Mister Carter**," (she emphasised these words for maximum effect) "who asked me to write to him after I got home as he wanted to keep in touch. And do you know what? I will accept the pendant and I will treasure it for the rest of my life in the knowledge that I at least thought of Sam with the respect he deserved and not of someone who would somehow buy favours from a younger woman."

She was just getting in her stride when Adam broke in. "Mrs Barnett, please sit down and listen to me. I owe you an apology for the way I intruded just now. I know it was wrong, but I had to be sure you were genuine. You see, my Dad's death has hit me and all the family hard. He didn't tell us about you and we only discovered your friendship after he died and we were given the details of his will and it was a bit of a shock to find he had left something that he valued highly, to a complete stranger. You talk about him as if you and he had a special bond and I'd like to understand that and know more about your brief time spent with him if you would care to tell me."

Adam turned to Mr Fearnley, who seemed to be about to say something and said, "James, I think we've taken up too much of your time already today. How about Mrs Barnett and I resume this discussion in a more convivial atmosphere? You've carried out your duties and I'm sure Mrs Barnett has other things she would like to be doing. Mrs Barnett, would you please consider having dinner with me this evening so that we can complete this transaction on a more amiable note?"

Both men looked at Sue, waiting for a response.

"Mr Fearnley, do you need some sort of receipt for the pendant? If so, please let me have something to sign and then I'll leave. Mr Carter, I am visiting London with a friend who is waiting patiently in reception and who I have promised to take out for dinner tonight. She has readily agreed to join me and I do not intend to let her down, so I am afraid I will have to decline your offer."

"Mrs Barnett, may I call you Susan? I would be delighted to take both of you out to dinner. I'm only here tonight and then I have to fly back to Canada in the morning. It's the least I can do after everything that's happened. Please say you will agree. I will pick you both up at your hotel so you don't have to negotiate the city unaccompanied at night."

Sue considered this for a moment while James produced a document for her to sign – in duplicate of course – one for her to take with her and one for his file. She looked at Adam and her face softened. *I'll be dammed if he doesn't look just like his father when he pleads with you,* she thought to herself.

"I'll need to speak to Jean first and then I'll call you at your hotel if you give me the details."

"That's great," he grinned, and took a page of notepaper offered to him by James and wrote on it. He handed it to her.

She glanced at it and laughed wryly. "I don't believe it. You are staying at the same hotel as we are – The Kensington Rise- that's bizarre. It's only round the corner so we walked it here earlier."

"You don't need to walk back – I'll get a cab for us."

"Absolutely not – er, thank you anyway but we would prefer to walk. I need to get some fresh air before I do anything else and clear my head. I will speak to Jean and then I will leave a message for you on reception before 6.00pm. Is that okay Mr Carter?"

"Please call me Adam, and, yes, that will be fine."

Sue rose and shook hands with James Fearnley, who was looking a little shell-shocked himself. She was about to leave when he said, "I think you are forgetting something Mrs Barnett." He handed her the brown envelope in which he had replaced the pendant and smiled.

Oh my God, the pendant, thought Sue, *I'd almost forgotten that what with everything else going on.*

She felt her stomach doing a flip at the thought of its beauty. How on earth was she going to explain all this to Mark when she got home? Before that she had to show it to Jean, but she'd wait until they were on their own in the sanctuary of their hotel room.

The efficient Laura entered the room on queue and accompanied her back down the stairs into the reception hall to the waiting Jean, who had apparently changed her mind and was just finishing off what turned out to be her second cup of tea. Sue gave Jean a 'knowing' look that said 'let's get out of here quick' and they soon found themselves standing out on Harrington Road in the fading brightness. Sue shuddered and Jean asked eagerly how it had gone and what was the item of jewellery.

It was 3.50pm and Sue apologised to Jean for the long wait. She said she would tell her in good time, but first she wanted a stiff drink in the hotel bar. Jean looked a little anxious and linked her arm in Sue's saying, "Come on then, I can't wait to hear what happened. You were gone ages and I was beginning to wonder if everything was all right. You do look a bit pale Sue. Are you okay?"

"I will be when I've had a glass of wine and time to come down to earth," replied Sue, and with that they headed back to the hotel.

Chapter 20

As they sat at a table in the far corner of the lounge bar, Sue took a long drink of the large glass of wine she had ordered. Jean sat next to her, waiting intently for her to tell her what had happened in the solicitors' office. Sue took a deep breath and began her tale. She left out the detail of the pendant telling Jean she would come to that shortly. Jean was mesmerised by what Sue was telling her. She interjected from time to time with an "Oh my God" or "I'd have run a mile. I wouldn't have known what to do." When Sue had finished her story, she produced the brown paper package and discreetly opened the red box under the table for Jean to have a peak at.

"Bloody hell!" said Jean. "Pardon my French but I've never seen anything like that before, it's beautiful! Sue, you must be thrilled to own that. I bet it's worth a bit you know. I think you should go to one of those swanky jewellers up the West End and get it valued."

"Jean, I just can't think of that right now," said Sue, closing the box and putting it back in the brown envelope. "I'm still in shock. What intrigues me now I've had a bit more time to digest what's happened is how an old farmer from an ordinary working background could afford to buy something like that. In fact there are one or two things that don't seem 'right' if you know what I mean."

"What other things Sue?" asked Jean.

"Oh, just this and that, for one thing, the solicitors' offices were rather up market didn't you think? They're not some small-time set up either. When I looked them up on the web they have offices in two other major cities and loads of partners and solicitors listed as working for them. Anyway, what about dinner tonight Jean? Are you up for it or not? If you don't want to I won't mind, but I must say there are a few questions I have for Mr Adam Carter that I didn't get the chance to ask this afternoon."

"I'm happy to have dinner with him so long as it's somewhere nearby so that we can get back here easily if there's a problem," said Jean finally.

"Well, I'll call him and suggest we eat in the hotel as we are all staying here and if he asks why, I can say that we are tired and he did say that he had an early start tomorrow. That way, we can beat a hasty retreat if needs be. I have to say though, Jean, he is rather a pleasant bloke and although we didn't get off to the best of starts, he had a bit of a way with him, if you know what I mean. He bears a striking resemblance to his father especially when he smiles."

"You don't fancy him do you Sue?"

"Oh for goodness sake no, it's just that I think he might be quite pleasant company and I'm hoping he'll pay as it is his invitation."

"When you put it like that Sue, it sounds a good plan. What shall we wear?"

Sue rolled her eyes and said, "That's the least of my problems at the moment. Anyway Jean, it won't matter what we wear will it? You're forgetting what we discussed on the train this morning – we're invisible!"

They both started to laugh uncontrollably and then Sue remembered something and became serious. "I promised to ring Mark to update him at teatime. How am I going to explain this little lot?"

"What's to explain? You just need to tell him that you have been left a rather nice pendant and the son of your friend has asked both of us to dinner as a courtesy – all perfectly innocent."

"A rather nice pendant! Jean, that's the understatement of the year. It doesn't even come close to describing it. Anyway, when you put it like that I suppose it sounds perfectly natural. Thanks Jean, I knew I could count on you to rationalise things for me."

"I do have my uses from time to time," said Jean grinning.

They finished their drinks and went upstairs to their room to prepare for the evening. It was now 5.30pm and as Jean prepared to make another cup of tea, they both realised that they hadn't really had much to eat apart from the snacks on the train that morning. That seemed so long ago now and Sue made a mental note of the things she needed to do next.

Number 1, ring Adam and confirm arrangements for tonight
Number 2, ring Mark and give him an edited version of the day's events
Number 3, drink her tea
Number 4, have a nice warm relaxing bath

Plan formed in her head, Sue set about the first task on her list and called Reception asking to be put through to Mr Carter, room number unknown.

Adam agreed that it would be sensible to eat in the hotel and said he would meet them both in Reception at 7.30pm if that was okay. Sue asked if it would be wise of him to check that the hotel could accommodate them at that time before they made a firm arrangement. He seemed a little amused at that and said, "Oh don't worry about that, they'll have room for us I can assure you."

With that she said goodbye and hung up the phone.

"You know, Jean, he's such a self-assured person. He laughed when I said he should check availability first. It's as if normal rules of convention don't apply to him. That's another thing he gets from his father."

Jean didn't answer – she was asleep on her bed.

Oh, well, thought Sue, *task number two here we go.*

Mark picked up on the second ring which was remarkable as he had a habit of leaving his phone lying about. "Hi ,Sue," he sounded quite bright, so she was somewhat encouraged by this and went straight into her edited version of events, telling him that the pendant looked like it was real diamonds but she would need to have it checked when she got home. She said that Sam's son was at the solicitors and he had invited both her and Jean to have a bite to eat with him later. She said she had accepted only because Jean was with her and she thought he would pay. Mark agreed that seemed a good plan and said he hoped she had a good night and a nice day tomorrow. He would give her a call at about the same time tomorrow to see how they were doing.

The call only lasted about ten minutes and when Sue put the phone down, she heaved a sigh of relief. Now, she would have that cup of tea, if it was still warm, then she would get in the bath while Jean was asleep.

Chapter 21

After much deliberation, Sue and Jean both decided that smart casual was the safest bet. They both opted for smart trousers. Jean chose a fitted blouse with a simple gold locket. Sue went for a black and white tunic that covered her bum and hid what she believed was her worst asset. Jean asked her if she was going to wear the pendant.

"Not on your life!" said Sue, giving Jean a 'don't go there' look "Actually, I'm wondering where to put it for safe keeping. Do you think it'll be all right in the room safe?"

"I don't see why not," replied Jean.

"I did wonder whether to ask at Reception for it to be put in the hotel safe but I don't want to draw attention to it. I know that might sound a bit daft. Having said that though, I can't take any chances can I? It would be terrible if it got stolen from my room even before I'd had a chance to get it home."

"Oh God, yes, especially as you haven't had it valued yet and you'll have to add it to your home insurance policy because it's bound to be more than the limit for a single item."

"Oh Jean, I hadn't thought of that either. This is becoming something of a burden right now. I will go and put it in the hotel safe. I'll do it when we go down to meet Adam. If we go a few minutes earlier, hopefully he won't be there to see me doing it, not that it matters I suppose, it at least proves that I intend to look after it."

At 7.20pm they took the lift down to Reception and fortunately, there was no-one waiting to be attended to. Sue asked to speak to the duty manager who appeared within seconds, as if by magic, from his office behind the desk. Sue asked if she could speak to him in private and he immediately ushered her into his office and offered her a chair, looking a little concerned at what she was about to say.

She produced the brown envelope and said it contained a rather precious item of jewellery that she would rather keep in the hotel safe.

"That's no problem at all, Madame," he said. He produced a log book and asked for a room number and name. "Madame, may I know the detail, just for the record of course. If, God forbid, anything should happen, we need as much information for our insurers as possible. I'm sure you understand."

"Of course," said Sue. "The box inside the envelope contains a diamond pendant on a white gold chain. Is that enough detail for you?"

"Yes Madame. That will be sufficient for my records." As he took the envelope from Sue he smiled a strange little knowing smile. Sue wondered if Adam had previously kept it in the hotel safe prior to taking it to the solicitor. After giving Sue a receipt for the package, the manager showed Sue out and wished her a pleasant evening.

Sue saw that Adam was standing by the reception desk talking to one of the members of staff. Jean was sitting on a settee waiting patiently. The manager instantly went over to Adam and shook his hand. "Good evening Mr Carter. How are you this evening? Are you dining with us tonight?"

"As a matter of fact, I am Max, actually with this lady here," Adam replied turning to Sue who was behind the manager.

"Ah, I see," said the Manager, with another of those little knowing looks that Sue was beginning to find rather irritating. He turned again to Sue and stood aside for her to pass. "Madame, I hope you enjoy your meal with us."

Sue noticed Jean looking a bit lost, still sitting on the settee and she said, "Thank you. Yes, my friend over there and I are joining Mr Carter for dinner tonight aren't we Jean?"

Jean sprang to her feet and came over to join them. Sue introduced her to Adam and he shook her hand. Jean looked a little flustered but she managed a 'pleased to meet you'.

The manager hurried away in the direction of the dining room and Adam pointed the way to the two ladies.
"The manager seems to know you by name Mr Carter," said Sue to Adam.

"Please, call me Adam, and I hope you will allow me to call you Susan and Jean?" He turned to Jean as he said her name. Jean smiled and said that was fine.

"Yes, the manager knows me because I usually stay here when I come to London on business, you know, to the solicitors and other meetings."

Sue wondered why a Canadian cattle farmer would need to come to London on business on a regular basis. That was another fact she found a bit odd, but perhaps the evening would reveal a little more information.

When they entered the dining room, the manager was deep in conversation with a man that Sue imagined to be the head waiter. The waiter was nodding his head and as the Maître d' approached the group, the manager swiftly exited the room. The dining room was quite busy but they were shown to a table on a raised level of the dining area in a corner by the window. As they reached the table an array of waiters and waitresses fussed around them until they were seated. Adam asked if he could be allowed to choose the wine, and Sue and Jean agreed as they were busy scanning the enormous menus put before them.

"Just have anything you like ladies," said Adam in a genial tone. "They do a very good fillet steak here and I should know a thing or two about that with my background shouldn't I?"

The ladies both agreed but Sue settled on a chicken dish with a red wine sauce and Jean plumped for poached halibut in a shrimp sauce. Both ladies declined a starter saying that they wanted to leave room for a sweet. Adam laughed. "That's just like my wife would do," he said.

The conversation turned to more general things like what Sue and Jean were going to do tomorrow and how the weather was still very cold. Adam remarked that they didn't know what cold weather was. Living in Canada at the foot of the Rockies was real cold. Temperatures plummeted in winter and the weather here in London was almost tropical by those standards he said. When they were having coffee, Sue broached the subject of Sam's death, asking Adam if he had been ill for a while. At the mention of this, Adam's mood changed a little and he became reflective.

"He'd had a bit of heart trouble the year before last and he was on medication for Angina. We noticed he'd slowed down a bit, but after all, he was 83. He seemed to slow down more just after Christmas, preferring to stay at home rather than go out to meet his old friends. Then, in the middle of February, he picked up a chest infection that eventually turned to pneumonia. That's what killed him officially, but he always said his heart was badly damaged after Mum died and it would never mend."

"During the time I spent with your father," said Sue, "he talked about your mother – Ellen he said her name was – and I picked up on the fact that he missed her terribly."

"They were inseparable. She supported him always in everything he did, even when things were tough, and they were tough in the beginning. Dad took over the ranch from his dad and it was in a pretty poor state then. My Grandpa served in France in the Second World War and Dad had to help my Grandma while he was away. When he came back, he was suffering from shell-shock and had repeated bouts of depression. He never really got back to normal after that and Dad had to assume much more responsibility to keep the wolves from the door. Dad married Mum in 1952 and they lived in a room at the old farmhouse. Not long after that my Grandpa died and everything was left to my Dad. Mum was his rock. He loved her very much."

Adam suddenly looked away and Sue felt a little awkward, like she had gate-crashed his memories. She looked at Jean who was also looking a little uncomfortable. Jean, as if reading Sue's mind, said that she was feeling rather tired and would anyone mind if she retired for the night.

"Not at all Jean," said Adam, and rose from his chair.

"Yes Jean, I think I'll join you. We've had rather a long day and I know you have an early start in the morning Adam." Sue got up and was about to make her thanks and farewells when Adam asked if he could speak to her alone for a moment.

Jean sensed the need to make herself scarce and said, "I must go now, I need the ladies room. It must be all that wine and coffee. Sue, will you ask the waiter to put our meal on our room number?"

"No, don't worry about it ladies. This was my invitation and it's all taken care of. I insist."

"Well thank you so much Adam, that's very kind of you," said Jean, "and it's been very nice to meet you. Sue, I'll let myself in. If you don't have your key card, just knock and I'll let you in." She turned and made a hasty dash to the door.

"Shall we sit in the lounge bar where it's a bit more comfortable?" said Adam, making way for Sue. She followed him into the lounge where they managed to find a table in one of the large bay windows.

"Would you like anything to drink Susan – a nightcap?"

"No thanks Adam, I have had more than enough tonight. It was a lovely meal and a very pleasant evening. You can call me Sue by the way, everyone else does. The only people who called me Susan were my parents and your father who insisted on it." She smiled as she thought of her conversations with Sam and sensing Adam's gaze on her, she brightened and asked, "What was it you wanted to talk to me about?"

"I just wanted to apologise for the way I behaved this afternoon in James Fearnley's office. It was very rude and not the way I normally am anyway. I'll be honest with you, my trip here was not entirely business related. When Dad passed away and our solicitor in Calgary, James' father, Robert, told us about Dad's bequest to you, we were all a bit suspicious. Dad had mentioned briefly meeting some interesting people on his visit to the Lake, but nothing else. So, when we heard that he had left the pendant to you we got a bit twitchy."

"And you were voted as the one to come to London to meet the scarlet woman that had stolen your inheritance," broke in Sue.

"When you put it like that it sounds like we are the vengeful children."

"What it sounds like is a perfectly natural reaction. After all, we are talking about a family heirloom being given to a total stranger. When I received Mr Fearnley's letter I was as shocked as you obviously were. I haven't been able to sleep for thinking about it. Thinking about what you would make of it and so I understand you would want to find out more about me. I hope now that you have met me, you will see I'm just an ordinary woman, as I said this afternoon, who met a very nice gentleman, old enough to be my father, and we just hit it off so to speak. Your father asked me to dine with him because he was in the concierge's office when I was trying to make a reservation for myself – unsuccessfully. He gallantly offered to share his table and after a bit of thought, I agreed. Actually, we went Dutch because I insisted on it. Then on my second evening, he asked me to dine with him again. He said I had made him a very happy man.

During those two days, we chatted like we had known each other for years. It was quite bizarre really, but I guessed he was lonely and I was on my own, so what did it matter? He kept saying that I reminded him very much of your mother when she was younger. Is there a resemblance?"

"Yes, Susan, er Sue, that's just it. You do look very much like my Mum. I can see why he was interested. I should remember that he was no-one's fool though, and he would not have written to you if he had not trusted you."

"Before we said goodbye on the second evening, he asked me if I would be a kind of pen pal and write to him when we got home. I agreed because I liked him and I confess I found him very interesting to talk to. When I got home I did wonder what on earth I was going to find to write to him about, but when I received his first letter, I started to look forward to hearing from him. He was a very wise man Adam, but I'm sure you know that. He was also a lovely man and made me think about my Dad whom I miss so much. He died about sixteen years ago.

Sometimes, the people who have the biggest impact on our lives aren't always the ones we know well. I've realised that over the years. I don't want to take something from you that you feel is rightly yours but I know that your father must have wanted me to have the pendant and it would be wrong to go against his wishes."

"You're right Sue, and now that I've met you I can see it from your viewpoint. I wanted you to be the gold digger type, as you so eloquently put it, so that I could tell you that it wasn't going to happen and that I was contesting the will, but you have proved me wrong. As far as the rest of the family goes, they'll take my word and abide by any decision I make. That's why they wanted me to come here."

"Just as a matter of interest," said Sue, "when was the funeral?"

"It was at the end of last week. Quite a lot of people attended from the local town because he had lived there all his life and was well known. Actually, that's something else I wanted to talk to you about. I have a favour to ask and if you say no then I'll understand. Dad requested that his ashes be scattered on Lake Louise as we did with Mum."

"Oh, so that's why he went back there. He must have known that he didn't have long and wanted to make another trip before he died. He talked about taking your mother there for their 50th wedding anniversary and he said it was ten years before and the last holiday he had with your mother before she died."

"Yes, she didn't tell anyone she was ill until the late stages. It really got to all of us. Anyway, as I was saying, we will be scattering Dad's ashes on Lake Louise during the first week of June and he asked for immediate family only to be there, but also you."

Sue took a couple of breaths to let this last piece of information sink in. "I'm not so sure that it would be right for me to join the family on such an intimate occasion. I'd feel like I was intruding. What do the rest of the family think about that?"

"Like I said, they will trust my instincts and decisions, so you don't need to worry about that. You also said if you remember, that if it is something my Dad wanted, then it would be wrong to go against his wishes."

"You know, you sound just like him when you are negotiating. Some of your mannerisms are him to a tee. I'll need to think about arrangements because I have to speak to my husband before I agree. It took me ages to book last year's trip to the Rockies, so I know how much it costs and what I have to organise."

"If you do come you would be our guest whilst staying at the Chateau, but anything else would be up to you."

"No, I couldn't possibly allow you to pay for me – really," said Sue.

"No, you don't understand Sue. Because this is a direct term of Dad's will, it's like the funeral and will be paid for out of the estate by the solicitors, so you would not be letting us pay for it."

"But it's such an expensive event. There won't be anything left of your inheritance after paying for this."
"Let me worry about that. Anyway, I think there might be a bit left over, even after a trip to Lake Louise."

Sue promised to let Adam know definitely by the end of the week, when she'd had time to talk to Mark. She thought to herself that she would also need to see how her finances were fixed for paying the flights and other accommodation that would be needed. She couldn't go all the way to Canada again without seeing some of the places she'd missed the first time. Then again, she thought it was the least she could do to honour Sam's memory, especially when he had left her that beautiful pendant. The other destinations on the bucket list would have to wait for now.

They parted with a handshake after Sue had taken a note of Adam's email address. On her way up the stairs to her room she smiled as she recalled Sam's admission that he would rather use hand written methods of communication than bow to the new-fangled web. Adam was not like his father in that respect.

Jean was waiting for her when she let herself into their room. "Wow! That was a long word you had. I've been waiting for nearly an hour. I was thinking of coming down to check you were okay. What did he have to say this time?"

"You won't believe it when I tell you but here goes."

Chapter 22

That night, Sue slept the sleep of the dead, until about 4.00am when she awoke from a nightmare. In her dream, she was being pursued by all Sam's family and friends who were trying to catch her to take the pendant from her. She was running on a cliff side path which eventually ran out and she had nowhere to go. She could see the sea below and the waves crashing on the cliffs and she was pushed from behind, but not before the pendant was torn from her neck. She began to fall, faster and faster until she almost touched the jagged rocks below and then she woke up.

She was soaking wet with perspiration so she got up and went as quietly as she could to the bathroom. Her heart was beating so fast and hard that she felt as if it was going to burst out of her chest. She ran the cold tap and threw the water over her face a few times. She then filled a glass and drank it down. She sat on the loo until the beating in her chest began to slow down and she felt calmer. After going to the loo and washing her hands, she crept back into bed, hoping she hadn't disturbed Jean. She could here Jean's rhythmic low breathing and was relieved.

However, that was the end of her night's sleep and she lay awake with a head full of thoughts and questions. Things didn't add up, for example, Adam didn't look or act like he was an average farmer. He was so – well, so worldly and business like. Sue had met many important business people in her years at the bank and he reminded her so much of the MDs and Chairmen she had come across. The hotel they were staying in was a very expensive one and although Sue had managed to get a special rate she had pushed the boat out a bit to pay for it, so how come he stayed here all the time? She wasn't completely convinced that it was just because it was close to the solicitors' office. All the staff seemed to know him well, and indeed they seemed almost reverential towards him. Why would a farmer need to come to London often anyway? No, there was more to Adam Carter than met the eye and she was going to find out when she went to Lake Louise.

Her thoughts turned to the return trip to Canada and how she was going to tell Mark about it and once again to the pendant. If she wasn't careful, she would be in danger of carrying it like a burden around her neck – literally!

Then she began to plan the trip anyway. She would go to Lake Louise and get that part over with and fulfil what she saw as an obligation to Sam. Then she would get a flight to Vancouver and spend a few days there, maybe even a week or so. She'd wished she had added a few more days onto her trip last year and spent them in Vancouver so this would be a good opportunity to do that.

What would she take to wear? She knew it could be cold up in the Rockies, so a couple of warm sweaters were a definite. She would take a formal dress this time so that she could eat where she wanted in the evenings. Then there would be the day of the scattering of ashes. Should she wear black? What would the family be wearing? Perhaps she could ask casually when she emailed Adam to confirm she would attend. Vancouver could be wet, as she already knew from last year, so a light raincoat would have to be included. The rest would be casual wear and she had plenty of that already.

It was 6.30am the next time she checked the bedside clock so she decided to get up and make a cup of tea. As she filled the kettle, Jean awoke.

"Good morning," said Sue. "Did you smell the kettle?"

"Morning Sue. I heard you stirring. What time is it?"

"Just after 6.30am. I hope I didn't disturb you in the night Jean because I've been awake since abut 4.00am. I had a terrible nightmare and since then I've been mulling things over in my head."

She proceeded to tell Jean about the dream and her thoughts.

"I have to say Sue, I think Adam is rather dishy don't you? I know what you mean though about him being very business - like. He seemed so cool and in control all the time, like he was used to being in charge. Maybe it's because he is the older of the brothers and he has to run things on the farm."

"Mm, maybe Jean but I don't know. Anyway, 'today is another day' as my Mum used to say and we have some serious sightseeing to do. Where do you want to go?"

"I'd like to go to the British Museum this morning and then we can go from there."

"Anything Jean, so long as it takes my mind off everything to do with yesterday's goings on. I don't want to think about the pendant or what it's worth or how I'm going to convince Mark that I should go back to Lake Louise or that there is nothing sinister in all this, although, as you know I have my doubts about that somehow."

They had their breakfast and set out to the British Museum to begin their day of sightseeing. They had lunch in Covent Garden and spent the afternoon on a sightseeing tour bus that allowed them to hop on and off. Finally, they arrived, exhausted but happy, back at the hotel at 5.30pm. As they were sitting having a cup of tea with their feet up on their beds, they talked about where they would go for their meal that evening.

"Although it's cold Jean," said Sue, "it's not raining or anything so if we get wrapped up we could go on foot and look down Kensington High Street for a little place to eat. What do you think?"

"That' sounds like a good idea so long as you know where you're going. You know me with directions!"

"Yes, Jean, only too well," laughed Sue. "Don't worry, we'll be fine."

At that point Mark called as arranged and Sue gave him a brief outline of the evening but focussing more on their day of sightseeing. She would tell him about the Lake Louise trip when she got home.

They didn't have to walk too far before they found a little bistro. Having checked the menu out, they went in and were shown to a table in the window. They both remarked at how different the atmosphere was from last night in the hotel, although they both agreed that they had enjoyed their meal last night. It was just that tonight they felt free from any pressure and they could be themselves and chat away to their hearts' content.

"You'd think we would run out of chat after today wouldn't you Sue?" said Jean as they were tucking into their main course.

"Yes, but I think true friends always have a lot to say to each other, but they also know when it's best to say nothing. I really appreciate what you've done for me Jean – coming down here with me and waiting around and then listening to me moaning about being given jewellery that's worth I don't know how much. How ungrateful I sound."

"Don't be daft Sue. I've had a ball and anyway, you've paid for most of it. You would do the same for me wouldn't you?"

"In a flash Jean, yes I would."

"Enough said then. Eat your dinner."

They exchanged glances and Sue held up her glass of Rosé wine to make a toast to best friends. Jean did likewise and they ordered another bottle. It really was very good wine.

"Tomorrow morning, Jean, I want to take a taxi to Marble Arch and go to Marks and Sparks for some retail. After all, I'll have to get one or two things to take to Canada won't I?"

"What are you like Sue? Okay then it's a plan. Cheers!"

Sue had a better night's sleep that night but it was mainly due to the amount of alcohol she had consumed with her meal. When she awoke, the reality of going back home, hit her and her mood dropped. She tried not to seem distracted at breakfast and concentrated on the morning's shopping trip that they had ahead. Retail therapy was a very good description for it. She would only buy something though if she really liked it she decided.

Chapter 23

They packed their cases and left them in the storage room behind reception and arranged to collect them before going for their train at 2.30pm. The receptionist reminded Sue that she had a package in the safe and said she had put a note on her case to that effect to ensure that whoever was on the desk when Sue collected her case, would see that she didn't forget it.

As if I need reminding, thought Sue.

The shopping expedition was not a particular success, mainly because Sue's mind was on her return home. She couldn't help feeling that she was going to find it difficult to get Mark to understand why she should go back to Canada for the scattering of Sam's ashes. She did buy a couple of items that she thought would be useful for her trip though, so not entirely a waste of time.

Sue slept for a good part of the journey home. She woke about ten minutes before their station and was feeling decidedly stiff and tense. They got a taxi which dropped Jean off first and then eventually, she was home, bags in hand, wondering what she had done with her door key. Mark was not in, so either he had worked late or had gone out to the pub. It was just after 8.30pm, so either scenario could be the case.

She had just taken her bags upstairs and made herself a cup of tea, when she heard Mark's van on the drive. He had been home already, as he had left the evidence in the kitchen sink –

his used plate etc. When he came in he accepted her offer of a cup of tea and asked if she had enjoyed her break.

She replied that she had, but that she was very tired because of the train journey preceded by the shopping.

"So, let's have a look at this pendant then," said Mark once he had his cup of tea in hand.

Sue went upstairs and got the brown paper package out of her handbag. She was beginning to feel a little uneasy for some reason. She produced the box and passed it to Mark to open himself. As he did so, he whistled long and low.

"Wow, that's a serious piece of jewellery. Sue, it must be worth quite a bit. Did you not take it to a jeweller while you were in London? That would have been the best place to get a valuation, especially somewhere like Knightsbridge."

"To be honest, Mark, I didn't want to carry it about with me in London and anyway I might have had to leave it and I couldn't do that as I was coming home today."

"Well, if I were you, I'd get it done as soon as, and then you know what to insure it for. You'll have to add it to the policy I think. That old fella must have liked you a lot to give you something like this. Are you sure you only met him briefly?"

"I've told you Mark, we shared a table the first night I was there because there was no room and then we just got chatting and we seemed to hit it off. He was just lonely I think and wanted someone to take his mind off it a bit. It's been a real shock for me, this, and I can do without you, of all people giving me the third degree about it as if I've done something wrong. All I've done is meet an old chap – old enough to be my dad by the way – and be his sort of pen pal for a few months. I didn't bargain for all this and it would be nice to feel trusted by my husband!"

"Okay, keep your hair on. There's no need to shout. It just seems strange that's all."

"Well, while we're talking about it, (and I'm not shouting), things are about to seem even stranger when I tell you that in his will he requested that his ashes be scattered on Lake Louise and I have been asked to join the family in June for that. Don't ask me why because I'm no wiser than you are. So, I said I would think about it and let his oldest son, Adam, know by this weekend. Apparently, the cost of the hotel and food will be paid for by the estate, but if I go and decide to stay on or go somewhere else, then obviously I'll pay for that."

"So, you've thought about it then? You're going to go are you?"

"Obviously I've been thinking about it, but I'd like to know what you think."

"What does it matter what I think? It's your money you'll be spending and if you can afford it then do what you want."

"You might sound as if you mean it."

"What do you want me to say? You've obviously made up your mind. Anyway, what was his son doing in London? Surely he didn't come all the way there from Canada just to ask you to go to some ceremony. He could have done that by email."

"Mark, no-one was more taken aback than I when he appeared on the scene."

Sue proceeded to tell Mark the full version of events in James Fearnley's office. He needed to know that she had considered refusing to accept the pendant and the reason why she then relented and accepted it. Mark listened quietly and when she had finished he simply said that he hadn't meant to accuse her of anything, he wanted to understand it a bit better.

Sue remarked that so did she and that was one of the reasons she was going to go back to Lake Louise. She felt that she must honour the old man's memory and his kindness, whatever anyone thought. They left it there – an uneasy peace. Sue said she was tired and was going to have a bath then go to bed. She would go to the family jeweller's tomorrow where Mark had bought one or two items for her in the past and get the pendant valued. They were very reputable and she felt she would get an accurate and realistic valuation. After that, she said she wasn't sure what she was going to do. One thing was certain though, Sue felt that familiar feeling of foreboding rising in the pit of her stomach as she climbed the stairs to bed, and again she was feeling sick.

Chapter 24

After unpacking her things the next morning, putting on the third load of washing and having a quick shower and change, Sue set off to the jewellers. The son of the jeweller was at the counter polishing a watch when Sue entered. Mark had bought her one or two things from this shop over the years so he knew the owners fairly well. The son greeted her with a smile and asked what brought her to the shop today. Sue pulled the red box out of the brown envelope. (It was strange but for some reason she felt she had to keep it in the envelope which was, by now becoming rather dog-eared). When she opened up the box she saw the look on the man's face.

"If you don't mind, I'll just get my Dad to look at this. It's rather a nice piece isn't it? Where did you get it?"

"I have been left it by a relative who has died," she lied. She had been anticipating this question and had decided that it sounded better than the real version.

The son disappeared into the office, behind the shop, and returned a minute later with his father who beamed in her direction and said hello. "Would you like to come through to the office dear? It's a bit more private and I'd like to hear a bit more about the pendant from you."

Sue accompanied the older man into the office and he offered her a seat. The office was rather small but it was crammed with old wooden filing cabinets all neatly labelled with surnames in alphabetical order. The desk was, in Sue's opinion, as old, if not older than the old man himself. Then she remembered that the sign above the shop said it had been established in 1902, so she guessed it was the previous generation of the family who had started the business.

"Now, Mrs? – I must confess I've forgotten your surname," he said.

"Mrs Barnett," said Sue. "My husband has bought one or two things for me in the past from you."

"Ah, yes, I recognise the earrings and the necklace you are wearing. You obviously like simple understated quality. I do think there is nothing to equal a good diamond. For me, the diamond is perfection. Anyway, now to this splendid pendant you have brought today. My son tells me you have been bequeathed this by a relative and you are looking for a valuation for insurance purposes is that correct?"

"Yes, I have only just acquired it and even I could tell that it was a bit special."

"Special is a good word for it. Can you tell me how long it has been in the family?"

"Not really, no. You see I didn't have any previous knowledge of the piece until last week. I only know that my relative bought it for his wife about twenty years ago as an anniversary present and as they had no daughters he left it to me. I was hoping you might be able to tell me a bit more about it."

"Well, what I can tell you is this: It is about thirty years old, so it was probably made for your relative as a bespoke piece. I think it is French and likely made by a jeweller in Paris. The chain is made of eighteen carat white gold and the diamonds in the pendant are mounted in platinum. I have to say the craftsmanship is the best. The diamonds around the perimeter are what we call cushion cut and each one will probably be about three quarters of a carat. There are twelve of them so that makes nine carats in all.

Now, to the oval one in the centre. That's going to be about three carats on its own, so you're looking at about twelve carats of top quality diamonds set in a platinum frame on an eighteen carat white gold chain. Some people might be put off by the fact that there are thirteen stones but I think it adds to the mystique a little don't you? Do you have any paperwork for it – maybe an invoice or something when it was bought?"

"No, as I said, I've only become aware of it last week. I'm afraid I can't help you there."

"Not to worry. I don't think in this instance that it will matter. In a sale this would fetch something like £50,000, but for insurance purposes, I'd say you need to cover it for £75,000. I know you won't want to part with it, so make sure you keep it safe, wear it when you can and love it. If you ever do want to part with it, come and see me and I'll deal with it for you. I have some good contacts who would just love that. There won't be a charge for this because it's been a pleasure to see it, and besides, if you do get rid of it you'll come back to me won't you?" He smiled as he said the words.

Sue was speechless. She had suspected it was worth a bit but this was far more than she had imagined. She must have blanched because she became aware of the jeweller asking if she was all right. She just managed a weak nod. The jeweller smiled and said it had been a long time since he'd had such an effect on a woman. He said he would send her a written valuation in the post once his wife had done the paperwork. He placed the pendant back in the box and handed it to Sue who immediately returned it to the tatty brown envelope.

Sue decided she needed a coffee, so she thanked the jeweller and went to a nearby café and hid herself in a vacant corner booth. She texted Jean to tell her the news and as an afterthought, she decided to text Mark as well. Her text would give him time to get over the shock before she saw him face-to-face.

As she drank her coffee and tried to make sense of the thoughts going through her head, her phone rang and it was Emma, James's wife, wanting to know how she had got on in London. She brought her briefly up to date and in between gasps and 'Oh my God', Emma was enthralled. "Oh Sue, that's great. You are so lucky to be given something so nice. It sounds fabulous. Will you call and let me see it on your way home?"

"Yes, okay," said Sue. "Put the kettle on, I'll be there in about half an hour."

On her way back to Emma's in the car, Sue's mobile phone pinged telling her that she had a message, and then straight after that, it pinged again. *That'll be Jean and Mark,* thought Sue.

Chapter 25

"It's like something from a novel," said Emma, as she admired the pendant in the box. "Have you tried it on for size?"

"Actually, no, I haven't," said Sue, the thought dawning on her for the first time. "I know this might sound a bit daft but I can't bring myself to think that it's really mine. It's as if I've just borrowed it or something."

"Well, we'll soon change that then. Come here and I'll put it on for you," replied Emma excitedly.

After much further persuasion, Sue agreed and just as she plucked up the courage to look in the hall mirror, her mobile phone rang. It was Mark.

"I told you it was worth a bit didn't I?" he launched in as she answered. "The old chap must have been worth a bob or two to be able to afford that, especially thirty years ago. Are you sure he said he was a farmer? Mind you, there are a few farmers around here that I wouldn't mind being a pound behind. They're a canny lot when it comes to money."

"Mark, I'm still in shock. I don't know the answer to those questions, but I'm sure as hell going to find out when I go to Lake Louise. I'm wondering if Sam got it on the cheap not knowing its full value. These things happen sometimes and it was a long time ago and people didn't know as much about stuff like this as they do now."

"Where are you now?" he asked.

"I'm just at James's having a cup of tea with Emma, why?"

"Having a cup of tea? You'd better get something stronger for later. Wait till James and Peter and Nicola find out. They'll have a fit!"

"I'll see you later Mark. What time will you be home this evening?" she asked.

"I might just finish a bit earlier today, maybe about 4.30pm. See you then."

Sue sighed and put down the phone. She turned to the hall mirror and just looked at the image before her. She had to admit, it packed a punch and made her feel good. She would be too scared to go anywhere with it on, and anyway, she had always been more than happy with the simple but classic jewellery Mark had bought for her.

Her mobile phone rang again and this time it was Jean. Her reaction was as excited as Emma's. She asked Sue what she was going to do next and enquired about her homecoming and discussion with Mark. Sue gave her a brief synopsis and said she would tell her the rest when they met on Sunday for a walk.

Sue didn't get much peace for the rest of that day. It started at 4.30 when Mark arrived home, followed a few minutes later by Peter and his wife, Lynne, then James half an hour later. After brewing the umpteenth cup of tea, Sue was interrupted by the ring of the house phone. It was Nicola.

"Hi Mum, just got in and heard Dad's message on my mobile. Is it true? Have you had it valued properly. Will you be getting it in writing?"

"Yes, it's true," said Sue somewhat wearily.

"What's up? You should be jumping about with joy. I certainly would be if I'd been left a priceless heirloom."

"Oh, it's just that I'm tired and overwhelmed by it all. I'm going to have to tell the insurance company and that'll cost me money won't it?"

"Don't be such an old grump, Mum. You can show off now when Dad takes you out."

That'll be the day, thought Sue. *When was the last time Mark took me out anywhere I could wear such a thing?*

"I don't do showing off as well you know. Anyway, changing the subject are you coming over this weekend? I just need to know when I go shopping if I need to buy enough for a siege."

"Try stopping me. Si and me will be there tomorrow afternoon about 4.00pm, after we've done a bit of cleaning up here. It's like a tip and past the point where I can leave it. See you tomorrow then. Love you, bye."

It was after 7.00pm when Sue and Mark were finally alone and Mark suggested a takeaway meal. Sue was relieved to hear this suggestion and agreed without hesitation, although she didn't feel particularly hungry. "As long as you go for it and make it sooner rather than later so that I can have an early night," *she said,* "I'm shattered."

"You're always shattered. I don't know what you'd do if you had to go out to work." Mark replied.

"Don't start that again, Mark. I can't be doing with it. Just because I've retired, doesn't mean I don't do anything all day.

Who does the washing and the cleaning and the shopping and the meals?"

"You used to do that anyway, and work if you remember?"

"Only too well and that's one of the reasons I was unwell and had to give up, so don't wind me up about it. You know it gets to me."

"I think you had a sense of humour bypass as well as everything else you had done. You can't take a joke."

"Go and get the takeaway or we'll be eating at midnight at this rate."

Sue turned on her heel and went upstairs to put the dry washing in the ironing basket. She heard the front door slam and sighed again. A thought came to her and she switched on her laptop. She composed an email to Adam confirming that she would attend the ceremony in June and asking for detailed arrangements so that she could organise her flight and the rest of her trip. Before she sent the email, she had an idea. She brought out Sam's letters from a small folder she kept them in and scanned each one in turn on her printer. She saved them into a file on her laptop and attached them to her email. Perhaps if Sam's family read his letters to her they would see that it was really he who was keen on them corresponding and that it was all truly innocent and above board. A part of her resented having to share her private correspondence with anyone, but she thought that this was necessary in order for them to see her in the right light. Just as she pressed the send button, she heard Mark coming back with the takeaway.

Chapter 26

After a very hectic weekend, when everyone and his dog seemed to descend on Sue and Mark, Sue started to plan her trip to Canada. However, she knew she could not finalise things until Adam got back to her with the itinerary at Lake Louise. She hoped it would be soon because she hated not being in control. It was something that took her well outside her comfort zone. She told Mark that she wanted to put the pendant in a safety deposit box at the bank but he insisted that he could get a good safe that he could hide somewhere in the house and keep it alarmed. Sue wasn't too sure about this but she decided to go along with the idea for now as it kept him quiet.

During the following week, Sue received an email from Adam. It read:

Thanks for your email and below are the arrangements for Lake Louise. The ceremony will take place at 6.00am on Monday 3 June followed by a family breakfast. (We'll need something after that early start). The reason for doing this so early is so that other hotel residents might still be in bed and the Manager has said that he can assure privacy at that time.

If you can be in Calgary on the Sunday morning, (2 June) we will collect you from your hotel and take you with us to Lake Louise. Kate and I will be in one car, the grand-kids will be in another, and Ryan will drive. Greg and Adele have said they want to go up a couple of days earlier and do some walking and biking.

Rooms have been booked for the Sunday and Monday nights with breakfast and dinner included, so no need to think about that part of your trip. You will be free to do whatever you want after the breakfast on the Monday. (There's a great spa in the hotel, but you probably already know that having been before). Kate and I will drive you back to Calgary when we return on Tuesday morning, but it will be fairly early, maybe 7.30am if that's okay. We can drop you at a hotel or the airport if you're travelling straight on.

By the way, thanks so much for sending copies of Dad's letters to me. It was very kind of you and you didn't have to do it.

If you have any questions in the meantime, let me know, and when you know your travel arrangements, drop me a mail and then I can be sure to make contact when you arrive to check all is okay.
Thank you for agreeing to come. I mean that.
Regards,
Adam Carter.

Sue's first reaction was one of alarm at the thought of spending a few hours cooped up in a car with Adam and his wife. What if she was resentful of Sue and showed it by ignoring her or being rude? If that happened Sue wasn't sure how she would cope. Anyway, it was 'a means to an end' as her mother used to say, and at least it meant she didn't have to pay for that part of her journey. Sue re-read the email and jotted down the dates on a piece of paper. Then, she went on the website of the travel company she had booked with for Canada the year before. In the end, she rang the number provided and discussed what she wanted with a very helpful young lady called Sarah, who said she would put a package together and email it to her later that day.

Sue's plan was to fly to Calgary on the Friday 31 May and stay in the hotel she knew from her last visit, Friday night and

Saturday night. That would give her a day to look around, something she hadn't had much time to do last year. She would go to Lake Louise as per the itinerary in Adam's email. She would return to the same hotel on the Tuesday, and on Wednesday, she would fly direct to Vancouver. She had asked Sarah to find her a hotel near to the waterfront in Vancouver even though she knew this would be a bit more expensive. She would stay there on a bed and breakfast basis for six nights, giving her ample time to explore the city and return home on Tuesday 11 June flights permitting. She didn't really have a budget in mind for the trip but hoped it wouldn't be too much. She wanted to do some redecorating at home and had originally earmarked the money for that.

As promised, Sarah sent her an email that afternoon with an itinerary that would fit her needs exactly. The price was within her rough idea so Sue rang Sarah and booked it. As it was not too far off, she needed to pay the full amount. She had anticipated this and had transferred some cash to her current account earlier.

When Mark came home that night she told him she had booked it. He didn't have much to say (as usual) but he didn't seem too concerned about it either. She wasn't sure that was a good sign or a bad one, but she was glad they weren't going to have another row. She'd had enough of that in the last week.

The following days passed rather quickly and Sue found herself looking forward to the trip but dreading it at the same time, especially the Lake Louise bit. As usual, Jean was the voice of reason and listened patiently to Sue's ramblings without judgement and with some encouragement.

Sue had not seen or spoken to her friend, Erin who lived in the south of England, since before she had gone to London and she felt rather guilty that she had not made contact, although she knew that Erin and her husband, Tom, were away from home for a couple of weeks. They should be back now so she decided to make a cup of tea and call her. The tea was essential when having a call with Erin as they tended to chat on for some time.

She brought Erin up to date on developments and listened to the now familiar reactions of shock and excitement from those she had told, which was mainly the family and Jean. Erin was the most reliable, caring and non-judgemental person Sue had ever known, even taking Jean into consideration. They had been friends for about twenty-five years, ever since they had worked together at the bank, even though Erin had moved away to accommodate Tom's family and work commitments. They had no family of their own but Tom had two children from a previous marriage, but they were grown up and lived away, one of them, a boy, in New York.

Sue asked Erin if she thought she was doing the right thing in going to Lake Louise and Erin confirmed what Sue had thought herself, that it would be wrong not to honour the memory of Sam, especially when he had been so thoughtful towards her. However, she also agreed that some things didn't add up and she urged Sue to be careful while away. She asked Sue to text her every now and then, to say she was okay. She also invited Sue to go and visit once back home, maybe in July. Sue readily accepted and promised to be in touch soon.

The next few weeks were going to be taken up with preparation for her trip (she couldn't think of it as a holiday, at least not the first part) and getting the garden looking good for the summer.

Time did pass incredibly quickly until, at last, packed and ready, Sue awoke on the morning of Friday 31 May. She was flying at 11.00am and so she had booked a taxi to take her to the airport about 7.00am to give her enough time. She said her goodbyes to Mark and told him there was plenty of food in the fridge and freezer and asked him to make sure the bedding plants in the pots and baskets were watered every day, especially if it got warm.

"I don't suppose there'll be much chance of that," he said rather gloomily, "this year's shaping up to be every bit as bad as the last one."

"Well, even if it isn't hot, the plants in the baskets and pots dry out very quickly so they'll need to be kept moist."

"I'll do my best but I can't promise. You know how busy I am at work. Anyway, have a good time and give me a ring when you get to Calgary, but not when I'm in bed."

"Of course I will and I know the time difference, so don't panic, I won't disturb your beauty sleep."

He didn't give her a kiss but that was nothing new, but he waived her off as the taxi drew away up the drive.

Brace yourself Sue, she thought to herself, *it's going to be a very interesting and challenging twelve days. You'll need all your reserves of courage and probably patience as well.*

A couple of days before leaving, Sue had made a conscious decision not to take the pendant with her. She didn't think it would be appropriate to parade it in front of the family, especially the females. It would seem like she was flaunting it and rubbing salt into the wounds because having thought about it since she first saw it, she was as sure as she could be that at least one of them would harbour a resentment of her having it. The only bright spot on the horizon was the fact that Adam, at least, seemed to be okay about it. The other reason for not taking the pendant was the obvious risk of loss or theft and she wasn't sure the insurance covered an item that expensive out of the home. She wasn't about to put the theory to the test.

As she neared the airport, her thoughts turned to brighter things, like what she was going to do with her free day in Calgary. She hoped the weather would be kind to her and she planned to read up on the sights of the city while relaxing on the plane. *Canada, here I come – again!* she thought and with that thought, she smiled and began to calm a little.

Chapter 27

Sue arrived in Calgary airport just about 6.30pm Canada time. Once she had negotiated her way through immigration, she headed for the nearest taxi. She had decided to get to the hotel as soon as possible and make contact with Adam carter. He had asked her to let him know once she had arrived. Sue wanted to be sure of the dress code for the ashes ceremony and if she needed to get anything, she could use her free day to do the shopping.

Her room was, co-incidentally, on the same floor as the last time she had stayed there but further down the corridor. The facilities were the same as before and it made her think back to her last trip. Such a lot had happened in the last year. Besides meeting Sam Carter she had made another friend in Valerie, from Australia, and they had emailed each other regularly. She had mentioned Sam's death but hadn't told Valerie about Sam leaving her the pendant or her current visit to Canada. She just didn't think it was appropriate for some reason.

She had a cup of tea and then rang Adam Carter on the number he had given her. He answered on the third ring and sounded somewhat relieved to hear her voice. "Thank you for getting in touch. I expect you will be tired after your journey, so I won't keep you. We will meet you in Reception on Sunday morning about 10.30am if that's okay," he said.

"Yes, that will be fine, but before you go can I just check something with you. This might sound a bit strange, but can you tell me if the dress for the ashes ceremony will be formal?"

"Hell no," he replied quickly, "we will be wearing smart outdoor gear. It will probably still be cool and especially that early in the morning. We don't want anyone to get cold and we did the formal black thing at Dad's funeral. This is more of a celebration if you like. It's what Dad wanted and we don't want to dwell any more."

"Okay, that answers my question. It's just that I wasn't sure and I don't want to stick out like a sore thumb. I'll be nervous enough as it is."

"Look Sue, there's no need to feel nervous about anything. There's only going to be the family and Robert Fearnley and his wife who besides knowing my Dad in his official capacity as his solicitor, both of them were good friends to my parents for many years and they are a great couple. He is my godfather as well, so he's a bit like family."

"Thanks, I'll see you on Sunday at 10.30 then."

Sue put the telephone down and heaved a sigh of relief. She had plenty of smart outdoor stuff and she had bought a cashmere and wool jacket in the sales at Christmas that would look just the part. She had always been a believer in dressing herself in the most appropriate and best way possible, especially at work when she was required to meet business contacts and prospective new clients. This gave her a feeling of confidence and it would certainly help her on this occasion.

That evening, Sue once again, chose to spend her first evening in the hotel restaurant rather than venture out into the city. She would get up early in the morning and check out the Heritage Park Historical Village. She was really looking forward to her day of exploration and hoped it would strengthen her mind for the ordeal she feared at Lake Louise.

Her choice of visit was a good one. The Heritage Park Historical Village was set in about 67 acres of lush parkland in the heart of Calgary. She enjoyed a cruise on the reservoir on the SS Moyie Sternwheeler and boarded a steam locomotive. She strolled down Main Street which was set out in early 20th century style and lined with stores and saloons. She bought one or two gifts to take home and when she finally arrived back at the hotel, she was ready for her evening meal.

She decided to call Mark first thing in the morning in order to catch him at roughly teatime at home. She had texted him on arrival the day before because she knew it would be night time and he would be in bed. He had texted back to say thanks for letting him know she had arrived and he hoped she had a good time. Well at least he had made contact.

She showered and changed, then went down to the Reception desk to enquire about places to eat that weren't too far away from the hotel. No point in being too cavalier and inviting any risk at walking through a strange city at night on her own. The clerk on the desk asked what sort of food she liked and when she told him, he suggested a place called Earl's on Fourth. However, he suggested she take a taxi as it would be inexpensive and better as she was on her own. He asked if she would like him to make a reservation for her and order her a taxi. She thought about it for a moment and decided she would like that.

Less than an hour later, Sue was enjoying a pre-dinner drink in the bar at Earl's on Fourth. The waiters were very attentive and the food was excellent. She had a lovely evening and once back in her room at the hotel, she decided to chalk that up as another achievement.

After a relatively good night's sleep, Sue arose and prepared to be collected. She had agreed with the hotel that she would leave her large suitcase in the storage room and only take a fold away smaller case with the things she would need in Lake Louise. She had just finished packing when she remembered that she had planned to ring Mark, so she did this before she went downstairs for breakfast. They spoke for about five minutes, just long enough to establish that each was okay and what the weather was doing. (Typical Englishman's topic of conversation – the weather). Mark sounded genuinely pleased to hear Sue's voice and by the time she had said her goodbyes and replaced the receiver, she felt a bit more relaxed.

She had a light breakfast and after making sure she had everything she needed for the next two days, she checked out, leaving her large suitcase at the desk in Reception and prepared to wait for Adam and his wife to arrive. Why were her teeth chattering and her knees knocking so much? She scolded herself for being so feeble. After all they were only farm people and ordinary like she was.

Chapter 28

A couple of minutes before 10.30am, a large 4x4 with tinted windows, pulled up on the forecourt of the hotel. Out stepped Adam Carter in jeans, white shirt and boots topped off with a Stetson hat and dark glasses. He was unmistakeable, even in the sunlight which shone behind him and clouded his face. He said something to the doorman outside and then went round to the passenger side of the vehicle and opened the door. The woman who stepped out was dressed in jeans and a pale blue cotton shirt. She wore trainers on her feet and she too wore sunglasses. She had shoulder-length fair hair that was tied back in a loose ponytail and she smiled at Adam as they walked towards the Reception hand in hand.

Sue couldn't help feeling a little envious in a strange sort of way. They looked so obviously happy in each other's company and chatted as they walked.

Adam greeted Sue with a shake of the hand and introduced his wife, Kate. Kate smiled warmly at Sue and said she had been looking forward to meeting her, especially since Adam had told her all about meeting her in London. Sue instantly felt at ease with this woman, who was wearing her fifty years extremely well. She had obviously been an attractive younger woman because the strong bone structure and her fresh skin were still very evident. She had either been very lucky or she had taken extreme care of herself. She still retained a youthful look and although she had what Sue's mother would have described as a large frame she was tall and carried her weight very well. Sue decided she would be a 'homely' type with a common sense attitude.

"Right," said Adam once the pleasantries were over, "let me take your bag and we'll get on our way. It shouldn't take us too long to get to the Lake as we'll mostly be on the Trans Canada Highway. We can stop for a coffee and a snack if you like Sue and we should get there mid afternoon."

"Oh, that seems quick. I seem to recall it took half a day to get to Banff and then another half day from there to Lake Louise last year. Oh, but of course we were sightseeing along the way and probably going on the scenic route. I'd forgotten about that."

They got into the 4x4 which was rather luxurious inside and their journey to Lake Louise began. Kate chatted to Sue quite freely about all sorts of things including family and children and the weather, but steered clear of any mention of Sam or the upcoming ashes ceremony. They stopped at a café diner just off the highway and then continued onwards to Lake Louise. Adam commented on some of the geographical and geological points of interest along the way. Sue remembered from her last visit that almost every peak (and there were lots of them) had a name and Adam seemed to know most of them. He was obviously well educated and more than a little informed about his surroundings.

They reached the road approaching the Château Lake Louise at about 2.30pm. As the Château came into view, Sue's stomach did a flip and the nerves began to return. Thinking about having to meet all the family was nerve racking. They pulled up on the forecourt right outside the entrance to the main Reception. A doorman dressed in the Tyrolean costume Sue remembered well, came to their assistance. Sue went behind the car to get her small bag from the boot, but Adam intervened and said that the staff would deal with that.

They went to the Reception area and Kate turned to Sue. "Come and sit over here with me Sue for a few minutes while Adam takes care of the check-in."

"But I'll need to sign in won't I?" replied Sue.

"Oh, that's okay, I think it was a block booking that Adam's assistant made, so he'll sign on your behalf."

Sue wasn't so sure but she did as requested and joined Kate on a large sofa to the right of the desk. She looked around her at the Reception area and marvelled yet again at the lavish décor and the sheer scale of the place. It was bustling yet there was a quiet and efficient calm about the staff carrying out their duties like perfectly tuned machines.

"I don't know about you Sue, but I'm going to have a stroll around the Lake once we're unpacked and then I'm going to have a long bath ahead of the dinner tonight. I think it will be in one of the function rooms across at the Conference centre, but don't worry, Adam will make sure you have all the details in good time."

"I didn't expect to be sharing dinner with you all tonight. I had planned to see what was on the menus for the various restaurants and then book something." Sue could feel the panic rising in her chest.

"Oh rubbish! You'll want to meet the rest of the family before tomorrow's schedule won't you? They're all looking forward to meeting you."

I'll bet they are, thought Sue and she said, "I haven't brought anything special to wear for tonight. I did intend to include a dress but at the last minute I changed my mind"

"Oh, smart casual will be fine. I'll be wearing a pair of trousers and a blouse. I don't do dresses if I can help it, so I know what you mean. The girls will probably be wearing something skimpy but you know what girls are like and Ryan will have designer Jeans and an open neck shirt probably. As for Adam, he'll be casual as will his brother, Greg and Mr & Mrs Fearnley. Adele may be the exception. She likes to flaunt her body if you know what I mean. Mind you, so would I if I had a body like hers. She was a gorgeous looking girl when Greg met her. In fact, she still is! She was Miss Stampede and she and Greg don't spoil a pair. Greg is a dish – I think I can say that even though he's my little brother-in -law. The first time they met at the stampede, she made a beeline for Greg and the attraction was obviously mutual because they got engaged and then married a year later. She's rather jealous though from all accounts. (I hear stories from some of the ladies in the town who socialise with them). Anyway, Sue, I'm sure you can hold your own where clothes are concerned so stop worrying about it. If Adele gets a bit too much I'll rescue you."

I hope I won't need rescuing, thought Sue, feeling even more nervous.

At that point, Adam joined them and handed Sue her key card for Room 712. "Everything's in order and your bag will be waiting for you in your room Sue. Has Kate mentioned the time for dinner tonight? It's 7.00pm for 7.30pm in the Condor Room over at the Conference Centre. If you just make your way across there, someone will show you to the room. Okay with that?"

Sue was about to say that she would be happy to eat on her own and she didn't want to intrude on a family gathering, when Kate cut in. "Yes, Sue knows where to go don't you Sue? We've just been talking about it as a matter of fact." She winked at Sue and turned toward the lifts.

Adam pressed the buttons for the seventh and eighth floors. *Oh, what a surprise,* she thought, *well, at least that confirms my position in this affair, one step below the family.* However, she was relieved at this as it gave her some degree of independence from what she saw as a fait accompli.

It was just after 3.00pm when Sue slid her key card into the lock of Room 712 and stepped inside. The room was very similar to the one she had stayed in last year but a bit larger if anything. It was also on the same side of the hotel so she knew that when she lifted the window blind, she would be greeted by that same heavenly site of the lake, except this time, three floors up. The view didn't disappoint and Sue gasped just as she had the year before, when her eyes fell upon the magical turquoise water surrounded by the still snow-capped peaks. She drank in the sight for a few minutes before turning to find her bag on the shelf next to the dressing table.

She unpacked her things and chose her evening's outfit. Smart navy slacks with a fine cream chiffon blouse over a delicate lace camisole. She would finish it off with her simple white gold and diamond earrings and tear drop pendant and navy patent pumps. She hung her evening outfit on the outside of her wardrobe so that she could keep focussing on the positive aspects of the evening. They included, looking as good as she could and ensuring she kept out of the way of Adele, who sounded positively awful. But she also reminded herself that she mustn't judge people until she had time to know them and she must try to discover a little bit more about the mystery that was Sam Carter.

Chapter 29

Sue took one final look at her image in the full-length mirror at 6.50pm. Well it would have to do because she couldn't think of anything else she could put on her face to make it look any less wrinkled. It was funny but she had taken to wearing her reading glasses when putting on her make-up. She would put on her foundation and then slip on the glasses to see where she had missed. She did the same with eye make-up and finally, lipstick. Another thing that bothered her was that her top lip seemed to be disappearing. She remembered her mother's doing the same and thinking that she would never let that happen to hers!

She looked at her watch again – 6.53pm. It would only take five minutes to get to the conference building and she didn't want to be the first person there. Similarly though, she definitely didn't want to be the last one. It would look as though she were making a grand entrance and they would all stare at her. That would be the absolute end! She settled on leaving her room at 7.10pm, so that there was a fair chance she would get it about right. She was greeted at the conference reception by a very smart man whom Sue guessed to be in his late thirties. He was, she thought, obviously the person responsible for seeing that everything went like clockwork because he had that air about him that positively reeked of efficiency and seniority. He greeted her warmly and asked if she was Mrs Barnett.

"Oh, yes I am Mrs Barnett, but how did you know that?" she asked.

"It's my job to know these things Madam and I'll let you into a secret, all the other guests on my list are here already." He smiled triumphantly and stood aside to point out the appropriate door.

So much for the plan, she thought and braced herself for the challenge ahead.

Thankfully, Adam spotted her at the door and walked over to her, but unfortunately, not before the various conversations ceased and all eyes were on her.

"Come in Sue. What would you like to drink? We have some champagne or you can have anything else you fancy." He looked at her expectantly and smiled.

She managed a very weak reply to the effect that she would have a glass of champagne and she remembered the evening she first dined with Sam when there was a bottle of it waiting on their table. A waiter appeared from nowhere with a tray bearing several glasses of champagne and Sue took one whilst desperately trying not to tremble as she did so.

"Now, come and meet everyone," said Adam, as he took her gently by the elbow in the direction of the first group, who were Kate and an elderly but distinguished couple, probably in their late seventies. Sue correctly identified them as Robert and Mrs Fearnley.

They looked rather well-heeled as Sue's dad would have said, but he was a solicitor after all, and in Sue's experience they were always well off. He was wearing a light coloured suit, white shirt and tie and Mrs Fearnley (Alice) was wearing a below the knee paisley patterned wool skirt with a white blouse and a string of pearls. Both of them smiled warmly and welcomed her to Alberta.

Moving swiftly on, Adam steered Sue to the other group consisting of two young ladies in their early twenties and a very good-looking young man of similar but slightly older age and a middle-aged but positively stunning couple who Sue thought must be Greg and Adele. Adam introduced Sue to them all in turn starting with the younger ones. They were all very polite and seemingly relaxed with her presence. Greg gave her a beaming smile and shook her hand. His piercing blue eyes positively bored into her and she had to stifle a gasp. *My God he's handsome!* she thought.

Adele's handshake was brief and limp and she looked a bit like she had just sucked on a lemon. She said a clipped hello and stepped back to summon the waiter for another glass of champagne. Despite the sour face, Sue had to admit that she was very beautiful. In fact, she thought her facial features were perfect in every way. Her hair was as straight as a ramrod, auburn and shiny and cut into a long bob. No wonder she had been Miss Stampede or Miss Calgary or whatever it was she was Miss of. As Kate had predicted, Adele was wearing, well nearly wearing a black velvet cocktail dress, cut very low at the front to display her assets to their best advantage, and very short to show off her perfect pins. She was wearing the most impossibly high, black, patent, stiletto heels that accentuated her toned calf muscles. She was tanned and probably weighed no more than about eight stones. This was enough for Sue to take an instant dislike to her, but she inwardly chided herself for being jealous of a woman who was probably at least fifteen years her junior.

Greg broke the ice by asking Sue if she had had a good journey so far. The others resumed their conversations but Sue was aware of Adele's attention in the background looking her up and down and scrutinizing every inch

"It's been lovely so far," said Sue, "I spent the day at the Heritage Park Historical Village yesterday and I enjoyed it immensely."

"Oh that's a great place to see if you're here for the first time. We used to take the girls when they were small. They always had a great time."

They made small talk for a few more minutes while Adele stood on the perimeter looking bored and not trying very hard to disguise it. Thankfully, they were summoned into an adjoining dining room for dinner.

The table was a rectangular shape, with three places on the longer sides and two on the shorter ones. To Sue's relief, she was seated between Robert Fearnley and Ryan on one of the longer sides. The two girls, Katherine and Sophie flanked Alice Fearnley on the opposite side. To Ryan's right sat Kate and Greg, and to Robert Fearnley's left was Adele and Adam. Thank goodness she had not been placed next to or opposite Adele. She felt rather intimidated by the woman already and she had only shaken her hand and said hello.

The meal consisted of four courses, each of which had a choice of three dishes. Sue opted for things that she felt would cause her least problems: soup for starter, poached halibut for the fish course, chicken and fresh vegetables for the main and meringue nest for the dessert. Of course the manner in which the dishes were displayed on the menu made for a challenging but in the end, successful translation. Each dish was accompanied by a different wine and to finish off coffee and liqueurs were to be served in the lounge area where they had gathered earlier.

Sue considered the meal as a whole and thought about the cost for ten people with all the added bits. This must be costing a small fortune and all being paid for out of Sam's estate. He must have saved well throughout his life because he had not stinted during his last visit to Lake Louise either. In addition to this, the assembled gathering was obviously used to dining well as they didn't seem to bat an eyelid at the splendour before them.

Robert Fearnley did his best to make Sue feel at home. He talked about England and asked where Sue was from (although she guessed that he already knew given that he had asked his son to write to her to tell her about the pendant) and said that he had read about the rolling Lancashire hills and the history surrounding the witches of Lancashire. Feeling on firm territory with this topic, Sue chatted happily to him and explained that there was more to Lancashire than the witches and the factories. Now that the factories had gone, she told him, tourism was a significant source of income and the forests and hills of the county were a magnet for keen walkers. It occurred to Sue that Canada has its own witches, one of whom was sitting not far away at this very moment! She stifled a smile at the thought and hoped that Robert hadn't noticed.

It was just after the main course had been cleared away and they were waiting for the dessert to be served, that Robert Fearnley excused himself and she found herself looking straight at the vision that was Adele. Adam had also left the table momentarily and so neither of them had anyone else to whom they could direct their conversation as everyone else was involved in some discussion with their other neighbours.

"I must say Sue," said Adele, leaning forward and with a faint smile on her face, "Sam was a dark old horse. He kept you quiet that's for sure. I always thought that he put Ellen on such a high pedestal that he would never consider another dalliance so to speak, especially with a married woman who's young enough to be his daughter. But that just goes to show, you never know."

"I can assure you Adele," said Sue rather too quickly, "that there was absolutely no dalliance between Sam, um, your father-in-law and myself. We simply met and shared a table for dinner and we found it easy to talk and enjoyed each other's company."

"Oh, I know, I've heard that version from Adam, but come on Sue, we both know what men are like when they're out on their own. Sam was a good-looking man for his age – that's where Greg gets his looks from – and I don't blame you at all. I just can't see him leaving a valuable item of jewellery that belonged to Ellen to some acquaintance he had dinner with. You must have earned it eh? I must say though Sue, you do disappoint me. I expected you to be wearing the 'object of desire'." She winked at Sue devilishly.

Sue felt her face turning red and hot. She didn't know what to say and she was floundering like a fish caught on the end of a hook. The thought crossed her mind that she should excuse herself and go back to her room, but before that thought could be turned into action, Adam returned to his seat next to Adele. He looked at Sue and then at Adele and seemed to sense the atmosphere. He asked Sue if the food was to her liking so far and she managed a weak response to the effect that it was delicious. Adele, meanwhile, turned her attention to her small clutch bag and produced a mirror and lipstick and proceeded to apply a new layer, apparently quite unaware of the mayhem she was causing, or maybe not. She gave Sue a sly knowing glance and took another sip of her wine.

Robert returned to his seat and Sue was grateful that her shield had been replaced and she could hide behind him. Throughout the remaining course, Ryan made an effort to engage Sue in conversation, telling her that he had visited England last year for a month. He had spent most of the time in London but also some in Liverpool, because he had read history at university and was interested in seeing the docks and learning more about the trade in slaves and how they had eventually been freed and settled there. He talked about his sporting interests that naturally included riding, skiing, snowboarding, and climbing. He was rather a nice lad (that awful word nice again) and he seemed very genuine, just the sort of offspring she would expect to come from Adam and Kate. The girls were also pleasant and Sophie commented on Sue's outfit saying how elegant she looked. At this point, Adele coughed slightly and buried her face in her napkin.

Once the meal was over, they retired to the lounge for coffee where Ryan, Katherine and Sophie asked to be excused. They were going over to the Glacier Saloon in the hotel to watch some TV and meet up with some other young people. They each said goodnight to Sue and left the older ones to continue chatting.

This was the point in the evening that Sue was dreading. It was only 9.00pm so how was she going to get away so early. She was still thinking about Adele's word to her and she was feeling rather angry, not only because of the blatant inference that she and Sam had had an affair but also because she hadn't been prepared enough to get back at her with a suitable response, but then again, that might have been a good thing because she would probably have said something she shouldn't have.

Alice Fearnley approached Sue and asked if she could sit beside her on the sofa. "I need to rest my legs a lot more these days my dear," she said with a wry smile. "How are you enjoying Canada for the second time?"

"Well, I'll be doing things a bit differently this time. When I get back to Calgary on Tuesday, I plan to do a little shopping and then I fly to Vancouver for the rest of my stay. I've been booked in at the Ocean Apartment Hotel, which I think is near Stanley Park."

"Yes, it is, I know it. Robert and I go to Vancouver once or twice a year. The firm has an office there and Robert goes for partners' meetings on occasion. Sometimes I go with him. Stanley Park is beautiful and well worth spending time there. If you're going to be in Vancouver for a few days you could go to Whistler on the Sea to Sky Highway. It will probably be a day's round trip if you go by coach, but well worth it."

"Mrs Fearnley, may I ask you something?"

"What's that dear, and it's Alice by the way. I don't like formality. I get enough of that at the Law dinners I attend with Robert." She grimaced as she said it.

"What was Sam really like? I only knew him for two days and then as you probably know, we corresponded for a few months after we returned home. Our conversations were mainly about topics of interest like our backgrounds and families, what we had been doing for the past week when we wrote our letters. Sometimes we would discuss what we thought about world affairs and what sports we liked – that sort of stuff – you know. I know Sam was a retired farmer and that his sons have taken over the farm. He talked about his late wife, Ellen, with a great deal of affection I might add, on numerous occasions. His face would light up when he mentioned her and he was sometimes close to tears. However, I just can't get my head around what made him want to include me in his will and request that I be here for the ashes ceremony. I know it must be equally unfathomable to his family and friends here. I also can't understand why an ordinary retired farmer could have bought such a valuable jewel even if it was a long time ago. What am I missing Alice?"

Alice Fearnley sat pondering for a moment before she replied, "Sam Carter was a canny old man. He worked very hard all his life and saved his money to spend wisely. He could see the potential of the farm and built it up after his father died so that he could leave his legacy to his sons. He knew cattle and he had a passion for raising them. He also had a wonderfully supportive wife in dear Ellen. We were very good friends for many years. She helped him through some bad times but it came good in the end. His sons are equally canny, especially Adam and they are carrying on his legacy. There's no mystery to that is there?"

"No of course not," said Sue, although she wasn't convinced by Alice Fearnley's response. It wasn't what Alice said but more what she didn't say that intrigued Sue. It was a reply that any politician would have been proud of. They were masters at saying a lot but not answering the question. She didn't have time to delve any further because Greg came over to talk to her. Alice rose and said she needed to talk to her husband and with that she left them alone. The waiter appeared with more coffee and Sue accepted another cup mainly because it was something to do with her hands.

"I hope we haven't overwhelmed you tonight Sue. It must be a bit daunting meeting all of us at once, but we don't bite you know, well most of us don't anyway," he joked.

"Oh everyone's been so kind," Sue lied. "I just feel a bit like a fish out of water. You must think it odd that your father requested my presence here. I feel like I'm gate crashing your most private moments. We did get on well, it has to be said and each time I got a letter from him I felt that we had some kind of affinity. We seemed to be able to talk about trivia and make it sound really interesting. I was quite upset and shocked when I learned of his death."

"My old man was one in a million and I don't mind saying that he knew people. He could read them well and it helped him through his working life. He would have weighed you up in the first few minutes of meeting you and he obviously had a favourable opinion of you – enough to want to spend some time with you, and let's face it, he knew he didn't have much of it left. We've realised that now because of the preparations he had made for his death. If I know my Dad, he knew exactly what he was doing leaving you that pendant, so don't feel guilty or beholden to anyone because from where I'm sitting, you are the kind of person who would have made him very happy and for that reason alone, you should have it.

Adam showed me the copy letters you sent by email. That was a kind and good thing to do because it showed us how he cared about you. I don't mind saying that at first, we weren't sure what to do about his bequest to you. Then Adam suggested that he mix a little business with an opportunity to see you in London and report back. It sounds like espionage doesn't it, but we needed to be sure. Adam reported back and we took it from there."

"I knew there was something going on, because I couldn't understand at the time, why Sam's son should be there at the solicitors. He was actually hiding in the next room and eavesdropping on the conversation. When he eventually barged in and interrupted us I was as mad as hell I can tell you."

"I know, he told me," said Greg with a laugh. "He said you were quite formidable and obviously not someone to mess with."

"Well, I don't know about that but if I think I'm justified I will make my point."

"You can consider your point well and truly made then Sue," he smiled broadly and added, "anyhow, it is good to meet you, and Adam and I are grateful that you came to Lake Louise. Enjoy the rest of your stay and of course your trip to Vancouver. I'll say goodnight as we have an early start in the morning. We meet in Reception at 5.45am."

"Goodnight Greg and thank you for talking to me like this, I feel much better now. I can make my excuses and go now that you are doing the same."

She went over to say her farewells to Adam and as she approached him, Adele, who was seated round a small coffee table with him and Kate, rose from her seat, turned her back on Sue and addressed everyone else in general. "I'm afraid you'll all have to excuse me. It's time I was in bed apparently. My husband has decreed an early night so I must obey." She made a mock bow of the head towards Greg who looked at her with a patience Sue felt he did not possess. He bent his arm at the elbow and pointed it out toward her and she linked hers in. They left the room with no more words.

The quietness that remained was broken by Kate, who turned to Sue. "Sue, I'm sorry I haven't had a chance to chat to you tonight have I? Have you enjoyed your evening?"

She motioned for Sue to sit beside her but Sue remained standing and replied, "Yes I have, thank you. Would you mind awfully if I left you to it? I'm shattered. It must be all the travelling I've done in the last three days."

"Of course, I wasn't thinking. Perhaps we can chat tomorrow over breakfast, or maybe you would like a short walk in the afternoon? The forecast is for dry and bright weather so we should be okay."

"A walk would be great, thanks Kate. I'll see you all in the morning and thank you again for a lovely evening."

They all wished her goodnight and she left, grateful that she had survived reasonably unscathed from that ordeal. As Sue made her way back to her room, she thought about her brief encounter with Adele. Sue's suspicions about her were proved correct and she decided that Adele was a nasty piece of work. Such a shame really, she had thought because the rest of the family and the Fearnley's were all really nice (that horrid word again) and friendly toward her. Well, after tomorrow she wouldn't have to see any more of Adele. However, she was looking forward to a good walk with Kate who seemed the complete opposite of her sister-in-law.

Sue made herself a note to remind her to ring Mark in the morning at 5.00am before she went to the ceremony. It would be about lunchtime at home so that should be okay.

Chapter 30

Dawn broke the next morning with a low mist hovering just over the Lake. As Sue looked out from the curtains, she could see the sun peering from behind the mountain and casting a strange light on the water. It was very still and quiet and a little eerie.

She checked her watch – 4.55am. She picked up the phone and dialled Mark's mobile number. She knew it would be expensive but he would be working so no good calling home. He answered fairly quickly and they exchanged the usual information about the weather. They were good at discussing the weather, but not much else these days. She told him about the dinner but not the details of conversations especially not the one with Adele. She reminded him that it was the ashes ceremony in an hour's time so she needed to get a shower and dressed. Sue said she would call him once she arrived back in Calgary at the hotel. That was it – end of conversation – no love you's or anything like that.

She showered and dressed and at 5.40am she was ready to go down to the Reception to meet the others. She took a last look out of her window and noticed that the mist had all but gone. The sun was almost up from behind the peaks and the Lake was like a mirror. Everything was still except for the Canada geese pecking on the grassy bank. It looked perfect. She thought about Sam and how he would have loved to be here now. But then of course, he was going to be here wasn't he? His ashes would be with them and then forever after his spirit would remain in this beautiful place.

She pulled herself up straight to quash the tears that were brimming in her eyes. She made a quick visit to the bathroom and dabbed her eyes before the mascara on them began to run down her face. She picked up her small purse and made her way towards the lift.

She was the last one to arrive in reception. Damn, not again! She thought she had timed it right but evidently not. The group was joined by the Vicar who introduced himself as Reverend Albright from the church in Lake Louise town. Everyone, except the vicar of course, (although she could see a pair of hiking boots peeking out from underneath the hem of his cassock) was dressed in smart outdoor gear so Sue's choice of smart walking trousers, cotton shirt and the wool and cashmere jacket were perfect. She noticed, however, that Adele was dressed entirely in black – black snow trousers, black sweater and jacket, all topped off with a black headband that pulled her perfect hair from her perfect forehead with make-up immaculately applied. She looked like a cover page model for designer outdoor wear. She was stunning.

Everyone wished her a good morning, but other than a discussion between Adam and the vicar, they remained quiet and reflective. Finally, a man who looked like the duty manager appeared from a room adjacent to the reception desk, carrying a small wooden casket. *The ashes,* thought Sue.

He gave the box to Adam and this was the signal for them to move outside. The vicar led the way, followed by Adam and Kate, then Greg and Adele. The two girls walked with Ryan, and Sue joined Robert Fearnley and Mrs Fearnley at the rear. As they stepped outside, the sharp coolness of the early morning air hit Sue's face. She shivered a little and pulled the collar of her jacket further up to cover her neck.

The tiny procession took the path up the grassy bank, passed the Canada geese that seemed to stop pecking at the grass and watch them on their way, like a guard of honour, then through the tree-lined part of the path that bordered the Lake. They walked for about ten minutes until they reached a break in the trees. The path sloped down towards the water's edge, and there, on a small pebbly banking, was a square wooden platform that jutted out over the water for about twelve feet. It was just large enough for the assembled group to huddle together in order to listen to the vicar speaking.

The ceremony lasted only a few minutes and after Adam had said a few words that he read from a piece of paper, he and Greg took out the handfuls of dust that had once been Sam Carter and scattered them on the Lake. The dust made a small floating monument and then began to disperse, wider and wider until it disappeared altogether.

Just at that point, there was a long, low rumble that appeared to come from the end of the Lake. Ryan pointed to Mt Victoria. "Look," he said, "there's an avalanche on the Victoria Glacier. Grandpa even managed to move that as well." There was a ripple of laughter and everyone turned to see the snow and ice crash down the mountainside as if it had been choreographed. The ladies in the group dabbed their eyes and Sue noticed that Adam was also tearful. The family hugged each other and even Adele managed to portray an air of sadness and respect for her dead father-in-law. It was a far cry from her demeanour last evening.

Sue felt surprisingly calm and in control of her emotions as if she was looking on from above. She felt the ceremony had been quite perfect and it made her more sure than she had been before that she had done the right thing in coming to witness it. She would never forget it and never forget Sam Carter.

After another few minutes, the assembled group started to disperse and return up the bank to the gravel path. Adam asked everyone to meet back at the conference centre where they had gathered last evening. He turned to the vicar and asked him if he would like to join the party for breakfast. The vicar declined saying that he had several visits to make and he needed to get back to the town, but that he wished everyone well.

The breakfast buffet was laid out on a long table at one end of the dining area in the Condor Room. A waiter was at the door to greet them bearing a tray of hot toddies to warm them up. Breakfast was much more informal and there seemed to be an air of lightness about the party that had not been there the evening before. Sue kept as far away from Adele as she could and chatted to anyone who happened to come and talk to her. This was everyone except for Adele, but this didn't worry Sue at all. She was glad it was that way.

Once breakfast was over and everyone had eaten sufficiently, Ryan and the girls were the first to make their exit. They were going snowboarding up in the mountains where there was still quite a bit of snow. Next were Greg and Adele who had planned a bike ride up the Great Divide Bike Trail. Robert and Alice Fearnley said they were going for a lie down as they had been up so soon, but would stay on for dinner tonight and travel home in the morning.

"Kate and I are going to the spa for a swim and a sauna. Would you like to join us Sue?" said Adam.

"Thank you, but I'd like to have a good look round the shops in the hotel. I didn't get much of a chance last time I was here and there look to be some interesting things."

"Go and enjoy a bit of retail therapy Sue, it'll do you good and you're right, there are some delightful things. Check out the knitwear design boutique. It's fabulous."
"I'll only be looking Kate. I suspect those prices will be way out of my league. You can tell they're expensive because there are no prices on them in the window. My Mum always said that if you had to ask the price you couldn't afford it. She was usually right."

"Well, you can have a good time looking can't you?" replied Kate. "What time do you want to meet up for that walk Sue?"

"Would about 2.00pm be okay?"

"Perfect. I should be done with the spa and had time for a snack, although I must say that breakfast has filled me up. I'll meet you down in reception at 2.00pm then," and with that she left Sue and Adam behind to go and get changed for the spa.

Sue was about to follow Kate out when Adam asked her to stay for a moment. "I have something I want to ask you Sue. Robert Fearnley has been sorting through Dad's stuff and he has a letter addressed to you that was never posted. He and I were wondering if you could meet us for a coffee about 11.00am in the Lakeview Lobby Lounge. He didn't mention it before now because he wanted to get the ashes ceremony out of the way first. Is 11.00am okay for you?"

"Yes, that'll be fine. I might have finished my window shopping by then," she said with a wry smile. They left together and walked across to the hotel in the pleasant morning sunshine.

"It looks like it's shaping up to be a good day Sue. Dad would have liked that."

"Yes, he certainly would."

Once Sue had left Adam to go back to her room, she pondered his request. She was slightly puzzled but decided that the letter must have been the last one Sam had written before he died and he never got the chance to post it. Why she needed to meet them to get it she didn't know, but anyway, she was glad of another opportunity to speak to Robert Fearnley whom she liked.

Chapter 31

The shops and boutiques in the hotel were every bit as expensive as Sue had feared. She spent some considerable time in the knitwear boutique. Kate was right – the merchandise was beautiful and so unusual. The rather too helpful assistant told her to feel free to try anything on that she liked. A rather lovely knitted jacket that would look perfect over a lace camisole for an evening event took Sue's eye, so she was persuaded to try it on. She had to admit it looked a million dollars and she felt really good in it. It was as light as a feather to wear yet warm and cosy - perfect for Christmas. She nearly had a heart attack when she was told it was only $780.00! Sue quickly removed it and said she would think about it. She saw some thick socks and thought she might be able to stretch to those, but she would come back later.

Surprisingly, Sue was rather peckish at about 10.00am, so she went to the twenty-four-hour Deli and got herself a croissant and a coffee to take away. She went outside on the terrace to enjoy her snack in the sunshine. The temperature had risen to about 20°C so she was able to sit with her book and relax for a few minutes. Her thoughts drifted to the last time she had been sitting here with Sam and she began to feel sad that she wouldn't be able to write to him again. She read a couple more pages of her book before remembering that she was due to meet Adam and Robert Fearnley at 11.00am. How odd that Sam's letter had only just come to light. At least it would be something to look forward to reading and it might give a clue to his state of mind just before he died. More importantly, it might tell her his reason for leaving her the pendant. She wondered again why Adam couldn't just have handed the letter to her at breakfast.

A few minutes before 11.00am, Sue returned to her room to leave her book and go to the loo, before her meeting with Adam and Robert Fearnley. When she arrived at the Lakeview Lobby Lounge, they were both seated in a corner, in deep discussion, both with serious looks on their faces. As they saw Sue approaching their conversation came to an abrupt halt and the serious faces changed to pleasant smiles.

Both men arose from their seats as Sue got nearer to them.

"Sit down my dear," said Robert Fearnley. "Would you like a coffee or something stronger?"

"No thanks, I've just had a coffee, so I'm fine." She seated herself between the two men on the sofa with its back to the wall and a perfect view of the Lake. Adam Carter glanced briefly at the other man who made a small nod as if to give sanction for him to speak.

"Sue, I mentioned a letter addressed to you that Robert had recently found in my Dad's things. Well, that isn't strictly true. You see, Robert has known about the letter since December last year. That was when Dad went to see him to make some changes to his will."

Sue was about to ask why she hadn't been given the letter sooner, when Robert Fearnley cut in.

"Sam came to see me about one or two things and he mentioned that he wanted to make a couple of changes to his will. One of those changes was leaving the pendant to you. That was the first time I had heard of you and the family still were unaware of your existence. I knew the pendant must be worth quite a bit and questioned his judgement. You do understand that don't you Sue? After all I was his solicitor as well as his friend and it was my duty to ensure that his interests and those of the family were protected."

Sue didn't speak but waited for Robert Fearnley to continue. He looked extremely uncomfortable but resumed his tale.

"I don't mind telling you, Sam was not pleased at my challenge and he told me to mind my own business. I asked him what he knew of you and he told me the story of your meeting last year. He spoke with such feeling that when he had finished his tale, there was nothing more to be said. I told him I would make the change, but then he requested another one. At this point you should know something about Sam which I suspect you don't already. He was a very wealthy man, and I mean wealthy. Oh, he liked people who didn't know him to think he was just a retired old farmer, which in essence, I suppose he was.

Well, the only thing that's true is that he was old, but although he didn't go out seeing to the cattle every day, he never really retired. He was probably one of the shrewdest men I ever knew. He could assess people so well and in a very short time and he never had time for fools. He built up his farm after his father died and he knew everything there was to know about cattle breeding. The Triple C Ranch is one of the largest in Alberta and I'm sure Adam will fill you in on more detail later if you want to know.

Anyhow, back to Sam's second request. He said he wanted to know that you would be able to afford to travel and he asked for a sum of money to be set aside for you. In short, he has left you £1 million sterling."

At this point Sue gasped and put her hands to her mouth to stop herself from uttering some expletive. She needn't have worried because she found that she could not speak. She opened her mouth but nothing came out. She obviously looked shocked because Adam signalled to a waiter to bring a glass of water and three whiskies.

The waiter appeared with the water within seconds and Sue took the glass with trembling hands. She almost choked on the first sip but recovered enough to take a larger gulp. Both men looked on anxiously as Sue struggled to recover some composure. Adam was the first to speak.

"Sue, I'm very sorry to do this to you. I, we, that is, Robert and I, we didn't want to upset you, but you see that's why we wanted you to come to Lake Louise so that we could give you the news face-to-face."

"You could have given me the news face-to-face when we met in London." Sue finally managed to say. This explained an awful lot. She now realised why Adam was in London and it explained all the attention he got from the staff in the hotel, just like his father in Lake Louise. She looked at both men from one to the other for a long moment and then when she spoke again, it was with quiet dignity.

"This charade has been about the family wanting to vet me hasn't it?" She didn't give them time to respond before continuing. "I had just about got used to the idea of the pendant and forgiven you Adam, for your performance in James' office in London. I deliberated long and hard before coming here but I wanted to honour the memory of a very special man, who I knew briefly but came to care very much for in the months we were in touch.

I didn't ask for any of this and if you knew Sam as well as you say you did Robert, then you would know that he wouldn't be taken in by some gold digger just out for what she could get. I sincerely hope he did want me to be here because if this was just a scheme to get me here so that you could all look me over and make judgement, then you are not the kind of people I want to have anything to do with.

This whole business has had a profound effect on me and my family. My own husband has doubted my fidelity. How bizarre is that? Sam was old enough to be my father and I have been put in the position of having to justify receiving the pendant. What my husband will say when he hears this I do not know.

My nerves have been shot to pieces in the last few weeks. I spent hours wondering what you would all think of me. Would I fit in? Would I wear the right clothes for heaven's sake? I can tell you this, I may not have much money and I may be ordinary but I would never treat another human being in this way. I hope I passed the test and gave you all some entertainment along the way."

Sue started to rise, but as she did so, her legs gave way underneath her and she staggered back onto the sofa. To her utter horror, she began to sob, heart wrenching sobs that would not stop. Robert Fearnley handed her his handkerchief and she took it gratefully because she wanted to bury her face in it and not emerge. It felt as if the whole world was laughing at her and she was powerless to do anything about it.

Neither man knew what to do. They were completely taken aback by Sue's response. Adam had been on the wrong end of Sue's tongue before but this was something else. She was perfectly justified, of course, he knew that much. He had acted with what he and his brother thought were the right motives, but it had gone horribly wrong. Robert had warned against keeping this from Sue at the beginning and if Adam hadn't have intervened in James Fearnley's office, James would have told her everything then.

Adam began to apologise and Robert Fearnley was so anxious about the whole thing that he downed one of the whiskies that had appeared during Sue's speech. After that, he remembered the letter and put it on the coffee table in front of Sue.

Sue looked up and dabbed her swollen eyes. She said, "Have you opened and read the letter as well?"

Robert Fearnley found his voice and replied, "Sue, I can absolutely promise you three things. Firstly, the letter has remained unopened since Sam gave it to me that day he came to see me. It has been in the safe in the office along with all Sam's other papers. Secondly, Sam did ask that you be here for the ashes ceremony. I can show you the part of the will that says so if you don't believe me.

Thirdly, neither I nor the family ever intended to cause you any distress or to humiliate you as you feel we have. We may have been guilty of being over cautious in dealing with this matter, but please believe me when I say that I am profoundly sorry. The letter is here on the table for you to take away and read when you feel you want to. Perhaps when you have read it you might feel a bit better about this whole thing.

If you don't mind, I'll leave you to talk to Adam. Listen to what he has to say before you do anything else and then let me know how you want to proceed. I very much hope to speak to you before you go home in the morning." He rose and retreated rather rapidly away from them and out of sight.

Sue and Adam continued to sit in silence until Adam said, "Have a sip of the whisky Sue, it might help you to feel a bit better. I certainly need mine after that dressing down."

"You're laughing at me again. Don't dare make light of all this. I have been forced to bear my soul to two near strangers and have made a complete fool of myself in public, so don't make it worse by joking."

"Sue, I wasn't trying to make light of anything. It was my clumsy way of saying how sorry I am. I want to apologise on behalf of myself and Greg. We made the decision not to tell you about the money or about my Dad's finances. Yes, as I said in London, we weren't completely sure that Dad hadn't had a flip or something and when I went back home after that, I talked to Greg and we agreed we would wait until you were here with us before telling you the rest. Please don't judge us badly."

"If Greg was so intent on waiting until I was here, why isn't he here as well?"

"He was going to come, but to be honest, he had some pressing personal matter to deal with. I can't tell you what but he was needed elsewhere this morning."

Sue guessed that the 'personal matter' might well involve Adele, as she was very drunk last night. That was not a happy marriage as far as Sue could make out, but not her concern right now.

"You must see how it looks from my viewpoint Adam," said Sue, a little more controlled now. "I can't begin to tell you how all this has affected me and Mark. He and I have been arguing about silly things and that's when we do talk. The rest of the time there's no conversation." She hadn't meant to say that but it just slipped out and she instantly regretted saying it.

"Sue, I'm really sorry to hear that and I do hope that you and your husband will accept the bequest in the spirit it was meant. Dad was wealthy, and now, Greg and I have inherited the Ranch and the associated businesses. We've been running things on a day-to-day basis, with the help of the Management Board but with Dad as the overall head. He had the final say but now we have equal shares. Despite what he led you to believe in his letters, he wasn't quite as detached from the businesses as he liked to make people believe. Dad knew exactly what was going on and would pounce on anything he thought looked a bit wrong.

I don't want to sound pompous or boastful, but the money is incidental. Dad was worth a fortune and £1 million won't be missed, so I don't want you to think that you are taking away our inheritance.

The grandchildren have all been provided for in trusts that will see them through their lives if they are wise with their finances. I don't know about the girls but Ryan has his head screwed on and he wants to be a part of the business so he's studying and learning the ropes at the same time.

As far as Kate is concerned, we share everything and you may have gathered she's not money orientated, so she's happy with the one or two personal items that Dad left to her. I was brought up to learn the value of money, and believe me, Dad made sure I had to earn anything he gave me when I was young.

Greg is like me, but he has an expensive wife to keep. She owns a stable in her own right with money that came from the business originally of course. She was a successful rider before she married Greg as well as being a bit of a beauty queen. However, she likes to live if you know what I mean and – well, some people never have enough money do they?

Please think about what I've said and once again, please try to forgive me for what's happened. Greg and I never meant any disrespect. We were just doing what we thought was right."

Sue looked at Adam intently and replied, "I need some time to be on my own and think about this. It's been such a shock. I still can't believe this isn't just a dream from which I'm about to waken any minute. Things like this don't happen to ordinary people like me, and quite honestly, I feel a bit queasy. I'm supposed to be meeting Kate at 2.00pm to go for a walk. Please apologise and say that I won't be able to come. It's after 1.30pm now and I must have some time alone with my thoughts."

"How about I tell her to meet you a bit later, say 3.30pm? That might give you time to work this out in your mind and then you can let her know what you've decided to do."

"You don't give up do you? You're just like your father you know. If he wanted something, he wouldn't let go until he wore you down."

"That was my Dad all right," said Adam, and his face broke into a wide smile.

Sue just shook her head and said she would meet Kate at 3.30pm because she would probably need some fresh air by that time. She picked up the letter from the coffee table and left Adam finishing off the third glass of whiskey that had been meant for her. She thought she might raid the minibar in her room when she was on her own. She needed something to help her while she read the letter from Sam.

Chapter 32

The envelope was the same as all the others she had received from Sam and she recognised the familiar handwriting on the front. Sue grabbed a couple of swigs of the Merlot that she had retrieved from the minibar and prepared to read the letter:

Mr S W Carter
Triple C Ranch
Caldrane
Bow Valley
ALBERTA
Canada

17 December 2012

My Dear Susan,

If you are reading this letter then I have passed away and I am once again with my beloved Ellen where I have always belonged. Since she passed away my life has lacked that sparkle it always had when she was around. Meeting you in Lake Louise brought that sparkle back if only fleetingly. You remind me so much of her when she was younger, and as I said, if I had been lucky enough to have a daughter, I just know she would have been like you.

There aren't a lot of people who would have put up with an old man on their holiday of a lifetime, listening to my ramblings and reminiscences. You were such good company and you made that last trip to Lake Louise very special for me.

Yes, it was the last one because I know I don't have too long to wait before I go to Ellen. I'm as ready as I can be and that's just fine.

Before I go, I want to do something for you in return for your precious time (yes, it is very precious and don't ever forget that) and your letters to me which have continued to cheer me through the last few months.

I have asked my old friend and solicitor, Robert Fearnley, to ensure that you receive the diamond pendant that I bought for Ellen all those years ago when we visited Paris for our wedding anniversary. I had it specially made for her you know. I know you will cherish it and please wear it when you can. It needs to be worn and I just know you will do it justice. You may wonder why I chose not to leave it to any of the females in the family. Well, Kate and Adele don't need any more than they already have and Greg's girls are too young to appreciate it. I'm happy that it's going to have a good home.

Also, I want you to have enough money to continue travelling to places you've never been and doing the things you like without worrying about the cost. You will know by now that I haven't been entirely truthful with you about my circumstances but I didn't think that telling you would add anything of value to our friendship, because you liked me for who and what you thought I was and that is the most important thing. Don't worry about what anyone else thinks about what I'm doing. No-one else's opinion matters. All that does matter is that you are happy and fulfilled.

One final request I have is that you return to Lake Louise one more time to join the family when they scatter my ashes on the Lake. Don't worry, they don't bite – except perhaps for Adele when she's had one or two drinks – but you can handle her I'm sure. This time, you won't have to pay the bill because it's all on me! You can't argue with me this time!

I'll let you into a secret. I am a shareholder in the company that owns the hotel so you see they have to suck up to me when I'm there. I know you wondered how I managed to get such good service and now you know.

Before I go, I wanted to say one more thing. You described yourself as an ordinary woman. Let me tell you that you are wrong. You are far from ordinary Susan. You have a rare gift of making people feel at ease with you. You treat everyone with respect no matter what their background might be. Never think that you are ordinary. You are very special and I'm so thankful that we met.

Please accept my gifts to you and enjoy them. I hope you and your husband are as happy as Ellen and I were. Don't give up on happiness, although you may need to fight for it.

When you travel to a new place, (first class from now on I hope) spare a moment or two to think of this old man and raise a glass of champagne to the memory of our brief friendship. You can afford the best champagne now so make sure it's something I would approve of!

I'll go now because I'm tired and I think I've said what I need to say.

God Bless you Susan,
Sam.

Sue put the letter down on the bed and for the second time today, she sobbed freely until she had no more sobs in her. She looked out of the window at the Lake and tried to picture Sam sitting on the terrace drinking his tea and reading his paper and wearing his Panama hat. So much had happened to her since she had met him that she felt as if she were being carried along on a strong tide to fantasy land, unable to make it back to reality.

£1 million! £1 million! The thought kept going through her head - round and round like a broken record. Just as she had been unable to stop sobbing, she found it equally impossible to stop the hysterical laughter that now burst from her lungs. She wondered how much more turmoil her brain could withstand. The feelings that were going round in her head were so diverse and at times perverse. How could she laugh like this yet at the same time feel unsure as to whether she should accept this gift to her? She finally realised that it was nearly time to meet Kate.

She went to the bathroom and looked at her reflection in the mirror. *Oh my God,* she thought. She looked like her eyes had been stitched in with red cotton! She quickly splashed her face with cold water to bring down the swelling and then hastily applied some foundation and a little lipstick. She completed the repairs with a comb of the hair and studied the result anxiously. It would have to do. She put on her trainers, picked up her small knapsack with her essentials in it, but not before replacing Sam's letter in its envelope and putting it in the desk drawer, then she made off to meet Kate in Reception.

Chapter 33

Kate was waiting for her when she arrived in Reception, looking very anxious so Sue guessed that Adam had told her about the meeting earlier. She felt really stupid because now they would all know that she had made a fool of herself. However, when she spoke, Kate was kind and, as usual gave Sue a balanced view of the situation.

"Look Sue, I think that what's happened is without doubt something unusual. I also believe that, we, as a family should have been more thoughtful about your possible reaction and if we could turn back the clock, we would have done things better. I'm using the global 'we' because although only Adam and Greg knew the full details, they acted on behalf of all the family.

Apart from all that, Sam obviously cared about you and your future and wanted to do something for you because he greatly appreciated your brief friendship and as everyone knows, he was a good judge of character and we should have respected that more than we did.

Please accept his gifts and don't give it another thought. You could do so much with the money couldn't you? Perhaps you would come and see Adam and I at least if you are ever in Canada again?"

She took Sue by the arm and led the way to the path that ran alongside the boat house. "Come on, let's have a good walk and some fresh air. You look like you need it and perhaps we can talk things through or if you want we can talk about anything but this whole business."

"Any other topic would suit me fine Kate right now. I'm worn out thinking about the 'other thing.'"

They walked for about forty-five minutes and then decided to head back to the hotel. They chatted about families and fashion, food and fitness, and by the time they reached the hotel, they were firm friends. Sue liked Kate a lot because she was a bit like herself – practical not airy fairy at all. She was a genuine sort of person and Sue could see that she would have got on really well with her father -in-law.

"What are you doing for dinner tonight Sue? I know you might want to be on your own but how about eating with Adam and I in the Lago? We've booked a table for 7.00pm so we could easily add you on."

"I had planned to do nothing tonight but I appreciate your offer and will be glad to accept, as long as Adam doesn't mind or tries to brow beat me again about the money."

"Oh, he won't mind. In fact he'll be delighted because he'll think that you've forgiven him and that you will give Robert Fearnley the go-ahead to transfer the money to your bank!"

"Let him sweat a bit longer Kate," said Sue. "After I have got over the initial shock I will agree that I can do a lot with the money. I desperately want to see more of the world and it would be great to be able to help the family a little. It's such a lot of money though and like the pendant I can't help feeling a responsibility for taking care of it. I will accept it gratefully but don't tell Adam though. I want him to stew a bit more but I'll call Robert later and confirm the details."

Kate smiled and gave Sue a squeeze of the arm before arranging to meet her in Reception at 6.45pm, then she left her and walked off in the direction of the Concierge's office.

Sue was about to press the lift button when a thought popped into her head. She walked through the door of the knitwear boutique and was met by the young assistant from earlier in the day.

"Could I please try on that jacket I looked at earlier today?" She admired her reflection in the full-length mirror once more and after a few moments deliberation said she would take it. "Oh, and I'll take a pair of those socks! You can charge it to my room – number 712."

Chapter 34

It was with very evident relief, that Robert Fearnley took a note of Sue's bank details. Sue could positively hear his voice relax in a matter of seconds. She did, however, ask him not to say anything to Adam as she was going to tell him when she was good and ready. She added that she was having dinner that evening with Adam and Kate at their request.

"Well that will be nice. Of course I will let you tell him. Thank you my dear. I'll see to the transfer first thing in the morning. The money will be in your bank within a couple of hours all being well. Alice and I will be dining in our room tonight and will be away early in the morning, so please accept our very good wishes for the future and if I can be of service to you at any time – you never know – just let me know, you have my contact details. It has been a pleasure to meet you, and Alice says she hopes you enjoy the rest of your stay in Canada. Goodbye Sue." With that, he hung up.

It was now 5.30pm and surprisingly, Sue felt more invigorated. She took a leisurely bath and then sent a text message to Jean. It read:
Having good time. Lots to tell. Going back to Calgary 2 morrow then onto Vancouver. See you soon. Sx.

She was tempted to tell Jean about the money but then realised that she would probably think it was a big joke. She would enjoy telling Jean all about this episode of her trip face-to-face. Jean was such a brilliant listener. This was going to blow her mind though. She would take her out for a cup of coffee and a cake, and then spill the beans. She couldn't wait.

Sue deliberated about whether to wear her new purchase, but then decided she would keep it for a night out in Vancouver. She settled on the same slacks as the night before but a different top. When she was satisfied that she couldn't do any more with her appearance, she left to meet Adam and Kate. Somehow, she felt much more light-hearted tonight, as if some pressure had been taken off her shoulders. She didn't feel the need to make an impression and she liked the feeling. Maybe it had something to do with knowing she was about to receive so much money. It gave her a feeling of confidence tinged with excitement of course. Perhaps she would be relaxed enough to enjoy tonight's meal properly.

Sue kept up her pretence about accepting the money from Sam throughout the meal and even as they were leaving the Lago restaurant and heading towards the Reception.

Adam said, turning to Sue, "I wondered if, on the way back to your hotel tomorrow morning you would like to stop off at the Ranch and see where Sam lived and I could show you around the place. That way, you might not feel so averse to accepting Dad's money when you see our tiny empire."

Before she spoke, Sue shot a warning glance at Kate who shrugged her shoulders and pretended to look for something in her bag.

"Yes Adam, I would like to see where Sam lived although I don't want to put you all to any further inconvenience. Besides, I'm sure the tycoons have had far too much time off in the last few days and will need to get back to check that all is still intact," she mocked.

"Hmm, very amusing I'm sure. Seriously, it would be a pleasure, and anyway, any tycoon worth his salt always has people to look after his empire when he's not there, and of course, Greg will be back there already. He and Adele left earlier in the evening."

"Okay, as long as Kate doesn't mind me taking up your time."

"I don't mind at all Sue. I have some jobs to catch up on and I'll be busy anyway. Adam can drive you back into Calgary after you've had a bite to eat with us."

"That's very kind of you and I'll look forward to it."

"Great," said Adam, looking like he had won a minor battle.

"I'll say goodnight then and see you here in reception in the morning. What time do you want to be away?"

"Can you be ready to go for about 8.00am?" asked Adam.

"No problem. I'll see you both then. Goodnight and thank you once again for a lovely meal this evening."

As Sue removed her make-up in the bathroom, she talked to her reflection in the mirror. "I'm a millionairess! Did you know that? Well I am. I know I don't look like one right at this moment, but believe me, it's true. I know I'm finding it hard to grasp as well." She looked at the face in the mirror and started laughing, but the laugh was a nervous one. Every time she thought about it, her stomach did a flip. She still wondered if this was a dream from which she would soon awaken. She pinched herself a couple of times and having satisfied herself that she was well and truly awake, she removed her make-up, got into her pyjamas and got into bed, putting the light out straight away.

She wasn't sure if it was the wine she had consumed or the fact that she had enjoyed the company of Adam and Kate last night or both, but she had slept better than any of the nights she had been away. She awakened refreshed and decided to get up early to enjoy one last stroll along the lakeside before leaving. It was 6.30am and there were one or two people with the same idea. It was another bright crisp morning that looked like it would turn into a warm day. The Canada geese were there, grazing on the grassy bank and there was the occasional click of a camera as keen photographers seized their opportunity to get that perfect early morning shot of the lake and the surrounding mountains, just as she had done when she was here last year.

She stopped off at the deli and got herself a coffee and croissant which she ate in her room before packing the last of her things, including the knitted jacket and socks. She felt a bit guilty about those but then decided that she deserved them after the ordeal she had been through. After all, she was a millionairess. The thought hit her again and her stomach flipped as if she had pressed a button. She was certain she would never get used to the idea. She handed her key card to the reception clerk and asked to check out of Room 712. As she got her credit card out of her purse to pay, the clerk said that there was nothing to pay. The bill had been settled by Mr Carter.

"Yes, but what about the extras? I bought some items in the knitwear boutique yesterday. Perhaps they haven't been added to the bill yet."

"Let me check for you Mrs Barnett. The items you mention are on the bill and it has all been settled, so there is nothing more to pay. I hope you enjoyed your stay with us at the Château Lake Louise and look forward to seeing you again maybe?" She smiled warmly and Sue replied that she had enjoyed it and it was her second stay. She thanked the clerk and went to sit down in the lobby to wait for Adam and Kate.

Oh no, now I'm going to have to confess to buying the jacket and socks, and Adam will guess that I've already decided to accept the money, thought Sue, as she waited. She would just have to pay Adam for them and say that she had always intended to get them anyway.

She only waited about five minutes before they showed up. Adam took Sue's case and they headed off to the waiting 4x4 that stood on the concourse. The door was opened by one of the doormen who took her case from Adam and put it in the back where Adam and Kate's cases were already packed in.

Another doorman came round the side of the vehicle and opened the passenger door for Sue to get in, touching his cap as he did so.

Adam shared a few words with both men and just as they were about to pull away, the duty manager appeared from the building. Adam handed him an envelope and he bowed slightly and said thank you. Finally, they were off and Sue looked back at the magnificent view of the Lake as they drove away down the long drive to the main highway. She said a silent goodbye to Sam and fought to quell the tears that began to well in her eyes. What a place this was. What an unbelievable couple of days she had just had. Who would ever believe what had taken place here? Her thoughts were finally broken by Kate who asked her if she had slept well. She replied that she had and added that she thought it might have been the wine she had consumed.

She plucked up courage to mention the knitwear and the settled bill. "Adam, I went to settle my bill for the extras and was told it had already been settled, so I will need to pay you for them. When we get back to Calgary, I'll sort it out with you then."

"There's no need for that Sue, it's done now."

"Oh, but there is a need Adam. It's a lot of money and I can't let you pay it."

"Call it a gift, Sue. Anyway, it's the least Greg and I can do after what we've put you through. I don't want it back and that's an end to it."

Sue sighed in submission and was at the same time relieved that he hadn't pursued the nature of the purchase any further. Perhaps she had got away with it.

Chapter 35

They turned off the main highway and passed through the town of Caldrane. It was obvious that the town catered for outdoor activities judging by the number of stores selling ski and walking gear. It was nestled at the foothills of the Rockies on the edge of the Banff National Park. Once through the town, they turned off again onto a smaller road and eventually, they approached a huge boarding advising of a right turn to a number of businesses. As they approached the boarding, Sue realised that the list of businesses were associated in some way to the Carter family. They included the following:

- *Triple C Ranch (Beef and dairy production)*
- *SW Carter & Sons (Beef exporters)*
- *Carter Cattle (Alberta Angus and Charolais Stud)*
- *A Carter (Stables & Stud)*

As Sue was taking this in, the 4x4 turned into a long driveway lined on both sides with maple trees. The drive went on for about two minutes before they rounded a sharp bend. At the bend, another road forked off to the right and was marked 'Commercial and Heavy Goods entrance only'. The main drive swept round to the left and revealed a huge archway built of stone about twenty feet high at the centre upon which was a sign saying 'Welcome to Triple C Ranch'.

They passed underneath the arch, and the first building Sue saw was a huge ranch style house with a gravel semi-circular drive around a perfectly manicured lawn. In the centre of the lawn was a water feature made from huge boulders. The water cascaded down from one ledge to the next until it gathered in a pool at the bottom. To the left of the ranch house was a paddock containing several horses and behind that a large bank of fir trees that seemed to stretch for miles in length.

They pulled up outside the stone steps that led up to the ranch house porch. Adam got out and opened the passenger door for Sue to get out. "Welcome to Triple C, Sue. This is the main house where Kate and I live. This is the oldest building on the land but we have made one or two changes in the last few years to bring it up to date a bit."

"It's magnificent," said Sue, taking in the features of the façade.

"When we've had some coffee or tea, if you prefer Sue, I'll give you a quick tour of the rest of the empire."
Adam smiled as he said this and Sue grinned back at his little dig.

As they walked up the stairs, the front door was opened by a middle-aged lady wearing an apron over her slacks and shirt. "Welcome home folks. I guess you'll be wanting some coffee after your drive. The machine's on, so I'll be with you in a few minutes. Did everything go okay?" At this point, the woman noticed Sue and introduced herself as Donna. "I'm a kind of cleaner come housekeeper for Kate and Adam. I look in most days and help Kate around the place, especially when she has guests."
"Donna, this is Sue from England. We are giving her a lift back to Calgary and Adam is going to show her round the place once we've had that coffee. Is coffee okay for you Sue or do you prefer tea?" said Kate.

"Tea would be good if it's not too much trouble, thanks," replied Sue.

"Coming right up," said Donna.

They stepped inside through the porch and into a huge square hallway with several doors leading from it. In the middle of the hallway a wide staircase rose up and divided into two separate wings. At the top of the stairs, was a long stained glass window, with a tall vase that rose about three feet from the floor, and contained an arrangement of silk flowers.

"We'll have our drinks in the small den Donna please."

"Okay Kate. I've been baking some oat biscuits this morning, so I'll put one or two of those out as well." Donna disappeared and Kate led the way to a cosy room on the right. It was obviously a room that was well used. The chairs and sofa were covered by tartan throws and there was a thick hearth rug that looked like it was used to people and dogs lying on it, in front of a high stone open fireplace. Sue had no sooner completed her instant appraisal of the room, when the door burst open and in came a huge hairy white dog that made straight for Adam, stood on his hind legs and proceeded to lick his face. Adam let him do this for a few seconds and after giving him a few generous pats, ordered him to sit, which he did immediately, although his tail continued to wag furiously.

"Sue, meet the boss of the house, Digger. He's two years old and he's a Japanese Akita. He's a good chap but he can get a bit boisterous, so look out."

"He's lovely," said Sue. The dog looked at her for a moment and then seemed to decide that she might be worth checking out. He bounded across the room towards her and put his front paws on her lap. Adam and Kate both called him off at the same time and he sat back looking at Sue, waiting for her to stroke him. She patted his head and said hello to him and he instantly began to lick her hands.

"He seems to like you Sue. Trust me, you would know if he didn't. He doesn't usually take to people straight away like that but he must think he can trust you."

"Perhaps you should have sent him to London instead of going yourself," said Sue, and flashed a wicked look at Kate who did her best not to laugh.

Donna arrived at that moment, carrying a tray with coffee, tea and biscuits. When she saw Digger, she said, "I'm sorry folks. I didn't know Digger had got in here. I don't know how he managed it. I had him closed in the pen outside. He must have sneaked passed me when I was brewing the tea. I'll take him out if you want."

"It's okay, Donna. He's just getting acquainted with our guest here," said Adam. He turned to Sue who was still patting and fussing the dog that was lapping it up.

"I'll leave you to it then. I need to get the washing out and then I'll get off if that's okay," said Donna to Kate.

"Yes, thanks Donna, that's fine. I'll see you tomorrow morning and we'll go through the list of groceries we're going to need for next weekend's dinner."

When Donna had gone, Kate explained that she and Adam were hosting a dinner party for some of the neighbouring ranchers and their wives. It was an annual event that she and Adam had started when Sam had officially 'retired' and they had moved into the ranch house.

As they drank their tea and coffee, Sue commented on the size of the ranch. "This is only the first bit that you can see from the main drive," said Adam. "There's a lot more to see and we'll need a set of wheels to get round. I'll go and get the Jeep pickup and come back for you in a few minutes Sue. I just need to check in at the ranch office first, but I won't be long."

Kate said she would make a light lunch of sandwiches and soup if that was okay with Sue. "You'll need something before you set off back to Calgary, and after Adam's bored you to death showing you around the place."

"Thank you so much for your support this last couple of days Kate. Does Adam still think I am in two minds about accepting the legacy?"

"Honestly, I haven't said anything and neither has Robert Fearnley because I overheard Adam talking to him on the phone this morning. He was asking him if he had heard from you and I'm guessing that he said no because Adam said that he would have another go at persuading you today."

"I'll put him out of his misery before I leave." Sue smiled and winked at Kate who returned the smile and said it was a pity she wouldn't be there to see him squirming. Adam returned after about ten minutes and he and Sue got into the Jeep.

"We'll start with a look at my Dad's place. It's just around the back of the main house, up the lane, to the left by those fir trees."

Adam drove the Jeep passed the paddock and towards the bank of fir trees that Sue had spotted when they arrived. The lane cut through the trees and as they entered Sue noticed a clearing to the left on which stood a small single storey timber framed house. It had a stone chimney stack on one gable end that rose from the ground and all the way up the centre of the gable and about three feet above the apex of the roof.
"Do you want to take a look inside?" asked Adam.

"Yes please, just for a minute."

"It will be just as he left it. We haven't had time to do anything with it yet apart from making sure it was cleaned. Sarah's been in so it should be okay."

"Your dad told me about Sarah. He said that you and Greg used to tease him by saying that she fancied being the next Mrs Sam Carter."

"Yes, that's right. We did rib him a bit. Sarah was distraught when Dad died. I think she loved looking after him because it gave her a purpose. Now, she has nothing to get her out of the house. Kate has said she will go and see her and try to get her involved in some voluntary work with her. She's a great one for a cause is Kate."

"She is a very good person, I think," said Sue.

Adam took a set of keys from the dash board and opened the front door to Sam's little house. There was a small hallway with two doors on the left side, two to the right and one at the end of the hallway. They entered through the door at the end that opened onto a modestly furnished lounge with a fireplace at one side and French windows that opened onto a wide covered veranda that ran the full length of the house. Through the windows she could see a table and four chairs at one end. In the middle of the veranda was a large wooden rocking chair covered by two fat cushions. Then she noticed the view. There was nothing at the back of the house but rolling fields dotted with cattle. In the distance were the foothills of the Rockies.

Sue stood for a long moment, taking in the view and picturing Sam sitting in the old rocking chair, surveying his land. He must have been so proud of the results of his work that he always wanted to be able to see them from his chair, even in winter when it was too cold for him to venture outside.

"I guess you're wondering just how big the ranch is. Well, we own just short of 10,000 acres. Some of it is scrub, some is woodland but most of it is prime grazing land. We have about 1800 head of cattle made up of Angus, Charolais and Hereford breeds. We also have some Jersey cattle for the milk and dairy side.

You'll have noticed if you saw the boarding on the main road that we produce and process or own beef and some dairy products – milk and cheese. We are a recognised breeder of Angus and Charolais, and we have won a lot of prizes for our bulls. Last year we won the prize for the best bull at the annual Bull sale in Calgary with a beast weighing in at 2400lbs. He sold for $21,000. He was an Angus.

I'll tell you more about the businesses when we move on."

Sue was still enthralled with the view and a feeling of peace that seemed to hang in the air all around.

"This is a beautiful spot. The house is something like I imagined it to be but the view is a revelation. I can see why your father wanted to be here."

"Yes, he loved this little place. He had it built when he decided to retire. I use the term advisedly because he never really stopped being involved. He and Mom had only been here a short time when she died. He said he wanted to be able to see his animals growing out on the pasture in summer and this was as good a place as any. The house has two bedrooms with en-suite facilities and a good-sized kitchen come dining room. That was all he needed he said. Shall we go now? There's a lot to fit in and Kate will have lunch ready soon."

"Yes, lead the way and then I'll be out of your hair at last. I'm sure you will be glad about that," said Sue.

As they locked up and walked back to the Jeep, Adam asked Sue if she had decided what she was going to do about the money. They got into the Jeep and as Adam let out the clutch and pulled away from the house, Sue turned to him and said, "I've been thinking about it non-stop since yesterday morning. I have already given Robert Fearnley my bank details so that he can have the money transferred. He said he would see to it today."

"You knew last night didn't you when we were having dinner but you let me carry on grovelling," Adam said, and then added, "well, it serves me right. It's no more than I deserve. But Robert must have known as well. He didn't let on."

"That's because I asked him not to tell you. Two can play at that game Adam," replied Sue with a wink.

"You should come and work for me Sue. I could do with someone at the negotiating table now that Dad's not here."

"I'm not so sure you need anyone Adam. From what I have seen, you can hold your own with the best of them."

They drove on and turned right through more fir trees until another large ranch house came into sight. "We won't go down there but that's Greg and Adele's place by the river at the bottom of the slope. She has her stables and stud down there. She's actually very successful at what she does, but she's not so good with the accounting side of things. Luckily, Greg is, and he does his best to keep an eye on things, much to Adele's annoyance at times. She's quite a handful."

Sue knew what a handful Adele could be, but that wouldn't be her description of the woman. Good manners and respect for her host prevented her from commenting.

They drove on and right as if going in a circle and Adam drove past a huge clutch of buildings that he said housed the abattoir, meat processing, and despatch areas of the business.

"We process all our own beef and dairy products but the dairy is housed further round. We export some of our beef to Scotland believe it or not and we're trying to do business with a large London company. That's why I go there often. We also supply beef to two large supermarket chains across Canada as well as a number of high class restaurants. We have our own fleet of container lorries and they are housed in the building at the end of that road down there. We have maintenance mechanics to ensure the vehicles are kept in good order."

They drove further on and came to another large building that Adam said was the dairy. "That's where we process the milk from the cows and make our own cheese which we sell to the supermarkets I mentioned earlier. Finally, we come to some of the sheds we use to house the cattle in the worst weather and where we keep an eye on new born calves. We have other sheds dotted around the pastures because it's not practical to bring the cattle all this way.

We are one of the largest employers in this area of Alberta. I think we have about 150 employees, but that can change in different seasons. We use seasonal workers to help with harvesting the hay for winter feed. So you see Sue, we are quite a big company.

Greg and I are helped by a team of people who also sit on the Management Board, but we are the only shareholders. There's the Livestock Manager, the Farm Manager, the Beef Processing Manager, the Dairy Processing Manager, the Transport and Logistics Manager, the Accountant and of course Robert Fearnley our Solicitor. In addition to those people we have Managers to look after Human Resources, Health and Safety Compliance, Marketing and Facilities. Last but definitely not least, we have a resident Vet. They all report on a monthly basis to the Board. Greg and I oversee it all and we personally visit our clients and customers at least twice a year.

Dad was on the organising committee for the Calgary Stampede and the Alberta Cattle Breeders' Committee . The ACBC have asked me to take his place. I'm thinking about it at the moment and I said I would let them know next week."

They finally arrived back at the ranch house after nearly two hours where Kate was waiting for them. Sue had said very little while Adam had been driving and giving his tour speech but she had taken in as much as she could and now she marvelled at the achievements of the old man she had met last year quite by chance. Little did she know then that she was in the company of a self-made multi-millionaire. He had seemed so quaint and modest. He had talked to her about everyday things and asked her to do him the honour of writing to him. She was the one who was honoured. He had mentioned nothing of his export business and his team of professionals headed up by his very capable sons. She was lost for words. She must have looked far away because her reverie was broken by Kate asking her if she wanted watercress soup with her sandwiches.

"Er, oh yes, that would be lovely, Kate. I'm afraid I was miles away just then. I was thinking about what Adam has just told me and trying to reconcile it all with the old man that I knew. He was truly an exceptional human being."

"He was," agreed Adam. "When I came back home after university, he listened to the ideas I had and although he had started to put some of the businesses you see today in place, he was open to new thinking and modern techniques to gain the efficiencies the businesses needed.

Even so, he never lost touch with his roots and the people who had helped him in the beginning. There is a community centre in Caldrane that he paid for. It's for the elderly people of the town and surrounding areas to meet and be given a hot meal. In winter, there is a team of volunteers helped by one or two paid staff who make sure that that those living in the outlying areas still get food and other help like being taken to the medical centre to get treatment. His legacy will live on even after his death because he has set up a trust fund to ensure that happens."

"You must be so proud of him," said Sue. "I wish I had known him longer than I did." The conversation turned to more mundane things like what time Sue wanted to get back to the hotel in Calgary. It was agreed that Adam would take her once they had finished lunch and she had freshened up. They agreed to keep in touch and Kate gave Sue a business card with their address and telephone numbers on.

At 2.45pm Sue said goodbye to Kate and Digger who wagged his tail enthusiastically in response. She and Adam set off in the 4x4 under the huge arch, back down the drive and onto the maple tree-lined road. They were silent for some time until the outskirts of Calgary came into view.

They pulled up on the concourse of the hotel and immediately one of the doormen came to open the passenger door for Sue. Adam handed her case to him and gave him a tip. Once inside the foyer, Sue turned to Adam to shake his hand. He took it but then pulled her to him and gave her a hug. He drew away and could see that she was somewhat startled. "Sorry, I didn't mean to be over familiar but I just wanted you to see that I really do appreciate what you did to make Dad happy those last few months. It's taken me long enough to come to terms with his death, let alone realise just how lonely he was. What you meant to him is evident by his actions and it's my way of saying that I hope you will finally forgive what Greg and I have done, and keep in touch with us, even if it's just the occasional email."

"Yes, I have forgiven you, just, and I will let you know how I'm getting on. The last two days have been eventful to say the least, but your generosity and that of Kate has knocked me out – really. Thank you so much Adam and maybe we will meet again if you come to London and bring Kate with you."

He nodded and turned to go. As he got to the doorway, he turned round and waved to her and smiled a broad smile that made him look even more handsome.

Damn if he doesn't look just like a younger version of his father, thought Sue for the umpteenth time. She sighed as he pulled away in the 4x4 and went to check back in and retrieve her other case.

She was back in the same room as before and her thoughts turned to home and Mark. He would be expecting her call. It was nearly 4.00pm and she tried to think what time it would be at home. She estimated it would be about midnight and so decided to send him a text message instead. He would pick it up in the morning and then she would ring him when she had eaten her breakfast, by which time, it would be about lunchtime at home.

She ordered her evening meal – a light snack – from room service and ate it watching the weather channel to see what it was going to be like in Vancouver. She had booked a taxi to take her to the airport in the morning. Her flight was at lunchtime and would take about one and a half hours so she needed to be ready to go at about 9.00am. She organised her clothes for the next day and had a long bath. She had a half bottle of wine and sat up in bed, watching TV and finishing off the last glass.

Eventually, she couldn't keep her eyes open and she put out the light and fell into a deep sleep. It didn't last long though because she awoke at 1.25am and instantly, she started to turn things over in her mind.

How was she going to tell Mark about the money? What would he say? Eventually, she decided not to mention it to him until she got home. After all, it wasn't the sort of news you could give on the telephone. No, she would wait until she was home so that she could gauge his reaction better when they were face-to-face.

She got up and made herself a cup of hot chocolate. She took it back to bed and watched a late film. It was an old black and white cowboy film – not the sort of thing she would normally watch, but perhaps it would be so boring that it would help her to fall asleep again. It was beginning to come light by the time she dozed off, by which time she was exhausted. She had set the alarm to waken her at 7.00am and when the shrill tone of the beeps hit her ears, she groaned and hit the button to turn it off.

Chapter 36

Sue's first task was to ring Mark. It would be mid-afternoon at home so she hoped to catch him on his mobile at work. He seemed pleased to hear her voice and said he had received her text message from the day before. She briefly outlined her journey back to Calgary from Lake Louise and mentioned that she had stopped at the *Triple C Ranch* along the way. She said that she had been surprised at the size of the ranch (the understatement of the year) and clearly Sam had been a man of some means (another understatement).

"I said he would have had a bob or two if he was a farmer," remarked Mark. "They've always got a bit stashed away that no-one knows about." He went on to relate a much used example of a local farmer at home.

"So what's your plan today, Sue?" he finally asked.

"I fly to Vancouver at lunchtime and it should only take about 90 minutes, so I should be checked in at my hotel mid-afternoon. I'll get a map and I've made a note of one or two places I want to see, but today I'll get my bearings and then plan something for tomorrow. I'm staying near a place called Stanley Park which is enormous, so I'll probably do that tomorrow. I'll give you a call before the end of the week – say Friday at about this time."

"Okay, enjoy your stay and I'll talk to you then."

They said goodbye and as she switched off her mobile phone, she heaved a sigh of relief that she had managed to carry off the nonchalant conversation. She hoped anyway that he had not picked up anything in her voice. She checked out of her hotel at 8.50am and climbed into the waiting taxi to take her to Calgary International Airport. As it was an internal flight, there wasn't too much of a wait and the check-in was relatively smooth.

The plane touched down in Vancouver just after 1.30pm and she was checking into her hotel an hour later. Although Vancouver has a reputation for wet weather, the day was fine with a light breeze and the temperature according to the pilot was a pleasant 19°C.

After unpacking and making herself a cup of tea, Sue headed out, map in hand, to have a look round her immediate surroundings in readiness for the next day's visit to Stanley Park.

****

Wednesday dawned overcast but still dry. Sue took her backpack and packed her shower proof jacket, because it folded into a small pack. She set off on foot, to find the Lion's Gate Bridge. This was the one that linked Stanley Park to North Vancouver. The weather was perfect for walking. This was just as well, because Sue headed for the Aquarium which was located a good distance from the Lion's Gate entrance.

Sue quickly realised that there was so much to see here that she could probably spend two days at Stanley Park, so she confined her day to the Aquarium with its many fascinating creatures including the White Beluga whales in the Arctic Canada exhibition. She strolled through the many different areas and had lunch in one of the restaurants. She finally made her way back to her hotel thoroughly exhausted but pleased with her day and decided that, after a relaxing bath she would find a restaurant near her hotel to have her evening meal.

On Thursday Sue returned to Stanley Park and this time she visited Prospect Point and the SS Beaver Centre.

She ate in the hotel that night and as she was sitting in the lounge bar, drinking a glass of rosé her thoughts turned once again to the money Sam had left her. She checked her mobile and as she had thought would happen, the bank had been trying to contact her, presumably to tell her that a large amount of money had been paid into her current account – one million pounds to be exact!

Friday, she decided, was going to be a shopping day. Downtown Vancouver would provide her with the perfect place to visit, even the most exclusive shops, and browse without feeling as if she was out of her league as far as prices were concerned. She wanted to see what it was like to know that you could afford anything on view even though you might not buy it. Yes, she thought it was going to be a revelation and something of an initiation that she felt she had to experience before she went back home.

Sue dressed in smart slacks and the *'Lake Louise jacket'* for her shopping trip. She wanted to look the part and enjoy seeing the reactions of the shop assistants as she casually strolled round the stores and browsed at the clothes and shoes.

She called Mark as arranged and they had their usual five minute conversation: mainly about the weather and what she had done the two days previously. After agreeing to speak again on Sunday, they said goodbye. Mark had said he would ring Sue this time because it would be costing her a lot to keep ringing him. Sue almost gave herself away by saying she could afford it now, but she remembered just in time and said it was easier for her to ring him because she would turn her phone off for the rest of the time as she wouldn't need it. She would just check it a couple of times a day for messages but usually there weren't any.

After breakfast, Sue set out on her favourite pastime – shopping! Marvellous!

Chapter 37

Sue estimated that she had walked as far on Friday as she had the two previous days in Stanley Park. She had a marvellous time though. She bought one or two things but nothing too expensive or heavy because she didn't want to have to pay excess baggage charges on the way home – even though she could afford it now. She wasn't going to be wasteful with the money she had inherited, but Sam would want her to have one or two little luxuries from time to time. She felt sure of that much. She bought silk scarves for the girls and smart T-shirts for the men. She would give the grandchildren some money when she got back. She wondered what to get for Jean and decided on a silver bracelet that caught her eye in a jeweller's shop window.

After an exhausting but very enjoyable day, Sue ordered a meal from Room Service and ate it watching TV.

The weekend weather was a mixture of sunshine and frequent showers, so Sue took the opportunity to visit the Vancouver Maritime Museum and the Vancouver Museum devoted to regional history and the First Nations. She was fascinated by the collection of arts and crafts on display.

On Monday the weather was dry and bright again so Sue went to Canada Place and took the SeaBus to Lonsdale Quay. The harbour waters were relatively kind to her stomach which was just as well because she was not the best of sailors. She enjoyed the fifteen minute crossing because it wasn't too long but it gave her plenty of photo opportunities. Lonsdale Quay featured a public market with fresh produce and a host of fast food restaurants from a wide range of cuisines. She had an inexpensive Chinese lunch and strolled through the gift shops and boutiques on the second floor of the glass fronted building.

She made the return journey and got a taxi back to her hotel. She had done enough walking these last few days. Her last night would be spent in the hotel restaurant and bar, and then she would be ready to go home and face the music on Tuesday. Her flight was mid-afternoon which meant she would get into Manchester about 6.30am on Wednesday. She had ordered a taxi back home so expected to be there before Mark went to work. She would ring Mark before she left the hotel in the morning to give him the details.

As Sue ate her meal that evening, she went back over the events of the last ten days. Such a lot of things had happened and she had gone through a wide array of emotions. It was no small wonder that she felt drained emotionally. She couldn't shake off the feeling of foreboding that lurked at the back of her mind, no matter how hard she tried. In the end, she left her meal half eaten and settled for liquid nourishment in the form of a whole bottle of wine.

Eventually, as she made her way to her room, the somewhat morose feelings seemed to be replaced by giddiness. She swayed slightly as she walked along the landing to her door and realised that she was colliding with the wall, re-bounding from one side to the other. She was relieved to negotiate her door key successfully without fumbling too much. She gratefully closed and locked her door, and once inside, she kicked off her sandals and flopped onto the settee.

She awoke about an hour later and after a few confusing moments realised where she was. She got up to go to the bathroom and staggered uncontrollably. Eventually, she was undressed, although she had just left her unfolded clothes on a chair, something she never did. She was too tired to worry about tidiness now and after filling and downing a tumbler of cold water, she refilled the glass and took it with her to bed. She got up in the night and was instantly struck by a thundering headache across her forehead. She took a couple of painkillers and got back into bed. However, the room started to spin and she felt quite nauseous.

She wasn't physically sick but she came close to it and when she awoke in the morning at about 8.00am, she groaned out loud. What a relief it was to know that she didn't have to rush because she knew she was incapable of anything faster than snail's pace today. The thought of food made her feel quite queasy, but she managed a cup of tea – just. She remembered that a drink of flat lemonade usually put the sugars back into her body, which was obviously dehydrated, so she opened a small bottle from the fridge and left it to stand for a while. She managed to stand in the shower long enough to have a quick splash and wash her hair. This made her feel a little better for a few minutes, but holding her hands above her head to blow dry her hair was a bridge too far! She flopped back on the bed and, still in her dressing gown she fell asleep again, this time for about two hours.

When she awoke, she felt much better, although still a little fragile. She wet her hair, which was standing on end and this time her blow drying attempt was much more successful. She downed the now flat lemonade, then she rang room service and requested some toast and butter and a pot of tea.

Once she had consumed both, she began to fire on all cylinders and started to pack her suitcase in readiness for checking out. She would get to the airport, check in and then get some food before the flight, so that she could manage with a light snack if the meal on the way home wasn't to her liking.

The taxi came on time and she left Vancouver behind with just a brief backward glance at the waterfront.

Chapter 38

On the way home, Sue tried to rehearse what she was going to say to Mark but whatever she said it didn't alter the fact that he was going to have the shock of his life. He wasn't going to accept that it was all very innocent, because things like that don't happen in real life – only in novels. She would tell him at the first opportunity, she thought one minute, and then the next minute she decided that she needed to wait until an opportune moment. But the thing was, there probably would never be a good time.

She tried not to think about it for a while and instead she read a few pages of her book. *Nothing like a good murder to take you out of yourself,* she thought. She dozed a little but images of her arrival home, standing at the door with no key and no warm clothes on her back crept into her dreams. She awoke with a start to find that she had dropped her book and the man in the seat next to her was trying to place it carefully on her table without waking her. He had failed. He smiled apologetically and she smiled back weakly.

The flight back seemed endless yet in a way she wanted it to be delayed so that it would, in turn delay her task. Eventually, the plane landed on a grey morning in Manchester. The clouds seemed to warn of foreboding and doom. She tried to pull herself together telling herself that she was being ridiculous and was overreacting. She wasn't giving Mark any credit for being reasonable at all. He would probably be really pleased after he got over the initial shock. After all, this was life changing. It would give them both the freedom to do what they wanted with their time. Yet, somehow, freedom didn't seem to be the one thing Sue needed right now. What she really needed was to know for certain that Mark loved her and wanted to spend time with her. She was becoming increasingly unsure about both those things.

The taxi was waiting for her as planned, and thankfully, the driver didn't want to talk much other than to ask her if she had enjoyed her trip. When she arrived home, Mark was still in bed.

She made herself a cup of tea and sat down quietly in the lounge waiting to hear him stirring. When she did, it was about 7.45am. She got up and made another cup of tea for herself and one for Mark.
He was surprised to see her when he came downstairs, even though he had known she would be back early morning.

"Hi," he said quite brightly. "I didn't hear you come in. What time did you get home?"

"About twenty minutes ago. I didn't want to waken you so I made a brew and sat down here."

"Well then, have you had a good time?"

"Yes, I have. It was eventful but really good. I got a chance to see much more of Vancouver than before and that's an amazing place. I'll tell you all about it when you're not dashing off to work." Sue knew she had chickened out of telling Mark. So much for telling him as soon as possible.
While Mark ate his breakfast and read the morning paper, Sue took her bags upstairs and started to unpack. She looked in the washing basket and saw it was quite empty, so she assumed Mark had been busy washing. When she checked the airing cupboard, the evidence was there – in a huge tangled pile. She sighed and closed the door. She would get the first load of washing on and then see what needed to be done next.

She knew she had to keep going today as long as possible before the jet lag took hold of her. She had just loaded the washing machine and was about to go and fold the clothes in the airing cupboard when Mark said he was going to work. At the door, he turned as if he had just remembered something and said, "There are several messages for you on the answer machine from your bank to ring them as soon as possible. It sounds like they need to speak to you urgently. I hope you haven't gone overdrawn on your account because they'll charge you a fortune."

"I don't think that'll be the problem. It'll be quite the opposite I should think," Sue replied, seizing the chance to get it over with.

"What do you mean?" he asked, and stepped back into the hallway.

"Well, I was going to wait until you weren't in a rush but something happened whilst I was away and I think you need to sit down."

Mark looked puzzled and even a little worried. They went into the lounge and Sue sat opposite Mark.

"It seems that the pendant wasn't the only thing that Sam left me when he died. After the ashes ceremony, his elder son, Adam, and the family friend and solicitor, the father of the one I saw in London, asked me to meet them in the coffee shop. Robert, the solicitor, told me that Sam had also left me a large sum of money – one million pounds to be exact. So that's probably why the bank has been ringing. The money's probably been paid in." She let the words sink in for a split second and waited for his reaction.

"Fucking hell!" was all he could manage and then, "this is a wind up right?"

"No wind up Mark, I can assure you. Try to imagine how I felt when I was told the news. I haven't been able to sleep or eat properly since last week."

Mark sat on the sofa and just shook his head as if to jumble up the thoughts to make some sense of what she had just told him.

"I know I said there were some wealthy farmers but this is not what I meant. Bloody hell, this is off the scale! Are you sure you've not been taken for a ride? Go and check your bank account on your lap top to make sure."

"There's no mistake but I'll check it in a minute. They are quite above board. On the way back from Lake Louise, the elder son Adam and his wife Kate took me to the Triple C Ranch where they live and where Sam lived. It's bloody huge. Apparently he was a very wealthy man and according to his son, one million pounds is a drop in the ocean.

They have a massive business, or I should say businesses. They breed top quality cattle for both dairy and beef and they export Canadian Angus beef all over Canada and even to Scotland. They are looking to export to England as well. They have their own abattoir and meat processing plant as well as a transport company. They own about 10,000 acres of prime grazing land and it's all managed by a massive team of people. I think they employ about 150 altogether.

So you see, he was a bit of a dark horse and it wasn't until they handed me a letter that he'd written to me in December last year, which was when he decided to leave the money and the pendant to me, that I discovered all this about him. In the letter he simply says he was grateful for my friendship and for writing to him when I got home, and he wanted me to be able to afford to travel when and where I wanted so he was repaying a favour."

"Repaying a favour? My god, I wish I could be repaid for a favour like that. What gets me Sue is how you've managed to keep all this to yourself for a week. You never hinted at anything like this when you phoned me."

"Obviously I didn't want to drop this into the conversation when I was on the phone. It's such a shock for both of us so I wanted to wait until I got home. I don't want to tell anyone else just yet, including the family, until I've verified that the money is in my account, so don't go texting or phoning them will you?"

"No, I won't if you don't want me to, but when are you planning to let them in on it?"

"I thought I might ask them round at the weekend and tell them all together. What do you think?"
"If that's what you want but I'm surprised you can keep it a secret for that length of time. I would have thought you would be too excited."

"I am but I'm also still trying to let it sink in. Like I said, it has been a tremendous shock for me and it's played havoc with my insides I can tell you."

"Go and check your account on-line and I'll put the kettle on. I need another brew before I go out to work this morning. In fact, if it wasn't so soon, I'd be having something stronger!"

Sue went on-line to check her account and sure enough, there it was, an automatic payment received into her account on the 6th June for one million pounds. She went back into the kitchen where mark was just finishing making the tea, and confirmed she had received the money. She said she would ring the bank later that morning.

"Well Sue, now that you're a woman of substance what are you going to do with all that money?" said Mark.

"It's not just mine Mark, it's for both of us to enjoy. You could retire if you wanted and we could do things together." This was as much a question as a statement from Sue who waited for his response.

"What sort of things did you have in mind? Anyway, who says I want to retire. I'm happy as I am thanks."

This wasn't the response she was hoping for.

"I was thinking we could go out a bit more and maybe have a break away somewhere together."

"Oh here we go. I knew that one was coming. Let's get some things straight Sue. Number one, I don't want to retire, not just yet anyway. Number two, I have no desire to go away on holiday. I've done without it for years and I don't want to start now. Number three, it's not our money it's yours. It was given to you for 'favours rendered' and nothing to do with me so don't go organising me. You can enjoy yourself as much as you like without the worry of the cost and that's fine by me. It also means you won't need my money to pay the bills, so I'll be able to spend my hard earned cash how I like and we'll both be happy."

There seemed to be no answer she could think of right at that moment so she opted for safety and simply shrugged her shoulders in resignation. She didn't want to have that conversation now, and besides, he would change his mind when he got more used to the idea. This subject was far from closed but she would wait until the time was right and have it out with him once and for all.

"Please don't say anything to the kids until we see them on Saturday will you?" she said.

"No, I've told you, if that's what you want I'll not say anything to anyone, but I hope you know what you're doing. Anyway, I'd best get going or I'll be so far behind, I'll be working at the weekend and that won't do will it, now that you're planning a major announcement to all and sundry."

"Don't be silly Mark. I just think it would be best to tell them all at the same time, once you and I have got used to the idea."

He shrugged and headed for the door, turning back just long enough to say he would probably be late in for tea, but didn't know exactly what time.

"Give me a ring when you're about half an hour away from being home so that I can get the tea started."

"If I get time I will. See you later." With that, he was out of the door and off to work.

Sue could have sat back down and brooded about their conversation but instead she forged ahead with the next of the day's many chores and made a note to call the bank mid-morning. Before Sue got round to making her call, the phone rang and she heard the voice at the other end announcing that they were calling from the bank to discuss a recent large payment into her current account.

Sue advised that she was aware of the payment but had been out of the country and so had not been able to call sooner. She said she would transfer the bulk of the money into her savings account for now until she had decided what to do with it longer term. The manager urged her not to delay and asked if she would like to make an appointment to see him to discuss her options. She said she would do that at some later date but that she needed time to think about it first. She had no intention of leaving the money in her savings account getting the minimum of interest. She would ask an ex-colleague to put her in touch with a professional person, who would give her some sound advice on tax efficient investments and trusts for the family.

She might be a wealthy woman now but if she didn't act wisely, she could lose a lot to the taxman and to people wanting to make money from giving her bad advice. She was going to make one exception to the rule of not telling anyone about the money and that was Jean. She would ring her at lunch time and see if she wanted to go for a cup of tea somewhere.

Chapter 39

Jean was surprised to hear from Sue so soon after her arrival back home. "I thought you would be too tired to bother with anyone so I was going to ring you tomorrow. How did it go? I got your text message thanks."

They had met at the bottom of the lane as they usually did and were walking down the path to the woods.

"I don't know where to start Jean, but I'll begin at the point I got picked up at the hotel in Calgary by Adam and his wife Kate to go up to Lake Louise."

As they walked Sue related her tale and Jean listened intently until the point where Sue was given the news about the letter and the money. Jean stopped walking and turned to face Sue, both hands over her mouth in disbelief.

"Oh my god Sue! Are you serious?"

"I'm perfectly serious Jean. I just had to tell someone, but apart from Mark you are the only person who knows at the moment. I plan to invite the kids over on Saturday to tell them."

"What did Mark say? How did you react when they told you? Oh my god, I can't believe it!"

"One question at a time Jean please," said Sue.

She continued with her story until she got to the bit where she went to the ranch. At this point they were walking on the path out of the woods and into the town. Sue suggested that they call into the café for a cup of tea and she would continue her story there. Jean agreed and once they were sitting at a table and Sue was pouring the tea because Jean's hands were shaking too much, Sue continued.

Jean interjected at intervals with comments like, "oh my god" and "what happened then?" She was mesmerised by it all, and excited and giddy all at the same time.

"Finally Jean, you asked what Mark had to say when I told him. Well, he reacted a bit like you except he used the 'F' word."

She didn't tell Jean about the rest of their conversation, but just left it that he had agreed to keep quiet until she had told the family.

"Does it feel like you've won the lottery?" Jean asked.

"It feels very weird Jean. It feels a bit like it's happening to someone else and I'm just the one who's standing on the edge. I can't take it in properly yet but I'll tell you one thing: I'm going to think very carefully for the next few weeks about what I'll do with it. Somehow it feels like a huge responsibility that I have to bear. I know that probably sounds silly to you but I can't quite explain how I feel.

When I was in Vancouver on the Friday, I decided to go shopping. I thought it would be great fun to go into all the expensive shops and know that I could afford anything I wanted. But to be honest, it was a bit of a letdown. I didn't buy anything except some gifts for the family. Oh, that reminds me – I've got something for you."

She put her hand in her pocket and handed Jean the little box containing the bracelet she had bought in Vancouver. Jean was thrilled and gave her a hug. "I love it Sue. Thank you so much."

"So Jean, like I said, it didn't really give me the buzz I had been hoping for. Perhaps it was because I was exhausted or maybe that I was on my own I don't know."

"Yes, I can see that you're very tired. It must have been an enormous shock. I don't know how I would have reacted to it. Anyway, the old man obviously saw something in you that he liked Sue and I bet reading his letter was a very emotional experience."

"Yes it was Jean. I can't and won't share the contents of that letter with anyone, not even Mark, but I can tell you that he was a wonderful man and I wish he were still alive."

Sue's eyes welled with tears and she dabbed them with her handkerchief. Jean looked like she was going to cry too and for a few minutes they were both very quiet, each trying to be strong for the other and not really making a good job of it.

Eventually, Sue found her composure and her voice and said, "I told you about Adele, Greg's wife, didn't I Jean? She was a right witch. It's a good job they weren't all like that. In fact, even their kids were okay with me. They were all very polite. I quite liked the solicitor, Robert and his wife Alice too. They seemed like 'old school' if you know what I mean. They obviously had money but I suspect nowhere near as much as Sam had. They did their best to make me feel comfortable and Robert was very concerned about me when they broke the news. I could see he was worried that they were going to have to get some medical help at one point."

"Do you think you will ever be in contact with them again?" asked Jean.

"Oh yes, I have Adam's and Kate's email address, postal address, and telephone numbers. I said I would keep in touch. Kate was lovely. She was very down to earth and we got on really well right from the start. Greg was a nice chap too, although I didn't see too much of him. I gather he had his hands full with the dreaded Adele. I'm not certain but I think they had a bit of a barny after the dinner on the Sunday evening. She was quite drunk but not so much when she dug her claws into me but later in the evening. I think he more or less told her she had to go to bed. After the ashes ceremony and the breakfast buffet on the Monday, they disappeared for the rest of the day and then they went home early.

I was quite relieved to be honest although, if she had confronted me a few minutes after I received the news of the money, I think I'd have got a few things off my chest and not been bothered about it. It was just as well she wasn't around. I will say this for her though – she was bloody beautiful. That woman could certainly wear clothes. She had some fabulous stuff. That was another reason for not liking her."

They both started to laugh and their mood lightened considerably. They finished their tea and continued on their walk back home, agreeing to meet on Sunday after lunch. On the way back up the path, Sue thought about her friend. *Thank goodness for Jean. What would I do without her? She's been my constant support throughout all this. I must do something for her when I get sorted out. On the subject of friends, I must ring Erin to say I'm back. I wonder if she will be up for me visiting her. I do hope so because I can tell her all about my trip (including the money) when I see her.*

Sue sent a brief email to Adam and Kate to tell them that she had arrived home safely and to thank them again for their hospitality. Mark didn't ring Sue so she started making their meal about 6.00pm. He finally arrived home at 7.30pm clutching a bottle of champagne. "I thought you might like a little celebratory drink Sue so I picked up this on the way home." He proceeded to open the bottle without waiting for

Sue's response and she went to the cupboard to retrieve two glasses. There was no point in arguing with him and at least he seemed to be in a better mood than he had when he left earlier that morning.

"Here's to you Sue, the woman of substance and of course to the old chap," he said, lifting his glass.

"To me and Sam," Sue responded.

Sue drank her champagne while Mark ate his rather dried up meal. It didn't seem to bother him so she decided not to comment about it.

"Have you invited the crew round then?" Mark asked when he had finished his tea.

"Yes, I've texted them all and I've had responses from them to say they'll be here. I told them to come about 7.00pm and said we would have a takeaway if that's okay with you. Peter's girls are out for the night on a sleepover at a friend's house, so it will just be the eight of us. I'm glad really, because I want them to agree not to tell anyone else about this. The girls are too young to appreciate how important it is that we don't tell anyone outside the family. It has nothing to do with anyone except the family and I want to keep it that way."

"Does that mean you won't tell Jean either?"

"No, it doesn't include Jean. In fact I've seen her this afternoon and told her but she's sworn to secrecy. I know I can trust her not to say anything."

"I knew you wouldn't keep it entirely to yourself until Saturday."

Sue pulled a face at him and he just laughed and went upstairs to have a shower. She had managed to stay awake this long but the jet lag was now definitely catching up with her.

Chapter 40

Sue spent the rest of the week getting the house back to some sort of order and finishing her washing and ironing. She also emailed an old colleague from the bank to ask who he could recommend to give her some financial advice. She didn't say much other than she was doing a bit of organisation of her finances (which was quite true) and wanted someone who would give her sound advice without charging a fortune. She also sent an email to Valerie to tell her she had been away to Vancouver. She hadn't told her about the events of the last three or four months but she did say that she had wanted to go back to Canada to see more of Vancouver.

On Friday she rang Erin. After the usual pleasantries, Sue asked if it would be possible for her to pay them a short visit. After checking diaries, Erin suggested two or three days in early July. Sue made a note of it and Erin said she would confirm for definite when she had spoken to Tom to ensure he hadn't anything planned that might conflict. They talked for about twenty minutes and it was all Sue could do to stop herself from telling Erin about the money. Erin, ever the intuitive friend, obviously picked up on something in Sue's voice and asked if everything was okay.

"It's absolutely fine Erin. I think I've got jet lag from the flight home and I did see and do an awful lot while I was away. I'm just a bit shattered. It was something of an ordeal meeting the family and trying to fit in, even though it was only for a couple of days."

She proceeded to tell Erin about Adele and her brief conversation with her. It certainly had made an impact on Sue and she had to admit that to herself later when she put the phone down. She was annoyed with herself for letting that awful woman get to her the way she had. At work she would have dealt swiftly and effectively with someone like that, but this wasn't work and she had to admit that she hadn't coped particularly well with one or two aspects of this whole business, the main one being her reluctance to stand up to Mark, especially on the morning of her return home. She really was a wimp when it came to dealings with Mark. He had always been able to get the better of her in a lot of things. She usually gave in to him for a quiet life.

She vowed she would eventually tackle him about his words and she would be assertive for once, but not yet because she was not ready for that. She would be practical and get sorted with one or two ideas for the family and helping them with some of the money she now had. She was looking forward to Saturday and seeing their reactions when she told them. She so wanted them to be happy about it, especially when she told them what she wanted to do for them. It was going to be so satisfying being able to help them financially and give them a boost in their young lives. She was determined they weren't going to have to struggle like she and Mark had done when they were that age.

She thought back to those times. They were certainly tough but they were also incredibly happy and they shared everything, from decorating at home, to Sue going to work with Mark in her holidays to help him with a big job. How they had taken pleasure from seeing their home improve and their children blossom into the good people they were now. What had happened to the laughter and the parties they had given for friends? She tried to think when it had stopped. Was it a sudden stopping or had they just drifted into the life they now had? Whose fault was it? She supposed it was a number of things with no one party to blame. She knew that some things had changed when she became ill. Mark didn't look at her in the same way as he did before. It was as if she was tainted in some way she felt. She knew she needed to get answers to some of these questions and there was only one way to do that.

As she finished her ironing, she rehearsed what she might say to Mark. She replayed a conversation in her head and for a while she was energised in her resolve to do something. It didn't last long though, because when he came home that night she just carried on as normal and after tea, she watched TV and he fell asleep in the chair. So much for her new found bravery.

Chapter 41

The first couple to arrive on Saturday evening were James and Emma, followed ten minutes later by Peter and Lynne. As usual, Nicola and Simon were last. Sue was used to this, because to her, they seemed to live their lives at ninety miles an hour. They crammed so much into their days yet always seemed to have plenty of vitality to spare. They had both been to the gym in the morning, followed by a spot of cleaning as Nicola liked to put it, and shopping later at the Trafford Centre.

When they had all arrived they agreed that they would have a Chinese takeaway. Mark rang the order through and he, Peter, James and Simon volunteered to go for it and to stop at the off licence on the way to get some beers. While they were gone, the girls helped Sue to set the table and get out the plates and the cutlery. Emma and Lynne chatted in the lounge and Nicola joined Sue in the kitchen to pour some more drinks.

"Mum, are you all right?" asked Nicola, quite out of the blue, so that it took Sue by surprise.

"Of course I am love, why do you ask?" Sue replied nervously.

"It's just that you look a bit peaky and you seem to be quiet. Emma mentioned that you looked a bit tired before you went away. I was just wondering if your illness was coming back."

"I promise that I'm fine but I am tired after the long trip I've had and all the sorting out since I got back. You know what your Dad's like when he's left on his own. He did some washing but that was it. I've just been busy. Don't fuss. Go and take these glasses in for the girls. The red wine is Emma's."

Nicola did as she was asked and Sue hoped that she had got away with her attempts at normality.

When they had finished their meal, Sue got up to clear the table and load the dishwasher. She looked across at Mark who raised his eyebrows in question. As if to answer his unspoken question she said, "I'll just clear these things away so that the house doesn't smell of Chinese food and then I've got some small gifts for you all that I've brought back from Canada."

There were calls for her to sit down and they would clear up later, but Sue ignored them all and started to do it anyway. James and Peter got up and helped her, and finally, Mark came into the kitchen with the tablecloth asking where Sue wanted him to put it. The boys all laughed at this point and Peter asked if he really wanted to know. The banter continued and Sue smiled to herself at their obvious ease with their father. She was so proud of them all. At that point she realised just how lucky she had been in her life and it put everything else into perspective.

She brought down several shopping bags with the gifts she had bought in Vancouver and handed them out one by one. There were baseball caps and T-shirts for the boys. Scarves and perfume for the girls. There were also one or two things for her grandchildren, Claire and Sophie. She had already given Mark his present of whisky and Levi jeans.

The gifts seemed to be a success and once things had settled down, Sue announced that she had asked them all here because it had been a while since they had all been together and she enjoyed seeing them. She added, "I have something I want to tell you all and I thought it would be best if I told you face-to-face."

They all looked at her with serious faces and she realised they were thinking that she was going to tell them that she had some terminal illness or something. She instantly tried to put them at ease by saying, "Don't worry, it's nothing bad. I'm not ill or anything.

You all know about the old man I met last time I went to Canada, and obviously that he left me the pendant and requested that I go back for the scattering of his ashes." They all nodded and murmured yes. "Well, it seems that he has also left me some money. It's rather a lot of money. In fact it's one million pounds."

At this point there were gasps and whoops and all sorts of comments including, 'is it for real?' and 'are you winding us up?'

"That's what I said when she told me," broke in Mark.

"It's absolutely for real and in fact the money is in my bank account right now. Now you can see why I wanted to tell you all together because I'm telling you, this is hard to keep saying and then fielding all the questions that follow after. I've had a hard enough time taking it in. I still have to pinch myself to make sure I'm not dreaming."

"This might be a silly question Mum," said James, "but why has he left you the money?"

"According to his letter to me, that he wrote in December last year and handed to his solicitor for safe keeping, he was grateful for my friendship and wanted to repay the favour. It turns out he was a very wealthy man and I'm assured his family won't miss the odd million pounds." She proceeded to tell them about her visit to the Triple C Ranch to try to give them some idea of the family's wealth.

"That's fantastic Mum and I'm really pleased for you," said Peter. He got up from his seat, put his arm round Sue's shoulder and gave her a big kiss on the cheek. The girls were all chatting excitedly and Lynne said they should have a toast to Mum and good fortune. They all raised their glasses and toasted her. She laughed and then said she had been thinking about nothing else for a few days but how she could use the money in the best way possible.

"Have a bloody good spend," said Simon and they all laughed.

"Just let me be serious for a minute please. I'll be getting some advice on how to make sure I don't lose loads of it to the taxman, but in the short-term I want to do something for you all. I want to give each of you some money to spend any way you want. I'll be making sure that some money is left in trusts for the girls Peter and that you all get a share if anything happens to me." She handed each couple an envelope containing a cheque for £25,000.

"I don't care what you do with the money I'm giving you now because that's just my way of treating you all and it gives me so much pleasure to be able to do it. Please take it and enjoy it and I love you all. The only condition I have is that you agree not to tell anyone outside the family. Peter and Lynne, I don't think it would be a good idea to tell the girls because they are bound to blab to one of their friends. The only people outside this room that will know will be Jean and my friend Erin. I know I can trust them both without question and I want to be able to repay them in some way for their friendship over the years."

They all agreed to keep it in the family. Nicola got up from her seat and threw her arms around her mother, tears flowing freely. She was followed by the others who were all overcome with emotion and gratitude for her generosity. Sue looked across at Mark while they all chatted about what they might do with their money and she mouthed to him that he would get something later. He smiled and mouthed back that he wasn't bothered about getting anything. He got up from his seat and went into the kitchen for more wine.

It was approaching midnight when they all made their way home in the taxis they had ordered earlier. Nicola and Simon were staying the night with James and Emma. Nicola said they would call back in the morning to collect their car before going home to Manchester.

"If you like, I'll make some bacon butties for you. See you tomorrow," said Sue waving them all off.

When they had all gone, Sue took the glasses into the kitchen and said she would do them in the morning. "I'm going to bed Mark. Are you coming up now or are you watching some TV first?"

"I'll be up in a few minutes. I'll just finish my drink and watch a bit of telly first. Did it make you feel good doing that tonight Sue?"

"Yes, it did. It's great to be able to do something for your kids isn't it?"

"I wouldn't know Sue, because I've never been in a position to do it. You're the one with the money."

"Don't be daft, Mark. The money's for both of us and anyway, you've done loads of things for them in the past. You've helped them get their houses into shape. They wouldn't have been able to do what they have without your help would they? I can't do those sorts of things."

"Whatever. You can do anything now Sue. Now that you've got money you can be as powerful as you want."

"It's nothing to do with being powerful. Now you're being silly. I'm going to bed. Goodnight." She knew it was the alcohol talking but it still hurt her to hear him talk like that.

There was no reply, just a snort and a sigh from the sofa and then the sound of the remote switching on the TV. Mark didn't come to bed at all and Sue realised this when she got up in the night to go to the bathroom. She could hear the television on low so she went downstairs to investigate. Mark was fast asleep on the sofa with a throw wrapped around him. His empty beer glass was on the floor beside the sofa. She picked it up and turned off the TV, then the light and closed the door. She went back to bed but it was a long time before she could get back to sleep.

Chapter 42

Mark was still asleep when Sue went downstairs in the morning, so she left him where he was, washed up all the used glasses from the night before and then prepared her breakfast. She took it into the conservatory and opened the French windows that led out onto the back garden. It was a fresh bright morning and the birds were busy looking for material with which to build their nests. They had a couple of boxes for the blue tits and she watched their frantic activity in and out of one of the boxes under an apple tree. After about twenty minutes, Mark stirred and poked his head around the door to the conservatory. He was looking rather sheepish and a bit hung over.

"Hi there," he said.

"Hello to you as well. What happened last night then?" Sue replied.

"It got a bit late and I didn't want to wake you so I covered myself up and crashed."

"Well you failed because I woke up and realised you hadn't come to bed so I came down to find the TV on, you covered with the throw and snoring your head off. It took me ages to get back to sleep so thanks for that."

"Oh," was all he said and then as an afterthought, "sorry."

He disappeared upstairs and Sue heard the sound of the shower being turned on. Sue finished her breakfast and by the time she had cleared her dishes away, Mark appeared in the kitchen to make himself a cup of coffee. She noticed it was black and very strong.

Sue spent the rest of the morning doing some weeding in the garden. After she had been outside for about half an hour, Mark got out the lawnmower and proceeded to mow the lawn at the back of the house. Sue knew that meant she would need to follow behind him and sweep the path because he always left a trail of grass afterwards. She knew she was being nitpicking but that was how she felt.

Nicola and Simon called about 11.30 am to collect their car. They didn't stay long and declined the offer of bacon butties but both of them thanked Sue again for their cheque Nicola hugged her and whispered in her ear, "You're brilliant – you know that don't you?"

Sue brushed it aside with a wave of her garden-gloved hand and said that it was only right that she should want to treat them all after her good fortune. She agreed, at Nicola's request to meet her in Manchester for lunch one day in the coming week and Nicola promised to text her which day would be best. After hugging her dad, she and Simon left.

By lunchtime the morning's work was evident and the garden looked neat and tidy. Mark had actually taken good care of the pots and baskets while she was away so they were beginning to look splendid. The azaleas were beginning to bloom and the clematis that covered one corner of the wall at the bottom of the garden was also blossoming nicely. She loved this time of year as it always made her feel hopeful. She certainly hoped the weather would be better than the last two summers had been but apart from the odd bright day here and there, it had been quite wet and cool again.

Her mobile phone bleeped a couple of times and when she checked it, she found messages from both Peter and James thanking her. She smiled at the thought that she had produced what she believed to be perfect kids. They were so grateful for anything Sue and Mark did for them and always showed their gratitude. How lucky she was really.

She made some sandwiches for lunch and called out to Mark, who by this time was tinkering with one of his motorbikes in the garage. "Great," she moaned, but not loud enough for him to hear, "just what I need, more dirty washing and the sink smelling of oil when he comes in to wash his hands – if he comes in that is."

A couple of minutes later and to Sue's surprise, Mark reappeared in the kitchen and went straight to the sink.

"Have you got anything planned for this afternoon Sue?" he said lightly as he splashed soap all over the worktop surrounding the sink.

"Yes, I'm meeting Jean and we're going for a walk up Black Hill. I'm going to take a carrier bag so that if the wimberry is out, I can pick some for a pie."

"Ooh, that sounds good. I love wimberry pie and custard."

"What are you going to do?"

"I just want to finish this job on the Velo and then I might cut the hedge at the back. You said you wanted it trimming a bit."

That's a sure sign of a guilty conscience, Sue thought, *he knows he's pushed me to the limit so he's trying to be good so that it'll get brushed under the carpet – again.*

Sue passed him a plate of sandwiches and brewed the tea. She marvelled at his ability to carry on as if he'd never been unreasonable the night before while she was still brooding about it. *He's like an ostrich sometimes,* she thought. *He thinks if he buries his head in the sand it won't happen – whatever it is he's ignoring at the time. It's so infuriating.*

She ate her lunch at the little picnic table on the patio outside the conservatory, and once finished, she went to put her walking boots on and get the car out. Jean was waiting for her, sitting in a deckchair in the garden when Sue arrived to pick her up. After the usual enquiries about each other's general health, Jean asked, "How did the family gathering go last night? Did you tell them all about the money?"

Sue went over the details of the earlier part of the evening while driving up to the car park where they would leave the car for their walk but said nothing about what had happened after they had all gone.

"They were so happy Jean," she said as they approached the flattened out patch of rough ground at the bottom of the hill that was used by walkers. There were only a handful of cars so there was plenty of room to park. They got out and put on their small backpacks.

"I'll bet they were. What's not to be happy about after all?"

They set off on foot up the tiny path that led onto the gorse covered hill. The day was warm and pleasant and they chatted as they looked for the precious wimberry that was so good and soon got picked once it started to show. They were lucky because there was quite a bit and it looked as if no-one had realised yet. Once they did, all the fruit would be picked in a matter of a few days. When they each had sufficient quantities in their bags, they put them in their backpacks and continued their walk – a circular one that went through a small village and then through the fields and back to the car park.

Sue and Jean had two essential rules for their walks and they were that there should be somewhere to get a cup of coffee en-route or at the end of it and along the way, somewhere to go to the loo. They often laughed at what they considered to be their age-related weaknesses and joked about how they would cope without a cuppa and a wee on a Sunday afternoon. Sue thought, not for the first time in the last few days, that the simple pleasures were all she and Jean had so far enjoyed together and even though now she secretly planned something a little more extravagant for them both – maybe an exotic holiday with no expense spared – she cherished these forays into the local countryside and the laughs and the companionship they shared.

She hadn't realised that she was daydreaming again until Jean gave her a dig on the arm. "Am I talking to myself? Where did you go to then Sue?"

"Sorry Jean, I've been doing that a lot lately. What were you saying?"

"I said how lovely it is just to be out in the warm sunshine for a change. We seem to have had such a lot of dark, damp weather lately. I do hope this summer is a better one than the last two have been."

"I was thinking that this morning when I was sitting in the conservatory looking at the garden. You're right Jean, we need some sunshine. How about a holiday in the sun – just you and me? Call it our little treat from Sam. What do you say?"

"It sounds fab but I can't let you pay Sue. You're always paying for things for me and you brought me that lovely bracelet. I can't do it."

"Please Jean. Do it for me. I would be really grateful and if it makes you feel better you can pay for all the coffees and the wine while we're away – that will cost you a bit!"

They both laughed and Jean finally agreed subject to hospital appointments etcetera on both sides. They agreed that Jean would come up to Sue one night during the week and they would have a look on the internet to see what was on offer. By the time Sue arrived back home, she was feeling much brighter and she told Mark what she and Jean had agreed as they ate their evening meal on the patio.

"That'll be nice for you. When were you thinking of going?"

"Sometime in September, I think – for two weeks. Jean's coming up here tomorrow night and we'll see what there is."

"Why don't you go for a bit longer? You can afford it now."

"Are you trying to get rid of me or something?" Sue asked, not looking up but continuing to eat her meal.

"No but if you're planning to go somewhere exotic you will want plenty of time to see what you want and I can't see the point of paying for two weeks when three might not be much more."

"So you're the holiday expert now are you? Since when did you know your way round a holiday website?"

She could see his point but was irritated that he stuck his oar in when normally he wouldn't have shown any interest.

"You don't have to go on holiday regularly to know that," he snapped back.

"It'll depend on whether Jean can do three weeks together."

"Well what else is she going to be doing? She's retired so her time's her own."

"Just because someone is retired it doesn't mean they don't have other things to do besides going on holiday."

"That's all you seem to be doing these days," he said, and instantly Sue knew he wished he hadn't.

Sue rose from her seat, snapped up her half full plate, and marched into the kitchen, scraping her meal into the bin and flinging the plate into the sink. She went back to the patio and retrieved her wine from the table and as she did so she launched into attack.

"Judging by the way you are acting lately, I would have thought you'd be glad to see me go away. I might as well be away for all the time I spend either on my own or in silence with you snoring on the couch. In fact, right now I'd much rather be as far away from you as I can!"

She drank down the last dregs of her wine and stormed off back into the kitchen to load the dishwasher. As she did, she made as much noise as she could, throwing the cutlery into the basket and clanging the saucepans. Her blood was boiling and she had just about had enough of what she believed to be his childish and unreasonable behaviour. Mark didn't retaliate. He simply finished his meal and quietly but deliberately brought his plate into the kitchen and placed it in the sink. Sue snatched it out again and threw it into the dishwasher then switched it on. She turned to go into the garden but then turned round and followed him back to the patio through the conservatory.

"And another thing," she resumed, taking him completely by surprise as he was about to settle back down on the lounger with his paper, "I won't be bringing you anything back from this holiday because you haven't even thanked me for the things I brought from Canada, you ungrateful, awkward, selfish bastard! I'm finding it very difficult to guess what it is you want from me these days. That's if you want anything at all besides your washing done and your meals made. I haven't stopped cleaning and washing and shopping since I came back last week and if you say once more that I have nothing else to do, I'll go into the garage and throw mud all over your precious bikes so that you'll have to wash them again, just like you seem to enjoy making work for me."

She rose from the table and walked off down to the bottom of the garden where he couldn't see or hear her weeping. She was so angry and frustrated with him that she couldn't control her trembling but she didn't want him to see her like that. She settled down on the swing seat near the garden shed and managed to calm down sufficiently to pick up the book and reading glasses she had left there earlier and began to read. After about half an hour Mark approached her carrying two mugs of tea. He offered one to her and she took it with a clipped "Thank you".

He sat down carefully next to her so that he didn't cause them to spill their drinks. Then after a couple of minutes, he told her he was sorry if he had upset her but he hadn't intended to do so. He thought he had thanked her for his presents. In fact he said he was sure he had done but maybe she hadn't heard him. He went on to say that he thought she was overtired and that she had seemed 'a bit off it' since coming home last week.

Sue put her book down and her cup of tea on the floor next to her feet and removed her glasses. She looked at him squarely in the eyes and said very quietly, "Yes, I am tired. I'm tired of treading on eggshells where you're concerned. I'm tired of always considering what you want first. I'm tired of waiting for you to show me any kind of affection. I'm tired of you explaining away my dissatisfaction by saying I'm 'a bit off it'. In fact, I'm tired of you. End of story."

Mark's expression changed from one of attempted conciliation to a thunderous glare. He didn't speak but got up and walked back into the house, leaving her to ponder their exchange. She couldn't understand why things were like they were between them. It seemed as if everything was fine for Mark as long as she didn't rock the boat by asking him to change a little. All she wanted was for him to have some quality time with her away from the house. They didn't even go out much these days. Occasionally they would go for a pub meal but after a few minutes they didn't seem to have anything to talk about. What was it Sam had said in one of his letters? Keep talking because when the talking stops that's when things go wrong. When did they stop talking? She couldn't even remember that much.

She felt very tired all at once and decided to empty the dishwasher and have a long bath. She hoped Mark wasn't having the same idea (the bath not the emptying of the dishwasher because there was no way he would think about that). She picked up her now cold cup of tea and threw it on the soil in the border and that made her think about watering the plants so she made that her first task.

It was late evening by the time she had finished her little chores because she had noticed one or two weeds that she had missed earlier and wanted to get them out rather than leaving them. When she went into the lounge, Mark was watching the TV.

He looked up at her and said quite calmly, "Are you feeling better now you've told me what you think of me?"

"Actually no, I'm not. I don't like falling out with you but I don't like being given the blame for everything either."

"Okay then, shall we agree that we are both at fault and move on? I can't even remember what we were arguing about."

"If I have to explain it all again to you it won't help me, so I can't be bothered. Let's just leave it at that Mark because I'm tired and I want a bath."

"I thought I might meet Steve and Chris down the pub for a pint if you're not bothered then."

"No, go ahead. Why should I be bothered? You work all week so you might as well have a pint if you want one. Anyway, I'll probably be crashed out by the time you get back, so don't wake me up."

"I wouldn't dream of it." Mark half smiled as he said this just to test the waters. Sue didn't respond but turned and climbed wearily up the stairs asking him to lock the door on his way out.

Chapter 43

Jean arrived at Sue's as planned on the following evening and they set about choosing somewhere to go on holiday. Sue enquired if Jean would be able to stretch to three weeks if they went somewhere further away, and although she protested about the cost going up all the time for Sue, she finally agreed that if required she would. They settled on early September mainly because it was the end of the normal school holidays and if they went somewhere hot, it might have cooled down a little.

That sorted, they talked about where they would like to go. A few places were thrown into the mix, but in the end, they settled for Corsica. This they thought would provide them with a beach location but also the opportunity to visit other towns and villages away from the sea and some good walking.

They chose their hotel – five-star of course – on the western coast of the island. Sue insisted that they fly first class. This meant that they would be provided with a chauffeur - driven limousine to and from the airport. As they progressed through the booking procedure on-line, Jean began to feel more and more excited but she kept reminding Sue of the cost. Sue's response to this was to wave her hand in the air in a gesture of rebellious abandonment. They settled on a date of Sunday, 1st of September which was just eleven weeks away and because they'd settled on a destination not too far away, they would have two weeks and return on the 15th.

After two and a half hours, everything was booked and Jean left, promising to call Sue later in the week.

Mark had arrived home late from work which was nothing unusual, especially on a Monday. He had arrived while they were planning their holiday and after finding his tea on a plate in the oven and eating it sitting in his armchair in the lounge, he had fallen asleep and was just stirring when Sue went in. She was still annoyed with him and although the atmosphere was less tense than the night before, she didn't really feel like being over-sociable with him. However, he asked if they had managed to book anything and Sue told him the details. "Is it on your bucket list?" He tried to sound reasonably enthusiastic, asking to see a picture of the hotel if Sue had printed one off. "Actually, no it isn't," she said, showing him the details. He whistled when he saw the luxuriousness of the hotel's interior and exterior facilities and remarked that they should really enjoy themselves. He was obviously trying to be amiable after last night. Sue had to admit that she would rather have that than the way he had been over the last few weeks.

Chapter 44

The next couple of weeks were busy ones for Sue. She met Nicola in Manchester on the Wednesday of the first week and she had worked in the garden keeping it tidy. She had done the most important thing and that was to get some advice regarding the management of the money she now had. Her colleague had put her in touch with a friend of his, who worked in a city brokerage dealing with high net worth customers. Apparently, you had to have at least a quarter of a million before they would take you on so Sue had no problems there. They had offices in London, Leeds, and Manchester but Sue had asked if she could deal with everything at home. He was only too pleased to acquiesce to her request and after three visits and lots of form-signing, the majority of the money had been dealt with. She had sorted out the trusts for her grandchildren. She also left provision for any future grandchildren (if indeed there were to be any) to have the same amount. She had agreed for some of the money to be invested in funds that were not too risky and of course a sizeable amount had been put into accounts that she could access if she wanted to work through her bucket list of travel destinations.

As part of the arrangement, she would meet every three months with the broker to review performance and make any changes as required. Finally, she had made a will to ensure that everything would be organised should anything happen to her. She felt much better knowing that this had been done. One thing that had bothered her was the fact that she couldn't get Mark to tell her if there was anything he particularly wanted. He seemed completely averse to any help from her and each time she broached the subject they would end up arguing. She finally settled on putting some money aside because she was sure that she would eventually manage to persuade him to accept it.

She went for a short visit to her friend Erin as planned at the beginning of July. Although it was only just over three weeks since she had returned from Canada, it had seemed much longer and she was glad to be getting away from the normal routine at home. Erin was waiting with sandwiches and a cup of tea when Sue arrived after a three hour drive. She hadn't even stopped to go to the loo preferring to get to Erin's as soon as she could. They hugged and asked each other how they were and, after bringing her bags out of the car and leaving them in the spare bedroom that Erin always had ready for her, Sue settled down to eat her lunch and catch up a little on news.

Once they had finished their lunch and they were enjoying their second cup of tea, Sue told Erin about her trip to Lake Louise and eventually, the money. Erin reacted in a similar way to Jean. "That's fantastic Sue! You must have had an enormous shock. How did Mark react?"

Sue started to say that although he was shocked he seemed pleased, but she knew she couldn't fool Erin. She was extremely intuitive and always sensed if something wasn't quite right.

"So why are you looking so tired and, might I say, a bit gloomy?"

Sue related most of the events of the last three weeks to Erin and waited for her thoughts on things.

"It sounds to me a bit like Mark is feeling surplus to requirements Sue. After all he's a man and they are stereotypically keen to be seen as the provider. I know your salary paid for a lot of things and kept you both afloat over the years when you were working, but now you are retired and maybe he saw that as his opportunity to be the main breadwinner. Now, as far as he is concerned that's been denied him because you have financial independence."

"That doesn't explain his anger at my suggestion that he works a bit less and spends some time with me."

"The best form of defence is attack isn't it? He's doing what comes natural to him, and it seems to me that until you sit down and have a proper talk with him, you are both going to make assumptions about each other that may be way off the mark."

"It's not just the last few weeks or even the last few months. Mark has been different towards me for quite a while now."

"Different in what way and for how long?" asked Erin.

"For a couple of years now he hasn't really shown me any affection. I get a peck on the cheek at Christmas and New Year if I'm lucky, but normally, he treats me like a sister. We hardly do anything together unless there is someone else involved: like the kids coming round for a barbecue, for example.
He seems totally indifferent to me going away and I even think he'd rather I wasn't there at home. The only thing he misses when I'm not there is someone to do his washing and have his meal on the table when he comes home in the evening. I think I can understand what you mean by him feeling surplus to requirements where money is concerned but I've tried to say that it belongs to both of us and we should enjoy it while we are still able to do so. Now, we've started to row fairly regularly and that's something we haven't done previously."

"Perhaps it will become easier as time goes on and he has a chance to get used to the idea. After all, it's only been a matter of weeks since you told him."

"I'm not so sure, Erin. Right now I'm glad to be out of his way and that can't be right can it? When I go away, Erin, I see couples walking hand in hand and obviously enjoying each other's company and I don't mean young couples, I mean people of our age. Look at you and Tom for example. You love your holidays together and although you have the odd disagreement, you show each other that you care.

I sit in restaurants enjoying the most delightful meals in some of the greatest locations in the world but I'm lonely and that's the bottom line."

Sue began to weep and Erin tried to comfort her, feeling her despair and wishing there was more she could do for her friend. After a few minutes Sue looked up with tearful eyes and apologised for burdening Erin with her sorrows.

"Don't be silly, Sue. I'm just worried about you, that's all. I wish there was more I could do but I think this one's down to you and Mark. You really need to have that talk."

"I know, Erin. You are right about that and I'm going to try to resolve this when I get back home. I'll go and wash my face and put some lipstick on and try not to get morbid any more. We have some serious shopping to do, with the odd tea and cakes stops here and there."

They both laughed and Sue got up to go and fix her face. When she returned from the bathroom in a state she felt was presentable, Erin suggested they go into Cambridge which was a thirty minute drive away. Erin's husband, Tom was working in London and wouldn't be home until tomorrow afternoon so he had suggested to Erin that she and Sue eat out tonight and he would pay. They decided to book a table at the pub in the village before they set off to shop in Cambridge.

Sue began to relax once they were on their way. Erin was driving as she always did once Sue arrived down there. She insisted that Sue should leave her car on the drive for the duration of her stay.

They had a great time trying clothes on and looking at jewellery etcetera. "Speaking of jewellery, Erin," said Sue as they were looking in a shop window, "I don't know how I could have forgotten to mention it but I have brought the pendant from Sam with me for you to see."

"Oh marvellous, Sue! I can't wait to see it. Well, not tomorrow evening, but the evening after, before you go back home, Tom has booked us a table at 'The George' in Stamford. It's rather a posh place and we go on special occasions. You could wear it then with your new dress that you've just bought."

"Believe it or not, that will be the first time I have worn it in public. I've been a bit scared to wear it and to be honest, I haven't been anywhere other than home since my holiday in Canada."

"That settles it then, it can have its maiden voyage so to speak."

While they were shopping Erin had admired a bracelet made of white gold with jade stones set in it. She had said that it would go with a blouse she had recently bought. This gave her an idea but how could she get it without Erin knowing? She knew that Erin would protest if she told her in advance so she needed an excuse to get away from her. Then quite by chance, Erin mentioned that she needed to collect a shirt that she had ordered for Tom, from a gentleman's outfitters. The store was just down the street from the jewellers' shop, so Sue suggested that Erin go on her own while she sat in the square on a bench for a rest for a few minutes and to call Mark on her mobile. As soon as Erin was out of sight, Sue hurried to the jewellers' shop and bought the bracelet. She had it gift wrapped to save time later.

As Sue made her way back to the bench, she could see Erin looking for her. She made an excuse about Mark not answering so she had decided to do a bit of window shopping further up the street and Erin seemed convinced. They found a small café and ordered tea, deciding against adding the rather delicious looking scones that were on display in case they ruined their appetite for their meal later.

It was late afternoon by this time, so they planned to make their way back home and be ready to make the short walk across to the pub for their meal at 7.00pm.

They enjoyed their pub food, which Sue insisted on paying for, even though Erin argued that Tom would be cross with her for letting Sue pay. As it was a warm evening, they strolled through the village making a circular path back home and spent the next hour sitting in the garden just chatting. It was amazing to Sue that she and Erin never tired of chatting and always had lots to say to each other. Whenever they spoke on the telephone or met, they just carried on from where they had left off last time. That, to Sue was the sign of a true friendship. It was like that with her and Jean as well. Not for the first time did Sue feel very fortunate to have two such people in her life. Coming to Erin's was like coming to a retreat where Sue could shed her worries and just relax and be herself. She felt completely at peace here and wished that the feeling it gave her would be with her at home, but she knew that wouldn't happen.

They spent the following day walking and had a snack lunch at a pub along the way. Tom had arrived home by the time they got back mid-afternoon. He and Sue chatted while Erin prepared one of her famous soufflés. This time it was cheese and spring onion which she served with new potatoes and a mixed salad, and washed down with a bottle of Prosecco that Tom had left in the fridge to chill. They ate their meal out on the patio in the warm early evening sunshine and when they had finished and cleared the dishes away, they returned to the garden where they spent the next couple of hours chatting about anything and everything. Sue and Tom always enjoyed bantering, but Tom, like Erin was very intuitive and he too guessed that all was not well with Sue. He didn't voice his thoughts to Sue but decided to ask Erin later.

The following day Sue and Erin went into Oakham which was only a short drive away. They grabbed some sandwiches from a local bakery and ate them sitting on a bench. They wandered around the shops and bought a cup of coffee at the Castle Tea Rooms café before returning home to have a couple of hours' peace and quiet before they went out in the evening.

At 6.45pm, just as they were ready to go, Sue appeared in the lounge wearing her new dress and the pendant. Tom and Erin were very impressed with it and complemented Sue on her appearance.

"You look lovely Sue," said Tom, "and I guess this is the famous pendant. It's fabulous and very you, if I might say so."

"Sue, I love it. What a wonderful gift to receive. You must feel a million dollars in it."

Sue laughed and joked, "Actually Erin, pounds not dollars."

They all began to laugh and then Sue turned to Erin, seeing she was wearing her new jade blouse with a black skirt and black high- heeled sandals.

"Erin, I love your outfit but I think there is something missing."

Erin checked herself over with a puzzled look on her face and then back at Sue questioningly.

"I think this might be what you need," she said handing over the small parcel containing the jade bracelet. "I got this for you because I think you will suit it and because I just wanted to."

Erin opened the box and looked at the bracelet then back at Sue. "Sue Barnett you are a very wicked lady! How did you manage to buy this without me knowing?"

"Sorry Erin, but I lied to you when you went to collect Tom's shirt in the shop in Cambridge. I went back to the jewellers and bought it. I wanted to give you something because you and Tom give me so much all the time. I do hope you'll wear it tonight."

Tom took the bracelet from its box and placed it on Erin's wrist while she told him about their discussion the other day in Cambridge. Tom said it was a wonderful gesture and he complemented them both on their taste. After hugs and thanks from Erin, Tom reminded them that they had better get going because it was getting late and it didn't do to be late for your dinner appointment at 'The George'.

They had a fabulous evening and from the moment Sue stepped in to 'The George' all eyes were on her. The dress she wore was a beautiful long sleeved, midnight blue, lace shift, with a lining of the same colour in silk. The style was famous in the sixties. It was making a revival and because it was A-line in shape, it suited Sue's frame perfectly. It was just above the knee in length and she wore flat black sandals with it. The pendant was shown off to its full glory. It shone and sparkled from every angle. In fact it was a real head-turner.

They ate and drank and talked and laughed until finally, at 11.15pm they made their way out, all remaining eyes of the staff and diners still there following them and particularly Sue. When they got into the car, Tom remarked, "My word, Sue, that pendant certainly made an impression. Did you see everyone looking at it and you? You looked wonderful tonight. In fact, as far as I'm concerned, I was sitting at the table with the two loveliest women in the place. I loved it and thank you both."

"Is that the wine talking, Tom?" said Erin teasingly.

"Certainly not, woman! Now just be quiet and drive!"

Sue remained very quiet in the back of the car. It was fortunate that it was dark because they couldn't see the tears running down her cheeks. Despite her best efforts to pull herself together, the tears continued, so she closed her eyes and pretended to fall asleep just in case they asked her a question. She couldn't remember a time when Mark had even noticed what she was wearing, let alone pay her such a complement. Erin was indeed fortunate to have a husband who lavished attention on her like Tom did. When they were approaching the village where Erin and Tom lived, Sue dabbed her eyes with a tissue and hoped that her mascara hadn't run too much. She announced that she was tired and would go straight to bed if her hosts didn't mind.

"Not at all, Sue, I'll be doing the same once I've sorted the table out for breakfast," replied Erin. "Thank you so much for the bracelet, Sue. I love it." She put her arms around Sue and felt her tremble a little. She pulled away and, with her hands on both of Sue's shoulders, she looked at her face and could tell that she had been crying.

"Please don't say anything Erin, because if you do I'll start again. I've had a wonderful night and thank Tom for me will you? I'll see you in the morning. Goodnight."

She pulled away before Erin could protest and went to her room. She stood in front of the full-length mirror for a minute, looking at her reflection. Apart from the messed up face make-up which did nothing to enhance her baggy eyes and wrinkled lips, she was pleased with her dress and the way it flattered her figure, even though she had gained a few pounds since she had retired. She didn't think her legs were too bad either. She'd always had shapely legs and thin ankles so the dress looked good. Then of course the pendant finished it all off and made all the difference. It was truly a fabulous piece of jewellery. What was is that Sam had said in his letter? 'Wear it whenever you can. It needs to be worn'. He was right of course. *Oh Sam, what am I going to do? I want nothing more than to be happy with Mark. What have I done wrong to make him treat me like this? I wish you were still around so that I could ask you.* She finally looked away from the mirror and got ready for bed, replacing the pendant in its red box and then in the now tatty brown envelope that she opened a few months ago in James Fearnley's office. It was odd but she couldn't bear to discard it, even though it was beginning to fall apart. Sam had handled it so she wanted to keep it for always.

She climbed into bed and fell asleep within minutes, but not before promising herself that she would tackle Mark as soon as she returned home. It had to be done.

Chapter 45

She didn't keep her promise. When she got home, there seemed so much to do and there was always a reason not to speak to Mark about their issues. Erin rang her a couple of days after she returned home, but Sue was reluctant to talk about anything but the most mundane topics like the weather and what needed to be done in the garden. Erin took the hint and let it go, hoping that Sue would take action soon. She promised to ring again in a couple of weeks.

Sue busied herself with the usual chores around the house and kept the garden in shape, leaving the lawn cutting to Mark. The summer was turning out to be a warm and mainly dry one, and she made the most of the weather by getting outside either in the garden or walking whenever she could. She also enjoyed some retail therapy at every opportunity. She bought loads of new things for her holiday. In fact, she bought far more than she would be able to take – even allowing for the extra baggage weight for first class passengers. She would need to have a decision-making session just before she started packing in a few weeks' time.

The family came round regularly and they had one or two barbecues at the weekends. On one of those occasions in early August, James and Emma arrived early and said they had something they wanted to discuss with Sue and Mark. They had decided to spend some of the money she had given them on IVF treatment. They talked about how they had wanted and tried for a baby for the last three years and had seen a consultant about it. They said that before Sue had given them the money they had already made their mind up to have the treatment, but it was to be on the NHS and they didn't know how long they would have to wait. In any event, if the first attempt didn't work, they would have had to pay for subsequent ones so they decided to seek a private route as soon as possible. They were starting the process the following week.

"So you see, Mum," said James, "the money is giving us an opportunity that we wouldn't otherwise have had and we wanted you both to know that we are so grateful to you."

Sue was so pleased for them and she gave them both a hug. Mark was equally enthusiastic about the idea but added, "It's all down to your Mum, not me. It's her money not mine."

Sue flashed him a warning look and Emma stepped in with, "Don't worry, Mark. You'll be doing your bit by making one or two alterations at home in readiness for an addition just as soon as we know if we have had some success."

He gave her a broad smile and said jokingly that she would have to get in the queue as he was very busy.

James looked at Sue and there was an unspoken question in his expression. Sue knew that he sensed some problem but he wouldn't say anything now. He would wait until the next time they were alone and she knew he would ask her what was wrong. She and James had always had this kind of telepathic sense between them. He was very much like her in his ways and they had an affinity she didn't have with either Peter or Nicola, even though she loved them all equally. The rest of the gang turned up so the conversation was cut short, thankfully as far as Sue was concerned.

Nicola and Simon announced that they had booked a holiday to Crete later in the month. They added that they had got a last minute deal via the internet and had saved nearly half the full price. Sue smiled to herself and silently approved of the practical approach displayed by her youngest child. *A chip off the old block is Nicola,'* she thought to herself.

Peter and Lynne said they were going to have a new and larger garage built at home and they had applied for planning permission. They hoped to be able to start it in a few weeks' time.

All in all, Sue considered her children's approach to finance. They were all practical, and as far as she was concerned, they all had a healthy sense of perspective and didn't take anything for granted. That was one thing she and Mark had done well. They had brought their children up to be well balanced individuals who all had common sense and good values. That was a real achievement in anyone's book and one they should be proud of. It was a pity they didn't seem to be able to join forces to heal their ailing marriage, because Sue was sure it was ailing and it was in serious danger of dying altogether.
When she came back from Corsica, she would definitely tackle Mark about things. She was brought back to the present by someone asking when there would be some food ready eat. She took a tray of chicken pieces outside and assumed her place at the barbecue, while Mark acted as barman and genial host. It was only four weeks from her holiday, so Sue thought that if she could get through this period without incident, she would return home refreshed and ready to tackle anything.

Chapter 46

Sue and Jean had the most luxurious holiday ever. They enjoyed everything from the chauffeur-driven limousine to the beach location of their hotel. They sunbathed, swam in the pool and the sea, walked for miles, and visited other locations escorted by a professional guide named Samio.

"I suppose it's a change from Jose or Marcel," said Jean when Sue told her that they were going to be driven around the island for the next four days and escorted by the driver as and when required.

"I don't know what he looks like or how old he is but the hotel manager assures me he comes highly recommended by other visitors."

"I'm not being ungrateful, Sue, honestly, but I hope he has integrity."

"Of course, Jean – but not too much eh?" said Sue with a wicked look on her face. (Well, she had been drinking red wine all evening).

Samio turned out to be an unmarried man in his early fifties. He was tall – about six feet – had thick dark wavy hair and the physique of someone half his age. He was of course, incredibly tanned and rather handsome in a rugged kind of way. He said that he was a true Corsican, meaning that he was among the ten percent of the population who actually spoke the Corsican language rather than the more common one of

French. He said the Corsican language was more closely related to Italian.

Sue was attracted to him instantly although she did her best not to show it to either him or Jean. He was very polite and spoke rather good English.

"Ladies, my Name is Samio. Welcome to Corsica – its nickname in English is 'The Isle of Beauty'. I am honoured to be taking two English beauties to see our beautiful island. If you will follow me I will ensure your first day is a memorable one. We will be visiting Porto-Vecchio and Bonifacio in the south of the island."

"Thank you, Samio," said Sue and she added, "please call me Sue and my friend here is Jean."

The look that passed between Sue and Jean as they walked towards the car was one of shared delight and anticipation. Jean whispered in Sue's ear. "Strike out what I said before. He can take me anywhere any time." Sue gave her a nudge and winked at her as she got into the rear seat of the car.
He proved to be very knowledgeable, stopping at intervals to allow them the opportunity to take photos and to obtain refreshments.

After they returned to their hotel at the end of the third day of the arrangement, Sue and Jean were sitting on their balcony overlooking the bay and watching the waves crashing upon the rocks below.
Jean announced that she was feeling a little nauseous and didn't want to eat anything. "You go and have something to eat Sue, but count me out. I think I might have had too much sun today and I'm absolutely shattered."

"Do you need me to get the doctor, Jean?"

"No thanks. I think I just need to lie down for a while and just drink water. Honestly, I'll be fine if you just leave me to it."

"How about I go and get something to eat when I've had a shower and then come straight back and see if you're feeling any better? I can order something for you from room service if you are."

"Yes, do that and I'll try and get some sleep for a couple of hours, so don't rush."

After checking for the umpteenth time with Jean that she would be okay until she returned, Sue locked the door and put on the 'Do Not Disturb' sign. She went into the bar first, in order to get a drink and sit until she decided which of the three restaurants she would eat in. She had just got half way through a white wine and lemonade, and was pondering the various menus in front of her when a familiar voice said "What are you doing here alone, Madame?" It was Samio. He had changed his cotton shirt and long shorts for designer Jeans, white T-shirt and pale blue linen jacket. On his feet he was wearing loafers with no socks. He looked wicked.

Sue explained a little breathlessly that Jean was feeling a bit under the weather and so she was going to get something to eat and then go back to check on her.

"That is indeed a shame, Sue," he smiled as he said it. "I too, am alone but I would be happy to escort you to a little place I know just down the road from here."

I bet you would, thought Sue but she astonished herself by asking, "How far down the road is this little place?"

"We can walk in about five minutes. I do not drive at night if at all possible." He smiled again and Sue's stomach did a little flip.

"Well I suppose it will be okay but I'll have to be back here before too long to make sure Jean is okay."

"I promise (at this point he put his hand on his heart and cocked his head to one side) that I will deliver you safely back here at 10.00pm."

Sue looked up at the clock behind the bar and noticed it was 7.15pm. "Right then, let's go," she said, and drank the remainder of her drink in one go, standing up quickly and nearly losing her balance as she caught her foot on the edge of the chair leg. He caught her by the elbow and steadied her. She felt a ripple of excitement run down her spine and smiled weakly at him.

He was true to his word and as he had said, there was a small café and bar about five minutes' walk away. The evening was warm and although there were one or two tables outside, Sue said she preferred to eat inside. Samio spoke to the waiter in French and they were shown to a table by the window where they had a perfect view of the sea.

After ordering an omelette and salad for each of them, Samio asked for a pichet of rosé. "This is a jug which is used to serve the local wine," Samio explained. When it came Sue thought to herself that he must be expecting her to pay. She gave herself a bit of a reality check until he said that he was grateful to her and Jean for letting him escort them and for treating him well. (They had bought his meals and refreshments while they were out). Tonight would be his treat and the only drink for a lovely lady was the local rosé. At this point he took her hand and kissed it gently. Sue's heart skipped a beat and she could feel herself going red and her body getting rather warm. Thankfully, the waiter brought a carafe of water and she took a few gulps of it as soon as it was poured.

The next two hours went in a flash. Samio was the perfect gentleman and they talked about their families and interests.

Samio exclaimed that she couldn't possibly be a grandmother. She was too young.

Too young – my god! she thought. She brushed his compliments aside, but inside she was revelling in every moment and every word. She drank several glasses of the rosé wine and abandoned any thoughts of how she might feel in the morning. Tonight was all that mattered and what a night she was having.

Samio paid the bill and they made their way outside. Sue looked at her watch and could just make out that it was 9.45pm. Darkness had descended but it was still very warm. As they started to walk back to the hotel, Samio slipped his arm around Sue's waist and pulled her closer to him. Instinctively she put her head on his shoulder, and to him, that was the signal he needed. He stopped walking and pulled her to him then kissed her full on the mouth.

Sue thought she was going to faint with delight. He started to pull away but she clung to him and kissed him back. The next few minutes were like being in paradise as far as Sue was concerned. It was such a long time since she and Mark had shared a kiss, let alone an intimate clinch like this and she realised in those few minutes what she had been missing. They didn't speak until he asked her if she would sit down on the nearby bench. Once seated, he took her hands in his and said, "Sue, you are a most beautiful lady. I do not do this with other women, believe me."

I don't believe a word of it but at this moment I don't care, she thought.

He continued, "I promise that I really honour you Sue. I am not out for anything."

"Well then, that's okay Samio, because neither am I. Let's just enjoy the moment shall we?" She couldn't believe she had just said that. It was like someone else was speaking through her mouth. He kissed her again and again. She thought she was going to burst. Her heart was beating so quickly and heavily that she was sure he could feel it.

Somewhere in the depths of her conscious mind, she suddenly remembered Jean and hesitated as his hand slowly started to descend towards her left breast. She stood up, rather too quickly as it happened and nearly fell over. He rose and stepped toward her to steady her, all the time apologising for what he had nearly done, wrongly thinking that this was why she had pulled away.

"Samio, you are a really gorgeous man. I would love to spend more time with you but I must go and see if Jean is okay. I have had a wonderful evening. You have made me feel so special and I thank you so much for that, but I have a husband at home who needs me and a friend who needs me right now, so please forgive me but I have to go."

She had to admit that it really was a bugger, but duty called and who knew how Jean was feeling at that moment. He dutifully took her arm and steered her back to the hotel. However, she allowed herself to grab his hand and squeeze it tightly to let him know that there were no hard feelings, well, not on her part anyway.

As they approached the hotel, she released his hand and turned to kiss him on the cheek, but changed her mind and kissed him full on the lips. He responded by pulling her into yet another embrace, and then, just as quickly, he was back to the daytime escort, asking her if 9.30am was okay to pick them up for the last day of their guided tour. She said it was and left him standing there, just watching her go into the hotel foyer.

She almost floated up to their room. She noticed the 'Do Not Disturb' sign still in place. She opened the door quietly, removed the sign and put it on the inside handle, and crept inside. Jean was sleeping soundly, still on top of the bed and dressed in the clothes she had worn all day. Sue heaved a sigh of relief and removed her shoes. She started to make a cup of tea when Jean woke and sat up.

"Oh hi Sue," she said sleepily. "What time is it?"

"It's almost 10.30pm. Have you been asleep all this time? Are you feeling better?"

"Yes, I do and I have been asleep since you went out. Did you get something to eat? I'm so sorry to leave you on your own."

"Don't worry about that Jean. I'm just glad you are okay. Would you like some tea?"

"Actually, I think I could do with something stronger and I might have some crisps or something like that."

"Steady girl," said Sue laughing, "don't go mad will you?"

"Do you want something from the minibar or are you up to an hour in the bar?"

"Give me a few minutes to have a quick wash and put something on that isn't creased and I'll be with you."

Fifteen minutes later they were sitting in the bar, Sue with a tonic water, and Jean with a gin and tonic, and a bag of crisps. She offered the bag to Sue who declined saying that she had eaten enough.

"What did you have Sue?" Jean asked while munching on a rather large crisp.

"Just an omelette and some salad."

"Did you talk to anyone or have you been sitting on your own all night?"

"Er, just one or two people, you know, passing conversation that's all."

"I really am sorry, Sue. I don't know what came over me but I think the sleep did me good. Perhaps it was the heat – it was very warm today – or maybe the thought of Samio made me come over all strange. He's a bit of a dish really isn't he?" She laughed and winked at Sue.

"I suppose he is quite good-looking – if you like that sort of thing."

"Well, I wouldn't say no if he knocked on my door."

"Jean!" Sue raised her eyebrows at her friend's uncharacteristic comment. "What's in that drink? Whatever it is, it's gone right to your head."

Jean laughed and said wickedly, "It's not my head that it's gone to Sue, well, not when I think about Samio. It's a pity tomorrow is our last day with him. I've got used to having him around. Never mind, all good things and all that."

Sue didn't know what to say, so she changed the subject. "Have you enjoyed yourself Jean?"

"Yes, it's been fabulous. Thank you so much Sue. Have you had a good time too? I have wondered because you've looked a bit far away a time or two. Are you missing Mark?"

"Good heavens no, and I have had a good time. I don't suppose he's missed me either. On the occasions I've spoken to him, the only conversation has been about how busy he is and the weather, which actually is very good apparently. He took great delight in saying it had been 26°C yesterday when we spoke this morning. Anyway Jean, tomorrow is our last evening here so I thought you might like to eat somewhere really posh and we can get dressed up. What do you think?"

"It's posh here Sue. I can't imagine we'll find anywhere better but if you want to go out that's fine with me and yes, we'll get dressed up. Have you brought it with you – you know the 'p' word?" Jean laughed again at her own little joke.

"Yes, I have, you'll be surprised to know. I plucked up the courage at the last minute, although I have been a bit worried that it might not be safe. I check it every night before I go to bed."

"Well, I sincerely hope you are going to wear it then. I bet you look fabulous in it, especially now that you have a lovely tan."

"Do you want another drink, Jean?"

"Yes, I think I will if you are having one. I need to make up for lost time don't I?"

Sue ordered another gin and tonic for Jean and a cup of coffee for herself. Jean frowned at her and called her a lightweight.
Little do you know what I've had to drink already and what I've been up to and with whom, thought Sue and she felt herself blush at the recollection of the events earlier in the evening. She had to admit to herself that even though she now felt somewhat guilty, she had enjoyed it. She hadn't done anything really bad though. It was only a kiss – well a few kisses and a bit of a clinch. He was about to go a bit further and he would have if Sue had not remembered the time and the fact that her trusting friend was ill in their hotel room. She pondered what might have happened had she allowed him continue. Would she have gone a bit further? She didn't know for sure but she had a sneaking suspicion that she might have done.

She felt herself getting hot at the thoughts of his hands on her body. *My god he was handsome and he certainly knew which buttons to press!*

"What are you smiling at?" asked Jean, bringing Sue back into the present.

"Oh, nothing. I was just thinking about all the lovely sights we've seen over the last few days."

"Hmm?" said Jean, but she didn't look convinced. Thankfully the drinks arrived at that moment.

Once they were in bed with the lights out, Sue went over the evening's events again and wondered if she could manage to be 'normal' tomorrow when they went out with Samio. She had to admit that it was going to be a real test of her composure. She felt a bit bad about not telling Jean, but she decided that this was something she should keep to herself. After much tossing and turning, she finally fell asleep.

Chapter 47

Sue was particularly pre-occupied at breakfast the next day and Jean picked up on it. "What's the matter Sue, you look like you've got something on your mind?"

"I didn't sleep too well last night Jean and I guess I'm a bit sad that our holiday is nearly over." She smiled weakly at Jean and tried to brush it aside. She didn't know how she was going to face Samio this morning and remain calm and casual. She was so embarrassed about last night and she wondered what he thought of her now. His manner had changed back to one of driver and passenger as soon as they got back to the hotel. *It's your own fault,* she told herself, *you can't let a bloke like that kiss you passionately then tell him there's no future in it and expect him to be all sweetness and light as if nothing happened. Stop wanting everything to be perfect all the time. You know it never is perfect.*

She brushed her teeth for the third time and went to the loo for the fourth, checked her hair for the fifth and then decided she couldn't put it off any longer. Sue and Jean made their way down to the foyer and waited. After about ten minutes of waiting and checking her watch which displayed 9.37am, Sue was about to say to Jean that she didn't think Samio was coming and she knew why. Just at that point, he pulled up outside the hotel and hurried in to meet them, full of apologies for being late saying that his mother was unwell and he had been delayed waiting for a neighbour to come and stay with her for the day.

"I hope she's all right Samio," said Jean. "Should you be with her?"

"Oh no, it is fine Jean, she is just old and sometimes she needs a little more looking after. My neighbour will take care of her and she will ring me if it is needed. Are you feeling better this morning Jean?" As soon as he had said it he knew that it was a mistake.

"How did you know I wasn't well?" Jean asked. Sue groaned inwardly as Samio replied, "I came into the bar to see the hotel manager about another job he has for me tomorrow and I saw Sue sitting on her own having a drink and she told me." He flashed a look at Sue and smiled briefly before opening the door of the car for them to get inside.

"Sue, you never told me you had seen Samio last night," whispered Jean to Sue, looking at her questioningly.

"Didn't I? I must have forgotten," Sue replied as nonchalantly as she could. Jean didn't respond but Sue could visualise the cogs whirring in her brain. At that point Samio started to tell them about the day's itinerary. He told them that today they were going to the island's capital and the birth place of Napoleon – Ajaccio. He added that Napoleon's ancestral home – 'Casa Buonaparte' was now a museum and it was well worth visiting. He said he would, as usual stop at places along the way for them to take pictures and also to get refreshments as they required. The weather was going to be as hot as the day before with a light breeze so he checked that they had their hats with them. He was the perfect guide once again.

Jean made conversation with Samio as he drove and this was a relief to Sue as she could try to relax a little. She was sitting behind him in the rear seat but she could see his eyes in the rear view mirror. Every now and then he would look into it in a certain way and she knew that he was looking at her rather than on the road behind him. When he did she turned and looked out of the window to her left.

As the day progressed, Sue began to relax and apart from the occasional smile in her direction when Jean was otherwise occupied, there was no hint of the passion they had shared briefly the night before.

All too soon though, the day was nearly over and as Sue and Jean were sitting outside a little café drinking a glass of water, Jean asked if she could give Samio the tip that they had agreed they would give him on the last day if he was a good driver. (Sue had already paid for the hire of his car and his escort service in advance).

"I think it's only fair that I give him the tip. What do you think would be appropriate?"

"Whatever you want Jean. How about twenty five euros?"

"I'll give him thirty I think – after all, he is worth it." With that she laughed and finished her drink.

Once back at the hotel, Samio got out of the car and opened the doors for them to get out. Jean was the first to thank him and she pressed the money into his hand, saying what a wonderful time she had had and she hoped that his mother was okay. He took her hand and kissed it gallantly. Jean nearly swooned with delight. Samio went around to the other door but Sue was already half way out of the car. As she stood up, their faces almost touched and there was that charge of electricity between them again. Sue held out her hand to shake his but as with Jean he took it and kissed the back of it. This time though, he held on a little longer and squeezed it smiling at her with those marvellous dark eyes that seemed to bore into her flesh. Her stomach flipped and she began to fumble with her bag.

"Thank you for your kindness, Sue and I hope you have a safe journey home tomorrow. Perhaps you will visit Corsica again one day?" he added, arching his thick dark eyebrows.

"You never know, we may visit again. We have had a lovely time haven't we Jean?" Sue replied, casting a look Jean's way. Jean nodded vigorously and with that, he turned, got into the car and drove away.

Sue felt her chest deflate and her eyes fill with tears. She dashed passed Jean saying that she needed the loo urgently and couldn't wait until they got up to their room. She hurried into the cloakroom just off the foyer and shut herself in a cubicle to weep. Jean followed her, not convinced that she was being entirely honest. She waited until Sue came out of the cubicle and seeing her red eyes, she began to put two and two together.
"Okay then Sue, spill the beans. Something happened last night didn't it? You've been acting strangely all day today. You might as well tell me because I think I know anyway."

"If you know already why do you need me to tell you?"

"I want to know the exact details with nothing left out."

They went up to their room and once inside, Sue shook off her sandals and flopped on the sofa. She related the events of the previous night, leaving nothing out. Jean listened without comment until Sue finally said, "So there you have it, Jean. Think what you like about me. I know it was wrong but I don't care." She gave Jean a look that would have rivalled a petulant child.

Jean thought for a moment and then she said, "Sue, I think you did something that I would probably have done (although I'm not attached). I can't say I blame you because he's fabulously good-looking and I bet he's even better when he's scrubbed up."

"Oh Jean he is, he was – absolutely divine."

"It's not that bad, Sue. It's not as if you did anything – you know – that."

"No, Jean, we definitely didn't do that, but I still feel like I've been unfaithful to Mark. If I don't come clean when I get home it'll be on my conscience all the time."

"Don't be daft, Sue. You only had a couple of kisses. It's no worse than New Year's Eve in the pub when the clock strikes midnight and everyone grabs the first person next to them."

"When you put it like that, Jean, I guess it isn't that bad is it?"

"No, it isn't. I am very jealous though, you dark horse. What I wouldn't give to have been in your shoes last night. What was it you said last night when I said he was a dish. I quote: 'I suppose so if you like that sort of thing' unquote and all the time you knew what you had done. Now that's bad in my book." She wagged her finger at Sue as if scolding a child and they burst into hysterical laughter.

Eventually, they regained some composure and Jean asked what the plan was for their last evening.
"There is a bistro-type place in the square. We could walk over and eat there tonight, or we could go into the really posh restaurant on the top floor here in the hotel," said Sue.

"I vote we stay here but do you think we'll get in. It's supposed to be very busy according to those two women I was listening to in the spa the other day."

"We'll get in," said Sue, "especially if I encourage them with a tip. It's amazing what money can do isn't it?"

"Right then, Sue, I'll go and have a shower first. Will you ring up to book?"

"Yes, I'll do that now while you are having your shower. Any time between 7.00 pm and 8.00pm do you?"

"Perfect. I'll check out the dress and the jewellery although I've got nothing to rival yours," she grinned.

Sue left Jean to ponder her wardrobe and called the number for the restaurant. She had no problem booking for 7.30pm and she asked for a table by the window so that they could have a view of the sea. That was no problem either so mission accomplished, she set about deciding what to wear with the pendant. She settled on a just above the knee coral coloured A-line dress with three-quarter sleeves and a simple scooped neckline. She had some cream sandals and small cream clutch bag with a diamanté clasp. It wasn't the real thing but it was far enough away from the pendant not to look too false. She felt better now that she had told Jean about Samio and she had to admit that she was looking forward to wearing the pendant tonight.

Chapter 48

"You look fabulous, Sue!" exclaimed Jean when they were ready to go. "I'll tell you something; that Samio has done wonders for you. You look positively radiant."

"I don't know about that but I think the sun and the sea air has really done me good. I'm beginning to feel quite full of energy at last. There's another thing as well, Jean. Whenever I put this pendant on it seems to energise me and transform my mood."

"I'm not surprised about that. I think wearing a £75,000.00 pendant round my neck would transform me as well!"

"Oh Jean, don't remind me of its value. Thinking of that makes me nervous in case it falls off or something."

"I don't think it's going to do that Sue. Stop worrying and just enjoy yourself. I'm willing to bet it gets noticed though. Just you see."

Jean was right. As soon as they exited the lift on the top floor and were met by the restaurant manager at the entrance, Jean noticed the looks of appreciation from anyone who came within a few feet of Sue. It wasn't just the pendant though thought Jean. It was Sue's general demeanour. It really did transform her and it went beautifully with that coral dress. It was perfect for Sue's fair hair and golden tan.

"Tonight, Jean," announced Sue once they were seated at their table by one of the huge picture windows overlooking the Bay of Calvi, "there will be no expense spared. We will have champagne to start and then anything you like after that. We have all evening and we don't need to rush. We can take as long as we want in between courses. I won't be rushed."

"Ooh that sounds marvellous," said Jean with a delighted look on her face.

The restaurant waiters were especially attentive under the watchful eye of the manager. The wine waiter brought them pink champagne and after Sue had taken a sip and approved it by smiling broadly in answer to the waiter's questioning look, they toasted each other, followed by a toast to Samio and his accomplishments (then they both burst into uproarious laughter at this point and were unable to stop themselves even though the other diners were looking at them).

"Oh, let them look," laughed Sue, "I don't care tonight. They're probably jealous that we're having a good time. Half of them look as miserable as sin."

"Perhaps one or two of those women could do with a night out with Samio. That'd loosen their corsets," said Jean and they burst out laughing again.

After a few minutes they managed to calm down enough to take a look at the menu. They thought they had better do this before they were asked to leave. The menu was in French but there was an English translation in brackets beneath each item. Sue chose a white onion soup followed by a chicken dish, while Jean fancied garlic mushrooms and sea bass. Sue chose the wine – a local red – much to the approval of the wine waiter. He said rather proudly that it was one of the best Corsica had to offer and she was obviously a lady of great taste. As he walked away, Jean looked at Sue and said, "Watch out, Sue, you're in there," and she winked as she said it.

"I think I've had enough elicit romance for now, don't you?"

"I don't know," Jean teased, "I think you've discovered yourself and this is only the beginning."

"Shut up, Jean and have some more champagne. Sometimes you do too much thinking."

The meal was delicious and the evening continued in much the same vein as it started, with both of them joking and making each other giggle. The waiters that attended to them picked up on their light mood and seemed to enjoy seeing them happy. Jean noticed that each time they came to the table they sneaked a look at Sue's pendant and she guessed that they were considering Sue's status regarding wealth. Perhaps they were also contemplating a large tip so that made them even more attentive. Once they had finished their coffees Sue asked for the bill and when it came, she charged it to her room and thanked the waiter. She left a good tip on the table and on the way out, she thanked the Manager personally. He inclined his head and smiled broadly, saying it had been a pleasure to see them and hoped they had a good journey home the following day.

"How did he know we were going home tomorrow?" asked Jean when they were out of earshot.

"They know everything, Jean, believe me. They're paid to know these things. It's called the personal touch, and hotels like this one take it very seriously."

"Yes, I suppose you're right. I didn't think about that."

"I don't know about you, Jean, but I'm not ready to go to bed yet. It's only just after 10.00. Do you fancy looking in at the bar downstairs where they have live music? I think it's a duo tonight and they're supposed to be very good. We could have a dance."

"I'm up for that, Sue. Lead the way!" and with that they made their way to the second floor, following the sound of an old Beatles song, 'Love Me Do' emanating from the bar in the far corner. They ordered some cocktails and managed to find a small table in one of the alcoves opposite the bar itself but where they could see the duo.

They stayed there until just after midnight when the duo finished their performance. They'd had another of the cocktails and had danced until they couldn't dance any more. They finally reached their room and kicked off their shoes simultaneously.

"Oh Sue, I've had a great time tonight. Thank you so much for bringing me with you."

"No problem, Jean. It's been a pleasure and thank you for being so patient with me. I can always rely on you to be there for me."

"Course you can, Sue. That's what friends are for eh?" As she said this Jean went towards the bathroom to brush her teeth.

Sue went out onto the balcony to look at the moon shining on the calm waters of the Bay of Calvi for one last time. She sighed and muttered to herself, *Back to reality tomorrow girl. Back to face the music.* She stood on the balcony for a few more minutes, fondling the pendant around her neck, thinking about Sam and, as usual, feeling sad at the loss. She continued to stand alone, soaking up the atmosphere and smelling the light sea breeze, thinking about the last couple of weeks and in particular Samio. When she finally closed the sliding door, Jean was sound asleep in bed.

Chapter 49

Mark was in the garden mowing the lawn when Sue arrived home late in the afternoon, on what was a glorious day. The temperature was still 21°C according to the weather station in the garden. He smiled and stopped the mower when he saw her. She felt a pang of guilt at the thought of her elicit episode with Samio but she smiled back and asked if he wanted a cold drink.

"There are some beers in the fridge. I went to Tesco yesterday and got some beers and a couple of bottles of wine. I got a rosé and a white. I hope that's okay. I also got some chicken and a bit of tuna to put on the barbecue, so when I've done this lawn, I'll light it. I'll have a bottle of beer now though if you want to pour me one."

Sue went back into the house and opened the fridge door to find it stocked with beer and wine that took up the whole of the top shelf. There was the chicken and tuna, and when she checked the salad drawer, she found a packet of mixed salad leaves, some tomatoes, baby peppers and coleslaw. She couldn't believe it. He had actually got some food in for them without having to be asked. She knew she would have to go to the supermarket for the basic stuff tomorrow but at least she was spared the task for now. Her mood lightened a little and she felt another pang of guilt. Perhaps he had missed her after all and this was his way of letting her know.

She poured him a glass of beer and then went upstairs to check the washing basket. She might as well put a load in the washer now and get it out before they had their tea. That was empty and when she looked in the airing cupboard, Mark's work things were piled neatly (well, neatly for Mark) on the shelf. Wonders would never cease. She opened her case and took out one or two things to wash. She might as well get a head start on her own washing.

While they waited for the barbecue to heat up, they sat at the patio table and chatted about what had been happening at home while she had been away. Mark said that James and Emma had called a couple of times and Peter had phoned twice, as had Nicola. He had been busy working as usual and had been out to the pub a few times. James and Emma had asked him to go to their house for tea last weekend but he said he had declined their offer because the pub had organised a barbecue and he had gone to that instead.

Sue told him how beautiful Corsica was and about hiring a taxi and driver for a few days to take them to other parts of the island. The weather had been fabulous the whole time and Mark commented on how tanned she was and it was obvious that the holiday had done her a power of good.

After they had eaten they spent a pleasant couple of hours pottering around looking at the garden plants and discussing what needed to be done. Sue had two or three glasses of the rosé and began to relax. It started to go dark and Mark said he would have a shower and go down to the pub for the last hour. Sue was busy clearing up the dishes and after she had loaded the dishwasher, she made herself a cup of tea and went to watch the TV while she drank it. Once Mark had gone out, she went to have a bath. She wasn't sure of it was the wine, the fresh air, the flight home or all three, but she felt incredibly sleepy. She fell into bed and went to sleep immediately. She slept all night, something that was unheard of for her. When she awoke at 7.00am the next morning, Mark was already up and having his breakfast. It was remarkable that she hadn't heard him come to bed. She must have been really tired.

After a couple of mumbled words about not knowing what time he would be home, Mark set off for work and Sue set about getting things in order. She would need to get some groceries, wash the rest of her holiday things, and at some point, check in with the family. Before she knew it, the day would be gone and she would be wondering what to make for tea.

She noticed Mark had left his mobile phone on the hall table and just at that moment, it rang. She looked at the caller ID – 'Diane'. She thought it might be a customer so she went to answer it. Before she got there, it stopped so she waited to see if there was a voicemail. There was, so she pressed the play back button and listened.

"Hi babes, it's only me. Just wondering if you got into trouble for being late last night. I'll be finishing work early today so I'll be in about 3.30pm if you want to pop round. Love you."

Sue almost dropped the phone. Suddenly, everything became clear. It was as if a blackout curtain that had been shielding her eyes, had suddenly been lifted and she could see flashing images of Mark and some unknown woman standing there in front of her. She flopped down on the chair in the hall and tried to think calmly and rationally, but her breathing was erratic and she had broken out into a cold sweat.

This explained everything that had happened over the last few months. How long had this been going on? She tried to think when she had first noticed something wasn't quite right and all she could think of was it was when she had retired. She had put their troubles down to Mark resenting her retirement in some way. In fact, she had blamed herself and wondered if she had been selfish in finishing work, while he was still working hard. But all that was just his excuse to be horrid to her because he, himself, had a guilty conscience and it was easier for him to deal with it if he could find something to blame her for and to argue about. No wonder they had rowed more in the last few weeks and months. No wonder he had been indifferent to her and obviously that was why he hadn't bothered about her going on holiday.

To think he had actually hinted that she had obtained the pendant and the money from Sam in return for sexual favours. The bastard! Her shock gave way to anger. She began to scream in frustration and rage. She ran upstairs and frantically searched his drawers and clothes looking for some sign of this woman. Why hadn't she noticed anything? She was, indeed, very stupid. She was angry with Mark, with this woman and with herself for being so trusting and so loyal. Her minor indiscretion with Samio (and it was minor – she now knew that), was nothing compared to what he had been up to. She wished she had let Samio whisk her off to his little hideaway hut on the beach to have his way with her. Then she realised that was stupid. Two wrongs didn't make a right, but it would have been so satisfying to tell Mark about it and see how it made him feel. She was suddenly overtaken by a wave of nausea and went to the bathroom to be sick.

The rest of the day didn't go to plan. No shopping was done and the washing stayed in the machine. She tried to drink a cup of tea but it made her sick so she sipped water and sat in the conservatory, staring at his phone, waiting for it to ring again.

Half way through the afternoon, Jean rang her to check she was okay. As soon as she heard Jean's voice she started to sob uncontrollably. Jean was of course concerned but Sue simply asked her if she could come down tonight. "Of course you can Sue, but I wish you'd tell me what's wrong. I'm so worried about you. Is it one of the children? Is someone ill? Is it Mark?"

Sue managed to say that everyone was okay but she needed someone to talk to and she would be down later. She put the phone down. She didn't know where Mark was working so she couldn't contact him. She would wait for him to come home. She was surprised he hadn't got in touch to say he had lost his phone. Just as she thought this, her mobile rang again. This time it was Mark ringing from a landline that her phone didn't recognise.

"Hi, Sue, it's only me. Have I left my phone at home by any chance? I've only just realised that I haven't got it with me."

"Yes, it's here," she managed to say in a clipped tone that he obviously didn't pick up on because he continued.

"Thank God for that. I was worried that I might have lost it. I might be a bit late home because I need to finish this job tonight. They're having carpets fitted tomorrow and they want me out."

"Liar!" she shouted down the phone.

There was silence at the other end and she continued. "Who the fuck is Diane? Don't tell me you don't know because she has rung you this morning and left a voicemail – Babes!"

"I'll be home in a few minutes." That was all he said and he put down the phone.

Chapter 50

Ten minutes later, Sue heard Mark's van coming down the drive. She tried to calm her shaking body but it was proving to be practically impossible. She couldn't let him get the better of her and she hated herself for being like this.

"Sue, we need to talk," was his opening line as he approached her sheepishly.

"Oh, so you want to talk to me now do you? That makes a change," she managed to say in a sarcastic tone.

"Look, Sue, arguing won't get us anywhere will it? I need to explain."

"Explain away then," she said and waited for his response.

"I'm really sorry you had to find out like this. I've been wanting, trying to tell you for the last few weeks but it never seemed the right time. Then you've been away a lot and I've been busy working long hours."

"Well, you've been busy but I'm not sure it was working and don't blame me for this. You encouraged me to go away. In fact, if you'd had your way we would still have been away. 'Oh yes Sue, go for three weeks and then you can see everything you want'. What you really wanted was for me to be away so that you could fuck Diane! How long has this been going on? Where did you meet her? Was she one of your 'jobs'?"

"Look, Sue, I never meant for this to happen. Yes, I did a job for her a few months ago." At this point Sue sniggered sarcastically.

"Okay, laugh if you want to but it's true. We just, well hit it off, a bit like you and the old man."

"No, Mark, it's nothing like me and the old man as you so eloquently put it. Ours was a true friendship, not some lurid affair."

"Well, anyway, we got on well and one thing led to another. She listens to me and she has a sense of humour. You're so boring, Sue. You're always tired and you never have a laugh any more."

"Boring? How can you say that when you won't do anything with me? You come home, have your tea and then fall asleep in the chair. Now I know why. You've been shagging Miss Perfect during the day or whenever you can. All I do is the drudgery – washing your dirty clothes, making your meals, shopping, cleaning up after the mess you leave behind you.

Is it boring to travel around the world seeing new people and countries and learning about them? Is it boring to do all that on my own because my husband won't come with me? Do you have any idea how much courage and imagination that requires? No, you don't because you don't give a damn about anyone except yourself. You are a complete arsehole, and right now, I could kill you and her!"

"I don' think this is a good time to be doing this is it? You are not exactly calm are you?" he said, just as Sue was getting into full swing.

"Not exactly calm? I wonder why that could be then. Perhaps it has something to do with the fact that I've just discovered my husband is shagging another woman. I suppose she's a younger model as well."

"She's fifty-three actually," he managed to say before Sue launched her fist at his face.

"I don't want to know!" she shouted and he took a step back more from shock than from pain.

"I think we need to put some space between us until we can discuss this rationally, I'll go and pack a bag," he suggested, trying to dampen down the tension.

"I'll put some space between us, Mark, don't you worry. I'll go as far away from here as I can. You can stay in the house. In fact, you can have it. It can be your divorce settlement because that's all you're getting from me. And another thing, two can play at this game, Mark. Boring am I? Well, that's not what Sam thought and nor did Samio. In fact, he was very complementary when he took me out to dinner and he's only fifty."

"Oh, great," Mark said as Sue was turning to go upstairs. "A pensioner and a Corsican taxi driver – two very good references I must say." He started to laugh but then Sue whirled round and slapped his face so hard, her hand felt like it was on fire. This time, he really felt it and his expression changed from mild amusement to cold hatred and shock.

For a few seconds they stood facing each other in complete silence and then Sue calmly turned around and walked up the stairs to pack a bag. She was so angry with him, but adrenaline was working for her and she calmly packed her overnight suit case with what came to hand first. When she went back downstairs, Mark was standing in the hall by the door.

"You don't have to do this," he said in much quieter tone.

"Oh but I do, Mark. I should have done it ages ago. I've been kidding myself and I realise I've wasted so much time. You can do whatever you want with 'whatshername'"

"Diane," Mark interrupted.

"I know her bloody name," she said quietly but with a venomous look. "I'll go and stay with Jean for a couple of days until I can find somewhere to rent for the time being. You can stay here. I'll be back for the rest of my things when I've got sorted with a place of my own. You'll have to get a takeaway for your tea – there's nothing in. I'm sure she will feed you."

"Oh yes, I forgot, how could I? You're a woman of means now so you can go and buy somewhere to live. I'm not sure I can run this place on my own. I don't have your money," Mark said.

"Well, you can always sell it and buy something smaller. After all, it's only bricks and mortar. It ceased being a home the day you decided to wreck my life. Alternatively, you could sell it and go and live with the new love of your life. I'm sure she'll be over the moon – Babes!"

Before he could respond, she left him standing at the door, put her case in the boot of her car and set off to Jean's house. As she drove, she thought of what he had said to her about being boring. That really got to her. She would show him. She would show everyone that she wasn't boring. She was Susan Barnett, millionairess, traveller and free woman. Why then, did she feel so terribly lonely and desolate?

She arrived at Jean's a few minutes later and parked her car on the drive. Jean held open the door as Sue walked towards her. When she got inside, she collapsed into Jean's arms and sobbed for all she was worth.

Chapter 51

It was a few minutes before Sue could speak clearly enough to tell Jean briefly what had happened.

"Oh my God, Sue. I'm flabbergasted. I never thought that of Mark. You two have always been the perfect couple as far as I knew. Even though you said he was acting strangely, I never suspected this. Now don't go blaming yourself, Sue. It's not you, it's him. No-one told him to go out with another woman did they?"

"No, but I can't help wondering what I could have done better. I thought I had tried to be a good wife and do the things a wife and mother does. Maybe it's the money he resents. Erin said a man needs to feel like he is useful. Perhaps it's made him feel surplus to requirements so to speak."

"Come off it, Sue, you said he had been acting indifferently towards you long before you knew about the pendant and the money. Do you remember our conversation on the train going down to London in April? It must have been going on for months"

"Yes, you're right, Jean. Why am I trying to blame myself for it all? He can't slither out of this one. He always manages to make me feel guilty when we fall out. Well, not this time."

"I think the kids will agree with you on this," said Jean, trying to make Sue feel better.

"Oh no, the kids! What am I going to say to them? It will devastate them, especially Nicola. She's the apple of her Dad's eye. James knew there was something wrong in July, when they came round for a barbecue. He sensed there was a problem. I wonder if he has known about this and not said anything?"

"I can't imagine him keeping it quiet if he did know," replied Jean.

"You know I told you that he and Emma were having IVF treatment. I hope this doesn't upset them enough to ruin any chance they might have. If it does, it will be Mark's fault and I really will go to town on him. I am so angry and upset and frustrated, and I feel sick all the time. He has no idea what this has done to me, Jean. All he cares about is his affair with this woman. He even tried to tell me that it was my fault for being so boring! What do you think about that?"

"You might be accused of some things, Sue but being boring is not one of them. I know because I've seen you in action – if you know what I mean."

They talked for ages until Sue asked Jean if she could stay for a couple of nights until she got somewhere to rent. Jean said she could stay as long as she wanted. She would make up the spare bed, and tomorrow, if Sue wanted to go and get some more things from the house, she would go with her.

Finally, Sue's head touched the pillow in Jean's spare room at about 1.00am. She was so tired but sleep eluded her. She lay awake, going over the events of the day and asking herself over and over why she hadn't realised what was going on. All the signs were there and she had not picked up on any of them. She had been so stupid and naive. She thought about her feelings of guilt over Samio and hated Mark all the more for putting her through the last few months. She cried again and again until finally, in the early morning light she dozed for about an hour.

When she awoke, it was just after 6.00am. She got up and put on her dressing gown and slippers. She crept quietly to the bathroom and then downstairs into Jean's kitchen to make a cup of tea. Jean heard her and joined her in the kitchen just as the kettle boiled.

"That's a real gift you've got there, Jean," said Sue, surprisingly light-heartedly as far as Jean was concerned.

"What is?" asked Jean.

"Always managing to turn up just as the kettle boils and someone is making a cup of tea. I've noticed it once or twice lately."

They smiled at each other both knowing that it was Sue's attempt at appearing more cheerful.

Jean made some porridge but Sue declined saying she wasn't hungry. In the end Jean made her promise to have a slice of toast, so just to keep her quiet, Sue ate half of it and left the rest for the birds.

Sue said she would wait until she knew Mark would have gone to work and then she would go and get some more clothes and some personal paperwork like bank books and documents for the car. She would bring them back here and then go into town to the letting agents and find herself a place to rent. She asked Jean if she wanted to come with her into town and the plan was agreed. She showered and dressed then drove back home. Mark wasn't in thankfully, so she gathered the things she had put on her list and took a look around the house. There were empty takeaway food cartons in the kitchen bin and Mark's breakfast dishes in the sink. She was about to empty the bin and clear the dishes into the dishwasher but stopped herself and left them.

"Bugger him," she said out loud, "he can do it himself. You're on your own now mister. Seen how you like that."

She went upstairs and could see that the bed had been slept in, so she gathered that he had stayed at home. She stopped short of contemplating whether the 'Devil Woman' as she had named her had also stayed because that upset and angered her even more. She considered leaving him a message telling him that he should get another skivvy to do his bidding but then decided it was sinking to unworthy behaviour, so she loaded the car and returned to Jean's. Once Sue had put her things away in the drawers Jean had emptied for her use, they set off into town to go to the letting agents. They decided to get some shopping and Sue said she would buy them lunch in Marks and Spencer's.

Sue picked at her toasted sandwich and left most of it.

"You need to eat something, Sue," said Jean, concerned at her friend's lack of appetite. "You haven't had anything today except a piece of toast and three brews. You are going to need some strength to get through the next few weeks you know."

"Yes, I know – don't remind me, but just at the moment I can't face anything. I feel so sick all the time."

"Well, it will probably wear off after a couple of days but I'll be keeping an eye on you to make sure you don't get anorexic."

"Jean, look at me. Do you think there's much chance of that happening? Now please don't go on at me and finish your tea then we'll go and find me a place to live."

Chapter 52

Sue and Jean toured the letting agencies looking in the windows at properties for rent. After dismissing a couple they headed for the one that showed most promise. Sue told the smart young woman in the office to which they were escorted that she wanted to rent a new apartment in a particular area – she had seen an advertisement in the window – and she wanted to complete the transaction as soon as possible due to personal circumstances. The woman, who introduced herself as Clare, was immediately interested because the apartments that Sue had mentioned were at the higher end of the market and they had only just been finished a couple of weeks ago.

"How soon would you like to be in situ, Mrs Barnett?" she asked.

"Ideally by the end of this month if all the paperwork can be done by then. I can provide all the references you need and I have ID on me at this moment in time."

"Well, it's a tall order, but we'll see what we can do," Clare replied eagerly. "Fortunately, I have some time this afternoon if you want to view. How does that sound?"

"Perfect," said Sue.

They agreed to meet at the apartment block in an hour's time. That would give Sue and Jean time to drop off their shopping at Jean's. They were outside the apartment block at 3.30pm that afternoon and following the guided tour around the apartment and getting answers to all her questions, Sue verbally agreed the deal. They returned to Clare's office to get most of the preliminary paperwork out of the way.

Sue left a cheque for the first month's rent – £800.00 – which Clare said she would hold on file until she had received two references: one from Sue's bank and a personal one from a professional contact. Sue gave her the name of an ex-colleague who was a Bank Manager and Clare promised to keep her up to date with progress.

The apartment was not far from Jean's house and it was on the first floor of a newly built two-storey building in a gated development. The workmen were just putting the finishing touches to the lawn in the centre of the four blocks of six apartments. The one Sue had chosen overlooked a small stream at the back that ran through some woodland. The lounge had French windows at the back leading onto a small balcony that was just big enough to fit a small table and chairs and a couple of pot plants. The window at the front of the lounge looked out onto the lawn and flower beds as did all the others. Each apartment had two numbered parking spaces allocated to the side of their respective blocks.

The accommodation comprised a small lounge, a dining kitchen, two good-sized bedrooms: one with en-suite facilities and a separate bathroom and airing cupboard.

When they arrived back at Jean's, Sue was looking through the brochure that Clare had given to her. "I think this will do me nicely, Jean. It's a good size and it's within walking distance from you, and handy for the bus route should I need it. What do you think, Jean?"

"I love it, Sue, especially the fact that it's gated and the gate is automatically locked with access just for key holders. That makes it more secure and although your car won't be in a garage, it will be relatively safe in the parking bay. There were plenty of lights around the outside as well, so even at night you should fell quite safe. I'll say this for you, Sue, you don't hang around do you? If that had been me it would have taken a lot more thinking about than that. Are you sure it's what you want?"

"Well, I've agreed to rent for six months initially, so it's not a disaster if I don't like it. I can just move to somewhere else if necessary, but this will give me some breathing space in the meantime."

"Changing the subject, Sue, how are you feeling?"

"Better than I was last night but I always feel better when I feel in control. I had to do this today because it gives me a sense of purpose. Although I'm shattered, I think I'm functioning on adrenaline. It will hit me when I stop though. Tomorrow, I'll make a list of all the remaining things, apart from the obvious, like clothes that I want from home. 'Home', it's not my home now is it?"

"Of course it's still your home, Sue. You own half of it and it has been a huge part of your life. You brought your children up there..."

"Oh Jean! The kids – I haven't told them yet. What am I going to say to them?"

"You just have to tell them straight – that you have left their dad because he has another woman and you are going to rent a flat for the time being."

"I can't come out with it just like that. They'll be very upset, especially Nicola."

"I don't see any other option, Sue. If you leave it to Mark my guess is they'll get his version and that might upset them more – being told their Mother has walked out on him and she hasn't been the same since she retired, especially since she inherited a fortune."

"You're right, Jean – as usual. I'll go and see Peter and James, but I'll have to ring Nicola and break it to her gently. I'm not looking forward to this, one little bit."

"You're not going anywhere until you've had something to eat and that's final. You haven't eaten anything much today, and like I said, you're going to need some strength."

Sue decided it was best not to argue with Jean about food, but the thought of it made her feel nauseous. She hoped she would get passed this feeling soon. She tried to force a few forks full of food down just to placate Jean. However, she only managed to keep it in situ long enough to leave Jean's heading for James and Emma's when she had to stop the car and get out and be sick. It was actually a relief to rid her stomach of the offending contents but she knew that it couldn't go on like this for too long.

James and Emma were upset as she had predicted. Emma expressed her sadness for both of them and said she hoped they might be able to sort things out. It should be noted at this point that Sue did not mention Diane. She had decided that it was up to Mark to tell them that bit of the news. James was quiet and only said that if she needed anything at all he would be there for her. She tried to sound upbeat and focus on the apartment that she had rented, saying that she would need some help getting it furnished. Emma offered her assistance and Sue said she would let them know when she had the keys. James asked if it would be okay for him to visit her while she was at Jean's.

"Of course you can, love. Jean won't mind at all."

Sue said she needed to go to see Peter and Lynne so she got up to leave. James showed her to the door and as she turned to say goodbye, he grabbed her shoulders and pulled her to him. He whispered in her ear that he loved her and he would check on her every day to make sure she was okay. It was all she could do to stop herself from crying, but somehow she managed it and asked him to check on his father as well. She didn't wait for a response but made a hasty retreat for her car. *One down, two to go,* she thought to herself.

Peter and Lynne were equally upset to hear the news, and Lynne also said if Sue wanted some company she would be glad to go out for lunch. They asked the obvious question – why? Sue simply said that they had been drifting lately and didn't seem to have any shared interests. She made some reference to it being difficult to adjust to retirement for both parties, so they had decided that they needed some time apart. Sue knew they weren't convinced but they said nothing else except that they hoped they could work it out. They also expressed their reservations at her getting an apartment this soon as had James and Emma. Sue explained that she needed to do something positive and it was what she wanted. She asked Peter if he would look in on his dad to check that he was okay and he agreed he would.

"I'll have to go, dears," Sue finally said as she stood to leave. "I need to go and ring Nicola now to tell her."

"She'll be very upset," said Peter, "you know how emotional she is and especially where Dad's concerned."

"I know and I'm not looking forward to telling her, especially on the phone."

As Sue turned to leave, Lynne asked why Sue had moved out and not Mark. Sue said it was easier for her to go somewhere else – like Jean's initially – and to get herself somewhere to live now that she had Sam's money.

"Do you think that has something to do with all this?" asked Peter.

"I really don't know, Peter, but perhaps when we can sit down and talk more about things we might find out, but for now, we each need some space. Now, I really need to go, so I'll be in touch very soon."

They each gave her a hug and she left to return to Jean's. She breathed a sigh of relief at having completed two thirds of her task but knew that the last third would be the most difficult. Sue asked Jean if she could use the landline to call Nicola as her mobile needed charging. "I'll pay the bill when it arrives, Jean."

"Don't be silly, Sue. It's the least I can do after all you've done for me. Just help yourself and I'll go and have my shower and put my PJs on."

"Hi, Mum, how was the holiday? I was going to call you last night but it's been so hectic at work and Si's been busy as well. Anyway, why are you ringing on a strange number?"

"I'm staying at Jean's for a day or two."

"Oh no, is she poorly?"

"No, love, I've left your Dad." There was no easy way to say it so she came straight out with it and waited for her daughter's response. At first Nicola thought it was a joke, but soon realised it wasn't. She launched into questions about why and inevitably asked how Dad was taking it. Was he okay? She would have to come over tomorrow night and see him.

That was typical of Nicola, and her reaction was no surprise to Sue. She tried to explain as she had done with the others but Nicola became upset and said that she thought Sue had been a bit selfish leaving him on his own so much lately to go on holiday while he continued to work. Sue wanted to tell her that he hadn't been working quite as hard as she thought but knew that detail would have to come from Mark. She would never believe Sue, and besides, this wasn't about taking the side of one parent or the other, it was about pulling together as a family in the face of adversity. Sue's main concern was her children whatever else happened.

The call lasted nearly half an hour, by the end of which Nicola had calmed down enough to ask Sue if she was okay. Sue told her about the flat and said she would welcome some input into the furnishings. After a short pause, Nicola half – heartedly said she would help her to choose some curtains and bedding if she wanted to arrange a time to meet when she was ready. Finally, Sue ended the call promising to get in touch in the next couple of days.

Jean appeared in her pyjamas and dressing gown and said she was making some coffee if Sue wanted one.
"Jean, I think I need something stronger than that after tonight. I'll open that bottle of wine we bought at the supermarket and then I'll fill you in on the latest."

"You shouldn't be drinking on an empty stomach, Sue," said Jean giving her a look of mild disapproval mixed with concern.

"Jean, I'm not going to turn into a raving alcoholic, and besides, we ate earlier." Sue didn't say that she had vomited most of it back up on her way to see James and Emma.

"You didn't eat very much, Sue but I suppose it has been a difficult day for you, but I'll be keeping my eye on you, madam. Have no fear."

Chapter 53

The next couple of days were taken up with arrangements for the apartment, including sorting out a telephone line and broadband. This reminded Sue that she hadn't checked her emails since she came back from holiday last weekend so she decided to go up to the house and do that while Mark was at work on Friday morning.

Peter had rung her the day before to say he had called a couple of times but Mark was not in. James had called at Jean's on the last two nights, on his way home from work to make sure Sue was okay. Sue had sworn Jean to secrecy about her lack of appetite because she knew that James would worry about her even more than normal and she didn't want to put any additional pressure on he and Emma while they were going through their first IVF treatment. Needless to say, she hadn't heard from Nicola. She guessed that Nicola had managed to speak to her father and therefore, she would be waiting for Sue to call her.

She pulled up on the drive and got out her key to let herself in. Everything seemed tidy as it had the other day when she had come to pick up more clothes. She went into her little sitting room that she also used as an office and switched on her lap top. There were thirty-five emails, over half of which were just spam. She quickly scrolled down the list of the remaining ones and noticed one from Valerie in Melbourne. Valerie was just checking all was well with Sue and family as she hadn't heard from her for a few weeks and she knew that Sue was having a holiday around this time so hoped she'd enjoyed it.

She also said, as she usually did, that she would be delighted to see Sue any time she wanted to have another break if Sue could manage it.

Sue felt a bit guilty at not having emailed Valerie before now but she fired off a quick reply to the effect that she would love to come and stay for a few days and she would be in touch soon. She wrote that her holiday in Corsica had been a lovely one and it had been very hectic at home since she returned.

Hectic! Sue thought. *That's an understatement if ever there was one.*

She switched off her laptop and packed it in its case ready to leave. She checked the hall table which was where they put any post that arrived to see if there was anything for her. There was a small pile of letters and she scooped them up to put in her bag. Just as she was about to leave, she heard the familiar sound of Mark's van pulling up on the drive behind her car. She stood in the hall waiting and after a couple of minutes Mark came through the front door. They looked at each other for an uneasy moment and then he said a quick "Hi."

Sue replied likewise and then she said, "I just came to access my emails and see if there was any mail for me. I was just leaving when I heard your van. Are you blocking me in?"

"Yes, but I'll move in a minute. I see you're taking your laptop with you. I didn't know Jean had broadband."

"She doesn't, but I'll have it installed when I move. I guess you will have spoken to Nicola so doubtless she's filled you in on the details of the apartment I intend to rent."

"Yes, she rang me to see if I was okay. It's good to know one of our children cares about me."

"Actually, Peter has called round twice but you haven't been in and I know that James and Emma have been very busy."

"They could have rung me," Mark said meekly.

"You could have rung them," responded Sue quickly.

"I suppose you've told them all about how I'm the villain of the peace and of course 'your boys' will take your side."

"Oh, stop being so bloody self-pitying. As a matter of fact, I haven't said anything about your affair because I thought you should be the one to tell them. Nicola certainly wouldn't have believed me if I'd said anything. I'm guessing you haven't told her either. I suppose you're too much of a coward to do that. If you didn't think you were in the wrong then you would have come out with it by now. 'My boys' as you call them are worried about both of us and all they want is to see us work things out."

"Well, I'd say there's not much chance of that, seeing as how you've already organised alternative living arrangements. You don't let the grass grow under your feet do you? But then again, money's no object to you is it?" He looked at her like a petulant child does to a parent when they won't give them what they want.

"Right now, Mark, I don't see any point in us talking to each other because we'll just end up rowing. You've hurt me more than you will ever know and even though I can't claim to be perfect, I can't think of any circumstances when I would do what you've done. We will need to talk at some point and try to get passed all this but not yet. In the meantime I think we should both do our best not to drag our kids into this. They all have their own lives to lead and their pressures. Nevertheless, I'm willing to bet that they are worrying like mad because they don't want us to split up. If you don't want the boys to think badly of you then talk to them honestly and try to explain to them what motivated you to do what you did. They'll respect you more for it. When you've done that, perhaps you will explain a few things to me without destroying any bit of confidence I have left."

Mark's expression changed and he took Sue by both arms. "I still care about you, Sue. You do know that don't you?"

"No, Mark. I don't know that. You haven't exactly shown your caring side towards me for ages now. In fact I've been walking on eggshells ever since I retired, because I could feel your resentment of my retirement. You would have been happy for me to continue working, keeping everything as it was and all the time you were carrying on with another woman."

"That's not true. I was glad that you retired. You needed to do that, I know, but it felt like you were giving up and let's face it, retirement is the last step before you die, isn't it?"

"It would be if you were a boring person who did nothing with your time, but contrary to what you think, I'm not boring and I can fill my time quite nicely, thank you. Perhaps it's yourself you're thinking about, Mark. Consider that. Now I have to go."

She picked up her things and opened the front door to leave. Mark took her car keys from her hand and opened the boot for her. As she closed the boot and held out her hand for the keys, he repeated that he cared about her and said he would help her move any of her things into her apartment when the time came.

"Thanks, I'll let you know if I need anything," she said and got in the car. He moved his van for her to back off the drive and waved to her as she drove off.

****

"He's definitely feeling guilty, Sue," said Jean when she told her about meeting Mark. "I bet he regrets what's happened. It won't last with this woman you know."

"Jean, the only thing he regrets is being found out and I don't care whether it lasts or not. She's welcome to him. At least I can please myself from now on and not have to put up with his annoying ways. His only other consideration is the fact that materially, he won't have my income to help him to do what he wants and live where he does. I don't know where she lives but I bet it's not somewhere he would choose."

"You might be right on that score but I don't believe for one minute that you don't care at all. You can't disregard forty-five years just like that. I know you, Sue Barnett and I think you would take a chance on him again if he gave up this woman and came to you on his knees."

"Jean, I'm not even going to talk about it okay?" With that, Sue went to her bedroom to read her mail and call Erin.

"Oh Sue, you poor thing," was Erin's first comment when Sue told her what had happened. "I'm relieved that you have Jean to take refuge with. If I was nearer I'd be there with you."

Sue assured Erin that although she was devastated by Mark's news, she was being positive and taking practical steps to sort out her life. She told her about the apartment and said the boys in particular were being very supportive. She added that Nicola was being – well – Nicola. There was nothing more to add because Erin knew how devoted Nicola was to her father. After talking to her for about twenty minutes, Erin promised to call Sue regularly to check how things were going and she repeated her offer of a bolt-hole if Sue wanted to get a bit further away.

Later, while Sue and Jean were eating a sandwich (well Jean was eating hers and Sue was nibbling at hers and struggling to get it down), Clare the letting agent called to say that the deadline Sue had set was not going to be managed. It would be the end of October, not the beginning before Sue could move in. Apparently, there was a problem with some work Sue had asked to be done prior to completing. The workmen on the site were busy sorting out a few remedial jobs for other tenants and this would mean they couldn't start Sue's work until the middle of October at the earliest. This wasn't the news Sue wanted to hear but she had fallen in love with the apartment and was prepared to wait.

Jean asked what the problem was when Sue finished her call and when Sue told her, she smiled and said, "That just means I'll have to put up with you a bit longer then, Sue."

"I can't do that to you, Jean. It isn't fair to expect you to have me around for nearly six weeks."

"Rubbish, Sue. Stop worrying about it and eat your lunch. Anyway, it will give you more time to go shopping for furniture and stuff with the girls."

Sue smiled and thanked her friend but inwardly, she was hatching another plan.

Chapter 54

The next day, Saturday, Sue went to visit James and Emma with her laptop.

"While I'm here, could I connect to the internet? I want to look at something and Jean has no broadband connection."

"Course you can. Here, let me have your laptop and I'll get you set up here so that if you want to use it while you're at Jean's you can come up here," replied James.

Sue and Emma chatted over a brew whilst James went to sort it out. Sue asked Emma how the IVF was going.

"Well, fingers crossed all seems to be going well according to Mr Sargeant the consultant. I don't want to say too much at this stage, Sue, but don't worry you'll be the first to know when we have some news. Of course, there are no guarantees that it will work first time or even that it will work at all but its early days and thanks to you we can afford the treatment. How are you anyway? Have you seen Mark since you left?"

Sue mentioned that she had called at the house to look at her emails and get her laptop the day before and she had spoken to him then. She added that they had talked briefly and he had offered to help her with her move into the apartment. She said that Nicola had seen him and told him.

"Blimey," was the response from James sitting at the dining table, "she's the only one of us who's managed to contact him then because I know Peter has been round twice and I've been once and he wasn't at home on any of the occasions."

"He's probably working longer hours than he did before, now that he's on his own," replied Sue defensively. "I know he has a big job on at the moment and he'll want to finish it as soon as possible so that he can get paid."

"Well, I left him a message on his mobile so I'm waiting for a call from him."

Emma jumped into the conversation as she could see Sue was reluctant to talk about it further. "I'm sure that you two can work it out. Perhaps you both need some time and space away from each other for a while."

"Well, I'm going to be as far away as I can for the next few weeks if I can get some flights organised. That's why I want to get onto the internet, so that I can book to go to Australia to see Valerie, my friend in Melbourne. Then I thought I might stop off in Sydney to see Steve and Grace."

"But what about the apartment? I thought you were moving into it at the beginning of October," said Emma.

"It's been delayed because of some other work that's going on so it's been put off until at least the end of October. Anyway, I can always ask them to hold it a bit longer. I might not come back until late November. It will all depend on whether Valerie and Steve and Grace can put me up."

James rose from the dining table and came into the lounge. "Well, I don't blame you, Mum and I've finished now so you should be able to sign on."

Emma and James exchanged a look that said 'it's more serious than we thought' as Sue made her way to the dining table. With James's help, she spent the next two hours going through the various websites looking at air fare availability, after she had sent off two emails to Melbourne and Sydney. If the times were okay with her friends, she was looking to go on October 4 and leave her return open until she knew more. Maybe she would look to coming home toward the end of November, just in time to get into her apartment before Christmas. That would give her six or seven weeks away – enough time for Mark to get used to her not being around at all.

She thanked them both for the tea and the use of the internet and agreed to leave her laptop there for now. After her car had pulled away James turned to Emma and said, "There's more to this than just not getting on with each other. Did you see Mum's face? It looks ravaged with those baggy eyes and I'm sure she's lost weight. I need to speak to Dad. Maybe he'll be a bit forthcoming."

"I know what you mean," replied Emma, "but I wouldn't bank on your Dad telling you anything."

"Things have been a bit dodgy, if you know what I mean, since Mum went to Canada. I noticed it when we went for that takeaway when she gave us the cheques. Then, when we went for a barbecue in July, I'd have sworn there was an atmosphere between them. It has something to do with the money. I think Dad resents Mum having it. He likes to be the one in control and I think it makes him feel vulnerable. Anyway, whatever it is I'm going to find out."

As James said this, he rang Mark's mobile and this time, he answered.

"Hi, Dad, I was just ringing to see if you're okay. Mum told us your news and I've called but you haven't been in.

Emma and I were wondering if you want to come round tonight and have some tea with us rather than being on your own."

There was a long pause at the other end of the line and James asked, "Are you still there, Dad?"

"Oh er, yes. I was just thinking. Would you mind if I didn't tonight? I said I would meet a couple of the lads from the pub. I'll tell you what – how about I come round tomorrow instead?"

"Just a minute, Dad, I'll check with Em first." He put his hand over the phone and asked Emma if she could manage tomorrow teatime instead. She said it was okay and he spoke to Mark again. "Yep, that'll be okay – say about 5.30pm?"

"That's good yes," replied Mark. "I'll see you then, bye."

Mark hung up and as James put the mobile back in his pocket, he couldn't help sensing the reluctance in his father's voice. He wondered why but didn't say anything to Emma. Later, James rang Peter to tell him about his mother's visit and that he had managed to speak to Mark.

"We might call round if that's okay, James," said Peter. "I've not managed to speak to him although I've called at the house a couple of times this week. Will that be okay? We won't come until after you've had your tea – say about 6.30pm?"

"No probs, Pete, we'll see you then."

"I had Nic on the phone last night," added Peter at the last minute. "She was really upset and worried about Dad but mainly she was having a bit of a go at Mum, saying that she thought she was being really selfish."

"What did you say to that?" asked James feeling irritated with his sister for taking sides.

"I told her that she was being unfair and I said that it was typical of her to take Dad's side when she didn't know all the facts. I was a bit mad actually and she went off with a flea in her ear because I didn't agree with what she said."

"Dad's always spoiled her, Pete. As far as she's concerned, he can't do anything wrong. I know it's their business and we shouldn't interfere but I'm determined to find out the reasons for this. It's bloody madness if you ask me. They've been together for forty-five years nearly and although I know they've had their ups and downs I've always thought they were solid."

"Me and Lynne think the same, James. I can't get my head around it. You don't think Mum's been having a fling with that old chap and she's told Dad about it?"

"I can't imagine Mum doing that but I suppose you never know. They say some women go through a funny stage when they get to her age." At this point, Emma, who was listening to the conversation, gave him a dig in the ribs and he winced.

"What's going on there, James? I can hear some funny noises."

"Oh, it's just Em getting violent with me again," he joked. "She thinks I'm being sexist."

They talked for a few minutes more about the football that was coming on the TV in the afternoon and how busy they had been at work, before saying goodbye.

"Pete thinks Mum might have had a bit on the side with the old man in Canada and that's why Nic's is saying she's selfish. That's rich coming from her. She can do a good line in being selfish when she wants," said James to Emma as he finished his phone call.

Emma nodded in agreement and said they'd better get off to the supermarket if Mark was coming for tea tomorrow.

Chapter 55

Jean was very understanding when Sue told her of her plan to go to Australia while she waited for the apartment to be ready.

"You don't have to go away again just because the apartment isn't going to be ready. You can stay here as long as you like. Besides, I like having the company. However, if you want to do that then I hope you have a great time."

"I can't impose on you for that length of time, Jean, and anyway, it's a good excuse to go and see Valerie and Steve and Grace. You've been so good to me this week, but you know Jean, when you've lived on your own for so long it can't be easy having someone living with you – even someone as lovely as me." Sue winked as she said this and they both laughed.

Sue rang the letting agents to tell them and it was arranged that the date for taking up the lease would be flexible but not before the end of November, subject to Sue losing her deposit of one month's rent if she didn't move in for any reason.

That evening, Sue and Jean watched a DVD as neither of them was interested in anything on the TV. Sue managed a small amount of food when they had their evening meal but Jean noticed that she pushed the rest of it round her plate and then she went to scrape what was left into the kitchen bin. She was becoming a bit worried about her friend. This was so unlike her as Jean knew Sue always looked forward to her food. She understood why Sue would not be hungry. After all, she had received a shock and although she was putting on a brave face of managing the situation and being practical, Jean was convinced that Sue was hurting inside and her emotions were all over the place. She also knew that there was little she could do to change the way Sue felt except be there for her as and when she needed to let off steam. That time would come sooner or later.

They shared a bottle of wine and spent the rest of the evening, like two couch potatoes, not wanting to move. Finally, just before midnight, they both retired to bed. Although completely worn out, Sue again found it difficult to get off to sleep. This time she was thinking about her possible holiday to Australia. She couldn't book her flights until she heard back from her friends to say the dates were okay – or could she? The thought occurred to her that even if she couldn't stay with her friends, she could always stay in hotels – she could afford it now so why not? It would be another adventure and maybe she would go to Alice Springs or up to the Great Barrier Reef. There was nothing to stop her doing what she wanted. She decided that she would book the flights tomorrow and worry about accommodation at a later date. She would go up to James's in the morning and do it on-line.

Eventually, after another hour of planning things in her head, Sue drifted off to sleep, but only for about four hours. It was just before 6.15am on a dull Sunday morning when Sue opened her eyes and decided to get up and make a list of what she needed to take away with her. By the time Jean came into the lounge at 7.45am, Sue had drunk two cups of tea and written a long 'To Do' list which she was perusing.

"You're an early bird this morning. Have you been up long?" said Jean as she saw the two empty cups on the coffee table beside Sue's pen and paper.

"I couldn't sleep, Jean so I got up just after 6.00am. I hope I didn't wake you."

"No, you didn't wake me. I was so tired last night and I thought you were too. Come to think of it you still look tired. Have you slept much at all?"

"I managed a few hours but I don't need all that much sleep anyway," Sue lied. "I'm just making a list of things I need to do and take with me on holiday. Six or seven weeks is quite a long time so I'll have to take enough stuff to last. It should be warm weather wise so hopefully, I'll only need thin clothes that don't weigh too heavy."

"Do you want some breakfast or have you already had something?" asked Jean as she strolled into the kitchen.

"Er no, I haven't had anything but I will get something later."

Jean whirled round and took Sue by surprise as she took her by the hand and marched her into the kitchen. "Sit there and don't move," she said as she pointed to the kitchen table. "I'm going to make some porridge and toast and you are going to eat it before I let you out of my sight. You have hardly eaten anything this week and I can see that you've lost weight. I know you say you aren't hungry but if you continue to starve yourself you'll get anorexic or something and anyway, you need food for strength or you won't be able to keep up this pace you're setting yourself."

"Jean, I promise I'm..." Sue started to say, but Jean held up her hand and continued, "Don't interrupt me when I'm in full flow! I have been watching you and I have to say I'm really worried about you so please let me make you some breakfast and eat it just to please me."

Sue sighed in submission and although she knew it would make her feel nauseous, she agreed to try some porridge.

"And a slice of toast?" asked Jean.

"Half a slice?" bargained Sue.

"Done," agreed Jean and made her way to the cupboard for the pan congratulating herself for being assertive and feeling like she had won a minor battle. Sue smiled to herself because she knew what Jean would be thinking. She sat patiently at the table like a dutiful child and she was reminded again why she treasured Jean's friendship so much. Ten minutes later, the steaming bowl of porridge was placed in front of Sue. After the first couple of mouthfuls Sue found that she could cope with the porridge and she almost finished the lot. Jean looked on approvingly as Sue took a bite of the toast and a sip of the tea that had arrived shortly after. When Sue had finished Jean said, "How was that?"

"It was good, thanks Jean."

"See, you just needed to get started. You'll be fine now. We'll have some chicken for tea tonight eh?"

"Don't get ahead of yourself, Jean. It's only a bowl of porridge and some toast. That'll do me for a while. We'll see about the chicken later when I've managed to keep this down." She gave Jean a look of warning and Jean took the hint to back off.

"When I've cleaned my teeth, I'm going up to James's to book some flights." She told Jean what she had been thinking while she was unable to sleep last night.

"Do you fancy a walk later?" she asked. "When I get back from James's we could drive over to the coast and walk on the beach – blow the cobwebs away. What do you say Jean?"

"Yes, that'd be good. I'll just do a couple of jobs while you're out and then we'll aim to go before lunch."

Sue pulled up outside James's house and as she walked up the path to the front door she thought about how all this was affecting her children. They shouldn't have to be worrying about their parents' relationship problems. It was supposed to the other way round wasn't it? Emma and James were pleased to see her but she got the feeling they were nervous about something. Then, James told her that Mark was coming round for tea.

"Oh good," she said. "I'm glad that you've managed to get in touch with him at last. Promise me you will take him for a pint while I'm away and don't be falling out. I know how you and he can argue at the drop of a hat."

"Why should we argue? Is there something to argue about?"

"No," she replied defensively, "but even though he and I are having a difficult time, I don't want it to affect his relationship with any of you. Now, I'll go and get these flights booked after I've checked my email account if that's okay."

She found a reply from Valerie who confirmed the dates were fine and she was looking forward to seeing her. She asked Sue to let her know the actual date and time she would arrive in Melbourne so that she could arrange to meet her at the airport. That was a good start so Sue went ahead with her plan. At least she knew that the first part of her trip was settled. She would check daily for a response from Steve and Grace. By late morning, everything had been done and Sue thanked James and left to call at Peter's before going back to Jean's. After having a swift cup of tea with Peter and Lynne, she promised to speak to them during the coming week and let them know she was okay. She thought about ringing Nicola but decided to leave it until the evening. There would be more chance of her being at home then.

Jean had packed a few sandwiches by the time Sue got back, so after a quick change they set off to go to Southport. It was flat and good for walking and they would get some much needed fresh air in their lungs. Sue hoped that it would help her to sleep because she was feeling really weary after the last few nights of restlessness and weird dreams.

The day turned out to be better than expected as the dull start changed into hazy sunshine even though it wasn't particularly warm. They walked and talked and ate their sandwiches en route – Sue even managed to eat one slice of bread followed by an apple. They found a wooden tea cabin on the beach and stopped for a cup of tea. There weren't all that many walkers and of course the tide was way out as it usually was at Southport. The owner said she was going to close at the end of September as trade was dwindling and she would be going to Spain until the end of March. She said she had an apartment there and quite a number of friends with whom she socialised in the winter. Sue told her she was planning to go to Australia for a few weeks early in October and this prompted envious comments about how she would like to go but couldn't afford it. After Sue had answered the umpteenth question about where she was staying and listened to the owner repeating how lucky she was to have friends in Australia, Sue looked at Jean and signalled it was time to go.

"Just think, Jean," said Sue as they were driving back home, "it's only been a week since we got back from Corsica. I can't believe it. I didn't think I'd have left Mark and be planning a life on my own only a week after getting home. It's been like a whirlwind. My brain is so saturated with thoughts that I'm actually finding it difficult to process normal stuff. To think that only six months ago everything was – well normal, but now everything's changed."

"I suppose it started when Sam died and left you the pendant," said Jean.

"Have I changed since then, Jean?"

"No not really, Sue. I can't honestly say you're any different than you were before all this. Why do you ask?"

"I think Mark considers that I have. He thinks that having money has changed me. Oh he hasn't said it in so many words but that's what he's hinted at."

"That's just his excuse for what he's been up to, Sue. Don't let him convince you otherwise. You have been generous to the kids and to me but you were always generous before. The only difference is that you can afford to be more generous now."

Sue fell silent and pondered on what Jean had said. Maybe Jean was right and Mark was looking for an excuse, but what if she had come across as flaunting her money at him and somehow making him resentful. Then there was the fact that she had retired. She thought about what he had said to her on Friday morning – about retirement being the step before death. Perhaps he was feeling insecure and vulnerable. What if he wasn't well and didn't want her to know? That might explain some of it. Then she reminded herself of his words to her the evening she left him. He said she was boring. That had hit her hard with the realisation that he had another woman whom he seemed to care more about. She couldn't cope with the feelings that awakened in her – jealousy, rage, hurt, betrayal, frustration – just about every bad feeling she could think of. Her thoughts must have taken her away somewhere because suddenly she heard Jean shouting "Sue, look out!"

She came back to the present just as a car coming in the opposite direction swerved into the side of the road and the driver flashed his headlights and sounded a continuous blast on his horn. Sue also swerved to the left just in time to avoid hitting him and she came to a stop on the grass verge. She sat motionless at the wheel, wondering how that had happened.

The driver of the other car came over and banged his fist heavily on the window. She pressed the button to lower it and a furious face thrust itself into the car and started to shout obscenities at her. Sue didn't speak but instead continued to stare out of the windscreen, while Jean tried to placate the angry man.

"What the fucking hell's up with you woman? he shouted. "You could have killed us all! You shouldn't be allowed behind a wheel if you can't steer straight. If you were a man I'd drag you out of that car and beat the shit out of you."

Still Sue continued to stare as if she was on her own. The driver continued to shout at her. Jean had seen and heard enough. She got out of the car and went round to the man who was still ranting at the window. She pulled him back and shouted at him to shut up.
"Can't you see she's not well, you moron? She's a good driver and if she was okay that wouldn't have happened! Leave her alone will you? There's no harm done, so bugger off unless you want to try beating the shit out of me!"

The driver stopped and stared at this diminutive woman in her sixties in disbelief. He seemed to regain his composure and his sense of decency and simply turned to walk away. However, he couldn't resist calling to her one last time over his shoulder. "She needs seeing to then if she's ill and she definitely shouldn't be driving." He got in his car and drove off and as he did so, Jean uncharacteristically stuck two fingers up at the car's rear end as it disappeared around the corner.

Thank god the road was quiet, thought Jean to herself as she opened the driver's door to check on her friend. She managed to get Sue to look at her and then she asked her to tell her what was wrong. Sue seemed to snap back into consciousness and she simply said, "Sorry, Jean, I don't know what happened then. I was thinking about Mark and..." Her speech trailed off and she started to sob.

It was heart wrenching for Jean to witness and she felt so helpless. She coaxed Sue out of the car and managed to get her to sit on the grass. She put her arms around her and held her while she continued to sob. Jean was afraid Sue was having a breakdown and she considered calling James or Peter. They were about half an hour away from home, so she weighed up the options which she decided were limited. She was about to make a call to James, when Sue pulled away from her, fell to her knees and vomited on the grass. Once Jean was sure that Sue had finished, she gave her some tissues to dry her face and found a half full bottle of water in her back pack. Sue eagerly drank the water and after about five minutes she seemed to calm down. She turned to Jean and apologised. "I'm so sorry Jean," she said in a rather weak, shaky voice. "I really don't know what happened. I'll be okay in a minute. Just let me sit here for a few more minutes and then we'll get on our way."

"Sue, I really don' think you are in any fit state to drive. I'll call James and ask him and Emma to come and get us."

"No!" shouted Sue. "Don't you dare call the boys. I don't want them knowing about this, do you understand?"

"Sue, I'm really worried about you. I only want you to be okay."

"I am okay. Now, get back into the car and we'll get home. I promise I'm okay to drive and I'll get you home in one piece."

Jean was not convinced but she got Sue to her feet and although at first she was a little unsteady, she walked unaided back to the car and got behind the wheel. Once they were both strapped in, Sue started the engine and drove off slowly at first but then she gradually gained speed until she was driving at a steady 40mph. She kept to the speed limits as she went along. Neither of them spoke as they completed their journey, but

Jean repeatedly looked sideways at Sue to check she was focussed as she drove. Finally, they pulled up on Jean's drive and Jean heaved a sigh of relief as she retrieved their bags from the boot of the car and dropped them onto the kitchen table. Sue was sitting on the sofa in the lounge, absent-mindedly unzipping her fleece jacket.

"I'll make us a cup of tea shall I?" said Jean tentatively.

"Thanks, Jean," replied Sue. She looked up at her friend and gave her a weak smile. "I can't tell you how sorry I am that I put you through that. I completely lost the plot didn't I?"

"You certainly gave me one hell of a scare but my main concern was you. That stupid man in the other car was shouting at you and he wouldn't stop until I faced up to him and told him to bugger off. I swear to you Sue, that I was ready to plant one on him. I wouldn't care but he had made his point more than once, he was like a dog with a bone. I bet he wouldn't have done that if you had been a man."

Jean went into the kitchen to make the tea while Sue continued to sit on the sofa trying to make sense of what had happened. When Jean returned with two mugs of tea on a small tray, she continued, "I was just about to call James when you were sick all over the place. I didn't know what else to do. I think this week has finally caught up with you. In fact not only this week but the last six months has taken its toll on you. It's no wonder you're not yourself. How about we go to the doctor's in the morning and see if there's anything they can do for you?"

"Thanks for caring, Jean, and I really mean that but I don't want to be taking tablets that will only make me more like a zombie than I was today. What I really need is a long bath and a good night's sleep."

"How about a light snack first?" Jean tried.

"Let's not have that conversation again, Jean. Besides, I'm likely to fetch it back up again and I can't cope with that right now."

Jean didn't argue this time because she could see the state her friend was in and she didn't want to make things worse by haranguing her about food. So she left her alone and instead she went to run a warm bath for her. As Sue tried to relax in the bath, she replayed the events of the last week in her mind. So much had happened and it was too much for her to cope with all at once. She was worried about her family too. They must be going through it as well as she was. She was heartened by the thought that at least the boys were trying to communicate with their father. Then she remembered that she hadn't rung Nicola. She made up her mind to do that before she went to bed. It was just after 7.00pm and so she guessed Nicola and Simon would be at home.

She was so relieved that Jean hadn't contacted James today. Not only did she not want to worry him but she knew that Mark was having his tea with James and Emma so he would have known about it as well. She hoped James and Mark had been able to talk to each other calmly. Perhaps James would take him to the pub for a quiet drink.

Chapter 56

Mark turned up at James and Emma's as arranged and they made small talk while they ate their meal. Just as they were finishing their dessert Peter and Lynne arrived. After asking Mark how he was and commenting that he had tried to contact him throughout the week, Peter suggested that he, James and Mark go for a drink at the pub while the girls watched a favourite programme on the TV. Mark seemed relieved to be asked and they left, promising to be back in an hour or so. Emma and Lynne didn't mind because they found the situation a bit difficult and were glad to be able to watch their TV programme in peace. Lynne said the girls were having tea at her mother's and she would be going to pick them up in an hour so the men had gone to the pub in James' car and would drop Peter off at home later.

James was pleased to see that the pub was quiet and after Mark got in the drinks, they went to sit at a table in the corner. Mark excused himself saying he was going to the loo. When he returned Peter opened up the conversation by asking Mark why his mother had left him. Mark was quite eager to tell them that he and Sue had drifted apart over the last few months, especially since she had retired. He said they had agreed that they didn't have a shared interest and she wanted things that he didn't. He added that now she had some money she seemed to enjoy being away and he was getting used to coming home to an empty house.

"But surely that's not reason enough to split up is it?" asked James.

"It's not just that, James, she seems different somehow. She never used to shout at me but she flies off the handle at the slightest thing. She never comes to the pub with me for a drink. Instead she goes off to bed really early and says she's tired."

"I think she might be finding it difficult to adjust to being at home instead of having to think about work," commented Peter. "After all, she worked hard, not only at work but at home looking after us. Then she was really ill for a while so I'm not surprised she's tired and I don't blame her for retiring when she had the chance."

"I'm not disagreeing with you Peter, but she certainly gives off the vibes that she'd rather be on her own. There's only so much of that I can take."

"I think you should both sit down and talk this through properly," said James. "After all, you've been married for a long time and you can't just disregard all those years. What does Nic think about it? I assume you've spoken to her."

"Yes, she called me on Wednesday night and she did say that she thought your Mum was acting strangely. She thinks she's being selfish."

Neither James nor Peter commented on this because they didn't want to admit that they already knew Nicolas's view and didn't agree. James continued to probe. "Has something happened recently to bring all this to a head, Dad?"

At this point, Mark's attention was diverted to a woman in her fifties entering the pub and going over to the bar. "Well, as you've asked, yes, something has happened. Just bear with me a moment and I'll be back." He got up from the table and attracted the attention of the woman at the bar. He motioned for her to come over to join them and when she approached the table he made his announcement.

"Peter, James, this is Diane, a friend of mine. Diane, meet Peter and James, my sons."

Diane held out her hand to shake theirs. Mark looked at them both expectantly, but neither of them spoke for a few seconds. Then, Peter said, "I don't want to be rude, love, but if this is what I think it is, then I can't stay here." He turned to James and said, "I'll wait for you outside, James." He walked passed Mark shaking his head and out of the door. James, on the other hand had plenty to say. "So this is the cause of the problem." James nodded in Diane's direction as he emphasised the words. "How did she know you were here? Did you ring her when you went to the loo earlier? Was this your idea of a good way to break the news that you had a bit on the side?"

Mark interrupted him angrily. "Don't be so bloody rude. Apologise now. I didn't bring you up to behave like that!"

"Dad, don't you lecture me in how to behave. You're a fine example aren't you? Now all is clear. No wonder Mum's left you, you sad bastard. You didn't have the balls to admit to us what you were up to so you brought her round here thinking we wouldn't say anything in front of her. You're not the person I thought you were. You've gone right down in my estimation."

"Look, James, sometimes these things just happen. I didn't set out to be unfaithful to your mother and neither did Diane. We just met by chance and enjoyed talking to each other."

"Don't waste your breath, Dad, because it doesn't mean anything. Just admit that you're a shit and have done with it. Be honest with us for once in your life instead of trying to blame Mum."

As he said this he got up from his seat and started for the door. Mark called after him as he turned away. "Just ask your mother, the saint, what she got up to in Corsica with the taxi driver! She's not so squeaky clean!"

James didn't look back but simply raised the middle finger of his right hand as he went through the door.

Outside, Peter was waiting next to James's car. They were both fuming.

"It's a good job I came out when I did," said Peter, "otherwise I would have decked him. The sneaky bastard! He hasn't got the balls to be honest and just say, 'Look lads, it's my fault, I've been shagging somebody else'."

"Well I said as much to him after you went out," said James. He rubbed his forehead, something he did when he was anxious and continued, "Emma and I don't need this at the moment. She's all stressed out with the IVF stuff and I'm trying to keep her calm and thinking positive thoughts. There's not much chance of that when Dad drops a bombshell like this one. No wonder Mum's looking like she is. I swear she's losing weight and her eyes are really dark underneath. She's probably not sleeping. I bet Dad expected Mum to tell us about the woman and when she didn't he thought he'd present her to us as a fait accompli."

"I agree," replied Peter, "Mum sounds weary, although I know she's doing her best to cover it up. So much for Nic's theory that Mum is being selfish. I bet he told her a right sob story and she's gullible enough to believe him. As far as she's concerned he can't do anything wrong. Well, she's going to get told when I get home. I'm going to ring her."

"Come on, I'll drop you off and then I'll get home. Oh no, I've just remembered, Dad left his car at ours. Well, no doubt he'll get her to take him to pick it up. I hope he doesn't bring her in to meet Emma. I'm not having her in my house, that's for sure."

They continued to discuss the evening's events as James drove Peter home. They agreed that they would both see Sue the following evening and check up on her. She was going to need all their support right now. As they reached Peter's he said he would text James after he had spoken to Nicola. James left him at the door and drove home. As he approached he could see that Mark's car was still parked in front of the house. He was relieved and after putting the car in the garage, he hurried inside and told Emma they were going for a short walk. He wanted to be out of the way when his father came to collect the car, which he knew would be very soon. When Emma asked what the panic was all about, he said he would tell her once they started to walk.

Chapter 57

Sue spent longer in the bath than she had intended and she almost nodded off. Jean knocked on the bathroom door to ask if she was okay and when she said she was getting out of the bath, Jean offered to make her a snack. The offer was declined but Sue then added that she would have some cereals and milk when she had dressed in her pyjamas.

I suppose it's better than nothing, thought Jean as she cleared up her plate that had contained beans on toast. She had given up on the idea of chicken for today but vowed to herself that she would get some proper food into Sue tomorrow. It was 9.00pm by the time Sue appeared in her pyjamas. She was about to call Nicola when Jean said she had heard Sue's mobile ringing while she was in the bath, so Sue checked her missed calls and saw that Nicola had left a voicemail message.

"Mum, it's me, just calling to see how you are. When you get this message can you ring me back? Love you."

"Hmm, that's a change in attitude from the other day, Jean," said Sue.

"What is?" enquired Jean.

"Well, you know I said Nicola was a bit off the other day when I spoke to her on the phone, her tone was much more of a concerned one and she finished off with a 'love you'."

"I wonder if Mark's told her about 'Devil Woman'," said Jean.

"I don't know, Jean but I think I might be about to find out. Here goes." She keyed in Nicola's number and waited. Nicola answered it after only a couple of rings.

"Hi Mum, how are you today?" she said, rather tentatively.

"To be honest, love, I've been better but Jean's looking after me well. We've been out to Southport today. We thought the fresh air would do us good. What about you and Simon? Have you been busy as usual?"

"Oh, just the normal stuff, you know. Mum, Peter rang me earlier and he says Dad is seeing another woman. Did you know when you spoke to me the other day?"

"Yes I did but I didn't think it was for me to tell you. I thought you should hear it from your Dad but I guess he didn't say anything to you either."

"No, he didn't and I'm sorry I was a bit off with you before. You caught me at a bad time and I didn't have time to digest what you were saying. Look, Mum, you know I love you both loads but I'm pretty mad with Dad right now and I'll be telling him so, when I next get hold of him. I was thinking of coming over next Sunday to see both of you. Will you still be at Jean's?"

"Yes, I will next week but the Sunday after I'll hopefully be in Melbourne."

"Melbourne in Australia?" exclaimed Nicola.

"Yes. My move into the apartment has been delayed so I thought I'd give Jean a breather and visit Veronica and then go on to Sydney to see Steve and Grace. I'm not absolutely sure about Sydney yet as I'm waiting to hear back from Steve to confirm they are okay with it. If they are, then I might stay there for a few weeks and come back at the end of November.

If not, I think I would like to visit the Great Barrier Reef and possibly Alice Springs but I'm not sure yet."

"My god, Mum, you're amazing!"

"Well, I don't know about that but I think putting some space between me and your Dad would be a good thing right now."

"Well, there's space and there's space. Don't you think it might be better to stay around and talk to Dad to try to find out what his motivation for this affair is?"

"No, I don't, and as far as I can see, his motivation is sex and thinking about himself as usual. Anyway, if you're going to be seeing him maybe you can find out why he has seen fit to shatter my life like this. But before you do talk to him again, you should know that I had a brief but very pleasant grope with a Corsican taxi driver while Jean and I were out there. Dad's bound to make a meal of it to try to divert any blame for this sorry mess away from him."

There was silence at the other end of the phone while Sue looked across at Jean who was falling about on the couch in fits. It took every bit of willpower from Sue not to start giggling on the phone but she managed to maintain some decorum as Nicola finally found her voice.

"Well, I'm lost for words and that's not normal. I take my hat off to you. Having said that, I really do think you two can still sort things out. Anyway, I have to go because Si wants to know what's going on. I'll ring you later in the week and I'll arrange something for Sunday. Bye ,Mum."

Nicola rang off and Simon waited to hear what the bombshell was.

"Si, I think my Mum's finally flipped." She related the conversation she had just had with her mother.

Meanwhile, as Sue finished her phone call, she turned to Jean who simply said, "One nil to you I think."

"My sentiments entirely, Jean," replied Sue and they burst into fits of hysterical laughter.

Later, when Sue went to bed, she thought about her conversation with Nicola, and particularly the realisation that Mark must have told Peter and James about his affair. She hoped he had handled it well and that they at least could see past the immediate situation and support them both equally. Her hope was in vain when she spoke to James on the phone the next day. She had rung him to check if it was okay to use her key to go in and use the laptop.

"Of course it is, Mum, I told you to help yourself," replied James. Then, he told her about the events of the night before. All Sue's worst fears were realised and after she had rung off, she began to feel very nauseous all over again.

She found she had a message from Steve and Grace to say they were delighted by her request to visit and they could accommodate her for as long as she wanted. They also asked, as they usually did, if Mark could be persuaded to come with her. She replied that he was very busy and that she would be travelling alone. She gave them the dates and the details then checked her current account just to make sure she had enough in it to cover the air fares and other expenses she would need while away. She transferred some additional money from her savings account just to be sure. The one thing that gave her some comfort was the fact that she didn't have to worry about funds. Sam had seen to that and she thanked him every day for it. Thinking about money reminded Sue that she should contact her financial advisor to let him know she would be going away for a while. She rang him and he confirmed that there was nothing to deal with at the moment so she should go and enjoy herself.

Sue could now concentrate on her next trip. She sent an email off to Valerie confirming dates and times. As she typed the message she began to feel less stressed and her thoughts turned to what she would need to take with her. She decided she would go back to Jean's and check her wardrobe. She hadn't taken everything with her and she knew she would need to go back home to get other things, but she would wait until she had seen what she had to hand at Jean's. On her way home, she called at the florist's to get a really special bunch of flowers for Jean. She was so grateful to her friend, not only for giving her a roof over her head but for saving her life yesterday – literally. She knew she had suffered some kind of emotional crisis and Jean had brought her back from the brink. A bunch of flowers seemed inadequate in the circumstances but it would at least be some recognition of Jean's unswerving loyalty – for now anyway.

She wished everything else in her life could be as easy to sort out but she had the feeling that she was going to need to be much more resourceful and strong in the coming months. Thank god for her friends, wherever they lived, they were all vital to her survival and none of them were ever found wanting. The thought made her cry but not in sorrow. Instead they were tears of thankfulness. She was doing rather a lot of crying lately. She would have to be mindful of the effect it would have on her facial features and she resolved to pay a visit to the spa for a mammoth service.

"That's it!" she exclaimed as she drove back to Jean's.

After she had presented Jean with the flowers, and Jean had finished hugging her, she told her that they were going to spend a day at the spa next Friday courtesy of Samuel Watson Carter!

Chapter 58

Sue spent the next day rummaging through her wardrobe at Jean's, looking over what she had there that she could take with her to Australia. She hadn't had time to put her summer things away since getting back from Corsica so she had quite a lot already. However, there were one or two things she would need to get from home, so she made a list and decided to call there later in the week. She had also left the diamond pendant in the safe at home because she had thought it would be more secure but now she felt that she wanted it close to her.

She made a pile of things to be ironed before being packed and took a jacket to the cleaners. She would travel in that along with some smart trousers and a blouse. She had booked first class flights so she wanted to 'look the part'. As a first class passenger, her baggage allowance was more generous but she knew she would want to buy new things while she was away, so she wasn't going to overdo the packing on her way out. Well, that was the theory anyway.

Jean continued to badger her about her appetite, or lack thereof, so she managed to eat just enough to keep Jean reasonably happy. She noticed, however, that when she got dressed in the morning, her trousers were quite slack on her waist. It was a similar story with T-shirts and cardigans. She went into Boots while out shopping to weigh herself and was surprised to find she had lost almost a stone in weight. When she considered that this had happened in a little over a week, she was even more surprised. She'd better not tell Jean or she would be doubling her rations and although she knew she couldn't continue to lose the weight, the thought of more food was unbearable. She never thought that she would refuse cream cakes and scones. After all, she was the queen of the coffee shops and her love of a good coffee and walnut cake was legendary!

As she walked through the shopping precinct she couldn't help taking glimpses of herself in the windows of the shops, and she had to admit, she liked the more slender version of herself. She had wondered what Mark's woman (she couldn't use her name) was like. She wanted to know but at the same time she didn't. If she turned out to be better looking and have a nice figure, Sue would hate her even more than she already did. As she sat in a café staring at the latte she had just bought, she had to admit, that her self-esteem was at an all time low. Mark had no idea what he had done to her or how his revelation had affected her confidence. What had he disliked about her so much that it made him want someone else? How could he possibly care about her when he was having it off with another woman? Yet that was what he had said the other day. She still cared very much for him even though she said she hated him. It was her defence mechanism coming into play and the anger helped her to cope more easily. However, the other feelings of hurt and rejection and even jealousy, were winning the battle over everything else. But she would show him what he had rejected. She would start at the spa on Friday, then she would just happen to bump into him when she was dressed to go out.

****

The spa day was a real treat for them, especially Jean, who didn't have the money to do it on a regular basis. Sue had pledged, when she retired, that she would visit the spa every couple of months as long as she could afford it. Now she could afford to do it every day if she wanted but she hadn't been for several weeks and that was just to get her nails gelled. Today, they were having the works. They would start with a full-body massage, followed by a relaxing sauna. After showering, they would be treated to special facials, manicures and pedicures and to finish off, a wash and blow-dry with the hairdresser, and full make-up. They began at 9.00am and it was nearly 4.30pm when they finally arrived home.

"I feel absolutely marvellous," said Jean. "That massage was something else. You'd never believe the strength that tiny girl had in her fingers."

"I know, Jean, its great isn't it? My girl said the muscles in my neck and shoulders were like a bag of ball bearings – all hard and knobbly!"

"Well, I'm not a bit surprised at that, Sue, after what's happened to you. But do you feel better for the treatments today?"

"Yes, I think I do. It's always good to pamper yourself every now and then. I think we should get our glad rags on and go to a pub for some tea and a few drinks. What do you say, Jean?"

"That sounds great, Sue, but not too many drinks for you unless you eat your dinner first." Jean said with a grin.

"You sound like my mother. I promise to be a good girl tonight ‚Jean," responded Sue pretending to be a little girl. She went into the kitchen and poured herself a glass of tap water which she drank down in three or four gulps. Jean followed and did likewise. "It's strange how it makes you thirsty when you've been to the spa isn't it?"

"Yes, apparently you get rid of all the toxins in your body and it makes you thirsty so that you'll flush your system out. You'll notice they plied us with water at every opportunity, especially after the sauna."

"Yes, I did, but there wasn't much in the way of food though apart from the plate of cracker things with some low fat spread that they gave us while we had the pedicure."

"No, but that's the whole point, Jean," said Sue shaking her head and laughing at her friend who's appetite never seemed to fade. Sue marvelled at Jean's ability to eat far more than she herself did without gaining any weight.

It didn't take them long to get ready, and at 6.30pm a taxi arrived to take them to a pub on the outskirts of town, The Shepherd. They were taking a chance that it would be quieter at this time and they would get a table without a booking, especially as there were only two of them. They asked the driver if he could pick them up again at about 10.30pm, and after checking his log, he said he would be outside waiting for them.

As they thought, the pub was relatively quiet and the manager showed them to a table in the corner of the dining room that overlooked a small garden at the back. They had both eaten there before so knew the food was usually good. After ordering their meal – no starters but a chicken dish for Sue, and salmon for Jean – Sue asked to see the wine list. After a swift glance through it, Sue asked Jean what she would like to drink.

"You choose, Sue. I don't mind as long as it's not red. I can't seem to cope with that these days."

"Well in that case there's only one thing for it – we'll have a bottle of Prosecco with our meal but how about now?"

"I'll have a vodka and tonic I think," replied Jean.

Sue ordered the wine from the bar and returned with two drinks – a vodka and tonic for Jean and a sherry for herself. Jean remarked that it was unusual to see Sue drinking sherry.

"I just felt like a sherry that's all. I sometimes have one while I'm making the tea at home." She stopped short for a moment, thinking that was something she had complained about – making the tea for Mark – now she wished that she was doing just that.

"Are you okay, Sue?"

"Yes, of course. I was just thinking about something but it doesn't matter."

The waitress appeared with the Prosecco in an ice bucket together with two fluted glasses. She offered it to Sue for tasting but she declined. "It'll be just fine. I haven't had a bad Prosecco yet."

The waitress looked a little disappointed at not being allowed to demonstrate her skills, but she left the ice bucket and glasses on the table and smiled as she walked away. The pub was beginning to get busy now as it was 7.30pm. Jean remarked how glad she was that they had arrived early because she didn't fancy standing about waiting for a table. Sue agreed. Their meals arrived and Jean tucked into hers with relish. The thought of the meal had seemed okay to Sue when she was ordering it, but now, faced with the reality on her plate, her enthusiasm for it waned considerably. However, she made a good effort at tackling it under the ever watchful eye of 'chief of food police' Jean. Sue poured the wine and in between sips, she ate minute quantities of her chicken, chewing it to death before finally swallowing it followed by another sip of wine. Finally, she managed to hide the uneaten chicken beneath a particularly adequately sized lettuce leaf so it looked like she had eaten more than she actually had. Jean seemed satisfied with the end result and the waitress came to clear their plates.

The dining area was now full and there were a number of other people waiting for a table, so Sue suggested, as neither of them wanted a sweet, they have coffee in the bar, where they could remain for the rest of the evening. Jean agreed and after ordering the coffee, then paying for their meal, they managed to find a small table in an alcove in the main bar area. They settled down to enjoy the rest of their evening.

One or two faces in the crowded bar were familiar to both of them and from time to time, someone would see them and waive or call out a 'hello, nice to see you'. Sue went off to fight through the crowd to get to the ladies and asked Jean what she wanted to drink next. "I'll get these, Sue, here's a £10 note."

Sue took it from her and headed off, first of all to the ladies. It took her a while to negotiate the crowds and on her way back she had to wait a few minutes to get served at the bar. She eventually made it back to the table where Jean was sitting looking a bit flushed.

"I think the wine's gone to your head, Jean. You look a bit flushed."

"Do I?" Jean responded but not really looking at Sue. Her eyes were focused on something in the opposite corner behind Sue, who noticed this and turned round. She started to say, "What's so interesting over..." Then she caught sight of Mark and a female sitting at the corner table. He had his arm around her shoulder and she was talking to him and smiling into his eyes at the same time. She immediately turned back and sat on a stool facing Jean. She almost dropped the drinks on the table but managed to avoid a disaster at the last moment.

"I saw them come in just after you went to the loo. They had drinks in their hands and were busy talking so they didn't notice me sitting here. They've been locked in conversation since they sat down and she's been staring into his eyes all the time." Jean said with a look of distaste on her face.

"What are they doing now?" asked Sue.

"Just talking and smiling at each other like two teenagers. Honestly, you'd think he'd have a bit more self-respect than that," Jean spat out. "Do you want to go, Sue?"

"No. Jean, I don't think I do. I've as much right to be here as he has. It's a free country. Anyway, he'll probably notice me if we get up, and at the moment, I have the element of surprise on my side."

"She's not as nice as you, Sue," said Jean after a few seconds silence. "Your hair's much nicer than hers. Did you say she was only fifty-three? Well, all I can say is she's had a hard paper round, Sue. You look much younger than she does."

Sue said nothing. She smiled at her friend. *Wonderful, faithful Jean,* she thought to herself. She knew what Jean was doing and she was grateful for it, but it didn't stop the queasy feeling she had in her stomach or the tightness in her chest. It didn't convince her that in a line-up, most men would pick the 'Devil Woman' over her if looks were what mattered. She took a sip of her wine and then she took another, much bigger one. She asked Jean, "How do I look?"

"You look good, Sue, why?"

Without another word, Sue rose from her seat, turned and walked over to where Mark and Diane were sitting. "Hello Mark," she said with a nonchalance she did not feel. "Have you come for a meal or just a few drinks?" Before he could answer, she continued, "Oh, and this must be Doreen."

"Diane," interrupted a stunned Mark.

"Well, I knew there was a 'D' in it somewhere. We meet at last." She did not offer her hand but gave her a sickly sweet smile. Mark was beginning to panic and finally he found his voice. "Yes, we thought we'd get something to eat here."

"We've already eaten – I'm here with Jean, by the way. I can recommend the 'Chicken a La Creme' Di, but it's very calorific and you know how we over sixties have to watch the cholesterol. You look a bit peaky, Mark. I hope you're getting enough nourishment. You know how irritable you get if you don't have your meals at regular intervals."

The 'Devil Woman' sat in silence and looked decidedly uncomfortable.

"Well, don't let me keep you from your meal. Before I go, Mark, I just thought I'd mention that I'll be calling at the house to collect a couple of things in the morning. I'm going off to Melbourne in a week's time. I don't know when I'll be back. Enjoy your meal won't you **'Babes'**?" She emphasised the last word just for effect and then turned and went back to sit down facing Jean. She took another huge mouthful of wine and said to Jean, "How was that?"

"Don't look now but they're leaving. I have only two things to say to you Mrs B. One is I don't know how you did that and two, I'd say that's two nil to you."

"Thank you, Jean. My sentiments entirely – cheers!"

It was definitely the wine talking as Sue was to realise later. She had another glass after that one and by the time the taxi driver opened the door for them to fall into the back seat, her head was beginning to spin. She managed to get back to Jean's just in time and she was very sick. Jean was not exactly sober either but she had eaten more than Sue and she hadn't had quite as much wine.

Finally, after vomiting several times, Sue went to bed with Jean's help. Jean left a large glass of water and a bucket by her bed and closed the door. For the first time in ages, Sue slept all night but when she woke up at 7.00am the next morning, her head banged and she had a raging thirst. She spotted the water by her bed and drank it down in one. She dragged herself out of bed and went to the loo. She was very dizzy and when she finally managed to focus on her reflection in the bathroom mirror, she groaned at the smudged mascara, red eyes and blotchy face.

My god, what was I thinking of drinking all that wine last night? she thought as she stared at the grotesque vision in the mirror. *I've just undone all the good the spa treatment did me. I have to stop drinking and start looking after my body better. That's it, no more alcohol until I'm on holiday. I need a complete detox this week.*

She went down to the kitchen where she found Jean making some toast. "Hi, do you want some toast and tea?"

"Er, no not just yet but I'll have some water. I'm never going to do that again, Jean. I was so drunk wasn't I?"

"Well, I wasn't exactly sober but I'd say you were much worse than me. I'll tell you what though, Sue, you were magnificent last night when you went over to Mark and 'Devil Woman'. I was proud of you the way you kept your composure. You could tell he was gobsmacked and not just because you said what you did but because you looked fabulous."

"Thanks, friend, but I don't feel fabulous this morning. Look at me. I look like an extra in Thriller."

Jean laughed and said, "You'll be okay after a shower and some breakfast."

"I'm going to have to do something because I'm going up to the house to get some things and I know Mark will be there. I can't let him see me like this."

"I hesitate to say this, Sue, but he might not be at home. He might have stayed the night with her."

Sue didn't want to think about that so she chose not to respond. Instead she drank more water and then went to have a shower. Nearly an hour later, Sue emerged from her bedroom with clean clothes and a little make-up. She had also washed and blow-dried her hair. "If I wear my dark glasses no-one will notice the bags under my eyes will they, Jean?"

"You look remarkably good considering how you were an hour ago. Now, you are having a cup of tea and a piece of toast before you go anywhere. Sit down and I'll do it for you."

Sue groaned inwardly at the thought of food but she said nothing and managed what she felt was nothing short of heroism by eating and keeping down a slice of toast. Before she left, she asked Jean if she needed some shopping.

"We could do with one or two things, so if I make a list will you be able to take me when you get back?"
"No problem, Jean. I shouldn't be long and thanks."

"Thanks for what?" asked Jean.

"Just thanks – for being you, for being here for me. I don't know what I'd have done without you this week."

"Oh get out before I start to cry, and be careful how you drive. You don't want to get stopped and breathalysed."

"I didn't think about that, Jean. I'd better get a taxi up to the house and then hopefully, I'll be okay later."

She waited about fifteen minutes for the taxi she had booked to arrive and then finally she left Jean to wonder how all this sorry saga was going to end. Jean wanted them to sort things out but after seeing Mark last night she wasn't sure it would ever happen. She didn't think that she would be able to forgive Mark if he was her husband, but Sue and Mark had been together for so long. Everyone thought they were the ideal couple even if they didn't do the same things as all their friends. She wanted to give Mark a good shaking and tell him to sort himself out before it was too late. Perhaps it was already too late but she hoped not.

Chapter 59

Mark was in when Sue arrived at the house. He was loading the washing machine with his work clothes and his manner was subdued as he said a quick "Hello." He had noticed the taxi and enquired why Sue wasn't in her car. "Well, I thought it best to leave it behind this morning as I had a few drinks last night and you never know if you're still over the limit the next morning."

"Ah, I see," he said and a smirk came over his face. "So that was the reason for the mouth in overdrive last night then?"

Sue chose to ignore the comment and replied, "We had one or two glasses but I'd say I'm entitled to enjoy myself from time to time don't you?"

He let the subject go and asked why she wasn't moving into the apartment the following week. She told him about the delay and said she thought Jean should be left in piece for a while.

"You don't have to go away to give Jean a rest, you could come back here. It's your home as much as mine and..." before he could finish his sentence, she interrupted, "...and you won't be spending much time here."

"That's not what I meant. What I was going to say was, you could come back here and it might give us a chance to talk things through. I don't want to fight with you, Sue. I meant what I said the other day. I do still care about you a lot even though you don't believe me. Perhaps there is a way to deal with all this mess."

"Mark, the only positive thing you could do is to end your relationship with 'whatsherface' and even then, I don't know if I could forgive you."

"Why can't you call Diane by her name instead of being childish?"

"Because, if I don't use her proper name I can pretend she's not real. However, when I have my sensible head on I know only too well that she is real. I hate her and I hate the fact that you prefer to be with her rather than me. There, I've said it – I'm jealous – happy now?"

She went upstairs to start sifting through her wardrobe for the few items she wanted to take. Mark followed her and sat on the bed while she looked in the wardrobe and retrieved one or two items on hangers. She tried to concentrate on what she was doing but the fact that he was watching her made her start to feel panicky.

"Have you lost weight, Sue?" he finally asked.

"I don't know really," she lied, "why do you ask?"

"You just look like you have, that's all. I noticed it last night – actually, you looked rather nice."

Sue almost let out a laugh but managed to stifle it and instead she said, "Oh, so now I'm nice am I? Well I suppose it's better than being boring."

"Did I say you were boring?"

"Yes, Mark, you did and at the time, you meant it."

"Well, we all say things we don't mean from time to time don't we? Anyway, I think you might have been swearing at me when I said that."

Without warning, he leapt up from the bed, took her in his arms and started to kiss her with a passion she remembered from years ago. She wanted to pull away but she was helpless to do so. It felt wonderful just for a few seconds to be held by the man she had always loved and she could feel his warmth against her body. Then, just as quickly, the moment was gone and she did tear herself away.

She fumbled with her scarf and tried to compose herself while he just looked at her and said nothing. She felt like a shy teenager after a first kiss, not knowing the right things to say or do.

"I have to get on with this because I've arranged to take Jean food shopping after," was all she could manage. He smiled and asked if she wanted a cup of tea, so she accepted just to get him away from her. While he was gone she finished going through the wardrobe and drawers and filled two carrier bags with the things she had gathered. She went to the safe and removed the tatty brown envelope that covered the red box containing the pendant and put that in her handbag. She relocked the safe and went downstairs to the kitchen where Mark was sitting at the table with his brew and the newspaper. There was another cup waiting for her on the table. She took it but didn't sit down. He looked up from his paper and placed it slowly down on the table, all the while looking straight at her. She turned away and went to the window by the kitchen sink to look at the garden. Finally, she plucked up the courage to speak and said, "Why did you do that?"

"Do what?" he responded, knowing full well what she meant but wanting her to say it.

"You know what – kiss me like that – like you wanted to."

"Because I did want to and I'm glad I did."

"Well I'm not glad you did," she said. "You're just playing with my emotions and it's very cruel."

"You didn't seem to mind," he said mildly.

"You are just one arrogant bastard, Mark Barnett. You think you can treat me any way you like. Well, not any more. Have you apologised to Peter and James for what you did the other night?"

"I don't think they'd be interested in anything I had to say just now to be honest, so I'm not going to bother. They'll come round eventually."

Sue wanted to slap that smug face of his but instead she turned round, picked up her bags in the hallway and opened the door to leave. Mark came to hold the door open for her and as she crossed the threshold she called behind her without looking at him, "I wouldn't be too sure of that, Mark. Even your devoted daughter is pissed off with you and it takes a lot for that to happen. Take a long look at yourself and think very carefully what you do next, because from where I'm standing you are going to lose their support and their respect for good."

As she stepped onto the driveway she suddenly remembered that she was not in the car. *Oh hell,* she thought to herself, *what am I going to do now? I can't carry this lot back to Jean's. I'll have to walk to the bus stop and wait for the next bus.*

As if Mark could read her mind, he offered her a lift. She was going to refuse – indeed, she wanted to refuse but she was torn between looking stupid struggling up the drive with her bags or allowing him to make her feel beholden to him. She chose the latter option and begrudgingly accepted his offer.

It only took about ten minutes to reach Jean's but it seemed like an eternity to Sue. She was so angry with him but even more so with herself for letting him get the better of her. He'd said she didn't seem to mind when he kissed her and the annoying thing was he was right. For god's sake she had loved it for a few brief seconds, but now she felt like she'd gone backwards emotionally. It was a good job she was going away where he couldn't distract her.

He got out and passed her the bags. As she took them from him, he said, "If I don't speak to you before you go next Friday, I hope you have a great time. Give my regards to Steve and Grace, and I hope you find whatever it is you're looking for while you're away." He turned and left, waving as he went.

What did he mean by that? she thought. Later she was to ponder what he had said and she knew exactly what he meant. As far as he was concerned, she was running away in order to avoid contact with him because she didn't trust herself to be strong. How bloody annoying it was that he was not a million miles away from the truth.

****

The next morning, Nicola arrived at Jean's as agreed when they had spoken earlier in the week. She hugged her mother and asked how she was. Before Sue could answer, she looked her up and down and said, "You've lost weight. I could feel your ribs. Mum, you've got to see the doctor!"

"Yes, I have lost a little bit of weight, but at my age it's good to carry a bit less around. Anyway, you've no room to talk, you're as thin as a rake."

"That's different, I'm well and you are definitely not."

"Where's Simon today?" asked Sue quickly changing the subject.

"He's gone to see his Mum because it's her birthday. I said that I'd meet him there later so I can't stay too long."

"Have you seen Dad?"

"Yes, as a matter of fact, I saw him yesterday morning when I went to collect a few things from the house." Sue omitted to tell Nicola about the Friday evening episode.

"Did you get much of a chance to talk?" she asked hopefully.

"Not really, love, I was in a hurry, but he seems okay. Anyway, I was wondering if you could meet me at lunchtime one day this week, say Tuesday or Wednesday. I want to get one or two new things to take with me and I don't want to leave it until Thursday because it might be too rushed and I'll need to check my emails and see if there is any mail to deal with before I go away."

"I'll text you in the morning when I get into work. I'm owed some hours so I'll see if I can get either afternoon off and then I could meet you about 12.30pm."

"That sounds good. Then we can have some lunch and a proper catch up."

Jean had left them alone and went to make a coffee which she now brought in on a tray with some biscuits. "Ooh thanks Jean, you're a star," said Nicola, eagerly grabbing a biscuit from the plate. They all chatted for about half an hour about nothing in particular until it was time for Nicola to leave. As she did so, Jean remarked at how full of life she was.

"She tires me out, Jean," said Sue, "she lives life at such a fast pace – like there's no time to waste."

"We used to be like that, Sue, when we were her age. Now, it seems to take me twice as long to do anything. I don't know how I found the time to go to work and I can't imagine how hard it must have been for you with three children to bring up. I didn't have any, but I was still busy all the time."

"Sometimes, Jean, I wonder that myself. Still, I wouldn't change any of them or any of my life to be honest. Well, maybe I'd change one or two little things but not much." She thought about the years she had missed out on holidays and travel but she was going to make up for it starting with her trip to Australia. She was quite excited at the thought of seeing Valerie and where she lived. She had heard that Melbourne was a beautiful city, so she would make the most of her time there.

Later, that evening Peter rang Sue to see how she was. He mentioned that Nicola had called on him and Lynne briefly after she had seen her father. "I think Nic's had a bit of a chat to Dad or rather she did most of the talking judging by the sound of it. Apparently she told him it was time he grew up and thought about what he was doing."

"I bet that went down well," replied Sue, feeling a little bit sorry for Mark being on the receiving end of one of her daughter's tongue-lashings. Also though, Sue was anxious because she didn't want any of the children to fall out with their father, but she knew that was asking a lot under the circumstances.

"Knowing Dad, I think he'll be feeling sorry for himself now and looking for someone else to blame. Honestly Mum, I could strangle him and that goes for James as well. Why couldn't he just be honest with us and let us think about it rather than being sly and evasive. He's going to have to be the one to apologise to us if he wants to regain any respect we had for him."

"Look, Peter, I know only too well how hurt you must be feeling right now and although I appreciate your support very much, it doesn't help me knowing that you are all at loggerheads. What's happened is for me and your Dad to sort out and no-one else. If I'm worried about you all while I'm away I won't enjoy anything, so please, for me, try to build some bridges with him. I'm not expecting you to be all pally with 'whatshername' – God forbid – but at least try to get on with Dad."

"I'm surprised to hear you saying that, Mum, but I guess you're right. For your sake only I promise to ring him soon. How's that?"

"That will do for me Peter and thanks. Please tell James what I've said as well. I'll speak to you later in the week before I go away."

James rang later in the evening and the conversation went in much the same way as the one with Peter. When she had finished her call, she was satisfied that she had done as much as she could to try to mediate. She hoped it would be enough.

Sue and Nicola met in Manchester on the following Tuesday at lunch time. Nicola had rung on Monday as agreed to confirm that she had managed to get Tuesday afternoon off work so they would have plenty of time to talk and shop. It was very unlike Nicola to be cross with her father because they were very close. Sue could see how badly affected Nicola was by all the upset although Nicola tried to play it down. Sue knew that when Nicola was anxious about anything, she developed a rash on her face and neck, and sitting opposite her at the table in the restaurant, she could detect the tell tale signs beginning to show. She didn't mention it because she knew that it wouldn't help but she did her best to reassure Nicola that her Dad needed her support just as much as always, but that at the moment, he was finding it difficult to find the right words. Nicola wasn't convinced but said she would keep in touch with him while Sue was away.

After lunch they toured the boutiques and in addition to buying herself one or two items of clothing that were a better fit than most of her other things, Sue treated Nicola to a new dress. All in all the expedition was a success and they hugged before Sue went to get the bus back home.

She might have plenty of money these days, but she still preferred to get the bus, and although she felt a little guilty using her free bus pass to Manchester rather than negotiating the city traffic looking for parking, Jean had said she should still continue to use it as she had worked all her life for it and was entitled to it.

Sue still couldn't get used to the idea that she was very wealthy because she still considered herself to be like any other ordinary woman in her early sixties despite everything that had happened to her. As she travelled home on the bus, Sue once again reflected on the events of the past six months, since she received the letter from James Fearnley advising her of Sam's death and asking her to collect 'a small item of jewellery' that Sam had bequeathed to her. Had that been the catalyst for the events that followed? She didn't know for sure but she strongly suspected it had played its part. Perhaps it had done her a favour by bringing the real problems in her marriage out into the open. But then she wondered if in fact she had brought out the real problems or their true cause. She tried to think of the time when she first thought that something was wrong with her marriage and she couldn't pinpoint it.

She guessed that her relationship with Mark was suffering long before she had gone to Lake Louise and met Sam but that she hadn't acknowledged it. She thought of all the things she might have done to cause Mark to find solace in another woman. Had she retired too soon? Had she been too willing to retreat into a predictable pattern of life that meant she was dull and uninteresting to Mark? Was she really boring? It was true that her illness had turned both of their worlds upside down but she hadn't considered how it had affected Mark because they hadn't talked about it.

That was it! she thought, *Sam had said something about talking in one of his letters to me. What was it? '...always keep talking because if the talking stops, so does the understanding and that leads to bad feeling and unnecessary conflict'.*

It was something of an eureka moment for Sue, although when she thought about it there was no great mystery in it. It was obvious really. She vowed that when she came back from Australia she would definitely sit down with Mark and clear the air. At least then they could both move on with their lives in whatever way they chose couldn't they? Then, she wondered if she actually wanted to move on and what it was she was afraid of. Whatever it was, she knew that she was running away from it by going to the other side of the world, just for now anyway.

Chapter 60

It was Thursday evening – the night before Sue was about to leave for Australia. She had been into town with Jean during the day and picked up her Australian dollars at the travel agents. Although she had transferred enough money from her savings account to her current account to last her for some time, she wanted to take a small amount of cash with her for her first couple of days in Melbourne.

They had also done some food shopping at the supermarket for Jean. As Jean didn't drive, Sue wanted to make sure she had taken her for a big shop before she left. While they were in town, they had lunch in Marks and Spencer. Sue told Jean it would save her the bother of doing tea when they got home, but the real reason was because she didn't want Jean to make her loads to eat. She felt so guilty leaving food on her plate when Jean had gone to the trouble of preparing it for her. Besides, Jean would only give her another one of her lectures and she wasn't strong enough to deal with it right now. She was apprehensive about her trip away, mainly because she wouldn't be able to be there for her family if anything went wrong. She didn't know if any of her children had tried to talk to their father and she was worried that things might boil over while she was away.

Nicola was the first to ring her to wish her a good trip and to tell her that she had spoken to Mark and he was going over to Manchester at the weekend to see her and Simon, "Without that woman!" she had added. They talked for a few minutes then said their goodbyes. Sue promised to email or text Nicola once she had arrived at Valerie's. Mark and James called together later in the evening, and to Jean's surprise, they brought her a bunch of flowers to say thank you for looking after Sue for the past couple of weeks. Sue was proud of them for being so thoughtful and she gave them both a big hug when Jean went into the kitchen to put the flowers in water.

While Jean was out of the room James opened up the conversation. "Mum, Pete and I have spoken to Dad and we're meeting him tomorrow night for a pint in the pub. He was a bit subdued when I spoke to him but he seemed genuinely keen to meet up and he said he would be on his own. I think he's got the message that we're not ready for being friendly with his woman just yet."

"Thanks, both of you. That makes me feel a whole lot better. I can go away without worrying too much about how things are."

"Don't get too excited – it's only a pint," added Peter.

"Well, it's a start and it's one less thing for me to stress about."

"What's to stress about?" said James, "You're going on a fabulous holiday in the sun while we are here putting up with all that England throws at us at this time of year. Just enjoy it and let us know how you are getting on."

They stayed for about half an hour then said their goodbyes, promising to make sure Jean was okay while Sue was away.

"They're good lads, Sue." remarked Jean after they had gone. "They make me wish all the more that I had children of my own but it never happened with me and Nigel. Never mind, I feel like they are partly mine when they come round and bring me lovely flowers."

"Thanks, Jean. Yes, they are good lads and I know I'm very lucky. Changing the subject, Jean, tomorrow, let's have a good walk – weather permitting – and then I'll have a shower and get changed ready to be picked up at 5.00pm. I think I'll need the walk to prepare for the long journey sitting in planes. It plays havoc with my back. It's a good job I can afford to go first class – at least I can stretch out a bit more."

****

The weather was kind the following day, so after having a light breakfast, Sue and Jean set off to walk down the lane and along the river bank, then through the woods back to where Jean lived. They chatted as they walked like they always did and before they knew it they were on the home stretch and ready for a drink. Jean tried to persuade Sue to eat something but all she could manage was a small bowl of soup and half a sandwich. Jean supposed it was better than nothing but she couldn't help worrying that Sue would need plenty of sustenance before her journey. She really was looking thinner and Jean felt that if Sue didn't keep a check on that she was in danger of getting too thin.

The car arrived to take her to the airport at 4.55pm precisely. The driver was a very smart man in his sixties. He said his name was Harry. As Sue hugged Jean on the doorstep, Jean whispered in her ear, "That's a good start, Sue." She pulled away and nodded in Harry's direction, then winked at her friend.

"Jean, you're incorrigible," replied Sue and laughed as Harry held open the rear door for her.

"Would you mind if I sat beside you in the front, Harry?" Sue asked the surprised driver.

"Not at all, Madam, if that's what you would prefer."

"It is and you can call me Sue," she added.

He looked at her in horror and said, "I couldn't do that, Madame. It's more than my job's worth."

"Well try just this once – I won't tell if you don't," she replied. He smiled and handed her the seat belt. As they drove off, Sue turned round in her seat and waved back at her friend standing on the doorstep. Once again, she thanked her lucky stars for a friend like Jean – always there, always constant. If only everything else in life was so reliable.

She chatted to Harry all the way to the airport and he seemed to like that. Sue guessed it was probably a change from his normal clientele, who were doubtless well-heeled and thought themselves a cut above talking to the chauffeur. Then, she remembered that she was among the category of the well-heeled and she laughed at herself. When they arrived at the airport, Harry put Sue's cases onto a trolley and escorted her to the Emirates first class passenger check-in desk. The man at the desk was very smartly dressed and processed her check-in with the utmost efficiency and courtesy. Harry said his goodbyes and wished her an enjoyable trip, then left with a touch of his peaked cap.

"Thank you, Harry," she said, smiling at him and handing him a small envelope containing a generous tip. He touched his cap again and said, "Thank you, Madam, it's been a pleasure."

The desk clerk led her to the entrance for departures and handed her a pass for the first class lounge together with her boarding card and passport. After going through the security check, she was free to make her way to the first class lounge. She had done this before so she was familiar with all its trappings and was looking forward to depositing her hand luggage at the reception desk and relaxing until her flight was called in another two hours.

She passed the time, strolling through the duty-free shopping area, reading her electronic book, and drinking the occasional coffee. She had decided not to have any alcohol preferring to save herself for the long flight to Dubai. There would be plenty of time for a bucks fizz or a glass of wine on the plane.

At about 8.30pm she heard her flight being called, so she went to the reception desk to retrieve her hand luggage. The very smart lady sitting at the desk advised her that there was no need for her to go to the gate yet because it was too soon and she would tell her when she needed to make her way there. After another two calls for passengers on Sue's flight, the lady from the reception desk came over to her and gave her the hand luggage telling her she could now go to the gate. She had just arrived there when first class passengers were invited to board the plane.

She had a window seat – seat 2A in first class. It was one of the new Airbus A380 planes and it was luxury personified. A female flight attendant was on hand to ensure she was seated and had her luggage stowed away and to offer her a glass of something fizzy to welcome her on board. With glass of champagne in hand, Sue toasted Sam and prepared herself for the first leg of her journey.

Chapter 61

Dubai airport at 6.30am was no less busy than any other time. There seemed to be people lying on the floor on mats everywhere Sue looked. She went through immigration and then made her way to the Executive lounge. After freshening up in the marbled ladies room, she left her hand luggage with the reception while she went to explore the airport shops. All manner of gold items were on sale at the most ridiculous prices. Watches costing thousands of pounds were on display in heavily guarded glass cases. Silk scarves and designer leather goods were equally impressive and although Sue knew she could afford to buy, she just enjoyed looking.

The two hours stopover soon went and she was called to her gate for the next leg of her journey to Melbourne – another fourteen hours or so. It would be early morning Sunday, Melbourne time when Sue arrived. That would be late Saturday evening at home. She changed the time on her watch once she was seated so that she would be prepared once she got to Melbourne. She hoped it wouldn't be too early for Valerie to meet her.

The first three or four hours seemed to drag, but when she checked her watch and saw from the in-flight information that there were only two more hours to go, she was quite surprised. She had slept in fits and starts, even though she had a flat bed seat that allowed her to stretch out completely and a privacy screen that could be put up or down as required. There was also a minibar and of course the seemingly endless meals and refreshments. The cabin crew were the epitome of efficiency and courtesy and nothing was too much trouble for them. Sue could even take a shower before the plane landed if she wanted to but she was happy with a quick freshen up.

Finally, the plane landed at Melbourne (Tullamarine) Airport at 6.40am on Sunday. It took nearly an hour for Sue to get through Immigration Control and then collect her baggage from the carousel. Valerie was waiting for her in the arrivals lounge. It was the first time Sue had seen Valerie since they had met on the train in Canada almost a year and a half ago, but Sue recognised her immediately. She was looking very well and beamed as soon as she spotted Sue coming towards her.

The airport was so busy that Sue was relieved to have someone who knew their way around to meet her. They exchanged hugs and congratulated each other that they looked so well, but Valerie asked Sue if she had been on a diet as she looked much thinner than she had remembered. Sue replied that she had eaten a bit less (the understatement of the year) and that she had been busy in the garden, both of which were true of course.

On the drive to Valerie's home, which was in a suburb north east of Melbourne called Eastlea, they caught up a little on what each other had been doing. Sue avoided too much discussion about family and stuck to more general things. The drive lasted about forty minutes and as the car pulled up the leafy suburban lane Valerie's bungalow came into view. It was situated in an area favoured by artists and called the gateway to the Yarra Valley. Valerie said her back fence bordered the Yarra Reserve and only a short walk away was the Yarra River which runs through Melbourne.

The front door opened into a central hallway from which there were several doors leading to the kitchen, three bedrooms all with en-suite facilities, a study and a spacious lounge. There was also a central courtyard separated from the lounge by huge sliding doors which gave the living area a greater sense of spaciousness and a lightness that radiated throughout the rest of the bungalow. Numerous solar panels provided Valerie with all the power she needed to heat the water which came from a huge tank in the garden and to run the house and so she didn't have to pay electricity bills. In addition, the whole place was double-glazed with large windows and French doors and was environmentally friendly. Valerie's late husband had designed the initial layout and a local architect had completed the drawings.

The town of Eastlea was known locally as the mud brick capital because most of the houses were made of mud bricks, but Valerie's was made from rammed earth which she thought had cleaner lines. Sue could tell from Valerie's in depth description of the property that she was very proud of it and rightly so, for it was a beautiful home. Sue thought about her own home and how she had loved it once, but now it didn't have the same appeal somehow. The heart and soul had gone from it as far as she was concerned.

"If you like walking, Sue," said Valerie, interrupting her reverie, "there will be plenty of that to do. Also as I said earlier, this area was much favoured by artists and still is. They established an art colony called Monsalvat which is quite near here so we can visit that as well. We'll go into Melbourne and see some of the sights there if you want to. We could always see what's on at the theatres and have an evening there or even stay overnight if you wish. How long are you planning on staying?"

"It's flexible Valerie but it really depends on how long you can put up with me. From here I intend to go to see my good friends in Sydney and they are on standby so to speak. However, I thought maybe a week or ten days? I have an open ticket from here to Sydney which lasts for about a month."

"That's fine then because you can stay as long as you like. It will be lovely to show you my favourite places and spend some time talking and walking with you. Oh, I almost forgot, I haven't introduced you to my house mate – Bella."

Bella turned out to be Valerie's six-year-old golden retriever who came bounding into the lounge from the courtyard where Valerie had left her earlier in the morning. She took a shine to Sue straight away and proceeded to lick her enthusiastically. "I hope you like dogs ,Sue, because that's my only stipulation about house guests – they have to love Bella."

"Yes, I do like dogs, Valerie, and I'm sure she and I will get on famously." Bella wagged her beautifully groomed tail in agreement.

After having a cup of tea and a biscuit (that was all Sue told Valerie she wanted at the moment), Sue unpacked her cases and sent a text message to Peter, James, Nicola, and Jean to tell them she had arrived safely. She told them that the weather was dry and sunny and the temperature was in the early twenties. *That will make them envious,* she thought to herself and she added to the kids that she would ask Valerie if she could use her email address to send them the occasional email. That done, she settled down to the task of enjoying her time with Valerie and trying to forget for now what lay ahead of her when she returned home.

Sue was suffering a little from jet lag, so for the rest of the day and the next two days they stayed within the area of Eastlea. Sue relaxed in the courtyard and slept in between walks on the nearby reserve. Bella and she became firm friends, and Valerie, sensing that there was something preoccupying her friend which she obviously needed to think a lot about, gave her plenty of space. She had noticed that she wasn't eating a great deal and wondered if Sue didn't like the food she was preparing or if she was unwell. She decided that a change of scenery might help.

After three days, when they were finishing their evening meal outside in the courtyard, Valerie asked Sue if she would like to take a trip into Melbourne, see some sights, go to a show and stay overnight or even two.

"What about Bella?" asked Sue, "who will look after her?"

"When I go on holiday, Bella stays with a friend of mine, Marjorie. I'll ring her to check that she can accommodate her. I'm sure she'll be able to have her." Valerie suggested that they go by train as it would be much less stressful for her than driving. Sue agreed and Valerie said she would make the arrangements in the morning so that they could go on Friday and come back Sunday. The arrangements were duly made and Marjorie confirmed she could look after Bella the next day and after discussing the cost, which Valerie sorted out up front Sue gave her half towards the train fare and the accommodation.

They were going to stay in a very comfortable hotel in the city centre close to Flinders Street Station.

They went into Eastlea to have a look around and get some last minute toiletries to take with them on their trip. They were sitting outside a small café opposite the library drinking a coffee. They were discussing their meeting on the Rocky Mountaineer train and Sue found herself telling Valerie about writing to Sam and then his subsequent death. She told her about the pendant because she knew that she would probably wear it and Valerie would be bound to ask her about it. She didn't however tell her any more as she thought it was unnecessary to do so.

Valerie then asked her if she was worried about something as she had noticed that Sue seemed rather preoccupied at times and didn't seem to have a huge appetite. After a few moments of thought, Sue mentioned that she and Mark were having one or two problems and she had taken the opportunity of getting away to think things over. Not wanting to pry, Valerie said that explained a lot and she offered an ear to listen if Sue felt she wanted to expand but added that she would respect her privacy if she preferred not to say anything.

"Let's just say that I needed to put some space between us for a while, Valerie, and it seemed a good opportunity to come and visit you and our friends in Sydney. I do apologise if I have been a bit quiet but I don't want you to think there is anything wrong with staying here with you – quite the contrary. The peace here is very therapeutic and it's giving me the opportunity to think about things in a more logical way. I'm not coping with eating much at the moment I know, but that's what happens to me when I have things on my mind. It's nothing to do with your lovely food – it's just the way I am right now. Enough said I think, and now, have we got everything we need for Melbourne? I'm really looking forward to it."

She put on a brave face but Valerie knew that it was just that. They finished their coffee and after browsing round the shops in Eastlea they made their way back home to pack for the following day.

Chapter 62

Sue awoke to a warm sunny morning. She looked out of her bedroom window onto the garden at the rear of Valerie's bungalow. The variety of birds that visited Valerie's garden was amazing. This morning she could see a pair of sugar gliders on one of the many tables and perches Valerie's late husband had erected in the garden. She watched them for a few minutes before putting on her slippers and joining Valerie who was already making some breakfast in the kitchen.

"Did you sleep well, Sue?" she enquired. "You looked very tired last night."

"Yes, thanks Valerie, I did as a matter of fact. It's so peaceful here, except for the odd bird that decides to give its voice an airing in the early hours." She looked at Valerie and smiled. "You are lucky you know living in a place like this. Eastlea is so lovely and the people are very friendly."

"You're right, Sue. I am lucky and I know it. I travel all over the world and see some fabulous places but you know I can't wait to get back here to my lovely home and I still get the same thrill as I did the day we moved in."

Sue's mind wandered to thoughts of her own home, although she found it hard to call it home any more after all that had happened. She wished she could wipe out the events of the last few months and carry on as normal. But then she knew that what had been 'normal' wasn't what she wanted because now she knew it was broken all the time. She had buried her head in the sand and hoped it would go away but instead everything had come to a head three weeks ago and there was no going back to what had been. She must have looked sad because Valerie asked her if she was feeling all right. She assured her that she was and that she was just thinking about the family and wondering how they were.

"Why don't you send an email before we go this morning? Then when we get back you might have some news from them."

"Yes, I think I will if you don't mind."

"Not at all dear, you know you can use the laptop whenever you want. I'll get us some breakfast while you do that. Would you like some tea or coffee now?"

"A cup of tea would be great, thanks."

Sue finished her emails to Peter, James, and Nicola, asking all of them to check on Jean and pass on her love. She also asked each of them if they had seen their father. She wasn't sure she wanted to know the answers to that question but she wanted to remind them to try to stay in touch with him.

After breakfast of a boiled egg and toast for Sue and muesli and toast for Valerie, they showered and got ready to get a mid-morning train from Eastlea station. Valerie had booked a taxi to take them to the station and she had left a note for Marjorie when she came to collect Bella – she had said that she would collect her nearer lunchtime after she had done her shopping. The taxi arrived and they set off for their short break in the city.

They arrived at Flinders Street Station shortly before lunch. They got into a taxi to take them the short distance to their hotel – The Victoria – aptly named with its Victorian era façade on a tree-lined boulevard. Above it, Sue could see the skyscrapers of the Central Business District, looking down on areas of landscaped gardens. Sue was struck by the charm of it despite the fact that the guide book she had been glancing at during the train journey had stated that Melbourne was Australia's second largest city.

They checked into their single rooms that were next door to each other on the 4th floor overlooking a walled garden area at the rear of the hotel. The window of Sue's room was open slightly and a light breeze gently moved the tassel on the window blind. She carried out her usual inspection of the bathroom and the wardrobe space, which, in her opinion could be very tiny in a single room, but in this case there was ample storage, especially as she had only brought a few clothes with her. She had decided that if she needed anything else she would just go out and buy it. This was becoming something of a habit she thought, but argued with herself that she deserved it after all she had been through.

She looked at her image in the full-length mirror on the wardrobe door. She had lost quite a bit of weight and her jowls were looking a bit saggy. Her bra was a bit too big for her in the cup and she could fit her hand comfortably in the waistband of the trousers that she had only bought a week or so ago. It was good to know she didn't look podgy but she had to admit that she was in danger of looking gaunt. She was eating a bit more, but the weight still seemed to be dropping off her by the day. She could visualise Jean's face and hear her scolding her for not looking after herself properly and she smiled at the thought. At least Jean cared about her enough to take notice. But that was unfair and she knew it. Her children were all concerned about her and they cared about her a great deal. The only person who didn't seem to be bothered was the one she needed to care the most – Mark. She wondered what he was doing right now. He would be in bed still, as it would be early morning in England. She started to wonder whether he was in bed alone and then quickly shook her head as if to banish all such thoughts. She started to unpack and then she knocked on Valerie's door to see if she was ready to go out.

Half an hour later they were making their way to Parliament Gardens and the surrounding area. The gardens were magnificently manicured and they spent some time, just walking and admiring the many plants and flowers on display. They crossed Lansdowne Street to the Fitzroy Gardens and Sue took some snaps of Captain Cook's Cottage. They stopped at a small café in the gardens and had tea and cakes in the late afternoon sunshine before making their way back to their hotel to prepare for the evening. Valerie had booked seats at Her Majesty's Theatre to see Billy Elliot. The performance started at 7.45pm so they had decided to eat a light meal in the hotel before grabbing a taxi to the theatre.

Sue enjoyed Billy Elliot tremendously and she found herself humming one of the songs on their way back. They stopped in the hotel bar for a nightcap and to listen to the female singer who was accompanied by a young, rather good looking pianist. Just for a while, Sue's thoughts were concentrated on the music which was a mixture of old and new pop music, so she sang along to them and laughed and chatted with Valerie. She was wearing the pendant and Valerie remarked that it seemed to attract attention from a number of quarters.

"Don't look now," she said quietly, "but you seem to be the topic of conversation among two couples over at the bar. I can lip read and they are discussing your pendant and saying how beautiful it is. One of the men told his wife that it went fabulously with the red dress you're wearing. I'm not sure she wanted to hear that bit because she's just given him a little tap on the knee."

Sue blushed instinctively and she and Valerie laughed wickedly.

"I must say, Sue," Valerie continued, "it's a real eye-catcher but it's not just the pendant that the men are admiring.

Take my word for it Sue, red is definitely a good colour for you, especially with a nice tan."

Just at that moment, another man who had been sitting on his own at a small table in the corner came over to Sue to ask her to dance. She was absolutely taken by surprise and when she told him she had two left feet, he laughed and said so did he so they would go together really well. Valerie urged her to get up and as she did, the man glanced over to the pianist and nodded. He started to play 'Lady in Red' as the man introduced himself as Geoff, took hold of her hand and put his other hand around her waist. Sue replied rather feebly that her name was Sue and stuttered for the first one or two steps until she found a little bit of rhythm.

About halfway through the song which was being sung perfectly by the pianist, Sue noticed that she and Geoff were the only two people dancing, while everyone in the bar stood on the edge of the dance floor and watched. Sue could feel the panic rising in her stomach but Geoff continued to guide her footsteps slowly but carefully around the floor. He told her she had lied to him when she said she had two left feet, because he thought she danced beautifully. She knew that was a lie because the only dancing she had done was in the hall at secondary school on wet afternoons when they would normally be out on the games field. She remembered how the boys would sit on one side and the girls on the other and Miss Simpson and Mr Briggs would demonstrate the dashing white sergeant while one of the prefects would be in charge of the record player. The girls although shy, would try to get to dance with the nicest boys but sometimes the teachers paired them off at random. Once she got paired up with Nigel Tattersall who was probably the ugliest boy in their year, if not the entire school. He had dark greasy hair and smelled of stale biscuits and his nose was always running. He would sniff continually and then wipe his nose on his sleeve. She inwardly shuddered at the memory but then Geoff asked her where she was from.

She replied that she was from the north of England and was visiting her friend.

"Oh, so you're travelling alone?" he asked and seemed even more interested. She told him she was, but that she was only in Melbourne for a couple of days then moving on to Sydney to see more friends there. She felt a little uneasy and wanted to let him know that she was very busy. The music finally stopped and the onlookers applauded them. Geoff thanked her and kissed the back of Sue's hand. She recoiled instinctively but then tried to recover her composure in order not to offend him. She smiled the best fake smile she could muster and started to make her way back to where Valerie was waiting. He seemed to hang about but Sue excused herself and said she was going to the ladies. She hurried away and once in the ladies, she sat on a buffet in front of the mirror to regain some composure. She applied a little more lipstick, washed her hands, and left.

Just outside the ladies door, she ran straight into Geoff, literally. The collision forced her to drop her handbag and as she bent to pick it up so did he. For a split second their faces were nearly touching and he put his free hand on her shoulder. They said nothing but then he hurriedly apologised. He said he was going up to the men's room and he had got the doors mixed up. Sue was anxious to get away from him so she waved her hand dismissively and turned away to go back to the bar. There was definitely something creepy about him and she sat down opposite a wide-eyed Valerie to have a swig of her drink. She put down her glass and waited for the inevitable comments from Valerie, but the only thing she heard was a gasp from her friend who said, "Your pendant, Sue, it's not round your neck!"

The world stopped in that moment, suspended in time. She instinctively put her hand to her throat and felt for the pendant that was not there. Immediately she knew it had been stolen and she knew who was responsible. She found her voice and shrieked "It's him – Geoff – the dancer!"

Mayhem ensued, with Valerie calling for the Manager to come immediately. Sue was looking on the floor and around the table in the vain hope that the pendant would be found, but of course, it wasn't.

A passing waiter came over to Sue to see what the problem was and he was quickly joined by several others. Finally, the duty manager arrived and calmly asked Sue and Valerie to accompany him to his office. As they followed the manager out of the bar, the other hotel guests who only moments earlier had been admiring Sue and her partner on the dance floor, looked on anxiously and started talking in groups about what was going on, shaking their heads and discussing the man they had seen with Sue.

The manager, Mr Fredericks, a middle-aged man with thinning dark hair and glasses, ushered them to seats in his well furnished office. "Ladies, please accept my apologies for this terrible incident. I can assure you that we are searching for the person who you believe has stolen your necklace, though I find it hard to believe that one of our guests could be responsible."

Sue broke in, "He must be a guest because he was sitting at a table in the bar prior to asking me to dance with him. I knew he was dodgy. There was something about him that I didn't like. He was too, well, familiar if you know what I mean. I can't believe I have been stupid enough to let this happen." She began to cry and Valerie took her hand to comfort her.

Mr Fredericks continued. "The police have been called and they will be here very soon. Meanwhile we are searching everywhere in the hotel for this man. Have no fear we will get your necklace back, Madame."

"He's bound to have left by now," wailed Sue. "That pendant means such a lot to me, you can never know just how much. I've only had it a few months and now it's gone."

Just then there was a knock at the door and in walked two men dressed in casual clothes. One looked a good deal older than the other. They approached the manager who seemed to know them and the older man whispered in his ear. He smiled broadly and turned to Sue. "Madame, please let me introduce you to Detectives Walker and James. I have some good news for you. The man has been apprehended and your necklace has been recovered."

The older of the two men introduced himself as Detective Sergeant Walker and removed a handkerchief containing the pendant from his pocket. Sue eagerly held out her hands to take it but he simply asked if it was hers and held it away from her. She confirmed that it was and then he explained that it was evidence and would need to be 'processed' before he could return it to her.

"How long will that take?" asked Sue.

"You'll have it back tomorrow after it's been photographed and you have given us a statement telling us exactly what happened here tonight."

Sue seemed content with that but then she asked, "How did you manage to pick him up so quickly? I would have thought he'd be long gone."

"Well, I should explain that Detective James here and myself have been working undercover and watching this guy for a few days. Mr Fredericks knew we were here keeping an eye on him. He's been a suspect in earlier thefts but we never seemed to get enough proof so we bailed him and kept watch. He checked into the hotel earlier today and we knew then that he was on the lookout for some unsuspecting guest to steal from. We were watching him on cameras in another office and we saw him bump into you outside the toilets. We followed him and after a few minutes, he led us to an accomplice waiting in a car down the street. We saw him take the necklace out of his pocket and arrested him and his mate there and then. We had a unit parked on the opposite side of the street because we knew he would try something sooner or later. He didn't disappoint us."

Sue and Valerie looked at each other in amazement. Neither of them had come to Melbourne imagining something like this happening. They both agreed to go to the police station at 10.00am the following morning to provide statements and to collect Sue's pendant. The manager apologised for the umpteenth time and said he would ask Room Service to deliver them a nightcap of their choice. They both gratefully accepted brandies and with that they got up from their seats to make their way back to their rooms. As they approached the manager's door, Valerie offered to sit with Sue in her room for a while and as she accepted, the manager stepped in between them.

"Ladies, in the circumstances I would like to offer you one of our suites on the top floor as a token of our appreciation of your understanding and to somehow compensate you for the ordeal you have had. If you wish to accept, then I'll have the housekeeping staff come to your rooms to help you remove your belongings."

They looked at each other for a moment and simultaneously accepted the manager's offer. It only took an hour before they were comfortably lounging on the luxurious sofas and sipping their brandies in one of the hotel's finest suites. Valerie looked across at Sue and said, "Are you okay, Sue? You've had an awful shock and I feel really bad that this has happened while you're my guest in my country."

"Don't worry about me, Valerie. I come from the north of England and they breed us tough there," she joked. But she was feeling a lot shakier than she would admit and Valerie knew it. She looked Sue square in the face and that was enough for her mask to slip and she began to cry. Valerie comforted her and after a couple of minutes Sue wiped her eyes and started to talk.

"Why does everything good have to be spoiled, Valerie?" she asked.

"What do you mean, dear? What's been spoiled?"

"The pendant. It was meant to be enjoyed and now this has happened I won't feel able to wear it with confidence any more because I'll be worried all the time that it's going to be stolen. The other thing is it has taught me a lesson. I was vain enough to think that someone was taking an interest in me but his only reason for asking me to dance was so that he could steal my pendant. I feel really foolish."

"I don't think you should feel that way, Sue," said Valerie. "You really did look lovely tonight and not just because of the pendant but because you are lovely. I'm sure your husband would agree with me there."

"That's another thing, Valerie. One of the reasons I've come away on holiday is because I've left Mark. He has been seeing another woman after forty-four years of marriage. He's only ever been the one for me and although we'd been having a bit of a torrid time lately, my marriage was precious to me and that's spoiled now as well. I don't think I can ever put this behind me, so you see I feel like everything that should be good isn't as good as I thought it was. I'm losing my grip on the things that matter most to me."

"Sue, I'm so sorry to hear about your marriage but you have to have faith that things will work out if you really want them to. You are right and forty-four years is an awful long time to be with the same person and you can't just dismiss it without a lot of very serious thought. Mark is still around and while he is you can talk to him but you have to want to do it. I don't have that luxury because Neville, my husband was taken away from me. He was all I had because we have no children, and for a time I thought that my life was over. I almost gave up but then I realised that I was still relatively young and although my perfect life had gone, there was a different one waiting for me but I had to want to take it and adapt. There isn't a day goes by when I don't think of Neville, and god knows I wish I still had him with me but I've learned to change, and now I feel happy and fulfilled with my life.

Just because some stupid man coveted your pendant enough to steal it from you, doesn't make it any less of a treasure to be enjoyed. Tomorrow you will have it back and you will enjoy wearing it again as Sam intended you to do. Your husband has done a stupid and hurtful thing and although you are struggling right now to cope with it you will get over the hurt. If your marriage means as much to you as you say it does, you will fight tooth and nail to save it. It isn't going to be the same as it was before but maybe it will be better because hopefully after you have talked it through with Mark, if he feels the same, you will have a better understanding of what each of you wants and needs. It seems to me that neither you nor Mark has talked and that's caused misunderstandings to occur. It's what doesn't get said that causes the trouble.

Now, I want you to enjoy the rest of your stay in Melbourne with me and after visiting your friends in Sydney, go home with a positive attitude and speak to Mark as soon as you can."

"I know you're right, Valerie. 'Tomorrow is another day' was a favourite saying of my Dad's and I won't give up without a fight. I just hope that Mark feels the same way. He knows that I won't consider any kind of reconciliation unless he ditches her. My friend Jean and I refer to her as 'Devil Woman'. You must think I'm very juvenile but it's the only way I can deal with the situation."

"No, Sue, I don't think that at all. What I do think is that you are very bruised and vulnerable at the moment and rightly so. You must feel like you are less of a woman because your husband has chosen someone else to be with. I can see it in your demeanour. It explains your poor appetite and the fact that you must be at least a couple of stones lighter than when I met you last year on the train in Canada. Your body is punishing itself and your head is telling you that you need to compete with this woman in some way. Is she younger than you?"

Sue nodded and Valerie continued. "I thought so. It's usually the case – a younger model but that doesn't mean she's a better person than you or that Mark doesn't still need you."

"I don't want him to need me, Valerie – I want him to desire me."

"In that case, Sue, you need to stop doing some of the things that you think he needs and start doing more of the things that make him enjoy being with you. Ditch the housework in favour of an evening in the pub. Be his best friend rather than his mother. You never know, you might even enjoy yourself."

They continued to talk for a while until Sue noticed it was nearly 2.00am. They said goodnight and Sue fell into her bed without bothering to remove her make-up – something she never did. She slept for several hours and eventually woke at 7.45am feeling rather better than she had for a few weeks.

After having breakfast in their suite (Valerie had ordered it when she awoke at 6.35am), they showered, dressed, and made their way to the police station to give their statements and retrieve the pendant. Valerie had suggested they get this out of the way as soon as possible so that they could enjoy the rest of the day.

Detective Sergeant Walker was waiting for them and asked Sue if she could identify "Geoff" whose real name was Thomas Gordon Jackson, from some photographs he was about to show her. She picked him out without any hesitation. Following that they were taken to two separate rooms with female police officers to make their formal statements. Finally, Sue was reunited with her pendant and after allowing the female officer to have a good look at it, she signed the receipt for it and away they went. As they made their way back to the hotel in the taxi, to deposit the pendant in their room safe, Valerie said she would keep an eye on the papers and let Sue know once the case had come to court and the suspect dealt with.

They had decided to make their way towards the Yarrow River and the Eureka Tower. At three hundred metres in height, it was, said Valerie, the tallest building in Melbourne. She managed to talk Sue into going up to the Skydeck on the 88th floor but Sue drew the line at taking the 'Skywalk' known as 'The Edge' which was a three metre glass cube jutting out over the city below. "You know I don't do heights, Valerie," said Sue as Valerie tried to coax her to try it. The view she had already was more than enough for Sue's head and stomach which began to flip each time she looked out.

Finally, feet firmly on ground level, Sue heaved a sigh of relief as they made their way to Federation Square to have lunch in one of the many cafés. The day was warm and sunny with a light breeze and perfect for walking aimlessly. They found a small restaurant that suited them both and spent the next couple of hours sitting, eating a very healthy lunch of goats cheese and mixed salad with a couple of bottles each of elderflower juice. They finished off with a cup of tea. Their conversation was easy as usual and Sue made a real effort to let Valerie know how grateful she was for her hospitality. Valerie waved it all away with her hand and said she had really enjoyed it and hoped she would return in the future.

"Try stopping me, Valerie," said Sue. "Perhaps we could meet up and have a holiday together somewhere new. What do you think?"

"That would be lovely and we can spend time thinking of places to go," replied Valerie enthusiastically.

"What would you like to do tonight, Sue?" Valerie finally asked.

"If you don't mind, I'd like to go to Chinatown for a meal and soak up the atmosphere there."

"That's an excellent choice and it's some time since I went. Actually, I've only been a couple of times since Nev died and that's almost eight years. We used to go a lot but it's not the same on your own is it?"

Sue agreed, thinking again about all the hotel dinners she had spent on her own. She couldn't help feeling that Mark had missed out on so much. He would have loved to eat in Chinatown because he enjoyed foreign food and especially seafood.

They spent the rest of the afternoon just strolling around, looking at the shops and occasionally stopping and sitting on any convenient bench. After the drama of the previous evening, Sue was happy to unwind and watch the world go by. Tomorrow, they had agreed that they would visit the Queen Victoria Market and the Old Melbourne Gaol before collecting their luggage and returning to Eastlea on the afternoon train.

On the way back to the hotel, they stopped at a small artisan gallery that sold paintings and pottery. Valerie and Sue admired the various pieces on sale and a small vase took Valerie's eye. Sue agreed that it was lovely and immediately she thought of a space in Valerie's bungalow where the vase would look just right. She had wanted to buy something for Valerie as a 'Thank You' present and this was ideal. She pretended it was for her, and as the shop assistant wrapped it, Valerie remarked how lovely it was and that she was envious of Sue for having purchased it first. It was, as were all the pieces a one-off so there was no chance of Valerie buying one like it. She decided she would give it to her when they got back from the city. The next thing she needed to do was to find a suitable card to go with it, but she decided she could do that back in Eastlea.

Chapter 63

Their evening in Chinatown was a fabulous experience for Sue. Gone were the cares of the previous evening and they both joined in the revelries of other visitors. The evening was balmy and so Sue had opted to wear her linen trousers and a silk blouse finished off with a comfortable pair of loafers. She was beginning to relax even more and they managed to get a table in the window of one of the many restaurants so that they could watch the passers-by. It was midnight when they returned to their hotel and it didn't take Sue long to drift off into a much needed blissful sleep.

The next day they packed their bags and left them with the baggage hold to collect on their way back to the station. They set off for The Queen Victoria Market and the Old Melbourne Gaol. The latter was the place of execution of the folk hero Ned Kelly in 1880. As they travelled on the Vintage Tramcar to La Trobe Street, Sue's thoughts turned to the family at home. Her first task when she got back to Valerie's would be to check her emails. She hoped the news would be positive from home. Valerie had talked a lot of sense the other night in the hotel and Sue had made up her mind to return home with a more conciliatory attitude. She knew she had to sit down and talk to Mark to discuss the future for both of them – whatever form that might take.

They visited the Old Gaol first and Sue was fascinated by the collection of death masks on show in the tiny cells together with the compelling case histories of the relevant murderers and their victims. Valerie said she found it very depressing and ghoulish but Sue had to admit that it captivated her macabre interest. After taking in some of the other exhibits on show, like examples of nooses and a scaffold, Sue looked at Valerie's expression and decided her friend had had enough. They moved on to the Queen Victoria Market further up on Victoria Street.

Sue marvelled at the diversity of the shops, many of which had been lovingly restored to their original splendour of the late 1870s. You could buy anything from new or used clothes to vegetables, fish and cheeses. Sue thought that the shoppers were every bit as diverse as the goods on sale and the atmosphere was positively bustling and noisy. Sue took a number of snaps in the market so that she could better describe the vibrant atmosphere there to friends and family back at home.

The highlight for Sue was the array of fabulous clothes and shoe shops and she spent a long time browsing. However, much to her own surprise, she didn't buy anything. She would save that pleasure for Sydney. Finally, they got a taxi back to the hotel to collect their luggage where the Manager was on duty. He made a fuss of them for one last time and then they were back in the taxi travelling to the station for their return journey to Eastlea.

****

Bella was extremely pleased to see them when they went to collect her from Marjorie's house that evening. She wagged her tail furiously and licked them both. "I think she's as pleased to see you as she is to see me," said Valerie as they led her to the car and said farewell to Marjorie.

"I don't think there's any contest, Valerie," replied Sue. "She knows who her mistress is and who takes care of her."

They arrived back at Valerie's and Sue asked if she could check her emails. She was anxious to hear the news from home. When she located her inbox there were two messages. One, from Peter and Lynne was from Friday and the other from Nicola was Saturday's date.

She opened Peter and Lynne's first. It was quite brief and simply said they hoped she had a good time in Melbourne and would be in touch again. They and the girls were going to the lakes for the weekend in their caravan as the weather had been forecast to be mild and dry. No mention of Mark.

Nicola's email was a little more detailed with the usual mention of how busy she and Simon were. Dad had cancelled his visit the weekend Sue had gone to Australia and she had not seen or heard from her dad despite ringing him and leaving him two messages. She would try again later that day and maybe arrange to see him on Sunday. She hoped Sue had bought loads of lovely things to wear and was having a good time.

She sent brief replies back to each email telling them she had enjoyed her stay in Melbourne and would be moving on to Sydney during the week – probably Wednesday – after she had confirmed it with Steve and Grace. She told each one that she would email again when she arrived in Sydney and asked Peter to make sure he checked on his dad. She did not mention the episode with the pendant.

Valerie asked her if everything was okay when she walked into the lounge after logging off the computer.

"Oh, yes fine I think, although there is no news of Mark. Nicola has left messages but he hasn't responded but Peter didn't mention him. He was supposed to be going out for a pint with Peter and James the evening of the day I flew out here. I do hope all is well with him and the boys."

"Don't worry so much about that, Sue. They will sort things out in their own way without you getting in the way. Now, what about eating?"

"I'm not particularly hungry at the moment. Valerie, but how about we get something delivered here later and I'll pay?"

"That sounds a great idea. Sue. It will give us time to unpack and have a shower or bath if you like. Then we can order when we're ready."

They finally settled on pizzas which were delivered after they had sorted out their luggage, showered and changed into their pyjamas and slippers. Valerie opened a bottle of Merlot with which they toasted their return home. (Well, you had to have something to toast and that was as good as anything). Sue managed to eat most of her pizza which she regarded as a great accomplishment and what she didn't eat she fed to Bella while Valerie wasn't looking. Bella didn't seem to mind one little bit and lay faithfully at Sue's feet hoping there might be a bit more.

"I'll need to sort out my flight to Sydney tomorrow, Valerie," Sue finally said.

"I'll be sorry to see you go, Sue. I've really enjoyed our few days together. You know you can stay as long as you like."

"I know that and I'm grateful to you but I need to move on and I know Steve and Grace are looking forward to seeing me."

"We'll get my travel agent to sort out the flight for you in the morning. She's a lovely girl and she'll do it in no time and save you the bother."

They started watching a film on the television but it wasn't long before both of them were dozing. Sue was the first to waken so she took the dishes into the kitchen and put the kettle on for a cup of tea. She filled the teapot with enough for two cups and took the whole lot into the lounge where Valerie was just stirring. They drank their brews and Sue made her way to bed. As she lay there in the dark, she thought about the weekend's events and particularly the theft of the pendant. Despite what Valerie had said, Sue knew that she would be more nervous from now on when she wore the pendant in public. She had felt really good in it the other night until that man had stolen it. Then she remembered what Sam had said in his letter about it needing to be worn.

Oh Sam, if only you had known what a catalyst of change that pendant has turned out to be. I wish I could have known you longer and got a better chance to tell you all that's happened to me since we met. She thought about what his reaction might have been to the man on the dance floor in the hotel. He would have sussed him out immediately. Not like her then, thinking she looked like the bee's knees when all the time all he was interested in was the pendant. She was a fool to think that anyone would find her in the least bit desirable. Mark didn't. No, he preferred a younger fifty-three-year old.

Her thoughts started to turn to her own feelings of jealousy and frustration and she began to get that awful nauseous feeling again. She got up and took a few sips of water, then got back into bed to try to think of more pleasant things, like seeing Steve and Grace again. Finally, she drifted off to sleep.

Chapter 64

It was the morning of Wednesday 16th October and the day Sue was flying off to Sydney. Valerie made her some breakfast of porridge and a cup of coffee following which, Sue packed the last of her things and prepared to leave. She gave Bella a few more pats and hugs and then passed a small parcel and card to Valerie. It was the vase she had purchased for her in Melbourne. Valerie was thrilled and teased her about being devious by pretending it was for herself. They hugged each other one last time and then set off for the airport.

"I don't want you to stay at the airport with me Valerie because you have to get back to Bella and I will only get upset if you do. I'll ring you when I get to Steve and Grace's and thank you so much for everything. It has been wonderful to see you and your lovely home."

"All right, if that's what you want I'll leave you now, but please take care of yourself and let me know how things go back home. Remember what I said to you about fighting for what you want. God bless and let me know when you are safely in Sydney with your friends."

Sue found a trolley for her luggage and waved as Valerie's car pulled away from the dropping off point. The tears stung her eyes and she dabbed them with a tissue to stop her mascara from smudging. She would have to do a repair job once she got inside the terminal and before she went through to check-in.
Once through check-in and security, Sue relaxed a little and made her way to the lounge for a sit down and a coffee.

She had about an hour and a half before her flight so she could text Steve and Grace to let them know what time she expected to arrive in Sydney. Once she had done, she tried to relax but kept thinking about Mark and the boys. Had he met them as planned or had he cancelled that like he had with Nicola? What was he playing at? She felt both angry and worried at the same time and it did nothing to quell the unease she felt in the pit of her stomach.

She had just been to the loo for the third time in an hour when her flight was called. She made her way to the gate, and after a fifteen minute wait, she boarded the plane. It wasn't full and Sue found the seat next to hers empty so she could spread out a little for the relatively short flight that passed without incident.

After going through security and collecting her luggage, Sue made her way to arrivals and found Steve and Grace waiting for her. They hugged her and Steve pulled back instantly, taking her hands in his and appraising her appearance. "My God woman you're skin and bone!" he exclaimed. "What have you been doing to yourself?"

Before Sue could summon up a reasonable excuse, Grace interrupted, "Steve, leave the poor girl alone she's only just arrived! You could do with losing some weight like Sue – she looks fabulous. Take no notice of him, Sue – he's only jealous." However, Grace inwardly agreed with Steve but she could see that Sue was not up to discussing her weight at the moment. She thought she looked quite gaunt underneath her golden tan. Her eyes were sunken somewhat and her neck was looking a little bit scraggy.

"Let's get you home and we'll have a snack and a brew while we decide what you want to do while you're here. It really is great to see you. Steve, get the luggage will you and I'll take this small bag. Sue, let me help you with that," she said, taking Sue's hand luggage from her and striding ahead towards the short stay car park.

Since Sue's last visit to Sydney, Steve and Grace had retired from their hectic careers in the city and had sold their enormous six-bedroom house in the suburbs. Their family – two sons – had long since left home and were married. The eldest, Patrick, lived in New Zealand with his wife, Maria. They had no children as yet but Grace was hopeful. Their youngest son Martin and his wife Trina had one child, a girl and they had moved to Adelaide a year earlier as Martin had received a promotion at the bank where he worked.

Steve and Grace were now living in a much smaller apartment in an area of the harbour called The Rocks. Their apartment was in a newly converted warehouse block and was situated on the seventh floor with a view of the harbour bridge. Sue contemplated the cost of such a place when they arrived and she got her first look at it. As if reading her mind Steve said they had used almost all the money they got for their previous home on buying this three bed apartment. "Location is everything, Sue. The good thing about this is the upkeep is much cheaper than the big place and we don't need to use the car too much when we are in the city. In fact we use it very little unless we go up to the cottage in Nelson's Bay."

Prior to retiring, they had purchased a small cottage further north up the coast from Sydney as a retreat from the hustle and bustle of city life. They still used it at the weekends as it allowed them to chill out and get away from the huge crowds in Sydney. Among other things they enjoyed walking and dolphin watching and the location of the cottage allowed both those activities.

Sue's room had en-suite facilities and was very modern, as was the rest of the apartment. The loft-style look was predominant throughout with solid wood floors and loads of rugs scattered around. In addition to the three bedrooms, there was a large entrance hall, and leading off from that, along with the bedrooms, was a small study, a kitchen diner fitted out with every modern convenience known to man and a good-sized lounge with an enormous floor to ceiling window looking out onto a balcony. From the balcony, there was a stunning view over the rooftops of smaller buildings to the Sydney Harbour Bridge in the distance. *No wonder this place cost so much,* thought Sue as she looked out on the view beyond. "This is fabulous," she said to Steve as Grace was preparing a snack in the kitchen.

"Yes, we love it and it's so easy to maintain. We have two parking places down in the basement so it's very convenient and safe. Changing the subject, how are things with you and Mark and the family?"

This was the question Sue was dreading but there was no avoiding it so she told him as briefly as she could what had happened. Grace overheard the conversation and broke off what she was doing in the kitchen to join them. She sat next to Steve and listened as Sue related the events of the last few weeks. She also went back to her first trip to Canada and the subsequent events including meeting Sam and his death then the bequests.

They listened in silence until she had finished and then Steve said, "Now I see why you look so tired, Sue. I must confess I can't claim to be an expert in these matters but it seems that both of you need to sit down and try to work this out. It makes me sad to think of both of you in this situation and I wish I could talk to Mark. Would it help if I called him to chat?"

"I don't want to be rude, Steve, but I can't see what good that will do unless you can find out why he felt it necessary to do what he has. He told me it was because I was so boring, and for a while I believed him, but I'm not taking the whole blame for this."

"It strikes me that you two have done precious little talking. Grace will agree with me that we have had our ups and downs but in the end we have managed to talk things through and work out an answer to our problems. If you don't talk, then you each carry on assuming things about the other without really knowing the truth and then the problem escalates."

Grace nodded in agreement and said that talking things through was the only way to sort things out. "I'd better go and finish that snack and the tea or you'll be gasping." She returned to the kitchen to finish her task and came back with a tray laden with sandwiches and tea a few minutes later.

As they ate the conversation about Sue and Mark continued with Steve repeating his advice and Grace agreeing with him. After eating half a sandwich and finishing her cup of tea, Sue finally said, "Can we talk about something else now, like how are things with you and the family?"

Grace brought her up to date with their news and Steve produced his *iPad* to show her some snaps of their granddaughter. They were very proud grandparents and Grace said they tried to visit Adelaide whenever they could and they talked to both their sons and families each week on Skype.

That reminded Sue about her emails and she asked if Steve could set her up to access them. He went into the study and switched on his laptop. After a few minutes he asked Sue her email address and told her he had set her up. She checked her inbox and was disappointed to find it empty. She fired off a quick email to all the children telling them she was in Sydney at Steve and Grace's place. She asked them all if they had seen or heard from their father and said she hoped to hear from them soon. Finally, she made a brief call to Valerie as promised.

She went back into the lounge to find Steve and Grace deep in conversation. They broke off when they saw her and Steve said they were discussing what to do that evening. Sue knew they were discussing her and Mark but she let it go and said she was open to any suggestions. Grace said they could walk down to the harbour and get an early evening drink in one of the bars and then go on to a café to get something to eat. It was agreed that this would be the plan and so that gave them a couple of hours to chill and get changed before they went out. Sue asked if it would be okay to go and have a lie down on her bed for a little while before getting changed and Grace told her to treat the apartment as her home to do as she pleased. She added that she thought Sue was looking tired so a short nap might make her feel better.

Sue kicked off her sandals and slacks and slipped under the bedspread. She felt drained and soon fell asleep. When she awoke it was 6.25pm and she jumped out of bed thinking Grace and Steve would be waiting for her. She moved a little too quickly and she fell in a daze to the floor. Grace knocked on the door and asked if she was all right, and before she knew it, both Grace and Steve were in her room and helping her up back onto the bed. She assured them she was okay and said she had been fast asleep and awoke with a start. She said she thought she had moved too quickly and it had made her dizzy but she felt okay now. They didn't look convinced but after she assured them several times that she was really okay, they left her to get changed.

Finally, at 7.00pm she was showered and changed and ready to go out. They decided to go straight to the restaurant which was only a short walk away. It took them less than ten minutes to get there and as it was mid week, it was relatively quiet. The cuisine was Italian and the atmosphere relaxed and this enabled Sue to put all thoughts of home to the back of her mind for a short time. They exchanged stories about their respective holidays since they had met last and laughed at some of the things Sue told them about herself and Jean.

Naturally, she didn't mention Samio. The evening soon passed and it was after 10.00pm when they made their way back to the apartment.

After a last cup of tea, Sue retired to bed and a much needed sleep. Before saying goodnight, Grace and Steve said they would discuss with Sue the following morning what she would like to do and see in the first few days with them.

Chapter 65

The next morning after breakfast they discussed plans for the week. Sue said she would be happy to just re-visit some of Sydney's attractions to remind herself of her last visit several years ago. She said she didn't expect Steve and Grace to accompany her everywhere while she was there. Steve could tell that she wanted some time to herself possibly to think through her problems with Mark, so he and Grace, having discussed nothing else the night before when they had gone to bed, decided that they would give her time to settle in for a day or two and then suggest a short holiday, possibly up to the Hunter Valley wineries. Steve also thought that he would try to contact Mark by phone to get his side of the saga. He didn't mention that part to Grace. He thought he would see what he could do before he said anything to her. If only he could persuade Mark to come out and visit them but he knew that was probably never going to happen.

Steve was probably Mark's closest friend but the years had passed so quickly since he and Grace had moved to Sydney, and apart from the occasional email or call and one or two visits back to England they hadn't had the chance to get together much. They could tell each other anything and Steve liked to think that if anyone could help Mark at this time it was he. He simply couldn't accept that a marriage as strong as the one he believed Sue and Mark shared could be cast off like an old coat without a real fight. He wasn't one for interfering but he had to have a try for both their sakes.

"I think that's a good idea, Sue," he finally said, "it will give you time to settle in a bit and then perhaps after the weekend we could take the car up to the Hunter Valley and sample some of the wines at one or two of the smaller vineyards. We can stay where we like and do what we like. How does that sound?"

"It sounds fabulous, Steve, and it will allow me to choose one or two bottles to take back home for..." she stopped mid flow because she was about to say that she could choose some wine to take home for Mark and then realised that she wasn't going home – well not to the one where Mark was.

That was enough to convince Steve that it was worth him speaking to Mark. He exchanged glances with Grace as Sue struggled to change the subject. "I think I'll get ready and stroll down to Circular Quay and have a look at the changes you say have been made since my last visit. Do you want anything bringing back Grace?" She tried to sound light and matter of fact but failed miserably and they all knew it. She disappeared into her room.

Once Sue had gone out, Steve emailed Mark – it was too soon to ring him because it would be turned midnight in England so he would email first to see if he got any response. If he didn't hear anything he would ring Mark in the early evening tomorrow in the hope of catching Mark before he went to work. Steve didn't know what he was going to say so in the end he opted for the direct approach and just said he was emailing to see if he was okay because Sue had told them about their problems. He said he wanted to help and asked Mark to respond either by email or phone.

Unlike Melbourne, Sydney was experiencing slightly cooler weather and especially on the quayside in Sydney harbour it was breezy too. She was glad she had put on her light fleece as it allowed her to stroll quietly rather than walk briskly without feeling chilly. There were several large white clouds above but when the sun popped out from behind them, she felt the warmth on her face. At that point she thought of Grace who was a stickler for covering up even in winter sun. She smiled at the memory of her last visit when they were in Nelson's Bay, trying to see the dolphins on a small boat. Grace wore her dark glasses and floppy sunhat all the time and was constantly warning Sue of the dangers of too much exposure to the sun. *Dear Grace,* thought Sue, *she was always looking out for me. There are so many people looking out for me. I'm so lucky.*

Sue reminded herself what day it was – Thursday – she would potter about today and tomorrow, she would visit the Royal Botanical Gardens. She would make herself a sandwich and take it along with a drink and her book and find that lovely spot to sit that she had found last time. It was so peaceful at the edge of a pond surrounded behind by palm trees that were inhabited by giant fruit bats. They hung from the branches like rows of overripe bananas during the day. Some people found it eerie but not Sue. At the other side of the pond were lawns intersected by pathways that led to the wall of the harbour. Behind the trees and to the left were the huge tower blocks of the city and ahead the harbour bridge and slightly to the left of that the Opera House just peeping through the trees. Yes, she would go and sit there – weather permitting – and try to relax.

She spotted a small café and stopped to get a coffee. As she waited for her drink to arrive, she looked out at the various boats making their way across and around the harbour. The Manley Ferry was just leaving and there were one or two harbour cruise ships that operated daily taking visitors on tours of the many harbours that constituted the port of Sydney. Her mobile signalled she had a message and for a moment she was startled at this unexpected event. She wondered who it could be then, as she took her phone out of her bag she decided it would probably be her network provider with a message of some sort. She was surprised to see it was from James and she was instantly on edge. Would it be bad news? Had he and Peter seen Mark and it had all gone pear-shaped again? Was Emma okay?

The message read:

'We are pregnant!!! It's X 2!!! All is well and will speak soon. LOL James + Emma.'

"Marvellous news!" cried Sue out loud. A young man sitting at the next table looked over and smiled at her. She realised she had called out and was embarrassed. She smiled at him and as if to confirm that she wasn't gaga she said, "I've just had some great news – I'm going to be grandmother again – it's twins as well."

The young man raised his cup of coffee in a toasting gesture. "Congrats and here's to you then, Grandma," he said in a broad Sydney accent.

"Thank you," Sue replied and lifted her cup in response. Then she quickly texted back to say that she would call them soon to get the details. That was the best news she'd had in ages. What a change it was to have some positive news and to think she had helped to make it possible – no **Sam** had made it possible with his incredible generosity. She continued to sit and take in the news. She knew she had a smile fixed on her face but she didn't care what anyone thought. She wondered who else knew. Did Mark know? Had they seen him? Her thoughts always came back to the same theme – Mark.

Sue changed direction and headed up toward George Street to take a look at the shops and the Strand Arcade. She wandered through the shops with a lighter step and found herself looking in the windows of any shop selling baby clothes or prams. She resisted the temptation to buy a cuddly toy (or two as the case may be) as it was obviously early days and anything could happen – God forbid. She bought a pair of sandals and a bag to match, and on the way back to Steve and Grace's she stopped off at a wine merchant's shop where she bought a bottle of very expensive champagne.

It was mid-afternoon when she arrived back at the apartment. Steve and Grace were relaxing on the balcony. They looked up as she walked in with the shopping bags and champagne.

"Are we celebrating something?" asked Steve, raising his eyebrows towards the bottle in Sue's hand.

"We certainly are," said Sue beaming at them both. She told them her news and said she was going to call James at home later.

"In that case, we should eat in style tonight," suggested Grace. "Steve, what about that Sicilian place we went to a while back with Patrick and Maria?"

"I'll give them a ring, and book a table for about 7.00pm or 7.30pm?"

"That'll give me time to call James and Emma," said Sue.

Grace went to put the champagne in the fridge and it was agreed they would enjoy it once Sue had contacted James prior to going out.

****

It was Emma who answered the phone when Sue called at 6.30pm Sydney time. It was early morning in England and Emma and James were just finishing their breakfast.

"Congratulations!" yelled Sue down the phone when she heard Emma's voice. "How is everything? How are **all** of you?"

"Hi Sue, it's lovely to hear your voice. Thank you, everything is just fine. The doctor thinks I'm about eight weeks so early days but things looking good so far. How are you? Are you having a fabulous time?"

"Yes thanks and the weather has been good so far. We have a bottle of champagne chilling here ready to drink before we go out for a meal to celebrate your news. How is James?"

"He's here and I'll put him on because I need to get off to work. James has a dental appointment this morning so he is taking the morning off. Take care Sue and we'll see you when you get back."

Emma passed the phone over to James who was obviously thrilled about the pregnancy and glad to hear his mother's voice.

"We owe it all to you, Mum, so thank you so much for giving us the chance to do this."

"Oh, don't thank me. You would have done it in the end anyway. Changing the subject have you seen your Dad?"

"Peter and I met up with him the weekend you went away. He was supposed to go over to see Nic and Si the day after but he didn't show. He was a bit quiet when we met him but it was okay. Don't get stressed, Mum, we didn't argue with him but we told him how we felt and he seemed to take it on the chin. He didn't mention **her** thankfully. We said we would meet again, but to be honest, things have been a bit hectic here as you can imagine, and although I've tried to reach him, we haven't heard from him since. I spoke to Pete last night and he hasn't seen or heard from him either. I wanted to give him the news about the pregnancy face-to-face but I'm going to have to text him. Don't worry – I'll track him down soon. You know what he's like. He's probably immersing himself in work as usual."

Sue was worried that no-one had seen Mark for a couple of weeks, and after she put down the phone, it was with mixed emotions. She relayed the conversation to Steve and Grace but tried to play down the absence of Mark as much as she could. She didn't want anything to spoil tonight's celebration. Steve had checked his email and had not received any response from Mark. He decided he would call him tomorrow night instead.

They had a lovely meal at the Sicilian restaurant. They specialised in fish and pasta dishes, all of which looked and sounded delicious. However, as usual, Sue opted for something plain to ensure her stomach didn't rebel too much. The restaurant was out of the city centre up on a cliff that overlooked a small bathing beach. It was very exclusive and the service was impeccable.

When they were on their way back home in the car, Steve remarked at the sky which was clear as a bell. The sunset had been fabulous and he said the forecast was for a spell of very warm weather starting tomorrow. "You should have a great day to browse around the gardens, Sue, and sit and read while you have your lunch. We could come and meet you around lunchtime if you wanted and then we could eat a picnic together. What do you say?"

"That would be lovely but I don't want to take you away from what you would normally be doing."

Grace commented that they would probably do very little so it would be a change for them to have a picnic. "I'll make sure I bring a rug to sit on and we'll find a good shade too. We don't want to get too much sun do we?"

You speak for yourself, thought Sue but she replied, "No, I suppose we don't, Grace."

Chapter 66

The next day dawned bright, sunny and warm, just as forecasted. After breakfast Sue gathered up her bag with everything she would need for the day. She plastered herself with a high factor sun lotion, much to Grace's approval and put on her sun glasses and hat that she had purchased the previous day. The wind had dropped so she was relieved that she wouldn't have to hang onto her hat all the time to prevent it being blown away. She said goodbye and agreed to meet Grace and Steve at 1.00pm near the restaurant, so that they could get a fresh cup of tea to take to a suitable spot to have their lunch. It was 9.30am when she strode off to walk to the gardens.

By her calculations, she would have at least a couple of hours to herself before she met her friends so she planned to write a postcard to Jean and one to Mark just to let him know that she was still speaking to him. She didn't really know why she was doing it but she only knew that she wanted to. She accessed the gardens from the entrance near the Opera House. She looked back on the stunning view of the harbour. The gardens were still reasonably quiet but Sue knew that come lunchtime, they would be full of workers running along the harbour walkway and through the gardens, getting their daily fix of fitness. She marvelled at their fortune at being able to enjoy this resource in the middle of their busy working day. It must be a great way to unwind before or after a meeting in the office or to relax before going back to work in one of the many stores and shops. No wonder the people were in the main so laid back.

She obtained a map from the visitor centre and made her way through the rose and herb gardens first. They reminded her of England and the scent of the roses was quite heady. She found the oriental gardens and decided to sit on a bench that was under a huge acacia tree. She drank frequently from the bottle of water Grace had insisted she bring with her. It was becoming quite hot now and she had to admit that Grace was right to insist. Grace was, after all, a native of Australia and so she knew better than anyone how important it was to take great care in the sun. She wrote her first postcard to Jean, telling her about the sights of Melbourne and her journey to Sydney. After about half an hour, she moved on, taking snaps of the various flowers and trees that she came across along the way. A couple of Japanese tourists – newlyweds Sue guessed by the way they looked at each other and held hands – asked her if she would take a picture of them next to a stunning display of azaleas. She fumbled with the high-tech camera that most Japanese seemed to own these days, but eventually, after three attempts, she managed to produce a snap that they approved of. They went on their way, thanking her with a succession of small bowing gestures and giggling at the snaps on their camera.

Sue found the spot she remembered from her first visit to the gardens and she sat down on the large rock that had been worn into a seat by years of people trying it out for size. She looked across the lawns at the Opera House and the bridge in the harbour and thought not for the first time how magnificent it looked. She started to write the postcard to Mark but after several attempts, she gave it up as a bad job. She couldn't think what to say and she thought how strange that was after living with him for forty-four years she was stuck for words – well the right ones anyway. She read a couple of chapters of her book and was surprised to see that it was a quarter to one. She packed up her things and strolled off to meet Steve and Grace making her way towards the Palm Grove area on the way to the restaurant. When she looked up to the gnarled branches of the Moreton Bay fig trees she could plainly make out the huge bats that hung from each one. At dusk they would come to life and hundreds of them would fly around the Palm Grove area of the gardens. Finally, she arrived at the restaurant and sat down on a seat to wait for her friends to arrive.

She wasn't particularly concerned when, at 1.25pm they still hadn't shown up. They were notorious for their erratic timekeeping, especially Steve. She smiled and remembered when she and Mark had known Steve as teenagers and the numerous times they had arranged to meet at a particular time only to wait around for ages before he finally showed up apologising and telling them a long story explaining why he was late.

The restaurant area had filled with lunchtime visitors and Sue looked carefully among the crowds of people milling around to make sure she didn't miss Steve and Grace. She waited patiently until about 1.45pm at which point she decided to call Steve's mobile to check that all was well. The call went straight to voicemail, so she left a short message saying she was waiting for them as planned. She had forgotten to take details of Grace's mobile so she couldn't ring her. At almost 2.00pm she became a little worried and tried Steve's number again but his voicemail message was all she could hear. She decided that she would make her way to the entrance by the Opera House as she knew that was the way they would come. The lunchtime crowds had dispersed and the area was much quieter again.

She gathered up her bag and hat, which she had put down on the bench beside her and started to turn towards the direction of the path that led through the Palm Grove. Just as she did, she caught a glimpse of a solitary figure walking towards her. She stopped in her tracks and looked more closely at the man who was about fifty yards away. There was something familiar about him and she squinted to get a better look. She found herself rooted to the spot, unable to move. The man held up a hand and waved. He was wearing jeans and T-shirt, trainers and a bush hat and sunglasses. He stopped about fifteen yards from her at the opposite edge of a lawn that separated them and removed his hat and glasses.

Could it be? No surely not. She was dreaming. It must be the sun affecting her vision. Sue shook her head and looked up once more. It was no dream. There, standing at the opposite edge of the lawn was Mark.

He smiled and called to her. "You'll have to come to me, I've come far enough. You can do the last few yards."

It was all Sue could do to stand up. She was literally weak at the knees with shock. Her heart was pounding and her head felt dizzy with emotion.

"Thank you," was all she could manage before she started to put one foot in front of the other until she was almost running towards him across the lawn. She had dropped her bag and her hat but she didn't care. He had come thousands of miles to see her at last. She didn't stop to think how he had managed it, she just flung herself at him and he caught her in his arms as she was about to fall forward. He held her tighter than she could ever remember being held before. She gripped his neck with both hands and kissed him passionately. There would be plenty of time for questions later. Right now she wanted to freeze time and keep this moment locked up in her mind. Finally, she whispered in his ear, "Have you come to take me home?"

"Well, yes, that's the plan," he replied, "but not before I have some time to get over the journey here and prepare for the one back."

They laughed and kissed again. It felt like it used to feel - all those years ago when they were young. She allowed herself one thought. *Could this be the first day of the rest of my life?* A little voice inside her head said, *That would be telling wouldn't it? You'll just have to wait and see.*

The End

(Or maybe not)